Those who Lived by the Sword

"The Illusion of Peace"

By J. Edwards

Edited by Shane Pope and Mariko Irving

Printed in the United States of America

First Printing, 2018

ISBN-13: ISBN-13: 978-0-692-04618-0

EireneBros Publishing LLC
4414 82nd St, Ste 212, -318
Lubbock, TX 79424

www.eirenebrospublishing.com

To those who care to listen

Those who Lived by the Sword

"The Illusion of Peace"

Chapter 1

Before the Sun Sets

"Jayden! Hello sleepyhead! Wake up already! It's seven in the morning; time for you to get ready for school!" His dad yelled.

"Hey! I said get up!" Still no response. "Okay, so you want to play this game? I know you're just pretending to sleep."

Jayden's father opened the blinds and yanked the blankets off his son's bed. "Still asleep, are you? Well, I have a solution to get you out of the coma in a jiffy. This bucket of ice water should do the trick".

"Whoa! Whoa! Dad, chill out. I'm awake now. Can you please tell me, what is so dang important that it couldn't wait til noon? I was busy having this awesome dream that I was a ninja."

"You do know that you have classes in the morning. Now I need you to get up, or I will accidentally put your TV out on the street."

"Dad, there is no need to do something so drastic. Plus my school is just up the street by Miss Mara's house, who just so happens to live just a few blocks down the road. It takes me a whopping thirty seconds to get there. Now explain to me why I have to get up at the butt crack of dawn?"

"Quit your yapping! I don't have time for it. Now get up and eat your breakfast," replied his father as he walked out of the room.

After yawning and stretching, Jayden was finally able to get out of bed with the grace and sophistication of a zombie. He stared blankly into his closet for about five minutes before he reached in and grabbed a red T-Shirt and a pair of jeans. Then he dragged his feet toward the shower. Once he turned the shower knobs on, he jumped in.

"Holy crap!" He screamed, "it's freezing in here! That's great. The hot water went out. Cold showers are just the greatest... said no one ever."

After an agonizingly cold shower, he stepped out of his torture chamber and began to dry off. As he got dressed, he began to comb his dark, curly brown hair. Flexing his tiny biceps in the mirror, Jayden smirked and said, "I am looking pretty darn good today. Sarah, your days of not dating me are numbered. I'm coming for you today."

"Dude, you've gotta talk to her before you can date her. You do know that right? Unless you believe the awkward silent treatment has been working," said a voice coming from just outside the door.

"Hey Tony, don't you doubt my system. I read somewhere that girls are really into the handsome, silent type. It makes you look mysterious," Jayden replied with his arms crossed.

Tony smirked, "you are lucky that we are friends because you are so weird. Let's hurry up and head over to school so I can watch you not talk to Sarah."

The boys sprinted out of the house with lunches in their hands, and made their way toward the school. Just as they arrived, he saw her. Sarah was chatting with her friends on the steps that led up to the school building. She looked stunning that morning; her beautiful black hair was blowing gently in the wind. Her hazel colored eyes were as entrancing as the stars in the night sky. Her voice was sweet and smooth as silk, and she had that beautiful smile that he just couldn't resist.

Instantly, his mouth became dry, and his hands started to get clammy. Jayden was so nervous and entranced by her beauty that he forgot to pay attention to where he was walking. "Ouch!" Jayden shouted, as his head began throbbing with pain. "What the heck was that?"

"Dude! You gotta watch where you are going. You about tackled that lamppost with your face!" Tony said as he was dying of laughter.

"Tell me she didn't see me make a fool of myself," Jayden said feeling thoroughly embarrassed as a crowd of students pointed and laughed at him.

Giggling, Sarah came up to him and asked, "Jade, are you okay? Why did you walk into a lamppost?"

Trying to sound confident, he replied, "well, the sun got in my eyes and I couldn't see."

"Isn't it pretty cloudy today? How did the sun get in your eyes?" She asked with a sheepish grin on her face.

"Oh about that, look at the time," Jayden replied while looking at the non-existent watch on his wrist. "I better get to Miss Mara's class. I can't be late for the third time this week."

***

The hours dragged on as the boys sat in class. Jayden kept staring at the clock praying that God would make its hands move faster. If he had to spend one more minute hearing about plant biology, he was going to shoot himself.

It's about time, he thought, as the lunch bell began to ring throughout the halls. Before the signal could stop ringing, Tony and Jayden were already out of their seats.

"So, are you going to go talk to her?" Tony chuckled. "Or do you plan just to keep walking into lampposts?"

Jayden replied, "I think after all of that I may just go back to using the silent treatment."

Tony punched him in the side. "Man up and go talk to her!" he demanded.

Jayden shrugged begrudgingly, "fine. I'll do it."

He scanned the schoolyard looking for her. There were children everywhere. Some were playing an intense game of a tag. There was a small group of boys playing dodgeball on the blacktop. One of those boys was lucky enough to be icing a freshly acquired black eye. Fortunately for him, Jayden thought, at least he has a valid reason to avoid talking to the girl of his dreams.

Jayden didn't need to look for her. He knew precisely where Sarah was. She always sat at the same outdoor lunch table near the soccer field with her friends. Jayden also knew that if he kept stalling, Tony would punch him again. Mustering up all the strength and courage he had, he began walking toward the soccer field.

As got closer to the field, he got the sense that someone was following him. Out of the corner of his eye, he noticed a shadowy figure was approaching from behind one of the school buildings. Suddenly, he felt the slight need to flee or to call for a teacher. Jayden opened his mouth to yell for help but became stifled as the shadowy figure tackled him to the ground.

"Get off of me! Get off! You're crushing me!" he cried.

"Jade, stop whining. It's not like you haven't been tackled before," said the strange tackler.

"Cain it's you! How have you been doing? It's been forever since I've seen you. How long has it been?" Jayden asked.

"It's been about five years now. I left when I was 13. What have you been up to these days? How old are you now?"

"Well, I'm 13. I guess you could say it's our lucky number. I am in the seventh grade right now. Man, you've gotten big. You look like you could lift a horse. And your hair got so long; it's longer than Tony's!"

Cain was the big brother that Jayden never had. He stood at just a little over six feet with broad shoulders and long black hair that extended to the middle of his back. He was wearing a black T-shirt with a pair of dark blue jeans. He looked menacing. There was something else that was different about Cain. There was a strange tattoo on his right forearm that caught Jayden's eye, but before he could ask about it, he heard a yell from Tony. "Hey Cain! How's it going?"

"I am doing fine Tony. I see you've gotten bigger too. I am digging that spiky hair you have. I bet the ladies are lovin' it," Cain replied.

"You know it. Unlike Jade, I don't give girls the silent treatment," Tony said grinning from ear to ear.

"I can talk to girls. I just don't sometimes," Jayden said defiantly. "So Cain, what have you been doing lately? I still don't quite get why you left all those years ago. By the way, that's a pretty cool tattoo on your arm. What is it? It looks like a scary monster."

"I haven't been doing too much lately. I chose to leave Eirene five years ago for my reasons. Who knows, you may end up doing the same thing someday," Cain said patting his young friend on the back. "Now the real reason I tackled you wasn't just to say hi. I was wondering if you knew where your father might be."

"O ya, he is helping to rebuild Ms. Tonya's fence," Jayden answered. "Do you remember where she lives?"

"Doesn't she live in that bright pink house? The one with the pink shed and the pink mailbox?" Cain asked.

Grimacing, Jayden replied, "Yep, that's the one. It's so dang pink you can see it from space. Anyway, we have to head back to class. The last time I was late, Miss Mara made me stay after class and clean the room."

As they watched Cain walk away, Jayden and Tony stared at him in awe. "So, what do you think he does for a living?" Tony asked.

"I am pretty sure he's a ninja or a superhero," Jayden replied.

"Jade, everybody knows there are no such things as ninjas," Tony said with a laugh.

Once they returned to their classroom, their teacher Miss Mara yelled," you boys are five minutes late! Now get to your seats. You have a math test to take. And guess what? You, gentlemen, get to spend some quality time with me in detention."

Two hours later, the boys emerged from the dungeon known as after-school detention. "The next time we see Cain, I'm going to kick him in the kneecaps for getting us detention," Tony said.

"You might just get your chance," Jayden replied as they walked down the street toward Cain.

From a distance, they could hear Cain having a heated conversation with someone on Main Street. Whatever discussion happened left Cain fuming as he stormed off.

"Well, there goes your chance to kick him in the kneecaps. Maybe you can kick him next time when he's not so angry," Jayden said.

"Hey Jade, wasn't that Cain and your dad talking? Man, he looks even more pissed than Cain did," Tony said.

Jayden's father looked distraught and drenched with sweat from his confrontation with Cain. He was so rattled from their conversation that his hands were shaking uncontrollably, and his heart was pounding in his chest. This can't be happening, he told himself.

How in the world did Cain know about *The Key*? What would he do with that kind of power? Out of the corner of his eye, he noticed Robert cautiously stepping outside of his tackle shop.

"Dion! What the hell was that all about? I could hear you two shouting from in my store. Is everything alright?" Robert asked.

"Ya, everything is fine. It was just a misunderstanding. I'm sorry we let it get a little out of hand," he replied. Robert eyed Dion suspiciously and decided that it was probably nothing to worry about and went back to his store.

If only it were nothing, Dion thought. He looked up and saw his son and his friend approaching him from down the street. Dion hoped that they didn't see what had just happened.

"Hey, dad!" Jayden yelled, "Are you okay? Why were you and Cain yelling at each other?"

Trying to look calm and reassure his son, his father replied, "ahh son, don't worry about that. We were just having a slight disagreement over something petty, and we both got a little heated."

"Are you sure? Cain looked like he was about to blow a gasket."

"Yes I'm sure. You know how he gets sometimes. Cain hates losing an argument. I need you boys to do me a favor and head straight home. I need you to stay there until I come to get you Jayden. Tony, I need you to head straight to your grandparent's house and stay there. Promise me you two will head straight home."

Looking at each other mischievously, "we promise," they said in unison. Turning around, they began their journey home.

Feeling a little lethargic, Jayden said, "hey Tony. I'm a little tired from detention. I'm going to head home and take a nap. When I get up, how about we go out and paint the town red?"

"Sounds like a plan man. Come get me when you're up," Tony replied.

***

After leaving Tony at his house, Jayden was almost home. As he walked, he had the faint suspicion that someone was watching him. That must be Tony, he thought. He must be trying to mess with me. He quickly turned around hoping he would catch his friend sneaking up on him. There was no one behind him or hiding in the bushes. He shrugged thinking that it must be his imagination.

Out of the corner of his eye, Jayden thought he saw dark shadows moving along the rooftops. He shook his head; I must be that tired. Without paying attention as to where he was going, he bumped into Cain. Expecting to feel his wrath, he nervously looked up at him.

The expression on Cain's face chilled Jayden to the bone. Cain didn't even bother to look at him. He just stared off into the distance with an empty expression; his slight grin was emotionless.

"Are you going home?" he asked in a monotone voice. Jayden nodded. "Good. Make sure you lock the door when you get in," he said as he walked past him.

Well, that was odd, Jayden thought. Once he reached his house, he crawled into his bed. The moment his head hit the pillow, he was out like a light.

Chapter 2

Blood, Sweat, and Fear

Once his nostrils flared, his consciousness dragged out of the world of dreams and back into reality. Even before he opened his eyes, he knew something was wrong. He sniffed the air as he opened his window. White ash blew into his room like snow in the winter. The air outside smelled like someone was having a bonfire.

As Jayden surveyed the world from his window, his heart almost stopped. He gazed on in horror as Ms. Rosa's house became engulfed in flames. Before he could yell for help, he heard a sound in the distance. At first, he thought it was just firecrackers going off in the night.

Jayden stuck his head out of the window just a little further and was shocked to see that there were other houses on fire, and then heard the screams. That's when he realized those weren't firecrackers he was hearing; that was the sound of gunfire. Jayden pulled his head back in the room, and he tried to cover his ears as he listened to a large explosion that shook his house so hard it knocked him off the bed. The windows shattered and his heart was pounding in his chest like a bass drum.

"Ow!" he yelled, "What the heck is going on out there?"

After another explosion shook his house, he jumped to his feet. Quickly he got dressed and ran out of the door. Once he stepped out on to his front porch, he instantly felt the heat from the deadly flames reaching into the sky.

Smoke rose from the rooftops throughout the town of Eiréné. Down the street, he watched as white lights flashed on and off in the darkness as the gunshots found their victims. For the first time in his life, Jayden knew fear. He understood it like it was his best friend. Fear was telling him to run, begging him to escape, but his legs were stuck, glued to his front porch. The anxiety he felt was almost too overwhelming; it made it difficult for him to breathe.

A sense of panic began surging throughout his body. Where was his dad? Where was Tony? He had to find them somewhere in this madness. Jayden glanced up and down the street frantically. He couldn't see either of them. He gulped down a heavy dose of fear and ran toward Tony's house.

As he ran up the street, Jayden's foot tripped over something in the darkness. He slammed against the concrete sidewalk as he hit the ground and scraped his knee. OUCH! That frickin' hurt! Why do I have to be so damn clumsy? With his knee throbbing from the fall, he crawled over to see what he tripped on.

Immediately his eyes widened, and the words he was searching for became caught in his throat. He couldn't believe what he was seeing, but there she was. Her ordinarily well-kept blonde hair was now matted and strewn across her face. Blood was dripping from bullet wounds on her left shoulder and her stomach. Her arms were spread at an angle as if she had just been running before she was shot.

The girl lying on the sidewalk was Stephanie. She lived across the street from him. She used to babysit him when he was younger. Even after Stephanie had stopped watching him, her family would always invite him over for food. She was one of the sweetest people he had ever met; she didn't deserve to die on the side of the street like a stray dog.

Suddenly her eyes flashed open, which almost gave him a heart attack. Stephanie turned toward him and said in a hushed voice, "Ja, Jayden. Hold my hand."

When he touched her warm hand, she gave him a weak smile. Then her hand went limp, and he knew she was gone. For a moment he sat there in silence as his heart became overwhelmed with anger and sorrow. He wiped a tear from his eyes, and then he noticed a bracelet on her right wrist. The bracelet was made with blue and white beads. It looked familiar. Then he remembered this was the same bracelet he gave Stephanie on her last day working as his babysitter. She wore it until her dying day.

The tears began to pour again as his heart ached like when he lost his mother. Gently, he removed her bracelet and placed it on his right wrist. Now she will be a part of him until his dying day.

A volley of rapid gunfire awoke him from his moment of grief. He checked down the street and saw Tony, and a glimmer of hope arose in his chest.

"Jayden!" Tony yelled, "get over here! Quick!"

Jumping to his feet, he began to sprint down the street. As he ran, he heard a low thump, and then the house to his left exploded launching him into the air and slamming him onto the ground. With his head spinning like a rollercoaster, he glanced up at Tony for a split second; then everything went black.

Tony ran to Jayden's side with his heart pounding in his chest, like it was about to burst. Please don't be dead. Please don't be dead, he pleaded.

"Wake up Jayden! Wake up!" Tony yelled, panic-stricken. "Get up Jade! I know you can do it! Now get up!" I can't afford to lose him, he thought. Not right after having to watch my grandparents get killed. What do I do? How can I help him? I wish my dad were here. As his pain and frustration became too much to bear, he shook his head. He was determined to make it through this.

Tony nudged Jayden's body and yelled in his ear, "Wake up!"

Jayden stirred, and he slowly opened eyes. With his head still spinning Jayden said, "hey, did you get the license plate number of the bus that just hit me? What the heck happened and why do I have this splitting headache? And why is my left ear ringing? I can hardly hear out of it."

"Don't worry about it, Jade. You just have a cut on your forehead and your ear is bleeding. Anyway, we have to get out of sight, let's go!" Tony said.

"Wait a second! Did you just say my ear's bleeding?" Jayden asked as he took a moment to notice the blood dripping on to his shirt.

"Shut up! We don't want them to hear us. Let's go!" Tony whispered.

Gunfire continued to fill the night as the boys snuck down Main Street. As they were walking, Tony noticed someone was running towards them with a rifle in their hand from across the street. Before he could tell Jayden to run, Tony looked back again and realized that it was Mr. Robert from the fish and tackle store in the center of town. Tony checked to see if Mr. Robert was hurt. The old man had a bruised lip, smelled like fish and cigarettes but, other than that, he seemed fine.

Robert pushed past them and tried to catch his breath. In between wheezes, he said, "man, I am getting too old for this." He lit a cigarette and took a puff, "my wife said these things would kill me one day. Maybe she was right. Now boys, I need you to follow me. We have to get off of Main Street."

He led them down a dark alley that was situated behind a row of the houses. It was unnerving for the boys, to hear the sound of rapid gunfire and small explosions coming from just a few streets away. Looking around, Jayden realized that he had forgotten something, "Hey guys, wait up. We have to go back and find my dad."

"Jayden, we can't afford to stop. We have to keep going!" Robert demanded.

"No, no, no!" Jayden replied with defiance. "I have already lost one parent. I don't want to lose another. You guys can go on. I'm going to look for my father."

Grabbing Jayden by the shoulder and turning him around, Robert looked him dead in the eye, "Listen here. We are going to escape into the Dragon Mountains as soon as we can get out of town. Your father will meet us there. He asked me to find you and take you there. You're going with me whether you like it or not. Now pick up your feet and let's keep moving."

"Fine!" Jayden replied as he dragged his feet and kicked the dirt like he was an angry six year old.

Robert stopped in his tracks and scanned the area around them. He raised his rifle as he glanced up at the rooftops. Shaking his head, he chuckled to himself. Isn't this ironic that this place is known throughout the Land of Eden as the "Town of Peace" and here we are caught in a war zone. How did this even happen? What did we do to deserve this?

The further they walked, Robert became more and more suspicious. He had a feeling that they were being followed. He didn't want to freak out the boys, so he gently flicked off the safety to his rifle and flipped the switch to 3 shot burst.

He ushered the boys to walk in a straight line to protect them. Robert was marching in the back of their line when he leaned forward and whispered to Jayden, "Look, you boys are going to have to go on ahead of me. We are not too far from the intersection of Grand Avenue and Main Street. I need you boys to run across Grand and duck behind the houses. Keep going until you can head up into the mountains. I will catch up with you okay. Nod your head if you heard everything I just said." Silently, Jayden nodded his head nervously. "Good. Now when I tell you guys to go, I want you to start running as fast as you can and make sure you keep to the shadows. Are you ready?" He pushed them forward, "Go!"

Jayden and Tony took off in a dead sprint just as Robert wheeled around with his gun raised. On the rooftops to his left, there were two cloaked figures aiming their weapons at him. Quickly, he squeezed the trigger on his rifle and fired off six rounds.

He managed to dispatch both of them and knocked one of them off the roof. Robert lowered his gun and felt slightly pleased with himself. Not too bad for a retired General, he thought.

He glanced up and noticed three more cloaked figures, heading in his direction. Instinctively he raised his rifle and fired six more shots. With blinding speed, they deflected the bullets with their swords. One of the rounds was deflected backward and hit Robert in his shoulder.

Stumbling backward, he grabbed his shoulder and saw that it left a small gash. How in the world were they able to move that fast? With his left arm trembling from the pain in his shoulder, he raised his rifle and took a deep breath. Aiming at the figure on his far left, he fired six more rounds. Immediately the man fell to the ground, howling in pain. One down, two more to go.

The cloaked figure in the middle stopped walking and turned to his fallen comrade, and he said coldly, "You're weak." He continued walking forward with his other comrade on his right only to turn and shoot the man on the ground in the head. "No sign of weakness will be tolerated is that understood?"

"Yes sir." said the other cloaked warrior.

While they were distracted, Robert had enough time to reload his rifle. He aimed and fired nine shots in quick succession and dispatched the cloaked figure to his right. Robert pointed at his remaining adversary and squeezed the trigger. Nothing happened. "Damn it!" he cursed, "the gun jammed!"

The shrouded figure approached him and said, "You have fought well old man. It is not easy to defeat my men. Let alone four of them. You should be proud to receive a warrior's death." With lightning quick speed, he reached into his cloak for a dagger and threw it at Robert. Robert leaned to the left and dodged it only to be run through by his sword.

Crumbling to the ground, Robert put his hand on his stomach as he bled from his wound. Breathing became more difficult for Robert, and he knew he didn't have much time left. Robert looked up at his attacker and smirked, "the funny thing is you think that you've won. I'm just an old man whose time has come to an end, but men like you will always fail."

"What makes you think that?" he asked.

Robert grinned, "well that answer is quite simple." He quickly slid a hand into his pocket, pulled out a pistol and fired.

"If I were any other man, you would have bested me," said the cloaked warrior as he spit the bullet out of his mouth. "As you can see, I caught it with my teeth. It is unfortunate for you that I happen to possess a rare charm that makes it pretty difficult to kill me. I do applaud your effort. I have enjoyed our little duel. Do you have any final wishes?"

Robert shrugged, "you can't blame a guy for trying. Hurry up and finish this. My lovely wife is waiting for me on the other side."

The cloaked soldier bowed respectfully; then an evil expression appeared on his face. In an instant, Robert's grin faded away and he felt genuine fear as a sword elevated above his head.

***

The boys were huffing and puffing as they drew closer to the intersection of Grand Avenue. Jayden glanced back just long enough to watch as a cloaked figure shoved his sword into Robert's chest, killing him. His heart broke and his eyes brimmed with tears as he watched the dark warrior clean his blade and fade back into the shadows.

Noticing that Jayden had stopped, Tony turned around to see what had happened. From a distance, he could see Robert's body slumped on the ground. Making a fist, he yelled into the night," you bastards!"

"It's not worth running anymore," Jayden whined. "How many people have died already? Where are we going to go? Let's just give up."

"Maybe you're right." Tony agreed.

A reassuring hand touched Jayden's shoulder. Looking up into the weary eyes of his father, he felt a small sense of hope again. Maybe they would be able to make it through this.

"Follow me, boys, let's get out of here," his father said calmly.

Taking a second look at his father, Jayden realized there was something different about his dad. A long black scimitar hung from his father's back, a row of throwing knives dangled from his belt, and he had a .45 caliber pistol strapped to his hip.

"Dad, where did you get all those weapons?" his son asked.

Smiling his dad replied, "I took them off one of the soldiers. Now we need to be quiet as we cross Grand Avenue. They are close by."

When Jayden crossed on to Grand Avenue, he glanced to his right and became aware of a group of cloaked soldiers on Main Street. They were surrounding seven members from town.

"Dad! Look over there! I think I can see Miss Mara with those people. Do you think you can help her and save the others?"

Dion ushered Tony and Jayden across the street. He hid them behind a tall two-story house.

"I will help them. But if something happens to me, you two must promise to head to Dragon Mountain without me," Dion said.

"But dad!" Jayden whined.

"You have to promise me. Remember, this isn't a game. This is real life. Promise me you will go there no matter what!" Dion demanded.

"We promise, we'll go," Jayden replied.

Dion embraced his son, and then made his way toward Main Street. He moved cautiously along Grand Avenue. Dion wasn't sure if there were any other sentries nearby. He couldn't afford to end up in a gunfight before he got to Miss Mara.

Dion ducked behind a dark alley by a corner store and cocked his .45. He looked around the corner to see what he was up against. Dion counted a total of eight soldiers surrounding some of the people from town. Dion needed to create a distraction if he was going be able to save them. He wanted to get their attention on him so that Miss Mara and the others could escape.

Dion raised his gun straight up into the air and fired off two rounds. The cloaked soldiers spun around looking for the source of the gunfire. Dion sprinted around the corner with his gun raised and sent bullets flying in quick succession. Immediately, he was able to dispatch three of the soldiers. Dion dove to his left to avoid the return fire. As he rolled, he fired five more shots finishing off the remaining soldiers.

Jumping back to his feet, he yelled, "you all have to get out of here quickly; they will be sending reinforcements here after hearing those gunshots. Miss Mara, my son and his friend are hiding behind that house down the street. Would you be willing to help get them out of here and take them to Dragon Mountain? I'm going to see if I can help anyone else get out of here and maybe lead some of the soldiers away so you can all escape."

Nodding her head, Miss Mara ran down the street and ducked behind the house. She saw the two boys and said, "Jayden and Tony, we need to get out of here. We just have to go past a few more buildings and we should be able to reach the dirt highway that will take us up into the mountains."

"Where's my dad? Is he okay?" Jayden yelled frantically.

"Your dad is doing just fine. We need to get out of here as quickly as possible. We can make it through this but we are going to have to work together to make that happen," she said firmly.

Jayden couldn't help but admire Miss Mara's strength and courage. Her look of determination helped to inspire the boys to press on. The way she guided them through town was masterful. It became harder and harder to believe that she was just a simple 7th-grade teacher.

Her blonde hair blew gently in the wind as she led them across a street. Miss Mara was only in her thirties, but the events of today seemed to have aged her a few years. Even though he was worried about his dad, her presence gave him hope that things might get better.

The bright lights from the burning buildings gave Jayden a greater appreciation for the damage that came upon his town. Houses and business centers crumbled from the damage caused by fire. Bodies of friends and neighbors littered the streets from where they fell. Gray smoke reached into to the sky signaling death's victory.

Somewhere in this living nightmare, his father was waging war against these cloaked warriors. Was it selfish for him to want his father to run away with them to the mountains? Instead of saving what's left of Eiréné? Maybe it was.

Before they crossed another street, Jayden nudged Miss Mara and said, "Thank you for doing this. I'm sorry for all the crap me and Tony have given you this year."

She smiled and said to them, "Boys, even though you have both given me a few gray hairs this year, I have enjoyed being your teacher. Now perk up, we're almost out of this town. Two more streets and we can hit that long dusty road into the mountains."

Miss Mara stepped out onto the quiet street with the boys at her side. Without warning, she crumbled to the ground. Tony rushed to her side, and Jayden watched in horror as a spot of blood slowly spread across her chest, and the light in her eyes began to fade.

Tears brimmed in his eyes as two figures in dark hoods crept out of the shadows with rifles in their hands. The two men laughed and cheered as they approached their next victims.

"Did you see that shot? I even closed my eyes for it. Kind of a waste though. She looks pretty fine minus the hole in her chest" said the taller soldier.

"Alex, you weren't supposed to kill her you moron. We needed to find out if she knew about *The Key*." said the smaller soldier.

"Thomas, who cares about her. Dion's son is that kid right there. He's gotta know about *The Key*," Alex replied.

Tony looked at Jayden, and mouthed, what are they talking about?

"Hey, you! Dion's kid, tell us where *The Key* is." Thomas demanded, "and maybe you won't end up like your lady friend."

With anger building up inside of his chest, Jayden yelled defiantly, "I don't know about any key and even if I did know, I wouldn't tell you crap. You just killed my teacher a-hole. I hope you and your buddy go to hell."

Thomas laughed sarcastically, "Talkative, are we. Where was all that bravery before Alex shot your friend? She might have stood a chance if you had that spunk earlier."

Consumed with anger, Tony rushed him and without hesitation, Thomas struck him with the butt of his gun. "Shit that hurts," Tony cried holding his forehead as it began to bruise.

"You young lads have got a little fight in you. I admire that," Alex said.

Thomas cocked his gun and looked at the two of them," We have to get back to the Dark Prince. These boys know nothing, and we can't leave any witnesses."

Grinning, Alex raised his rifle and said, "say cheese."

Before he could pull the trigger, a sword pierced through his chest, and a gun appeared from behind him and fired two rounds into Thomas's chest. Alex fell to the ground, and the hero standing behind him was Jayden's father.

Running to him, the boys wrapped their arms around Dion, and all the tears they had been fighting up until this point came pouring out.

"It is going to be alright," Dion said calmly with the sword and gun still in his hands.

"Dad, can we please go now and just get away from here!" Jayden pleaded between sniffles as he held his father.

Taking a deep breath, his father replied. "Son, I know that you don't want to hear this, but I will have to catch up with you two later. I need to slow them down so you two can escape."

"Dad! Just come with us! They won't catch us!" Jayden cried.

"Son, remember when I made you promise to head up the mountain if something happened to me. I need you to promise to go there. I will catch up with you," his father said.

"Promise me that you will meet us up there. You know you can't break your promises."

Looking into his son's eyes, he smiled and said, "I promise. Now go!" Letting them go, Dion turned and ran down the street.

For a moment, Jayden stayed there in the middle of the street watching his Dad run off to save the day. His glowing sense of pride for his father was slowly becoming a victim to a growing sense of dread. Will I ever see him again? He wondered.

While Jayden was thinking, Tony grabbed him by the shoulder and said, "I know this sucks, but we promised that we would go. Hey, I bet you I can beat you over to the mountain, you slowpoke."

Then for the first time in a while, a smile formed on Jayden's face. Shoving Tony to the side, he dashed towards the dirt highway. "See if you can catch me."

As Tony caught up to him, he could hear the faint sound of gunfire echoing into the night. Jayden seized a moment to look back at the town he once called home. He watched as bolt of lightning struck down in the middle of Eiréné, and it began to rain. That's great, he thought. As if today couldn't get any worse, now it's raining.

Chapter 3

A Royal Obsession

The capital city of Eden is Central City. Central City is the second largest city in the country of Eden and it stretches on for miles. Central City's eastern border touches the ocean known as the Crystal Sea, and its western border ends at the Forest of Dreams. The Capitol is protected from the north by a mountain range of volcanos, known as the Scorching Mountains, and from the south by the Imperial Marine Corp base. The Royal Palace resides at the northern end of the city, and it is protected by a twenty-foot tall spiked fence. Members of the Imperial Guard stand watch at the gate and the four corners of the wall.

An army soldier began to approach the palace's front gate. The young warrior stood at 5'10 and was twenty years old. He wore his navy blue officer's uniform with a Gladius hanging on his left hip. The sword had a golden hilt that shined beautifully in the afternoon sun.

Three guardsmen stood at the entrance. The High Commander looked up at the soldier and shouted, "halt! What brings you to the Royal Palace soldier? What is your business here? You need documentation to enter."

This guy takes his job way too seriously, the soldier thought. Standing up straight, he replied, "I am Sergeant Jason. I am here to meet with King Aelius."

"Where are you stationed, Sergeant? Do you have a formal invitation to be in the King's presence?"

"Yes I do, and I am stationed at the Western Army airbase," Jason replied while handing the guard his invitation.

"The Western Army Base, you say? You're a little far away from home, aren't you? What is your business with the King?"

Smiling, he replied, "That sir, would be classified."

The guard shrugged and gestured for him to enter the gate. Walking toward the Palace, Jason took a moment to take a look at its immense splendor. The palace had two enormous windows on each side of the Palace doors. The two palace doors were bright red and twelve feet tall with solid gold handles. The doors opened by themselves slowly as Jason approached.

The palace itself divides into three sections. On his left was the hall that led to where the Parliament assembled. The hallway to his right led to the war room and the cafeteria. The King's suite was in the center of the building.

Jason was guided to the King's suite by a beautiful red velvet carpet. Walking down the hall, he examined the many portraits on the walls as he approached the King's room. He recognized the images of the previous Kings and Queens of Eden. To the average tourist or diplomat that may visit the palace, these portraits would have inspired patriotism and would instill confidence in all who entered.

The young sergent knew better as he glared at each of their smug faces. He knew about their untold stories, their lies, and dirty secrets that many of the residents of Eden never knew, and fewer would believe. Jason knew about their stories of betrayal, infidelity, and their unbridled lusts for power. If only the people knew the truth, they wouldn't follow such filth. There needed to be a change in regime.

Jason continued down the hall, and when he reached the top of the stairs, he stopped in front of a door made of white oak and inlaid with gold. Behind that door was the King's office, and his living quarters. Taking a deep breath, he knocked on the door. No response. He knocked again and heard someone yell, "come in!"

Jason entered the room and staring out of his window was King Aelius. The King was observing the immense beauty of the Palace Garden. The garden was three acres wide and was home to a plethora of beautiful plants, flowers, and three large fountains made in the shape of a Phoenix. King Aelius wore a dark blue suit with a matching tie. The King looked like a man in his forties; he had slightly graying hair that was slicked back. To the untrained eye, he looked like a pure politician. The King was a man of ambition, and he usually kept a compact high caliber pistol under his coat.

Smiling as he turned around, the King said, "I almost didn't recognize you without your longbow and quiver of never-ending arrows. It is nice to see you again Jason."

Bowing respectfully, Jason stood up saying, "they tend to frown on me wearing my combat uniform in the palace. I could say the same thing to you. Why aren't you wearing the royal robes? Don't tell me they have fallen out of fashion."

Laughing the King replied, "I find your humor amusing. In these modern times, I find that my subjects are less threatened by a man in a suit, than a man in flowing red and white robes. Anyway, enough of the small talk, do you bring news from out west?"

"That I do. I bring with me some good news and some bad news."

The King's demeanor changed immediately. His brow furrowed and his face was slowly turning red. "What do you mean bad news? Don't tell me they didn't find *The Key*!"

Jason grinned, "No they did not find it. However, they do believe that Dion must have moved it not too long before the attack on Eiréné. They are trying to chase down where *The Key* was relocated to."

The King slammed his fist on the desk and yelled, "So you're telling me that I allowed a foreign military group to walk around Eden for no good reason? They were supposed to find *The Key*, and then we were going to take it from them. If word gets out that I allowed Eiréné to be wiped out, we will both be tarred and feathered."

"Don't worry." Jason said calmly, "They believe that Dion's son will be the best bet for finding it."

"Well, where is his son? Go get him and make him look for it."

"They tracked his son going into the Dragon Mountains two days ago. We believe that he is staying in the monastery up there."

The King was growing increasingly frustrated, "what is the problem then? Send them up there to get the boy or get some of our troops to bring him here."

Typical politician Jason thought. So ignorant and blinded by his greed. He smirked and replied, "the reason they won't go after him is that when the boy becomes a man he will find *The Key* and bring it to us. Plus, attacking that monastery would be a one-sided battle. Those monks are trained in martial arts and magic. They have the high ground. If your military showed up at their doorstep, the other monasteries in Eden would rise against them, which would lead to a civil war and us getting tarred and feathered by the monks. Does that sound even remotely pleasant? Be patient your highness, let the boy find *The Key*. He will be too motivated by vengeance not to."

The King took a moment to think and shrugged, "well I guess it isn't a complete loss. I am willing to wait until the boy grows up. The power that *The Key* will give me is worth waiting for. While we wait, I need you to send some soldiers from the northwestern outpost to Eiréné. I want them to stay there, so it looks as if we are responding to the situation properly. Also, so that they can keep an eye on the movements of the boy." The King took a moment to adjust his tie when he heard a knock at the door. "Come in!" He yelled.

The door opened as a beautiful woman stepped into the room. Her light brown hair was straightened and came down just to her shoulders. She wore a navy blue cape that came down on her right side. Her arms and legs were covered in armor made of the most beautiful steel. She was equipped with a three-foot-long rapier that hung from her belt against her left hip. She carried a stern facial expression and possessed a quiet intensity.

"General Floriana, I presume? What brings you to my neck of the woods?" The King asked.

"My Lord, I am honored to be in your presence. I bring you some disturbing news. An unknown force has destroyed the town of Eiréné. I have soldiers ready to retaliate. This insult cannot go unpunished. I apologize for having to reveal such disturbing news," she said firmly.

"As it turns out, Sergeant Jason traveled all this way to inform me of these disturbing events. You should be proud of your Sergeant; you have trained him well."

Turning to Jason, she replied, "I am quite impressed Jason. So how should we respond to this attack my Lord? I had some family members who were killed there, and I want them avenged!" She said with her fists clenched.

"My lady, we have already decided on how to proceed. Jason will be stationing some soldiers at Eiréné. They will be there to investigate to see what happened and we will proceed from there. Our initial thoughts are that the invading force came from our enemies on the other side of the ocean. We believe the Aggeloi were searching for something and sent one of their black ops teams. I will be giving a press conference in the next hour so that we can get the support of our people. I am sorry for your loss; we will have them avenged. What I need you to do is to inform your soldiers to be on alert." Nodding her head in agreement, she turned on her heels and walked out of the door.

The King poured himself a drink. Taking a sip, he walked to the window. "If she ever discovers the truth, I want you to kill her."

"Yes, sir," Jason replied before bowing and exiting the room.

***

General Floriana stepped out of the Palace, and she couldn't quite shake this feeling that something fishy was going on. She felt as though there was something the King hadn't told her. She couldn't understand why Jason would contact the King before she had the chance to. The inconsistencies in procedure and many questions began to pile up in her mind. Looking at the time, she had a few minutes to spare. So she decided to wait outside of the palace until Jason came down.

Watching him walk out of the palace, she gestured for him to come to her. "Jason, may I ask you a question?"

"Yes," he replied.

She's already getting suspicious, he thought. Floriana was only two years older than him, but she had climbed the ranks even faster than he had. Aelius was an idiot to believe that he could keep her fooled for long.

"Are you hiding anything from me?" She asked.

"No."

"We've known each other for many years. You would tell me if you knew anything more wouldn't you?" At that moment she stopped addressing him as a fellow soldier, but as a friend.

"We have known each other for quite some time. If I knew any more, I would tell you. However, I do need to get going. I have to get those troops organized to start this investigation. I will see you back at the base."

Watching him walk away, she still couldn't shake away her suspicions. Jason wouldn't lie to me, would he?

***

The King took the stairs from his office and walked toward the rear exit of the palace. He stepped out on the patio and noticed that they had set up a podium with a mic. Once he approached the stage, he was blinded momentarily by the flashing lights from the many cameras. He could hear reporters shouting out question after question, begging for him to acknowledge them.

Stepping onto the podium, he glared down at the crowd of reporters. A part of him died on the inside every time he had to address these blood-sucking vermin.

One of the reporters raised their hand and asked, "what are you going to do about the economy?"

Another reporter asked, "how are you going to increase the availability of jobs?"

Yawning, he ignored their questions. So trivial he thought, he was on to bigger and better things than merely dealing with the economy.

A tall reporter in the back asked, "what are you going to do about the destruction of Eiréné? Was it the Aggeloi? Or was it one of the terrorist groups?"

Bingo he thought. Finally, a question worth his time.

"What happened to the beautiful people of Eiréné is a tragic loss for us all. For those of you who may not know, the Town of Peace became a war zone three days ago. An unknown group of assailants attacked the residents of this town, and burned it to the ground," he said while fighting a grin. The King forced himself to sniffle and caused a tear to fall from his eyes. "Our current reports say that there were no survivors. This is my fault; I dropped the ball. I will never let this happen again!" He slammed his fist on the podium, "I have ordered troops from the Western Army base to mount a full investigation into this incident. We believe that the group responsible were affiliated with the Aggeloi. They have denied responsibility, but I, King Aelius, will not rest. I will not sleep until the men, women, and children of Eiréné are avenged. We, the people of Eden, will learn from this tragic event and we will rise above it together, stronger than ever before!"

For the first time in about twenty years, the King was unanimously supported by the press cheering for him.

"Long live the King! Long live the King! Long live the King!" they shouted in unison.

Smiling, he waved to the crowd, as the cameras flashed. Stepping down from the podium, he walked toward the palace. That should keep them happy for a while.

Chapter 4

The Broken Promise

Dion sprinted down Main Street and about 30 yards in front of him, he saw a mob of cloaked figures approaching. There were some twenty troops from what he could see. Some of them were carrying rifles, while others had swords strapped to their backs. These aren't high odds, he thought, but I have to give my son enough time to get away. He ducked behind a house quickly to reload his pistol. Taking a moment to check his knife belt, he took a deep breath. I guess it's now or never.

He burst out from behind a house and began firing his pistol. The rounds found their targets, striking two soldiers in the chest. The cloaked figures responded and returned fire. He dove forward and as he rolled, he threw three poison-tipped knives which hit two soldiers to his right. They fell to the ground and began convulsing. That's four down, sixteen more to go.

The mob continued to fire back at him. Dion pulled out his scimitar from his back and used it to deflect bullets, while he shot rounds from his pistol. He managed to drop two more soldiers, dispatching one by deflecting a shot into a soldier's eye.

Diving to his left, he hid behind another building as they continued to fire. Sticking his head out from behind the building, he fired four more shots, then pulled his head back just in time to avoid another volley of lead. As they were reloading, he ran back onto the street.

The mob of cloaked warriors was now less than fifteen yards in front of him. For a moment, they halted and lowered their weapons. Their leader stepped out from the midst of the group and drew his sword from its scabbard. The longsword radiated with magical power, and it's platinum hilt shined ominously. "Dion is it? You have me at a loss. For just being part of a one-man band, you fight with the ferocity of a whole army. It's a shame that things must end this way. If it weren't for you hiding *The Key*, your beautiful town would still be standing. I have been impressed by the resolve of the residents of this town. They have put up quite the resistance. I couldn't have imagined, that I would lose as many soldiers as I have. In hindsight, I should have recruited more fighters from your town; they have proven to be quite capable. Back to the situation at hand. Dion, I don't often make deals, but I am willing to do so for you. If you tell us where *The Key* is, I will promise not to harm you or your son. We know that he is heading up into the mountains."

"I would love to help you all, but I haven't seen *The Key* in years. Also, I never got your name?"

"Well, that is quite unfortunate. I was hoping that finding *The Key* would be a piece of cake" pulling his hood back he replied, "They call me the Dark Prince." His spiky blonde hair blew gently in the wind. He had a handsome face and blue eyes that were cold and expressionless. "We are on a pretty tight schedule. So, I will just have to kill you now." With his sword drawn, the Dark Prince advanced on Dion.

With blazing speed, Dion flipped backward and fired two rounds at the Dark Prince, causing him to stop his advance. Then Dion jumped 30 feet into the air, and he swung his sword over his head.

"Monsoon! "He yelled.

Thunderclouds began rapidly forming in the sky above him and rain started to come down in sheets. As Dion descended, he slashed down with his sword, and three lightning bolts slammed into three of the cloaked soldiers below. Then he threw a knife at the Dark Prince that cut his left cheek.

Touching his left cheek, he examined the blood with a detached curiosity. Smiling, he said, "I have to admit, you are quite good, maybe even one of the greats. That storm magic was a nice touch. I can do it too. The last time someone made me bleed I was just a child. Bravo," he said coldly.

Looking up at Dion, his blue eyes flashed red from anger. Rushing at Dion, he slashed left and right. Their swords clashed sending sparks into the air. Dion ducked a sword swipe and swung his leg at the Dark Prince for a front sweep. The Dark Prince back flipped over the sweep, then summoned a gust of wind that knocked Dion backward. Stumbling backward, he tried to regain his balance and then he felt it. A cloaked figure standing right behind him stabbed him in the back. Dion fell to the ground and he threw his remaining knife at his attacker. Striking him in the shoulder and sending him to the ground bleeding and in pain.

Standing over Dion, the Dark Prince said, "I'm guessing that last stab about did it for you, but you know what they say, all good things must come to an end." As the Dark Prince raised his sword to finish the deed, Dion quickly raised his pistol and fired two shots. Swinging his sword, the Prince deflected away one of the bullets; the other caught him in the shoulder. His anger burned towards Dion, and with his sword, he made a sideswipe that created a massive gash across Dion's chest.

Smiling cruelly, he turned to the crowd of hooded soldiers and pointed at one, "you, come here and prove your loyalty."

Stepping out from the crowd, came a soldier with a five-foot-long spear in his hand. He stood over Dion and a small tear barely even noticeable fell from the warrior's eyes. Raising his spear, Dion opened his eyes for one brief moment and with a gentle smile he said in a hushed tone, "I forgive you." Then it all went black.

***

The boy woke up screaming and in a cold sweat.

"Jayden! Jayden! It's okay; it was just a dream. You were screaming in your sleep." Tony said, trying to comfort his friend.

Wiping his eyes, he tried to erase the images of his dad dying in his dream. It was just a dream he told himself. Looking around the room he noticed that he was in a dormitory. There was a bag filled with jeans and a T-shirt next to his bed. Across the room, he saw that Tony's bed had begun to gather some clutter. Then a thought jumped into his head, where the hell am I?

"Tony, where are we? Whose bed is this? Tell me this is just another dream and we are secretly at my house."

Laughing, his friend replied, "God no. We are staying at the Dragon Monastery."

"Dude! What in the world! Why in the heck are we here? Did we lose a bet?"

"Well, don't you remember? Yesterday, Eiréné was destroyed by a group of people in darkly hooded pajamas. We escaped into the mountains as your dad asked us. Two of those jack-holes followed us into the mountains. Then you tried to play hero and ran into a tree. Successfully knocking yourself out, I might add. Then some monks from the monastery came and saved us. It was pretty awesome! They beat those guys up and then sent them walking home in just their underwear."

"Well, that sounds awesome! Are you sure I got knocked out? I've been bulking up a lot lately. I don't see that being a possibility." Once those words exited his mouth, all of the images from the previous night came flooding back. His anger grew and he became deeply concerned.

"Tony," he said in a hushed tone, "where's my dad?"

Without meeting his eyes, Tony's tone changed and replied softly, "we don't know."

I need to find him, Jayden thought. My dad must have just got delayed. Maybe he forgot how to get here and he's just a little lost. Jayden quickly removed his covers, jumped up and ran for the door.

Once he stepped out of the dormitory, he found himself in a courtyard. Hundreds of feet up the mountain, the Grandmaster's Temple loomed above them. The building shined in the morning light, like a beacon of hope. He had seen it before when he had gone hiking. Usually, the splendor of the mountains and the light fog would make him stop and stare at the glorious beauty, but his mind focused on finding his dad. Unfortunately, he had no idea how to get out of this place. Jayden decided to take a left and was able to find some marble steps, which appeared to lead down the mountain.

"You must be Jayden, it is nice to see you up and about," said a voice from behind him.

Turning around, Jayden saw a monk in a red martial arts uniform, with a yellow sash that hung on his left side. Standing face to face with a monk, rendered Jayden speechless. The power and wisdom radiating from this man were overwhelming.

Jayden cleared his throat nervously, and said, "um Hi. How's it going? And you are?"

"They call me Master Thai. I help to train the next generation of Dragon Warriors."

"What the heck is a Dragon Warrior?"

"A Dragon Warrior is the title and rank given to warriors who have successfully been trained here at the Dragon Monastery."

"Well, that's cool. I guess"

Moving closer to Jayden, Master Thai took a moment to examine the boy and smiled. Okay, weirdo, Jayden thought. Who knew monks were such creeps. "You look a lot like your father," Master Thai said.

Well, maybe Master Thai wasn't so creepy after all. Wait a minute, how does he know my father. Reading his expression, the monk said, "I've known your father for many years. We trained here together. He informed us that you and Tony might end up coming here someday."

Talk about random. How did his dad know that he would end up here? None of this makes sense he thought.

"Mr. Thai, it has been nice meeting you and thanks for giving us a place to stay. But I have to find my dad. He may have gotten hurt and might need help."

Noticing the worry on Jayden's face, Master Thai smiled and put his fingers to his lips and whistled. Then seemingly out of nowhere, three more monks appeared at his side.

"Jayden, we will go down the mountain with you. We believe the invaders are gone, but you can never be too careful."

Tony came out of their room and ran after them. He was moving so fast, that he bumped into Jayden and made him take a tumble down the mountain. Catching himself, Jayden. Glanced up at Tony and said, "If you're going to try and push me down the mountain, you're going to have to try harder than that." Tony shoved Jayden again, and the boys laughed, as they began their journey down the mountain.

Ash fell from the sky, like a haunting snowstorm, as they descended the mountain. The smell of smoke was so thick in the air; it was difficult to breathe. With every step they took, Jayden's mind began to race. The events from the previous night played over and over again in his mind. He tried covering his ears to shut out the sounds of gunfire and people screaming into the night.

Jayden felt uneasy, as they passed under the sign that said, "Welcome to Eiréné." His heart was pounding in his chest, and he felt sick to his stomach. He wanted to find his dad, but his mind and body wanted to be as far away from Eiréné as possible.

He shook his head in disbelief, hoping and praying that this had all just been a dream. Then he saw her, and he knew that there was no way, the other night was anything but a nightmare. Lying on the ground, where she fell was Miss Mara. Bending over, he touched her once warm hand. His heart broke, as he remembered how she was willing to give her life to protect him and Tony. With a tear in his eye, Jayden said, "This isn't fair. It's not fair that you had to die trying to save us. Maybe if I were a little stronger, I could have done something. We will never forget you!"

Letting her hand go, he wiped the tears from his eyes. Tony put his arm around him, "Don't blame yourself. There was nothing we could do".

Together, this odd band of monks and two teenagers began to head down Main Street. In the light of the day, it became clear how devastating the destruction was. Smoke was still rising from the holes in Ms. Tonya's pink roof. There were whole neighborhoods that burned to the ground. Many of the houses and stores were peppered with bullet holes and blackened from the fire damage.

Eiréné was beginning to remind Jayden of the documentaries he saw in school, about the cities bombed during the last war. The scene looked hopeless. The warm spirit of the people that once filled the town, had been replaced with sorrow and death. Were there any survivors, he wondered? Did the others get away? Or were they hunted down like him and Tony? Passing by Tony's house, Jayden turned to him and asked, "Did your grandparents make it?"

Without looking up to respond, his friend just shook his head. He grimaced at the thought. Jayden had been so caught up with his problems that he failed to realize that Tony might be hurting too. He started to pat his buddy's shoulder when he almost tripped over his own feet because Tony stopped walking without warning.

What the heck was that for? Who just stops in the middle of a road? Carefully he followed Tony's line of sight. When he saw what Tony was staring at, his jaw dropped. He felt queasy on the inside, and his heart began banging in his chest like it wanted to escape.

Resting further down the road was a body, lying on the ground with a spear sticking out of it. As they got closer to the body, time felt like it was slowing down. Jayden was getting more nervous the closer they got. It became harder and harder for him to breathe. When he couldn't take it any longer, he sprinted to the body.

Jayden was hoping beyond hope. Please let it be someone else, anybody else. When he got there, his heart stopped, and his knees became weak. His hands were shaking and for a moment, he didn't know what to do. He was praying to God that his eyes were playing tricks on him, that what lay before him was part of some elaborate prank.

The body resting on the ground was his father. There he laid with his arms spread wide, his sword and gun were resting on each side of him, with a spear protruding from his chest. His eyes were closed and his face looked calm as if he was just asleep.

Jayden fell to his knees, as he began to sob. His heart ached more than it ever had before. The tears flowed like a river of sadness leaving his body. His hands continued to shake as his new reality was starting to become too much to handle. He wanted to run away; he wanted to escape to anywhere but here. His sadness began to meld with the growing rage that was building up from deep inside of him, and he couldn't take it anymore.

Staring at his dad's face, he yelled, "You promised! You said you would find us, but you didn't! You chose to stay here, and now look at you! Why did you leave me!" as his sobs were beginning to overcome him, he cried out, "You promised!" His head fell on to his father's chest as the tears continued to flow. Tony sat down beside him and shed a few tears with his best friend.

It felt like they had sat there for hours. While time passed by, their sobs became fewer and farther between. Suddenly, they heard the faint sound of engines rumbling off in the distance. The sound grew louder, and the monks glanced in the direction of the disturbance.

Master Thai said, "Cars are coming this way, we have to go."

Feeling both emotionally and physically drained. Jayden stood up and without waiting for the others, he started walking back toward the mountain. Master Thai indicated for the other monks to pick up Dion's body, "We will give him a proper burial."

Jayden was the first one out of town. He just kept on walking; maybe he would just keep on walking forever he thought. Tony finally caught up to him with his backpack jingling as he ran.

"Hey! Turn around!" Tony said, "Look at those cars driving into Eiréné."

Turning around Jayden looked at the caravan of vehicles. They had the Western Army base insignia of a Phoenix holding a dagger on their doors. The soldiers jumped out of their vehicles armed to the teeth. That's just great Jayden thought. If only they could have shown up sooner. Maybe his dad would still be here.

He shook his head in silent frustration and kept walking until he reached the base of the Dragon Mountain. Master Thai signaled for them to stop. The monks began to dig a grave and placed the body into the ground. Then they covered it up. By using two sticks, they laced them together with weeds to make a cross for a headstone. Then they gather together and formed a circle around the grave.

Master Thai took a deep breath, "Dion, I have known you for many years. During that time I never thought that I would be the one giving your eulogy. You were a great warrior, an amazing friend and a one of a kind person. You cared for anyone that you came into contact with. You showed mercy to those who didn't deserve it. You gave your life to save others and I am truly honored to have known you. Though your days on this Earth are gone, you will live forever in our hearts. May your spirit find rest, as we carry on your memory. From ashes to ashes. From dust to dust." Bowing respectfully, each one of them slowly began the trek back up the mountain

Jayden was the last one to leave. Standing by his father's grave, the tears began to brim in his eyes once more. Trying to fight them, he said, "I miss you, dad. I just can't believe that you're gone. I know you're in a better place, and I wish I were there with you" as his anger began to build up inside of him, he clenched his fists, "I will never forget you! Never! I will never forgive those that did this to you. I will get strong dad, I promise. You will be avenged." Touching the cross, he whispered, "I love you."

Chapter 5

New Beginnings

Seven years have gone by, since that fateful day. When Jayden's peaceful world came crashing down in a fiery flame. Since that day, the people of Eden and the Aggeloi were slowly growing closer and closer to war. *The Key* that many were searching for has still not been found. Jayden and Tony have been training in the Dragon Mountains, since the destruction of Eiréné. It was November, Jayden had just celebrated his twentieth birthday the day before, but today was going to be even more special. November 18th was the day in which Jayden and Tony were to complete their trials and become official Dragon Warriors.

Jayden stood at 5'9 with his curly brown hair cut short. He examined himself in the mirror, and he couldn't help but smile. Flexing his biceps, he said to himself, Jayden you're looking good. Staring at his reflection, he said, "Jayden, you can do this. Yes, this will be your second attempt at trying to complete the trials, but this one is special. Remember, think slowly, use your training, and remember always to have the eye of the tiger out there. You are the best Dragon Warrior to come through this monastery. Remember that."

"No you aren't," said a voice coming from behind him, "You are twenty years old and giving yourself a morning pep talk. I don't think I've walked in on anything funnier in the last year." Tony said, falling to the ground laughing

Turning toward the laughing monkey on the floor, Jayden said, "Laugh all you want. You won't be laughing when I complete my trials in record time."

"If you can complete the trials in record time than anything is possible. Maybe I can flap my arms and go to the moon." Tony said sarcastically. "Anyway, you need to hurry up and get ready. You move slower than a turtle."

Jayden opened his drawer and pulled out his lucky black Dragon Warrior shirt, and red pants. He wrapped his white sash around his waist, cracked his knuckles, it's game time he thought.

Stepping out of his dormitory, he made a right and took the steps up toward the Dragon Warrior temple. The Dragon Monastery was made up of three large temples. The Dragon Warrior Temple, was where young warriors were taught hand to hand combat, and how to use various weapons, and firearms. The second temple which was higher up on the mountain is The Temple of Magic, where the highly adept students, were trained to use fire and storm magic, and that's also where they learn philosophy. The third building was the Grandmasters Temple, where the Dragon Sage resided. The temple of the Grandmaster sat near the summit of Dragon Mountain. Jayden had only seen it and wasn't allowed inside. Only warriors that were worthy could be in the presence of the Dragon Sage. One day that warrior will be me, he thought. Without paying attention to where he was going, he bumped into Master Thai.

Master Thai did not look amused, "Jayden, do you know what time it is?"

Smiling mischievously, Jayden replied, "Morning time?"

"Oh, you got jokes this morning. I hope those jokes help you in your trials. I would hate for you to get embarrassed again like you did last year. In all my years of training fighters. I've never seen my pupils fail so badly. Make me proud today, or you will be cleaning out the Temple bathrooms until you're forty!"

"Don't you worry Master Thai. I'm wearing my lucky Jade necklace. And I went to bed before 2 a.m. last night; you should be proud."

"Enough chitchat, let's get the show on the road. Tony has already started his trials."

"What? Let's go!" Jayden yelled as he ran toward the temple.

The Dragon Temple was made of bronze and on top of its roof, sat a gigantic statue of a dragon. The dragon was 25 feet long, with razor sharp claws that were made of crystal. The dragon's body was made of emeralds and gold. The statue was an immaculate piece of art, and how these broke monks could afford to build it, Jayden had no clue.

The first time he laid eyes on that statue, he found it intimidating. This morning, it seemed like the dragon's eyes were judging his every move. While he stared at the dragon, the white temple door, opened by itself.

The temple that morning was filled with activity. Young warriors ran from one side of the room to the other. While the Masters stood in each corner of the room, leading their students in hand to hand combat drills. One lucky student even had to practice cartwheeling across the balance beam. Jayden remembered, the first time he had to that, he could still feel the bruise he got from falling off it. While he was momentarily distracted, Master Thai grabbed him by the shoulder and led him out into the temple garden.

The Dragon Temple's Garden was separated into two sections, by a cement wall. The western side of the Garden was a rock garden filled with a plethora of bonsai trees. The eastern side of the garden was filled with beautiful flowers, vegetables, and fruit trees. A series of pillars made of granite were placed throughout the flower garden. These pillars were fourteen feet high, and they were stationed five feet apart from each other. There was a total of ten pillars. Resting on the furthest pillar was a red sash.

His first challenge involved jumping from pillar to pillar until he reached the red sash. Sounds pretty simple right? Wrong! There was a little catch to this obstacle. Jayden had to carry an egg on a spoon, and that egg had to survive him jumping from pillar to pillar. If that didn't sound bad enough, the pillars would wobble and lean when a person landed on them. For this challenge, Jayden would be given three tries to complete it.

Master Thai turned to Jayden, "Are you ready?"

Jayden nodded as he placed an egg on his spoon. With ease, he jumped up and landed on the first pillar. The pillar swayed gently back and forth. Not too bad so far, he thought. Then his mind flashed back to the previous year when he was unable to complete this task. He shook his head and said to himself, I can do this.

He beamed with confidence and proceeded to jump from pillar to pillar with ease. He made it all the way to the final pillar and picked up the sash. With a grin on his face, he yelled, "I did it!". Master Thai shook his head and pointed at the spoon.

Crap, the egg had fallen off. Oh well. Jayden jumped back down and grabbed the second egg. Then he leaped back on to the first pillar. When he landed, the pillar swung more violently, than he was expecting. So both the egg and Jayden fell to the ground. Luckily the pink and white daisies broke his fall.

"Jayden, when Tony did this earlier he completed it on his first try. You can do this; you have to focus on balance. Don't try and complete the task; you need to find your balance. "His master yelled.

Dusting himself off, Jayden grabbed his third and final egg and placed it on the spoon. Jumping up on to the first pillar, it wobbled even more than it had previously. Just as he about to lose his footing, he propelled himself forward to the second pillar. He continued to jump from pillar to pillar with ease.

Once he landed on the eighth pillar, it tilted back and forth violently. Jayden glanced over at the final pillar, and he could see the red sash gleaming in the sun. I'm almost there he thought. Then as the pillar swayed backward, his egg fell out of his spoon. With blazing speed, Jayden was able to catch it before he lost it.

Master said that I need to focus on balance, and not on the victory. He closed his eyes and took a deep breath to regain his composure. Then Jayden front-flipped on to the ninth pillar, and as it swung backward, he leaped forward. Jayden was beaming with pride as he landed on the tenth, and final pillar. He reached out and picked up the sash and exclaimed, "I did it!"

"Well done," Master Thai said, "Now don't get too confident, remember you still have two more challenges to go. For those tasks, you will only be allowed one chance to complete them."

One chance? I hope they get progressively easier, Jayden thought. Master Thai led him back into the Dragon Warrior Temple. They took a right and entered a small room. In the center of the room was a white pillow used for meditation. That's odd Jayden thought, what kind of challenge is this? Oh please tell me that it's a napping challenge.

"Master, seeing as I have never made it past the first challenge. Can you explain to me what I am supposed to do here?" Jayden asked.

"You are to sit on that pillow, and you are to meditate for the next two hours. You are not to say a word. You may not adjust how you sit on the pillow. Once you pick a position, you must stay in it for the remainder of the time. You may begin at any moment."

"Well, that sounds easy enough. I'm pretty good at meditation." Jayden replied. He placed his knees on the pillow, closed his eyes and began to meditate.

Time felt like it was going by slowly, or maybe it was going quickly. Jayden couldn't tell if he were there for five minutes or thirty hours. Just as his back began to get stiff from sitting, he heard the faint sound of a water faucet start to drip. A few minutes later, the sound grew louder, and the drops occurred more frequently. God that sound is annoying, he thought.

Then he heard the beautiful sound, of nails, scratching on a chalkboard. He cringed as the sound mixed with the noise of the faucet. These people are going to drive me crazy! Maybe that's the point, a stupid point at that. I've got to focus on meditating, he reminded himself.

Then he heard the sound of laughter, not just any laughter, the sound of children laughing. Creepy children laughing that is. As the creepy laughter grew louder, additional sounds were added all at once. He heard the sound of jackhammers pounding the concrete, people yelling, and the sound of someone sawing wood. The chaotic sounds were unbearable. He wanted to scream, "Shut up"! But, he knew he couldn't.

Jayden knew he had to find his focus, so he decided to focus on finding his calm. Breath in the good, breath out the bad, breath in the good, and breath out the bad. With every deep breath he took, the obnoxious sounds became less distracting. Even though it was difficult to ignore the sound of nails grinding against a chalkboard, Jayden was able to find a sense of peace. Now all he had to do was maintain this calm for just a little longer, and he would be home free.

As Jayden took another deep and calming breath, a raspy voice whispered gently in his ear and said, "You're the reason your father died." Immediately, his sense of calm was unraveling; he wanted to hurt whoever said it. Just when he was about to lose it, Master Thai said, "Your time is up."

Opening his eyes, he looked around the room. All he could see was his Master sitting in the corner. "What the heck was that?" Jayden shouted. "What was making all of that noise?"

Master grinned, "What noise? I didn't hear anything. Let's go to your last and final task."

Jayden was absolutely livid. The anger he felt made him want to explode. He wanted to slap his master so hard that his head would spin. Why would Master Thai make him do that? Does he want me to think I'm going crazy? Were all of those sounds, just in my head?

Master Thai signaled for Jayden to follow him. Jayden was being led back out into the garden, to face his final challenge. They traveled along a stone path that led to one of the gardening sheds. His Master opened the door and stepped in. Before Jayden joined him, he had a thought. Why is my last task in a storage shed?

Once he stepped into the shed, his nostrils flared from the musty scent of the wood. The shelves that stored the gardening tools were stripped bare. Since nobody was doing gardening work today, Jayden was a little concerned as to what his final task might entail.

He stood in the corner of the room and in his hand, he held an old machete. In the center of the room, a person was wearing a black coat, with a matching hood, sitting on their knees. As Jayden crept closer, the cloaked figure seemed more and more familiar. He knew he had seen him before but from where?

"Jayden, you have completed two out of the three tasks. Are you ready for the third and final challenge?"

Jayden began to panic on the inside. What was he supposed to do with that old machete? Is that rust on it? Oh my God, don't tell me the final task is to get tetanus.

He glanced up at Master Thai and nodded yes.

"I have to hear you say it with conviction. Are you ready for your final challenge?"

Gulping down his fear, he stared at his master dead in the eye, "Yes Master, I am."

He gestured for Jayden to stand in front of the cloaked figure in the center of the room. Once he stood in front of the cloaked figure, he heard the man whisper quietly, "Please, whatever you do, don't do whatever he asks."

Jayden began to feel sweaty, his hands became clammy, and his mouth felt dry, as he started to understand what his next task was. He was going to have to execute this man.

Master Thai gave Jayden the machete and nodded his head. As Jayden gripped the blade, the reality of his task weighed heavy on his mind. The machete felt like it weighed a million pounds in his hands. This weapon should feel lighter, he thought. Maybe his mind was playing tricks on him again.

Jayden examined the cloaked figure, and he began to wonder if this man had a family or any friends. Would anyone even notice if this guy died? Jayden knew that he would, and that's what made doing this difficult.

"Jayden! Quit your stalling! This man deserves to die!" Master Thai shouted. "He was with the group that destroyed your town and killed your father."

Instantly, Jayden looked at this man with a different set of eyes. His magical power began to skyrocket, and red flames swirled around the tip of the machete. Jayden adjusted his grip on the weapon, and it felt lighter and more powerful in his hand. He was going to hurt this man. He wanted to watch this man bleed for his sins.

Pulling the machete back, he prepared to swing it, and send this guy to Hades. With all his might, he swung that rusted sword and just as it was about to connect, he stopped as the blade grazed the man's neck. He dropped the machete, and it clanged as it hit the ground.

Jayden slumped to the floor and shook his head in frustration, and said," I just can't do it. I can't kill this man. How do you know he was even there? No matter what he did, I just can't

47

kill an unarmed man. I'm sorry master; I failed you...again." Jayden bowed his head in shame.

Smiling with pride, his Master approached him and touched his shoulder, "Jayden, I am so proud of you. You passed the final test, congratulations. Now head over to the Wyvern fountain in the garden. I have something to present to you and Tony. Don't feel too bad, the guy in the hoodie is Master Tanaka."

Jayden stared at his hands, "Could I have gone through with it? Could I have taken his life?" he said softly.

Dusting himself off, he got up from the floor, but he couldn't quite shake the feeling of rage he had. It was almost uncontrollable. The amount of power he was able to channel from his anger frightened him.

Jayden pulled the shed door open and stepped outside. The moment his shoes touched the pavement, reality struck him. I've officially completed my trials, he realized. Suddenly, the world seemed hopeful and filled with opportunities. The sun shined just a little brighter, the flowers in the garden, seemed to bloom as he walked by. There was a spring in his step that he had not had in quite some time.

Jayden found his Master, who was now standing by the Wyvern fountain. He noticed that Master Tanaka was standing with him. Tony was kneeling in front of the two of them and was bowing in respect. Jayden came up beside his friend and knelt down.

"Arise my students. I want you to know that I am very proud of you. Don't feel discouraged that it took you two attempts, over the last two years to complete your trials. Personally, it took me three tries, and I turned out alright. Before I present you with your sashes and rank, I want to talk with you about the trials you faced. I want you to understand their deeper meaning. First off, I want you to understand that being a Dragon Warrior does not make you better than anyone else. It does not make you invincible. However, it does require you to be a servant and helper of humanity. You are to be part of the good in this world. The first challenge was about focusing on the task at hand. When you didn't focus, you forgot the little things, and that would cost you. In life, if you do not keep your focus, sooner or later the cost of forgetting the little things, will be greater than you can imagine. The second task was about blocking out all of the distracting noises in your life and finding peace. Focusing on the good things when bad things surround you, will keep you centered. The final task was specifically designed to attack your deepest and darkest desires. You two have experienced traumas that most will never understand. Your temptation and desire for revenge, has helped to motivate you here. That feeling isn't bad, letting it consume you is. Letting it control you is. You need to be able to extend mercy to those who don't deserve it. You young men did well at rising above your desire for vengeance, but remember, just because you were able to do that today, does not mean it will be easier to do tomorrow. To be a Dragon Warrior is to bless those around you, even when it's not easy."

Master Tanaka handed Master Thai one of the red sashes. Master Thai bowed respectfully and gave Tony, his red sash, and then he gave Jayden his. Then Master Thai said, "Congratulations, you both have completed all the training needed to receive the rank of Dragon Warrior. I have been honored to watch you young boys grow into men. Now, that you two are of age, you are welcome to leave and explore the world. You are also welcome to stay and train to become Dragon Masters."

Whey their excitement became too much to bear. Jayden turned toward his friend, jumped up and gave him the biggest high five of the century. "We did it! We did it!" yelled.

His Master smiled with pride, "Now before you run off and celebrate. There is one more thing you must do. I almost forgot to give you your surprise. Stick your right arms out."

They did as he asked, smiling from ear to ear. Then he snapped his fingers and magical energy filled the air.

"Ouch!" They screamed. Then they quickly glanced down at their arms, as dragon tattoos began to form on their forearms.

"Those tattoos are to remind you of the power you possess. The red dragon on your arm Jayden signifies your ability to use fire magic, and the fiery spirit that you possess. The twin dragons on your arm Tony, one of them white and the other blue, signifies your ability to use storm magic, but to remind you to wrestle with the storm inside you."

The boys both admired their new tattoos, with a sense of awe and amazement. They continued to give each other high fives and rejoiced for the next hour or two. Once they had split up for the evening, Jayden found himself going toward Master Thai's study. He had made his decision, about whether he would leave or stay. He knocked on the door. "Come in," his master said.

When he entered the room, his mentor was sitting at his desk. Master Thai was reading old manuscripts written in some language that neither Jayden nor anyone born in this century could understand. His Master turned to him and said, "I was wondering when you would show up." He gestured for Jayden to sit in a chair.

"Master, I have decided that, I want to leave and explore the world."

"Is that really why you want to leave?"

"No. I want to chase down the people that killed my father and destroyed everything I love."

"The road of vengeance, is a lonely one to travel."

"I don't care! I need to know that my dad and all of the people from Eiréné died for something! I owe it to them, to bring them justice."

Master Thai reached into his desk and pulled out a paper with some writing on it. He handed it to Jayden. Jayden looked at it, and said, "Skyline Apartments Rm. 205. What is this?"

"That is an address to an apartment in Mirage City. The person living there will help you on your journey. And remember, no matter how far you travel, you can always come back here. The Dragon Temple will always be a place that you can call home."

Jayden thanked his Master and bowed respectfully before he left the room. Once he left his master's study, he ran toward his room to pack for his journey. While loading clothes into his duffle bag, he began to reminisce about his time spent at the monastery. He felt honored for having been there. The monks, took him and Tony in, without a second thought. Master Thai even helped him to bury his father. I could never thank him enough for that, he thought.

While packing his bag, he grabbed the katana he made during his second year. Pulling the sword out from its black scabbard, he admired the power and craftsmanship of the weapon. The blade was made of magically infused dragon steel and was exceptionally sharp. Near the hilt of the sword, it said in gold cursive letters, Jade Blade. Smiling with pride, he placed the weapon into his bag.

He reached over to his bed, for one last item, his red sash. The crimson fabric of his new sash shimmered in the light of his room. This was the ultimate symbol, of his accomplishments. All the blood, sweat, and tears he spent trying to get this, were all worth it. Now he had the power, to change the world, and bring hope to the hopeless. While he was lost in thought, he heard the bedroom door open.

"So you're leaving then?" Tony asked when he entered the room.

"Yes, I am. You should go with me."

Tony shook his head, "After doing the trials today. I'm finally at peace with what happened all those years ago. If I go on that trip with you, that's only going to make keeping that peace impossible. You should stay here."

Jayden's caramel skin turned red and he clenched his fist. "I can't stay here! Every night when I go to sleep, I see flashbacks from that terrible night. I need to know there was a reason for it. I won't be at peace until I find out why."

Tony crawled into his bed, and rolled over so he couldn't see Jayden, "Good luck."

Wow, that was a terrific way to say goodbye. It's nice to know my best friend isn't going to miss me that much. Maybe I should have left sooner, Jayden thought.

Chapter 6

Two Steps forward and One Step Back

The morning sun greeted Jayden with a beautiful orange and yellow hew. The boys slept with the windows open, and Jayden was awakened, by the sound of birds chirping, and the wind brushing gently against the trees. Dragging himself out of bed, he glanced over at his friend's bed. Tony, had already left for the day. He didn't even leave a note saying goodbye.

After a ten minute shower, Jayden got out and put on a black shirt and jeans. When he got back to his room, he stopped once he crossed the threshold. Resting on his bag, was a black sword and a pistol. The closer he got to his bed, the more he recognized those weapons. They had belonged to his father. They were in pristine condition. The black scimitar was recently sharpened, and when he picked up the pistol, he noticed that it had been loaded with hollow points. There was even an extra magazine resting on the bag. Staring at the two weapons made emotions that he kept buried rise to the surface. He began to tear up, and his mind played back the moments from the worst time in his life. The sight of his father on the ground, the sound of gunfire, the heat burning buildings, and the smell of smoke. All of those repressed memories, came flooding back into his mind with a vengeance.

"So, you saw them?" Said a voice from outside of his room.

Turning around Jayden saw standing Tony in the doorway

"What do you mean?"

"The sword and the gun. They were your dad's."

"Ya, how did you know they were here?"

"I put them there. They were a going away present. When we saw your dad on the ground, I decided that it would be good to take them with us. I knew that they might be useful to you down the line. So I waited until you guys were far enough away, then I took them. I've kept them maintained over the last few years because I knew that eventually, you would want to leave. I was hoping that no matter where you were, that these weapons would make it, so you won't ever forget where we came from, what we've been through.

Jayden gave his friend a big hug. "Thanks, man, I couldn't ask for a better friend. I wish you were going with me, but I can understand you wanting to stay. I will send you letters, so you know how I'm doing."

Tony nodded, "Be safe man and remember if you ever need anything you know where to find me. And knowing your luck, you're going to need it" he said slapping him on the back. Smiling, Jayden gave him one more hug. Then he grabbed his bag and set off on his journey down the mountain.

***

After hours of hiking, Jayden was about half way down the mountain. He sniffed the air. The fresh smell of the pine trees was intoxicating; it was as if the Dragon Forest was saying goodbye to him in its special way. He was going to miss spending nights on this mountain and falling asleep under the stars. However, he wasn't going to miss, running up and down this mountain for training.

Jayden pushed his way through a thicket of pine trees and stepped into an open area. The trail that he needed to take to get down the mountain was about twenty yards in front of him. Large trees surrounded the path on both sides. As he got closer to it, he had the feeling that he was being watched. On his right side, there was a large field of tall grass. He stopped for a moment to listen, and that's when he heard the sound of a low growl.

Stepping out of the tall grass, was a lone wolf. Her beautiful white fur made her stand out, against the green back drop. She slowly crept closer to him. That's when he realized she wasn't an ordinary mountain wolf. The creature that was stalking him was an ice wolf.

He remembered learning about Ice Wolves in school. They were large pack animals that were able to run very fast and had a bite that would make the strongest man in the world cry. That wasn't even the worst part, these majestic creatures also possessed the magical ability of frost breath, which could turn your fingers into Popsicles.

The animal growled again as it crept closer. Jayden knew that he needed to act quickly. If he reached for his weapons, the animal would overcome him before he could even put up a fight. On the other hand, he could summon a fireball and turn this wolf into a hot dog. He didn't particularly, like the idea of roasting this animal. So what other options did he have?

He reached into his right pocket slowly, and rummaged around, hoping to find something useful. Jayden frowned, as his hand found the beef jerky in his pocket. He was originally planning on saving it, for a midday snack. Now, this jerky was going to be used to save his life. Jayden grimaced, as he pulled out the jerky begrudgingly. The enticing scent of the jerky seemed to catch the wolf's eyes. Great, she wants it, Jayden thought. He was secretly hoping wolves didn't like beef jerky. Well, if it keeps her from eating me for another five minutes, it might be worth the sacrifice.

Jayden closed his eyes and tossed the jerky at the wolf. The animal quickly snatched it out of the air. Then Jayden sprinted towards the trail. Don't look back, don't look back he told himself. So he decided to look back, just in time to see that the wolf had finished off the jerky and was now chasing him. The animal was gaining on him, and Jayden was within five feet of the nearest redwood tree. Bending his knees, he jumped as high as he could, which after years of training and a little magic, was pretty high.

Jayden grabbed the first branch he could reach and pulled himself up. He climbed as quickly as he could, and ducked just in enough time, to avoid a blast of cold air. His jaw dropped when he looked up to see that the branches above him now covered in snow.

He looked down and figured that he was now forty feet up into the tree. The ice wolf was drooling with anticipation, as it circled the tree. The creature let out a soft bark, and four more wolves appeared beneath the tree.

Smiling and feeling pretty impressed with himself, Jayden laughed at the hungry wolves. "Sucks to suck!" He taunted, "human is off the menu for today." For security reasons, Jayden chose to spend the night in the tree and used his bag as a pillow.

***

Ouch!" he cried, as a rock hit him in the face. "Ouch!" he yelled again, as he was pelted with more rocks. What kind of a jerk throws rocks at someone sitting in a tree, at 7 in the morning?

Jayden opened his eyes cautiously, and he realized two things. One, the sun was way too bright, and two, Tony was a jerk. Standing at the base of the tree, was Tony holding a handful of small rocks, and a devious smile on his face. Leaning over on his branch, Jayden yelled, "Hey, you jerk! I was planning on sleeping for another six hours". Unfortunately, he leaned a little too far and fell gracefully out of the tree. Luckily three branches broke his fall. Jayden hit the ground with a thud and Tony fell back laughing,

"Hey Jade, you would make a great pine cone. What were you doing up in the tree? Were you bird watching?" His friend asked.

"Well if you must know, I was chased up the tree by a pack of 1000 wolves. I climbed up in the tree because I don't believe in cruelty to animals."

"Sure you did. Well, the wolves are gone now. You might want to start carrying a weapon on your person because next time you might not have a giant redwood to climb up in."

Jayden reached into his bag and pulled out a six-inch knife which he strapped to his belt. Turning to Tony, he said, "So what made you want to come join me?"

"O that's easy, Master Thai told me that you would be helpless without me. He even told me which tree you were sleeping in. I thought he was kidding." Jayden smiled and continued his trek down the mountain with Tony at his side.

Once they reached the bottom of the mountain, Tony stopped and asked, "Where exactly are we going?"

Jayden replied, "We are going to Mirage City. Master Thai gave me the address to some apartment there. He said that someone living there would be able to help me in my search. The best way to get there is going through Eiréné, then taking route 25 south."

Tony shrugged, "Sounds good to me. We were very young when we lived there. I wonder how much has changed since then."

When the rusted "Welcome to Eirene" sign came in to view, it became apparent that his hometown had changed. Nature was well on its way, to reclaim what was left of this ghost town. Green grass and weeds protruded through the floors of the damaged houses. The smell of smoke was long gone. If it weren't for all of the devastations, Eiréné would have appeared mildly pleasant.

They stopped outside of Jayden's house. As they admired the place he once called home, he realized that there was something unusual about it. Out of all the buildings in town, his was the least affected by the damage. There were no burn marks from fire, not even a bullet hole.

With their curiosities piqued, they entered the house, and he noticed that it had been trashed. Whoever had been here last, must have been looking for something.

Jayden made his way through the living room and entered the hallway. He was half tempted to go into his bedroom, but he noticed that the door for his Dad's room was left ajar. Cautiously, they opened the door and entered. Just like the rest of the house, the room was trashed.

"What the heck were they after?" Jayden asked. And did they find it?

"Jayden!" Tony yelled, "take a look at this".

His friend was pointing at the closet. Jayden moved beside him and gazed into the closet. Tony must be losing it he thought, everything in the closet seems normal. To appease his friend, he stuck his head further in the closet, and that's when he noticed that the rear wall of the closet was missing. Taking a moment to look closer, they saw that the back wall for the closet was actually a sliding door that had been pushed aside.

On the other side of the closet was a small stair case. Tony led them down the stairs, and they found a small room. In the center of the room was a metal table, with some papers strewn across it. Along the walls and in lockers, were weapons of varying types. From swords to guns, to spears, and arrows.

"Do you think this has been here the whole time?" Jayden asked.

Tony's eyes widened, as he was entranced by a vast array of weaponry in the room. He turned to Jayden and said, "It doesn't look like these weapons have been touched in quite some time. I can't believe your dad had all of this, and we never knew. It's like he was preparing for a war. I think we should take some of these with us."

Jayden grabbed a military grade bolt action rifle and put it in his bag, along with over a dozen throwing knives. Tony pulled down from the wall, a combat shotgun and placed it on his back. As they climbed back up the stairs, they both wondered, what had Jayden's Dad been up to all this time? His dad was just a glorified handyman, wasn't he?

***

An army soldier was patrolling the area that he was assigned to monitor in the town of Eiréné. The young warrior hated having to walk around this ghost town, month after month. He didn't spend all his time training to join the army and waste it having to watch the grass grow. No one has even lived in this town for years. Just a few more days, he thought, and I will transfer elsewhere.

His ears perked up when heard the sound of voices coming from Main Street. He noticed two peculiar looking young men stepping out of a house. They weren't dressed like any soldiers from his unit. When he took a second glance, he realized that the house they stepped out of was the home that belonged to Dion. He remembered from his briefing, that Dion's house was off limits, and that if anyone was caught entering that building, they were to be detained. The soldier reached for his radio and said, "I have two young men coming out of Dion's house. Should I detain them?"

"Yes, but use caution, we will bring the truck around to meet you," his commander said.

The army soldier approached the two young men cautiously. "What are you two doing here?" He demanded. "This area is for military personnel only. I am going to need you to come with me."

"Wait! What? Why do we have to go with you? You guys didn't even leave a sign up for people to know. Plus we used to live here. We were stopping by for nostalgia's sake," Tony replied.

"I'm sure you two did, and I'm also the tooth fairy. I need you two young men to get on your knees and put your hands behind your head. So I can pat you down. The detention truck should be here soon to haul you off." The soldier said

They both got on their knees as he padded them down. "That tickles" Jayden smirked, "My back is itchy, do you think you could scratch it".

"Excuse me! Do you think this is a joke? I have the right to shoot you for trespassing."

"Well sorry, with our hands behind our heads. I can't scratch my back."

The soldier gestured to the black detention truck. "Well ladies, your chariot has arrived."

Chapter 7

A Frosty Welcome

General Floriana, was standing near the northern entrance of Western Army Base. She was perusing through some forms that required her signature and was looking forward to her busy day coming to a close. Floriana looked up, just as the sun had begun to set, and noticed a black truck was coming through the gate. When the truck passed by her, she was able to see the outline of two individuals through the tinted windows, sitting in the back seat of the truck.

That's odd she thought, I don't remember being informed about any prisoners coming onto the base. She ran to the gate to speak with the guards. "Where was that truck coming from? Who is in it? Why wasn't I informed about this?"

Saluting her, the guard said, "General Floriana that truck came from Eiréné. The detainees in the truck were found coming out of one of the houses. Sergeant Jason told us to keep it quiet, because of the ongoing investigation."

Very interesting she thought, why would Jason not tell her about this? The suspicions she held about him, were slowly rising to the surface, after having remained dormant for years. Quickly turning on her heels, she marched toward the Army detention center. Swiping her card, she spoke with the soldier at the front desk. "Where are the detainees that just arrived being kept? And where are they going to be interrogated?"

"Due to the sensitive nature of the investigation. I cannot give you that information. My apologies General, I have an order from the King." The guard replied while handing her a letter with the King's seal

Her face turned a bright red. What is going on here, she wondered. Whatever it is, I will get to the bottom of it. Trying to calm herself, she forced a gentle smile. "I do need access to the armory in the detention center to do inventory. Will you open the gate, so I can get through?"

Nodding his head, he flicked a switch to open the gate to the detention center. As she walked away, he picked up a phone and made a call. "Sergeant Jason, you told me to inform you if anyone was asking about the boys you are detaining."

"Yes, I did. Did anyone ask about them?"

"Yes sir, it was General Floriana. Is everything alright?"

"Yes, it is, thanks for touching base with me." Jason hung up his phone, as he entered the interrogation room.

There was nothing particularly special about the interrogation room. The room consisted of a pale green table in the center and three small chairs. The walls were made of cement bricks, and resting on the table, was a small digital voice recorder.

The two boys were joking with one another until he stepped into the room. The young man on the right was shorter and had spiky, black hair. The other young man sitting in the left chair had dark curly hair, and he looked a lot like Dion.

Jason sat down at the table and opened the file on the two detainees. The young men were picked up with no I.D.s, and they had two duffle bags filled with food, clothes, and weapons. When he finally he looked up at them, with his blue eyes. He said, "So, explain to me why you two were marching through Eiréné with a bag full of weapons?"

They both glanced at each other, then stared back down at the table nervously.

"Just as I suspected. You, gentlemen, are nothing but looters, stealing from abandoned houses. You do know, that at one time those houses were not abandoned. You stole from people who were murdered. How does that make you feel?"

Tony lifted his head, "We didn't steal anything! The weapons we took, belonged to his father." He shouted, pointing at Jayden. "We used to live there. So, we took a little trip down memory lane. We didn't know that our former town had become a home for the army".

"So you're telling me, that you two both lived there? According to our reports when Eiréné was attacked, there were no survivors. You two would have been about 13 at the time. Explain to me, how you two could have survived this long, on your own?"

Jayden spoke up and said, "We were rescued by monks from the Dragon Monastery, and we have been living there ever since."

Grinning, Jason replied, "Don't worry, you two aren't in trouble. I just had to double check that you were telling the truth. I am still heading up the investigation, on the attack on Eiréné. Unfortunately, we haven't had any leads because we haven't had any witnesses. I need to know if those men that attacked your town said anything important to you. Were they searching for anything in particular?"

They both looked at each other again, as they tried to remember the events from that night.

"I know this must be difficult for you to recall the events of that night. If you can remember anything, it might help us find out who did it and why." Jason added.

Jayden looked up and said, "I can sort of remember these two guys mentioning a key. But we really didn't know what they were talking about. What kind of monsters would invade a peaceful town over a key?"

For a second, Jayden thought he saw the soldier interviewing them, smile briefly at what he just said. Something about this situation didn't seem right. He had a feeling this guy wasn't completely honest about what he knew. Jayden nudged Tony, and they both silently agreed, that if an opportunity for them to escape arose, they were going to take it.

"I'm sorry sir we never got your name," Jayden asked.

"Sorry, I forgot to introduce myself. I am Sergeant Jason, of the Western Army. Now those men did they tell you about where *The Key* was or why they were looking for it."

"Why all of a sudden are you interested in *The Key*? My issue, Mr. Jason, is that a group of men in black hoodies were able to make it all the way to Eiréné without any of the military outposts seeing them. I know there are at least two outposts in between here and Eiréné. I also don't understand how they can leave without anyone seeing them. I also don't understand how your troops can show up after it happened, and not be able to track them down." Jayden said with his voiced raised.

The room went silent as Jayden's words hung in the air. Smiling Jason replied, "Excuse me, I have to make a quick phone call. Please wait right here for just a few minutes. I'm also going to get the paperwork ready, so I can have you released."

Stepping out into the hall, Jason reached into his pocket, and pulled out a black phone, and pushed a button.

"Hello brother. Yes, they brought in the boys from Eiréné. Yes, one of the boys appears to be Dion's son. I plan to keep them here for a few hours until a few of your men get here, and you can force him to find *The Key*. I know we can't afford to fail again brother. I promise we will get the power we need and we will fulfill our calling". Hanging up the phone, he went down a hall and headed toward his office.

Chapter 8

Integrity and Suspicion

General Floriana was stomping down the halls of the detention center. Her mind was going a mile a minute as she searched. Where are they she wondered? She had already checked each of the interrogation rooms they typically used. Then she had a thought, Jason is trying to hide them. Where would be the best place to interrogate them in secret? They must be in one of the old interview rooms that they no longer used.

She made her way toward the west wing of the detention center. General Floriana began to remember why they no longer used the west wing. Water dripped from old pipes, and it smelled like mold. Some of the holding cells were thoroughly rusted. The interrogation rooms were the most pleasant part of the west wing.

She checked the first two interview rooms, and there was no one there. Then she checked to make sure that she wasn't being followed. The coast was clear, so she swiped her card and entered the room.

When she entered the interrogation room, she saw two young men sitting at the table. They both had surprised looks on her face when she walked through the door.

"Where is Jason? He said he would let us go." The boy with the short dark hair asked.

"Who are you two? And why did Jason bring you here?" She demanded.

"I am Jayden, and this is Tony. And we don't know why we are here. I thought this was a free country still. One moment we were visiting our old stomping grounds, minding our own business. In the next moment, we ended up here in this fancy interrogation room".

"Old stomping grounds?"

"We are from Eiréné? Who are you?"

"I am General Floriana of The Western Army and Leader of the Death From Above Glider Unit. If you young men are truly from Eiréné, did you know a man named Robert? "

"Yes, we did. If it weren't for Robert, we would be dead." Jayden replied

"He was my uncle." She said with a struggle

"We are sorry. If only we were strong enough then, maybe we could have helped him, and he wouldn't have died." Tony said while sinking into his chair.

"Do you two know why Eiréné was destroyed?" She asked.

"We believe they were searching for something. We also think that your soldier buddy knows more about what happened than he is letting on" Tony replied.

"What do you mean? How dare you accuse Jason, he is a sergeant in the army and a decorated soldier. I will not allow you to run his name through the mud, without evidence that says otherwise." She said defiantly

"How is it that you can stand there and defend him when he didn't even tell you why we are here, or even who we are? He is keeping you in the dark for a reason. You're a General. Isn't it your job to know what's going on?" Jayden asked

For a moment her stern expression wavered, and she felt doubt, mixed with the sense of anger. Am I not a General? Have I not earned the right to know the inner workings of this country? Have I not shed enough blood and tears in the name of the King? This insult cannot stand, if Jason is in the wrong, then I must inform the King.

"Jayden, I will help you two escapes. You must do exactly as I say."

"Why don't you just come with us?" Tony asked.

"I'm a soldier. I must inform my King of deception within my ranks. However, I am duty-bound to do what is right. Therefore, I will help you escape. I will guide you down the hall and tell you where to go and the rest you must do on your own."

They nodded, as she led them out into the hall. Jayden didn't pay much attention to the detention facility when they walked in, but looking at it now, he was glad to be leaving it. As he examined the cells they were passing by, Floriana suddenly stopped in her tracks, and Jayden was of course not paying attention and walked right into her. "Ouch!" she shouted and shot him a look, which said do it again, and I'll kill you.

He glanced around her to see why she had stopped. Approaching them from down the hall was Jason walking with two soldiers at his side.

Jason smiled, "I was hoping you would stay out of this Floriana. Now I have to arrest you and bring you before the King."

She dared at him with fury in her eyes, "I don't like you keeping me in the dark. All of this cloak and dagger is unacceptable. I am a General, you conducting an investigation behind my back, is something I will not allow. Your integrity is in question. You three have one option, turn around and head back to your stations that is an order!'"

"Due to the nature of this investigation, I will opt to ignore your request. My order from the King supersedes your request."

"That is very unfortunate....for you," She said with a smile. General Floriana pulled out her rapier and pointed it at the floor beneath Jason's feet, and yelled "Flash Freeze!" The ground underneath him and the two soldiers quickly turned into ice. They slipped and fell, which caused Tony and Jayden to laugh hysterically. She turned to them and mouthed, "Follow me."

Together, they raced down the halls of the detention center. After making a few turns, Jayden was already lost. Luckily, he was able to keep Floriana in his eye sight. She quickly made a left turn and stopped in front of a steel door. The young General swiped her card, and they entered the evidence room.

Jayden stopped and stood in amazement, at the sheer size of the evidence room. It was designed like a large warehouse. The building was filled with shelves that stretched as far as the eye could see.

How are we supposed to find our duffle bags in all of this nonsense? As if she could hear what he was thinking, General Floriana ran off for about five minutes and came back with their bags.

"How did you find our bags so quickly? This place is huge! By the way, was that frost magic you did back there? That was pretty awesome, I guess you could say you put them on ice" said Jayden, laughing at his own joke

Tony elbowed him, "That was cheesy dude."

Fighting a smile, Floriana said, "I am still a General, and if you don't chill out on the cheesy jokes. I'll put you on ice."

Jayden turned to Tony, "Did Captain Serious make a joke? That's our department."

Floriana signaled for them to stand next to a set of shelves that were tall enough to reach the ceiling." We have to climb up this shelf, at the top is an air vent that will lead us outside. Once we are out, head for the fence and we can go from there."

Jayden smiled, "Whoever makes it to the top first, gets to have the last chocolate in my bag."

Chapter 9

A Glimmer of Hope

Together they hopped a fence as the alarms from the base blared into the night. Grass and weeds crunched under their feet as they sprinted into the darkness. The darkness of the night provided excellent cover for them, but it also made it very difficult to see, as Jayden found out the hard way, by accidentally tripping on a rock.

"Get up Jayden! We need to put a few more miles between us and the base", Floriana yelled.

"Well, General pain in the.."

"Ahem," Tony said, "Watch your language Jayden, she did save our rear ends."

"I mean, General Floriana. I am having trouble seeing in the dark" said Jayden as politely as he could.

"Well, if you like Jayden, we can use a flashlight or a torch so that the army can find us in five minutes. It will help you to see better until they find us."

Jayden wanted to kick her for her sarcasm, but he remembered his dad telling him not to hit girls, and especially not to hit girls that have sharp swords.

"Fine, I'll watch where I am running."

"Great, then we have an accord. Now pick it up, my grandmother runs faster than you two."

They ran for ten miles straight before they stopped. Jayden and Tony crumbled to the ground from exhaustion. While sitting in a circle, Floriana turned to Jayden and said, "I thought Dragon Warriors were supposed to be in shape."

Jayden looked at her nervously, "How did you know we were Dragon Warriors?"

"I saw your Tattoos. Some of the soldiers in the Western Army were also trained by Dragon Masters."

"Well, if you must know, we Dragon Warriors are trained for combat, not for running marathons."

"So where were you two planning on going, before you were brought to the base?"

Jayden handed her the note that Master Thai had given him, "Our Master told me that someone at that address would be able to help us on our journey. We were on our way to Mirage City. You should come with us. I'm sure the Army wouldn't like you coming back after turning part of the detention center into an ice rink."

Taking a moment to respond she said, "I will travel with you to Mirage City, but from there we must part ways. I need to speak with the King."

"There was something else we didn't tell you about our interview with Jason," Tony interjected. He took the next few moments, to explain to her about Jason's interest in *The Key*.

"So do you know what this key is?" Floriana asked.

"Nope, we have no idea. The guys who asked us about it during the attack on Eiréné didn't feel the need to share specifics."

"Hmm...that's interesting. Well, I will need to present this to the King. By the way Jayden, I believe you owe me that piece of chocolate. I did beat you to the top of the shelf."

"That's because you had a head start. Unfortunately, I already took a bite out of it, so now you will only get half of it."

Taking the chocolate, she took a bite, and for the first time since meeting her, they saw her smile. Even though it was tough to see in the dark, she did have a beautiful smile.

"I was beginning to think you didn't know how to smile," Tony said with a grin.

"O shut up and go to sleep. We will be getting up at 0500," she replied. Jayden grabbed a rock and placed his bag over it to make a pillow. Once his eyes closed, he was out like a light.

While Jayden dreamed, he felt like he was sleeping on a boat. He could feel his body swaying back and forth like he was riding a gentle wave. Then he thought he could hear an annoying voice in his ear. "Wake up Jayden!" Floriana yelled in his ear, while she shook him out of his deep sleep.

"What the heck is your problem? It's still dark out, which means it's bedtime." he snapped and rolled back to sleep.

"I told you he wouldn't get up so easy," Tony said, as he proceeded to throw cold water on Jayden's face. With a jolt, Jayden got up and muttered some things under his breath that would have gotten him detention back in grade school.

Floriana stretched out her hand to bring Jayden to his feet. "We will be taking an around about way to get to Mirage City to avoid the Army and anyone else that might be searching for us. We will go through Downer Pass." She said.

The wise General was leading them toward an area known as Downer Pass. This old dirt highway was originally a main thoroughfare, situated between two small mountain ranges. Over the years, Downer Pass became notorious for being unkempt, a den for robbers and an overall blight, on the Eden continent. Jayden had heard stories about it; he was hoping they weren't true.

The closer they got to Downer Pass, the more landscape began to change. The green grass and lush trees were replaced with weeds rocks and dirt. If beauty were in the eye of the beholder, you would have to be blind to find any source of beauty in Downer Pass.

Jayden's stomach started growling. I'm so hungry, he thought. "Hey, can we stop and eat?" he whined. Ignoring him, Floriana continued walking.

"Alright, ignore me; I'm just going to eat these crackers myself," he said. Grabbing a handful, he almost shoved them into his mouth before she grabbed his wrist.

"We need to ration the food. We still have another 30 miles to go before we make it to Mirage."

***

After a few hours of nonstop hiking, they were nearing the end of Downer Pass. Tony heard the sound of vehicles rumbling off in the distance. He glanced around and saw nothing. Then seemingly out of nowhere, six motorcycles and three dune buggies were approaching them from the rear.

Moving to let them pass, Tony had a bad feeling about this group of travelers. Most of them wore black leather jackets, and all of them had tattoos. A few of the bikers wore bandanas on their heads, while others had their faces covered with them. That wasn't the disturbing part. What scared him was that all of them seemed to be carrying a weapon of some sort. A few of them had sub-machine guns slung over their backs, and the rest had short swords. He was grateful because the motorists passed them, without even acknowledging their presence.

Stepping out of Downer Pass, they continued down the dirt highway. On both sides of the road were large dunes and hills that went on for miles. Something about them seemed just a little off.

As they passed by a large dune, a group of motorcyclists jumped out from the other side of the hill. Three more of them sprang up from another dune, and stood in the middle of the road, blocking their path. More bikers appeared, and immediately they were surrounded.

The tallest biker of the bunch, with a red dolphin tattooed on his neck, approached Jayden. With a smile on his burly face, he smacked the young Dragon Warrior with the butt of his pistol, sending him to the ground.

"What the heck was that for?" Jayden whimpered, as his face was throbbing with pain.

The other two bikers raised their pistols and forced Tony to his knees, and they had him put his hands behind his head.

"I feel like this same thing happened to us not too long ago. Pistol whipping you was a nice touch though," Tony laughed.

Wincing, Jayden replied, "I could do without that. Who are you people and what do you want?" Looking around, he said, "Hey! Where did Floriana go? Some General; she runs off as soon as the trouble starts."

Five more men appeared on the hill. The large man in the center was carrying a sawed-off shotgun.

"We are the Desert Rats. We travel throughout Eden causing mayhem and anarchy. My name is Samson. Consider yourselves honored."

"Desert Rats, what kind of name is that and why should we feel honored?" Jayden asked.

"First off, Desert Rats is an awesome name. Secondly, you should feel honored because today we will rob you and beat you mercilessly."

"11 against 2, your mothers should be very proud," said Jayden.

"She is proud. Now, you two, check their bags." Two of the bikers standing on the hill descended and began perusing through their duffle bags.

"Do they have anything good?" Samson asked.

"Yes. They've got a few swords, throwing knives, and some guns."

"That's interesting. Where are you boys headed? Are you planning to fight an army? Either way, it doesn't matter. It's been nice spending time with you, but you aren't the only lucky travelers we have to rob today." Samson turned to his men at his men, he nodded.

Jayden was starting to freak out; he knew they needed to act quickly. He quickly glanced at Tony, he mouthed it's now or never. With lightning speed, Jayden grabbed the arm of the man behind him and flipped him over his shoulder, and then he hit him in the throat. Jumping up, Jayden pulled his knife out and slashed the man to his left in the chest. Then he spun and kicked him in the head sending him to the ground. Samson and the men on the hill raised their guns. Just before they could fire their weapons, Tony flicked his wrist, and a dust storm appeared in the midst of armed men. The cloud of dust made it impossible for them to see.

Copying Jayden, Tony flipped the man that was behind him over his shoulders and punched him in the face, knocking him out cold. Standing up, he ran toward the bikers that were standing by their bags. The large men fired a volley of bullets at him. Tony jumped over them, then spun around and did a front sweep sending them to the ground. Three men were left on the hill as the dust storm began to die down.

Jayden summoned three fireballs and threw them at the men on the hill. He struck them in the chest so hard their shirts were burned, and they fell to the ground.

Struggling to recover from the force of the fireball, Samson stood up, "We...We give up. You guys get to live another day. Desert Rats roll out."

A few moments later, their attackers left, bikes and all. Tony and Jayden watched them drive off, followed by the cloud of dust that their vehicles left behind. "I give your dust storm a 3 out of 10. It looked cool for a minute, but then it ran out of steam."

"Oh, that's funny. Your fireballs were really effective. They almost kept you from getting pistol whipped. Oh wait; they didn't. Plus, I managed to dodge a barrage of bullets. I think that makes me the winner of this bout."

Laughing, the boys picked up their bags and started back down the highway.

"Hey! Are you gentlemen just going to leave me, out here in the middle of nowhere?"

Whirling around, they saw General Floriana. Jayden noticed that there was something entirely different about her. She was no longer wearing her military camo. She was now dressed in metal armor and had a blue cape that hung over her right shoulder. Her hair was no longer in a ponytail; it was hanging just past her shoulders. She looked like a combination of beauty and raw power.

"Where were you? We almost got mugged, and Jayden got smacked with a pistol, which actually knocked some sense into him," Tony said

"I was over there," she pointed out into the distance.

"Doing what, picking daisies and straightening your hair? "Jayden chimed in.

Smacking him in the back of the head, she replied, "That group of bozos, had a sniper trained on you about fifty yards that way. I went to dispatch him for you, and I had to change into my combat uniform." Showing them her rapier, they could see stains of blood on it.

"Why didn't you tell us what you were doing? And why didn't you help us afterward? Also, where did you get those clothes? You don't even have a bag with you, "he asked.

"Oh well, I do know more than just ice spells. I'm also trained in transformative magic," she said. Snapping her fingers, her clothes changed back into her camo. Snapping again, she was back in her combat uniform. "Plus, I knew you two would do fine. That was a nice dust storm Tony; I've always been impressed by storm magic."

Grinning, he dusted his shoulders off. "I do what I can General Floriana."

"Did you not see my fireballs?" Jayden pleaded.

"Jayden, anyone can start a fire. By the way, you two need to be better equipped as we travel. You can't just leave all of your weapons in your bags. A knife and magic saved you this time, but will it the next?"

Opening their bags, Tony grabbed the combat shotgun and slung it over his back. Jayden grabbed his Dad's .45, and for a moment, he sat there to admire the weapon. He wondered how many battles it had seen and the places it had traveled. At that moment, he vowed to make his father proud. Then he strapped the weapon to his right leg.

As the day turned into night, a full moon rose into the sky. The moon's beautiful light shined so brightly, that Jayden half expected to see witches on broomsticks streaking across the sky. Once they had found a nice place to camp for the night, he laid his head down on a nice comfy rock and fell asleep.

***

He was in a deep sleep until he felt a warm drop of liquid on his forehead. Followed by another, and another. Please don't tell me it's going to rain, he thought. We are in the middle of a plain, and there is no cover for miles. Forcing himself to wake up, he looked up and saw two bright glowing eyes gazing down at him. He couldn't see what it was, because dark clouds had covered the moon, dampening its beautiful light.

Tony and Floriana were both still fast asleep. I must still be in a dream, he hoped. Then, he heard a snarl come from those eyes looking down on him, and another drop fell on his face. It felt warm and gooey. Drool, he thought. That is beyond gross. Wait, what in the world is drooling on me? Fear began to rise deep inside of him. Slowly, he moved his hand to his knife, just as the clouds moved aside. The moon's magnificent light shined, allowing Jayden to see what was standing over him finally.

The creature standing above him was a dark goblin. This goblin stood just a little over 5 feet. The creature's frame was small and skinny, but it's dark arms and legs were full of toned muscle. The dark goblin's teeth were yellow and razor sharp. It had five claws on each hand; they were pointed and about 4 inches long. With the moon shining, he could see that it had long pointy ears and spikes going down its back.

Jayden had never seen a dark goblin in real life before. Rumor has it that the bite from the female goblins is very poisonous. The goblin moved its head closer to take a bite out of Jayden. I need to let it get a little closer before I can strike, he told himself. The goblin's face was almost a foot from Jayden's; the smell of its breath was worse than anything he had ever smelled or wanted to smell.

He stealthily removed his knife from its sheath and slashed at the goblin's throat causing purple blood to spurt from its neck. The goblin attempted to howl as it choked on the blood. Jayden kicked it in the face, sending it to the ground. The monster squirmed for a few seconds before it drew its last breath and stopped moving.

Then he stood up and realized that he had woken up Floriana and Tony. Looking around Jayden realized that they were surrounded by goblins. The thick clouds covered the moon again, and all he could see was 30 sets of glowing eyes surrounding them.

Quickly he grabbed his pistol and fired three shots into the darkness, striking two of monsters.

He felt a sharp pain, as a goblin scratched him across the back of his neck. Rolling forward, he turned and fired four shots into another goblin. To his right, he saw Tony firing off shells as goblin after goblin rushed him. On his left, Floriana just sent an icicle through the chest of a goblin, then spun around and decapitated another goblin. How many were left, he wondered?

He lowered his gun for a moment and was immediately tackled by two goblins. He shot the one on his right, as he landed on the ground. The goblin on his left opened it's mouth and bit Jayden on his shoulder. Pain shot through his body. He wanted to scream, but before he could yell in pain, his training took over, and he rolled over on top of the monster and dispatched it with a squeeze of the trigger. Diving forward, he reached into his bag and grabbed his katana. Turning around, he swung and defeated two more goblins.

The clouds moved again, and he was able to see that there were still five more left. Two goblins were moving in his direction, and the other three rushed Tony and Floriana.

In the light of the moon, he could see that the dark goblins' mouths were watering as they tried to make Jayden into their midnight snack. The goblin on his left jumped in the air, and Jayden sidestepped him and then cut him in half. The other monster, slashed Jayden's chest, with both claws leaving deep scratches. Jayden jumped back as his chest and shoulder were burning from the pain. As soon as he regained his balance, his vision became blurry. His muscles began to weaken, and he crumbled to the ground right in front of the goblin.

Out of the corner of his eye, Tony saw Jayden fall. Sprinting forward, he jumped over the goblin standing in front of Jayden, then he raised his shotgun and fired. He quickly rolled forward and fired two more shells at the remaining goblins. Floriana rushed to Jayden's side, touching his forehead. She looked at Tony, "He has a fever, and he's lost some blood. We have to get him to a hospital. He's been poisoned by the goblins bite. We will have to carry him the rest of the way to Mirage, or he will die. You grab the bags, and I'll carry him. We have about two hours to save him and five miles to go."

Time seemed to slow down, as they rushed to save Jayden's life. For Tony, it felt like it took hours to go one mile. He was so lost in his mind, that he was shocked when he looked down and saw that the road beneath them had changed from dirt to pavement and Mirage City appeared off in the horizon.

The city's tall skyscrapers reached into the skies like the hand of God. Though the sun was coming up, it was still very dark, but the lights of the buildings shined in the darkness, offering him a glimmer of hope.

We must be almost there, Tony thought. Jayden you have to hang on, he said to himself. I can't stand to lose another person I care about. Tony looked around as they were passing rows of houses while running through the suburbs of Mirage City. Each of the houses had red shingle roofs, many of them were two or three stories. He figured this must be where the upper middle class lived. Large bushes aligned the boundaries of the properties, green freshly cut grass covered their front lawns. In any other situation, Tony would have stopped to explore, but right now they needed to get to a hospital quickly. Jayden's life was hanging by a thread.

Ten minutes later, they entered the metropolitan area of the city. They zoomed past building after building and crossed street after street. Floriana took a right turn; they were now on a street that curved left and went up a hill. At the top of the hill was a hospital with a white sign that said, Mirage General.

As they approached the hospital, they saw an ambulance and paramedics standing outside. Tony waved his hands and yelled, "Hey! We need help! My friend's hurt badly." Grabbing a gurney, the paramedic rushed to them. Placing Jayden onto it, they ran into the building.

"What is his name, and what are his symptoms?"

"His name is Jayden, and he was bitten by a dark, female goblin. He has a fever, and he can't move," said Floriana.

"Alright, we will get him to the anti-venom ward. They will do what they can."

"Do what they can?" Tony mumbled. What does that even mean?

They ran into the hospital lobby, and Tony glanced at Jayden as he lay on the gurney. His caramel skin had developed a pale tint to it. The bright smile he normally carried, was completely gone, as his life was slowly fading away.

The paramedics reached the double doors, which led to the emergency rooms and the anti-venom unit. Two of the paramedics pushed Jayden through the doors; the third turned and put his hand up for Tony to stop.

"We can't let you go any further; this area is for medical staff only. We will let you know what happens."

Tony punched a wall, "That's my friend; I need to be in there with him."

"Sir, the best thing you can do for your friend is to stay here."

Floriana pulled Tony back, "We can hang out here in the lobby."

Tony was fuming, he wanted to do something, but he knew he could do nothing. He hated this feeling of helplessness; he hadn't felt this helpless since Eiréné was destroyed. He remembered having to watch his grandparents being dragged out into the middle of the street to be executed, while he hid in the house. Tony felt utterly powerless back then, and now he felt useless and unable to save the people he cared about.

General Floriana watched Tony sulk as he sat in the lobby; it tugged at her heartstrings. She had a feeling that she should say something to him. Sitting down next to him, she opened her mouth and said, "Don't worry, he will be fine. As a soldier, I have spent a fair amount of time with my brethren in hospitals. Your friend is strong; he will make it." What is going on with me, she thought. Why do I even care about what happens to these boys?

Having been recruited at such a young age, all she had known was the military life. In the last few days, she had risked her life for people she hardly knew, for reasons that had nothing to do with the military. The concern she felt for Jayden was similar to what she felt for the soldiers that had fought alongside her. It was weird for her not merely to be fighting for her country; she was beginning to fight for people she cared for.

Jayden, you have to make it through this, and not just for Tony's sake, she thought. Shaking her head, I have to control my emotions. I'm a soldier for crying out loud. With a gentle voice, she said to Tony, "You should walk around a little bit, to get your mind off things."

Standing up, he walked around the lobby. Passing by the front desk, he did a double take as he stared at one of the receptionists. She was just a little shorter than he was, and she had beautiful long black hair, with highlights. Her skin was light, and she wore a red bow in her hair. She glanced up at him and smiled. Awkwardly, he quickly looked away, then looked back. Man, she looked so familiar. Wow, this girl probably thinks I'm a creeper now, he thought.

"I'm sorry, I didn't mean to stare at you like that. You look like someone I used to know." He said.

Smiling, she responded, "You look familiar too. What's your name?"

"Tony." He glanced at her name tag, and it said, Sarah. No way, he thought. It couldn't be her? Could it? "Are you from Eiréné?" He asked.

Her jaw dropped, "Tony, is that you? You've gotten taller, and your hair is as spiky as ever." Overcome with emotion, she jumped over her desk and gave him a big hug. Tears streamed down from her face, "I didn't know there were others who made it out."

"What's going on here? Tony, who is this girl?" Floriana asked sounding curious.

Embarrassed, Sarah released him, and wiped her eyes, "Sorry about that; it's just been so long. My name is Sarah; I grew up with him. Where is Jade? Did he not make it? Is he dead?" she asked.

Tony hesitated to answer. Then, a surgeon approached them, "Were you two that brought in that Jayden boy?"

"Yes, that was us" Tony replied.

The doctor gestured for them to sit. Sarah joined them.

"First off, does he have any family members for us to contact?" The doctor asked.

Tony shook his head no. "We are the closest thing to family he has left."

"Alright, well, I do have some news for you about his condition. Are you ready to hear it?"

Tony wanted to say yes, but he couldn't bear to hear any more bad news. His life had been filled with too much bad news. From his father leaving to the death of his grandparents and his home being destroyed, this would be too much. Gulping down his fear, he nodded his head.

"Well, right now we are prepping him for surgery. That's the good news. However, he's not out of the woods yet. By the time you brought him here, the poison had spread throughout parts of his body and into some of his vital organs. As of right now, he has fallen into a coma, and we are hoping to be able to bring him out of it. His heart rate and blood pressure are constantly fluctuating. The anti-venom has helped to slow the spread of the poison and to combat some of his symptoms. Understand, that with goblin poison, there are no guarantees. He may make it; he may not. Hope for the best but be prepared for the worst. Again, are you sure he doesn't have any family members we can contact? They may want to be here, just in case. Normally, we don't allow this, but you are welcome to come back and watch the surgery."

Chapter 10

A Temporary Jubilee

Slowly, he opened his eyes; his vision was a little blurry from sleep. He felt cold and tried to sit up. Looking to his right, he thought saw a girl sitting near the edge of his bed. Her image was a completely fuzzy, but she looked breathtaking.

"Are you an angel?" he asked sounding groggy.

Giggling, she replied, "of course, you have died and gone to heaven!"

"Wait, I died? Where the hell, I mean, heaven am I?" He asked. Jayden rubbed his eyes; his vision became clearer. He realized that the girl sitting in the room with him looked vaguely familiar. "If you're an angel, why don't you have a halo? And if this is heaven, why does it look like a hospital room, and why do I have this needle in my arm?"

Smiling, she replied, "In some ways, you've changed a lot, and in others, you're still the same Jade."

"How do you know me by that name? Who are you?"

She looked offended and punched him, "You jerk! How dare you forget who I am! It's me, Sarah."

"Sarah who? I've met so many Sarahs over the years. Which one were you?" She proceeded to punch him again, "Ooh, now I remember. Don't hit so hard; I'm in the hospital you know."

She shook her fist at him and said, "I'll put you in a coma if you ever think about dying on me again!"

As Jayden took a better look at her, she looked as if she had been crying for quite some time. Her mascara was smeared, and there were Kleenex on the table she was sitting by. Leaning in, he hugged her, "I'm sorry, I promise to never put you through that again."

Tony and General Floriana came into the room. "You gave us a little bit of a scare back there," Tony said. "The doctor told me to give these to you when you woke up." He handed him a lollypop and a teddy bear that had a big red heart on it.

"I'll take that," Sarah said while grabbing the teddy bear. "I'm keeping this to teach you a lesson to not get bitten by goblins anymore."

"So, when am I allowed to get out of here? This bed isn't comfy at all, and the hospital food they left me tastes like plastic."

Floriana put her arm on his shoulder, "The doctor said if you are feeling up to it that he will clear you to leave. Where do you want to run off to anyway?"

"Well, I want to go see whoever lives at the Skyline Apartments," Jayden said.

"Why do you want to go there?" Sarah asked.

"Our Master told us, that someone who lives in room 205, would be able to help us on our journey, "Jayden replied.

"Hey, that's where I live." Sarah chimed in

"Oh really?" He said unenthusiastically. "How can you help us?"

Feeling flustered and offended, Sarah got up and walked out the door, slamming it.

Shaking his head, Tony said. "Wow dude, that was not cool." Floriana proceeded to take Jayden's pillow and smack him with it.

"Ow, what did I do? Did I say something wrong?" Jayden asked.

"Ya man, that was rude. Do you not realize that she spent two nights in this room while you were comatose? She wanted to be the first one you saw when you woke up." Tony replied.

Jayden felt horrible, "I was trying to make a joke. Well, I'll apologize to her when we go to that apartment. Now, where is that doctor? I'm ready to get out of here."

Jayden was happy to be able to leave the hospital finally. He had never been a big fan of hospitals. The rooms were always too cold, and the beds were terrible, and of course, he hated the doctors who liked to poke and prod you with needles. Then they expect you to thank them at the end of the day.

Once Jayden had showered and changed, they made their way out onto a busy street. Cars were everywhere, honking and blaring their horns. Pedestrians walked past them as if they didn't even see them. One also bumped into him and didn't even apologize. What a jerk! Jayden thought. The last time Jayden had been in the city was when his mom was alive, and they came here with Tony to go to the fair. Life was so much simpler then.

While walking down the street, a mugger grabbed Tony's bag and took off with it. "Big mistake," Tony said with a grin. He ran after the thief and tackled the guy. Taking his bag back, he looked down at the guy who had this mortified look on his face.

Tony said, "Thanks for taking my bag; I needed a good morning jog. You need to work on your cardio sir. You should consider spending less time taking purses from old ladies and consider getting a gym membership." Patting the man on the head, he added, "Have a good day."

Turning to Floriana, Jayden asked, "So, do you know how to get to the Skyline Apartments?"

Shaking her head, no, she replied, "Most of my time in Mirage has been spent either meeting with military officials or in the hospital visiting soldiers. What we need to do is hail a cab." Putting two fingers to her lips, she whistled, and a bright yellow cab parked itself next to the curb in front of them.

Looking at his wallet, he said, "Floriana, would you be willing to help with cab fare? The Bank of Jayden is feeling a little empty."

"Sure, just remember you owe me a favor," she said with a devilish grin.

The sun was starting to set as they traveled to their destination. The Skyline Apartments were on the northeast side of the city. Approaching the complex, Jayden could tell that this was the rougher side of town. Homeless people congregated down some of the alleys. A group of them stood around a fire. Drug dealers were standing up against the walls, waiting for some poor soul to get their fix.

The apartment complex itself was a medium gray color, the S on the Skyline sign was hanging off to the side. It's neon lights flickered off and on sporadically. Jayden looked at Tony, "For a girl who works at the hospital, I'm surprised she lives in this part of town."

Floriana paid the cab driver, and they stepped out on to the curb. There was a seven-foot tall iron fence that surrounded the complex. Pushing the gate open, they went up the stairs and stopped at a door that had the number 205 on it.

This must be it, Jayden thought. Knocking on the door, he heard a woman on the other end yell, "Be there in a minute."

Unlocking the door, she opened it for them. They were greeted by a woman in her fifties. She had brunette hair that was graying in some areas, and she had it up in a bun. In her right hand, she was holding a green towel and was using it to dry a plate. Once she got a good look at who they were, she dropped the plate and wrapped her arms around Tony and Jayden. The strange lady gave them the most painful hug they've ever had. Once she released them, they saw that she had tears in her eyes,

"Boys, I thought I would never see you again. What brings you two to Mirage City?"

It took Jayden a minute to realize who it was. "Ms. Tonya? Is that you?" She nodded her head, yes, and they both proceeded to give her another hug before entering the apartment.

The inside of the apartment was a lot larger than it appeared from the outside. Her living room had a three-seated couch, a love seat, and a recliner that sat in front of a large television. The kitchen was connected to the living room, and the bedrooms were down the hall. She looked as if she had almost finished doing the dishes before they had arrived. Ms. Tonya gestured for them to sit.

"And who is this lovely lady in the military garb?"

"This is General Floriana," Tony said enthusiastically, which was followed by him getting an elbow and a death stare from Floriana.

"Don't worry, your secret is safe with me. I have something for you boys that your dad gave me this on the day that Eiréné was attacked." She went back to her room and came back with two leather bags that jingled as she walked. Dropping the bags at their feet, they fell open and inside was cash, gold, and silver coins.

Jayden looked up and asked, "Ms. Tonya did you steal all this from a leprechaun?"

Laughing, she replied, "Boy, one of these days your mouth is going to get you in trouble that you won't be able to talk your way out of. But to answer your question, no I didn't. This money is from both of your fathers; it was to be given to you when you reached adulthood. Your dad knew that sooner or later, you two would come walking through my door. Now tomorrow, you two are to head to the bank and deposit most of the cash and coins. If you don't want to have to lug all that money around, you can use these." From her purse, she pulled out two money cards with their names on it and handed it to them.

Taking their cards, Jayden turned to Tony and said, "We're rich!" He gave his friend a big high five.

Looking at the money and the card would usually make any young man happy, but Tony couldn't find any joy in it. His dad chose to leave him with cash, instead of leaving him with a father. He mumbled to himself, "I don't care that he's left me with all this. If I didn't need it to get by, I'd give it all away."

Then Floriana spoke, "Ms. Tonya, Jayden was told that you might have some information for him. Do you know of anything that we could use?"

Taking a deep breath, she turned to the boys and said, "How much do you know about your fathers? I bet you don't know as much as you think you do, especially you Tony. You can choose to believe what I have to say or not. Your fathers, along with Sarah's parents and myself are members of a secret society known as "The Witnesses." It was started a long time ago, right after the Great War. A small group of the Elders, created this organization to keep a war like that from ever happening again. Many of The Witnesses are descendants of The Elders. One of the byproducts of that war was that many of the magical weapons that were used in that war are still around. Our job is to keep those weapons from being found and to keep mankind from destroying itself. The group that attacked Eiréné is known as the Daimonia. They can usually be identified by a tattoo of a demon on their arm. They're a group that broke off from ours. They believed the best way to keep humanity from destroying itself, was by acquiring power and seizing control."

Tony elbowed Jayden who was falling asleep during Tonya's lecture. Tony looked up and asked, "who are the Elders?"

"The Elders are an older race of elves and humans that lived on a large southeastern island chain. They are the ones who started the Great War, which was mainly between them and the younger race of humans and dwarves."

Jayden perked up and asked, "Wait a minute. There are such things as elves and dwarves? What does any of that have to do with this key they are searching for? And why did they kill my father and destroy our home?"

"*The Key* is a tougher concept to explain. So I don't put you to sleep with the details, I will give you the condensed version. *The Key* itself is not a powerful object, but what it does do is it makes the acquisition of power possible. *The Key* was made by the Elders shortly after the Great War began. Years ago, your fathers were part of a strike team that went after the people who found *The Key*. After retrieving it, your father kept it for some years. The precise reason that Eiréné was destroyed is because they believed your father had it. But we know now, that he had moved it since then. Your father, Tony, may have an idea on how to find it. Believe me boys when I say, that it needs to be found and destroyed if possible. The Daimonia aren't the only ones looking for it."

"How can we help? We don't even know where Tony's dad is." Jayden said.

"Ya, and personally, I don't want to have anything to do with him. I don't care what information he has. We can figure it out another way." Tony added.

Smiling, she said, "Boys and girl, don't worry about that right now." She stood up, "It's time for you all to get ready. I have two bathrooms, one down the hall and the other in my bedroom. You boys most definitely could use a shower."

General Floriana looked perplexed, "What are we getting ready for?" she asked.

"To go out on the town. You three have earned a break and a little bit of fun. Sarah has some clothes you can wear, so you don't have to go out with all that armor on."

Floriana looked mortified at the thought, which made Jayden and Tony laugh. I can't imagine her dressed like a normal person, Jayden thought. This will be rich.

Having taken a shower, Jayden put on a pair of black jeans, a nice red button up shirt, and black shoes. Stepping back into the living room, he noticed that Sarah had arrived and was already dressed. Man, she looks good, he thought. Sarah curled her hair and replaced her red bow from before, with a white one. Sarah was now dressed in a white T-shirt, with jean shorts and white shoes. She smiled as Jayden stepped into the room. I guess she's not that mad at me anymore, he thought.

"So how do I look?" Said a voice from down the hall.

General Floriana appeared in the room; her beauty diverted all the attention in the room from Sarah to her. She was wearing a red buttoned-down T-shirt, with a black skirt that came to just above her knees, and she wore a pair of black boots. Her hair was braided, and it hung over her shoulder. "I'll take the boys' jaws dropping as this looks alright?"

Sarah looked at Jayden and raised an eyebrow, which caused him to pretend that he was staring at the wall instead of the beautiful woman standing in the living room. What am I now, chopped liver? Should I change into something different? Who would have guessed that G.I. Jane would clean up so well? Floriana did look pretty nice in her black skirt, Sarah admitted to herself.

"You look wonderful," Jayden said to Floriana while trying to avoid making eye contact with Sarah, who seemed to be giving him the, I'm going to kill you, stare.

"Yeah! I agree with Jayden's professional opinion," Tony added.

"Yes, my dear, you look stunning," said Ms. Tonya who stood up to get a better look, "Now, Sarah, where will you be taking them for the evening?"

Finally, I get a little bit of attention, Sarah thought. Standing up, she put on a smile and said, "I plan to take them shopping in the fashion district. Then we will head to the fair for the rest of the night." Taking Jayden by the wrist, "it's time to go folks; we're burning daylight. We can't let all this beauty go to waste right?" she said, winking at Floriana.

Going with the girls to the Fashion District of Mirage City, seemed like a great idea Jayden thought. Now he knew what it must be like to be tortured for hours on end. All the stores they went to blended into one nightmare for Jayden. Not only did the girls try on everything they saw, but the ladies also found it important to make Jayden and Tony try on clothes, which was cool for about five minutes until they were coerced into buying some of them. When did Floriana become a girly girl all of a sudden, he thought.

"Floriana, I thought you liked manly things. You're a soldier, remember? Don't let Sarah corrupt you. You were so awesome before all this." Jayden said.

"I'm ignoring you." she replied with a smile, "Hey Sarah take a look at these dresses."

"Do you want to go check out the jewelry store next door? They have the most amazing earrings and engagement rings," she said winking at Jayden, which made him feel a little squirmy. Engagement rings and jewelry, he thought. This store should be less painful to endure than the last fifteen shops they went into. Boy, was he wrong. After spending what felt like hours in the jewelry store, they finally started walking in the direction of the Mirage City Fair.

Drawing closer to the fair, Jayden began to remember the first time he had come to the fair when he was six. The joy he felt spinning on the merry go round, sitting with his dad on the go-karts, and taking pictures with his Mom and Tony. Now as an adult, he could see that the fair had expanded since then. A humongous Ferris wheel stood in the middle of the complex; it shined in the night with bright yellow and red lights. At the far end of the fair was a roller coaster. Part of the coaster struts were planted in a manmade lake owned by the fair. The roller coaster was called "The Widow Maker" because it was the second fastest wooden roller coaster in the world. It had tight turns and a wicked drop that went into a tunnel under the water, and if that wasn't scary enough, there were large fresh water sharks in the lake.

Tony turned and said, "Hey Jayden, I bet you five gold pieces and cotton candy, that you will wet your paints riding that thing."

"I'd like to get in on that bet. If you scream like a girl on that roller coaster, you have to win me a giant teddy bear and go with me on that Tunnel of Terror boat ride," Sarah added.

"Fine! I'll take that challenge, and when I succeed, you must admit that I am the man and get me a funnel cake and a corn dog."

They were greeted by a clown with a bright red nose and green hair as they entered the fair. He was walking on stilts, which made him look nine feet tall. "Welcome! Welcome! Test your luck at our games! Now for you lovebirds, take a romantic ride in the Tunnel of Terror. The scares and frights will bring you two together. If you are feeling brave, ride the Widow Maker!" he yelled.

Leaning in, Jayden whispered to Sarah, "I hate clowns."

"Aww, Jade that's cute. I didn't know you had a fear of clowns."

"I'm not afraid; I don't like them."

Sarah grinned, "Well Jade, today is your lucky day." She approached the clown and looked up at him, "Hello mister, my friend over there would love to take a picture with you." she said pointing at Jayden.

Grimacing, "I hate you." he muttered.

"Let's go on the Ferris wheel first. Tony, you're riding with me" Sarah said, which caught Tony completely off guard. Grabbing his arm, they ran to the Ferris wheel.

That's weird, Jayden thought, I figured she'd want to go with me. Turning to Floriana, "Well I guess you will get to ride with me," he said locking arms with her.

Rolling her eyes, "Lucky me," she said unenthusiastically.

"You know you're secretly happy about getting to be my Ferris Wheel buddy."

"Jayden, even under the threat of torture, I would never admit such a thing," she said defiantly while trying to cover up a smile.

Passing through the turnstile, Tony and Sarah found their seats on the Ferris Wheel. "All aboard!" yelled the Ferris wheel operator, pulling on a crank. The ride came to life.

"I'm surprised you didn't want to sit with Jayden," Tony said.

"Huh? O ya well, I felt it would be good for us to hang out some. When we were young, I feel like we didn't hang out much." She replied.

"You sure that's why? You're not still mad at him, are you?"

"To be honest, I really wasn't that mad. I couldn't stand being in that hospital any longer. It was tough thinking everyone I had ever cared for was dead, and then I saw you in the hospital, and I found hope again. And seeing Jayden fade in and out was almost too much. Watching him come out of that coma will be a moment I'll never forget."

"He must mean a lot to you. For you to felt that way after all of this time?"

She nodded, "He does, maybe that's what scares me. After all, that's happened, I don't think he's the same Jayden I used to care for. He doesn't seem to have the same joy, he once had. And, I don't think he will ever go back to the way he was."

"Will any of us?" Tony replied, "You should still give him a shot. He could really use a friend." Putting his arm around her, she rested her head on his shoulder.

"Maybe, you're right," she replied.

***

What if she doesn't like me like that, Jayden thought. Watching Tony put his arm around her, and seeing her lean against him, made Jayden feel a little jealous. Is she into him now? Why did she spend those nights in the hospital, only to switch up for Tony? Women are so confusing. Looking at Floriana, he decided to take a shot, while yawning, he put his arm around her.

"O look at that, how did my arm get there?" Jayden said trying to be slick.

"So, that was your move? You're better than that Jayden. I'm going to let it slide this time. Next time you had better at least bring me flowers."

"Wow! When did you become such a girly girl? Where did Ms. Soldier of Fortune go? And what makes you think that I'll try again?"

Putting a knife to his throat, she said, "If you tell anyone that I like girly things, I will cut you. And I know you will try again because this face and this outfit are irresistible. You can trust me; I'm a General."

"Why would you bring a knife to a fair? The only people you have to worry about here are the clowns on stilts."

"Anyway, it's nice getting just to have fun. I've spent so much time in the military, that I haven't had too many opportunities to do things like this. Despite the trouble you two have caused me, I'm grateful to be here. So, why does she call you Jade?" Floriana asked.

"It's a nickname that some people in Eiréné would call me."

"Isn't that a girl's name?"

"No! It's unisex, and the ladies love it."

"Do they now? That's news to me. So how come you aren't riding the Ferris Wheel with your lady friend? Aren't you afraid she might get jealous?"

"She wanted to go with Tony; I doubt she cares at all. But it's okay; I'm enjoying my time with you."

"Don't get used to it Jayden; this is the only shot you're getting. So make it count." Too mean Jayden thought, sinking in his seat.

Leaving the Ferris wheel, they headed toward the roller coaster. The wait to get on the ride was 30 minutes to an hour. Jayden looked up as the trains raced around on the coaster track, and he could hear the sound of riders screaming into the night.

"The Fair will be closed, by the time we make it to the front of the line" Jayden whined.

Seemingly out of nowhere, the line started to shrink. "Sweet!" Jayden yelled as they rushed to the front of the line. When he reached the roller coaster, he realized why the line had shrunk. The ride was now closed for repair. "Well, that's just great. I guess that means bet is off."

"O, you're not getting off that easy Jayden," said Tony. "Let's do the rock wall."

Pulling Jayden aside, Tony whispered, "Let's make a new bet. Whoever makes it up the wall first, gets to go on The Tunnel of Terror ride with Floriana."

"Alright, I'll take that bet," Jayden replied.

They put on their harnesses. Looking up, Jayden guessed that the wall was about 30 or so feet. Turning to Floriana, he said, "Kiss for Good luck?"

"No, I prefer for you to have bad luck when it comes to heights."

"That one hurt right here," he said, pointing at his heart.

The rock wall operator, turned to Jayden and Tony and asked, "Are you two ready?"

They nodded yes.

"Go!" He yelled.

Immediately, Tony jumped ten feet in the air and started climbing, and Jayden only jumped five. Before Jayden was even halfway up, Tony was waiting for him at the top. "Did you let me win?" he asked.

Jayden winced, "Heck no. I got a leg cramp before I jumped."

Tony rolled his eyes, "Whatever helps you sleep at night."

Tony walked away with Floriana at his side. Leaving Jayden alone with Sarah for the first time since he was in the hospital. "Do you want to see my favorite part of the fair?" She asked.

"I would love to, as long as it's nowhere near the clowns."

"We can go there after," she said with a wink.

Grabbing him by the arm, Sarah led him to the southeastern corner of the fair. They stepped out into a large square that was surrounded by Victorian styled buildings. This was the area, where merchants were selling souvenirs. In the center of the square was a fountain, with twin dolphins made of crystal. About twenty yards behind the fountain, was the lake, and the light from the full moon shined gently upon the waters. They sat down on a bench which overlooked the lake.

"After Eiréné was destroyed, this was the place I would go just to think. Something about the water helped to calm me on tough days, and it gave me hope that things might get better," she said while placing her hand on his. "That moment when you and Tony came back into my life, has helped me to see the silver lining finally."

"I meant to apologize for what I said earlier today. Tony told me you spent two nights in the hospital with me while I was out. Were you really that worried about me?"

Blushing, she replied, "I'm going to kill him for telling you that. But, yeah I was worried; the doctor said you had a very low chance of survival. The idea of losing you again was almost too much to take. Plus, I knew my mere presence would inspire you to get better."

"I didn't know you cared for me that much."

"Jayden, you know I do, and I always have. Since like third grade, we've always ended up sitting next to each other in at least one class. It's a shame you spent more time sitting next to me than trying to talk to me."

"I'm sorry, I was shyer back then. Plus, I was nervous. I did tell you jokes and drew pictures for you from time to time. I should at least get points for that."

"Ha! I'll give you half a point because your jokes were funny half the time. Why were you nervous around me? You've known me for a while."

"Well, because back then I was a growing boy learning about the world. And I accidentally liked you a little bit."

Smiling, she elbowed him, "Well why didn't you ask me out then? Why didn't you tell me that you accidentally liked me a little bit?"

He smiled, "Well I was afraid, that if I told you I liked you. You would try and get me to marry you. I wasn't ready for that type of commitment. Did you like me back then too?"

Grinning, she nudged him, "You're funny. Well, I guess now you'll never know."

"You're a devil woman. What If I asked you out now?"

For what felt like forever, his words just hung in the air. After what seemed like hours of silence and awkward glances, she turned to him on the bench, and she looked him dead in the eye, "Can I ask you a question?"

"Sure," Jayden replied nervously.

"Can I join you and Tony on your journey? I know I'd be able to help you guys out. Plus, after your incident with the goblins, you could use all the help you can get."

"Are you sure you want to do that? It's been dangerous so far, and I have a feeling it will get more so. You could get hurt or worse."

"Jayden, I've already experienced my fair share of dangers. I can handle it, plus the best way for me to know you're safe is for me to go with you."

"Fine! You can join us. But you never answered my question, what would you do if I asked you out now?" he asked, as he tried to put his arm around her.

She pushed his hand away, "Jayden I can't answer that right now. I'm still working out some things."

"Is it because you're into Tony now?"

"Maybe, I don't know."

"Is that why you want to go with us? So you can hang out with him? Is that why you asked me?"

She stood up, with tears in her eyes, "It's not like that at all. You're such an ass sometimes." She stormed off, leaving Jayden sitting alone on the bench, as it began to drizzle.

Chapter 11
Red Eye

My life has become a chick flick, he thought. One moment I'm having fun with the most amazing woman in the world, the next I'm sitting alone on this bench in the rain like an idiot. Ms. Tonya was right; my mouth would get me into trouble. Who knew it would happen twice in less than 24 hours to the same person? I shouldn't have questioned her motives. I shouldn't be surprised that she wants to travel with us.

Floriana sat down next to him on the bench. She rested her head on his shoulder and put her hand on his. "What happened to that bright smile of yours?"

"It ran away," he replied.

"Well, let me know when it comes back; I was starting to get used to it."

"Why did you come find me? I thought you were hanging out with Tony."

"I was until Sarah came up to us with tears in her eyes. So I just assumed you said something stupid."

"You might be right. Wait, so you walked all this way just to check up on me. That's pretty sweet of you. First, you're checking up on me. Next, you'll be wanting to marry me. It's too much, too fast Floriana."

Laughing, she replied, "Jayden, please, you couldn't afford my wedding dress, let alone my wedding day."

"Ha! I'm not sure if you heard but, I just came into money."

Floriana looked into his eyes and smiled, "I'll think about it. You can ask me again tomorrow."

***

Sarah stepped back into the square and her clothes were now completely soaked from the rain. If walking around with wet clothes wasn't annoying enough, she was still a little upset with Jayden. He just had to go and make everything more complicated. On the other hand, maybe Tony was right; maybe she should have given Jayden a chance. Would it really have been such a horrible thing to try?

As she got closer to the bench, she realized that Jayden was no longer alone. In fact, he was now cuddling up with a pretty brunette. Did she just kiss his forehead and is she holding his hand? I'm going to choke him, she thought. I've been gone less than 10 minutes, and he's already moved on.

She breathed a sigh of relief, when noticed that girl sitting with him was just Floriana. If it was any other brunette she might be worried. Then another thought popped into her, was Floriana trying to make a move on him? The more she thought about it, the more she knew it couldn't be true. The General was way to classy for that.

Sarah cleared her throat and awkwardly waved at them, just in case she was wrong. Then she said, "I was told by one of the staff that they will be closing the fair in twenty minutes, because of the rain. We will meet you at the exit."

She left quickly, before they could even respond. Once Sarah made it out of the square, she made a beeline for the exit. She stopped when she saw Tony standing outside of one the gift shops. He opened his gift bag and showed her the new whoopie cushion he got. Together they made a plot to prank Jayden, before the night was over.

She glanced up momentarily from their conversation, to see Jayden and Floriana heading their way. Sarah leaned in and asked, "Tony, what is she carrying?"

He shrugged, "I guess Jayden must have won her a gigantic teddy bear."

"Jayden," she said, as he approached her with a big smile on his face, "Where did you get that?"

His beaming with pride, "I won it doing the ring toss."

"That's cool" she replied, with as little enthusiasm as possible. "I thought you were going to try and get me a bear."

"I did try, but I was only able to get you this Slinky." He replied as he handed it to her. "I think they rigged the game, so you can only win the big prizes once in a lifetime."

Sarah took the Slinky in her hand, secretly wishing that it was a teddy bear. She gave him thankful hug and tried to give him the most appreciative smile she could muster. Even though she absolutely hated Slinkys, she would try to use it on her apartment's staircase at least once, for his sake.

Tony linked his arm with hers and said, "Let's get out of here. I think Ms. Tonya is probably worried sick about us by now. Hopefully, she will make her famous hot chocolate with marshmallows for us."

Together they made their way to exit. On their way back to her apartment, they explored the city for just a little while longer. When they made back home, Ms. Tonya gave each of them hot chocolate as they walked through the door. By one in the morning, they were all exhausted and went to bed.

***

The alarm on his clock was blaring and Jayden was pulled out of his amazing dream world. He sat up and stretched to wake himself up. Their bedroom was complete mess, with their clothes from the previous night, strewn across the floor. They probably should have hung those up, hopefully they don't mold.

Tony stood by his bed rummaging through a backpack. When he noticed the Jayden was awake that Jayden was awake, he threw a backpack at him.

"What is this for?" Jayden asked.

"It's a backpack for storing things in," Tony replied.

"I know that, but why are you giving it to me? I already have a duffle bag."

"O, I forgot you were asleep when we got these. Ms. Tonya gave us these bags. Apparently, they have this special enchantment that allows the bags to store up to 300 pounds worth of stuff. The bag can expand internally and won't externally. The best part is that the bag will still only feel like it's just a couple of pounds."

Jayden opened the bag and looked inside. The interior appeared the same as any other backpack since the beginning of time. There is nothing special about this bag; maybe Tony is trying to prank me. "Tony, you almost had me. There is no way a bag could do what you described. You're such a trickster."

Tony shook his head, "Jayden, sometimes I wonder if you bumped your head when you were little. But then you talk, and my suspicions are confirmed. Yes, the bags do work; you should give it a try, for once, I am not trying to mess with you. These are goodbye presents from Ms. Tonya; she just about cried when she handed one of the bags to Sarah."

The memories from the previous night started to come back, and he remembered making Sarah mad at one point. Is she still angry with me, he wondered. "Hey Tony, what the heck is an enchantment?"

His friend shrugged, "I don't know; maybe it's some kind of Voodoo."

What in the world is voodoo? Trying to sound smart, Jayden replied, "Ahh Voodoo magic that explains everything."

Sarah came barging through the door, to grab something from the closet. Jayden noticed something different about her, "Hey Sarah, you shouldn't come barging through a room full of dudes. You may see things that you can't unsee. Also, did you do something to your hair, because you look different today?"

Sarah gave him the creepiest smile in the world and said, "Jade, don't you remember that I spent two days with you in the hospital, while you were sound asleep." Her response was so off-putting, that it made Jayden quickly cover himself up under the blanket.

Then she flipped her hair back and forth for him, with a level of sass that he was unaccustomed to seeing. "And yes, I did do something different today. I'm glad you noticed." Sarah turned around for him. Then he noticed on her that she had two short swords strapped to her and attached to her hips by a leather belt, was a pair of 9mm fully automatic pistols with what appeared to be 30 round magazines. Suddenly Jayden felt inspired to never be mean to her again, mainly because he had this deep seeded fear that Sarah could now stab him in his sleep.

"Sarah, can you remind me never to make you angry again? On an unrelated note, where did you get all of that?"

"O, you like what you see?" She said with a smile. So now that I'm the only woman in the room, he finds me pretty again, way to go Jayden. Sarah was still a little angry with him partially because, he let his mouth get him into trouble, and because he won a giant teddy bear for Floriana. All she got was a slinky that broke when they got home. "Well I got the guns at the grocery store, and the swords came with this cute skirt I bought yesterday."

"Really? I didn't know you could get guns at a grocery store."

"No you moron, I was kidding. The guns and swords belonged to my mom and dad."

"Well, they look pretty impressive."

"See Jayden, sometimes that mouth of yours can say the sweetest things, and other times it makes me want to throttle you. On another note, you need to get up; we are leaving in 30 minutes. Make sure you take a shower; you may not get to for a while."

I guess I could get out of this bed, he thought. "Wait, where are we going?"

"We are going to the Water Temple. It's going to take 18 hours of driving, and then we have to hike the rest of the way for another day or so."

"Why there? When did you get all this information?"

"That's where Tony's Dad is, and we discussed this during our meeting this morning."

"Where was I during this meeting?"

"Sleeping like a bear in hibernation."

Jayden began to transfer all of his equipment into his new backpack. The enchantment seemed to work incredibly well.

"Hey Jayden, Floriana says that we need to be better equipped as we travel. So load on to your person anything that you might need quick access to." Jayden noticed that Tony had slung his four-foot long broadsword to his back, along with the shotgun. Grabbing his dad's pistol, he strapped it to his hip, and put the "Jade

Blade" on his back and attached two throwing knives to his belt. Once they were all loaded up, they set out on the highway.

Jayden and Tony decided to rent motorcycles, and the girls got a red convertible. They stopped off at a gas station to fill up and to stock up on food. "Jayden, if you try and run us off the road again, I will cut you in half," Floriana said.

"I will try my best not to; the bike has a mind of its own."

Having finished gassing up and getting food for the road, they prepared to leave. All of a sudden, the roaring sound of bikes echoed throughout the desert. Ten bikes appeared over the horizon, speeding down the highway. Something about this group seemed very familiar. As they drove by, Jayden waved at the passing caravan of motorcyclists; they didn't acknowledge his gesture. Well, that was rude, he thought.

Jayden and his group sped away from the gas station, kicking up dust into the air. Once they were about twenty miles down the road, they spotted the group of motorcyclists off in the distance. They were congregating on the highway, creating a roadblock. Jayden glanced at Tony with that here we go again look.

Standing in the center of the group of bikers was their leader who had his back to them. Turning around, the man had a big smile, which immediately vanished once he recognized Jayden and Tony.

"Samson? Is that you?" Tony asked.

"Aww, not you two again. Last time we saw you two, we ended up having to go to the hospital afterward. And we are still upset because you killed our sniper, Tommy. This time we won't let you off that easy."

Floriana stepped out of the convertible and said, "They weren't the ones that killed your little buddy. That was me." A big grin spread across her face as she slowly drew her rapier. "Are you boys looking for round two? Last time I let these two have all the fun."

Samson hesitated as he saw the two pretty ladies stepping out of the red convertible armed to the teeth. "Well, this should be interesting. Let's make a deal. You ladies join us, and we won't beat up on your boy toys too much."

"As great as that offer sounds," Sarah replied turning to look at Jayden, "we would prefer to take two of your fancy motorcycles, that convertible was starting to feel cramped."

"Just two motorcycles? Is there anything else you'd like your ladyship?"

"Personally, I would love to have that Chrome 44mag, you have," Jayden interjected.

"Well if your lady friend can come and take it from me, you can have it and the bikes."

Smiling, she stepped toward Samson. Sarah cracked her neck and her knuckles. Samson grabbed a metal baton from his bikes saddlebag. "This might hurt a little bit," he said.

"I hope it does," Sarah replied, as he rushed her. He swung at her wildly as she proceeded to duck and dodge each swipe. Then he swung for her legs, and she did an aerial flip over it and did three back handsprings to get some distance from him. Sarah waved for him to attack her. As he swung, she sidestepped and grabbed his arm, and hit him in the throat. He fell to the ground grabbing his neck. Sarah bent over and grabbed his pistol and the two magazines he had and threw them at Jayden.

"Thank you, Sarah."

"Remember you still owe me a giant teddy bear, and you can add a nice dinner to the list."

Once Samson could breathe again, he yelled for his men to help. Quickly Sarah snapped her fingers, and a yellow ball of energy appeared in her hand, then she threw it at the approaching bikers. The ball of energy exploded as it hit the ground, sending them flying into the air, and then crashing to the ground hard. Floriana pointed her rapier at the remaining bikers, and they were turned into ice cubes.

Samson was the only biker left that was still conscious. He looked up at them and said, "You can have two bikes and the gun, just don't hurt us anymore. And unfreeze my buddies."

Floriana pat his head said, "don't you worry. We won't hurt you anymore. And your buddies, they will finish thawing within the hour okay."

Sarah hopped on to one of the bikes, and it roared to life.

"Hey what kind of magic was that? And where did you learn to do that?" Jayden asked her.

Sarah dusted her shoulders off and said,"It's called explosive magic, and I learned it from Ms. Tonya. I'm going to use it on you the next time you decide to be a jerk."

"You're joking about that, right?"

Smiling back, she replied, "I might be."

Driving into the night, they approached a fork in the road. The paved road to their left led northeast to Central City, and the dirt road that veered to their right led to the Forest of Eden. Stopping at the edge of the Forest, Floriana got off her bike and said, "Let's camp here for the night. In the morning I will need to head to Central City. I still need to talk to the King."

Jayden was saddened at the thought of Floriana leaving them, but he understood that she had her duty. It was going to be weird not seeing her after tomorrow. Will they ever see her again, he wondered.

He found a nice flat area of ground to lay on. Using his bag as a pillow, he closed his eyes. Since his dad's death, Jayden often had nightmares that would leave him screaming in his sleep. Little did he know, that he would soon wake up to a living nightmare.

***

The peaceful night was broken, by the sound of a stick snapping. At first, Jayden thought it was just an animal; then he heard another snap five minutes later. What could it be? The last time he opened his eyes on a night like this, he got bitten by a dark goblin. So he was less inclined to open his eyes and investigate the creepy noise.

Jayden heard another snap, followed by a scream, he opened his eyes, and rolled as he grabbed his sword and drew it from its sheath. Glancing up, he saw two hooded figures were holding Tony and Sarah with black knives to their throats. Three more figures attempting to grab Floriana. Unfortunately for them, she struck down one of them with ease and stabbed another in the stomach, before being tackled by the last man.

"Lady Floriana," said a hooded figure who just stepped out from the tree line. "If you would kindly stop resisting, we can make this as painless as possible." Turning to Jayden, he removed his hood, revealing the tattoo of a demon on the back of his head, and suddenly Jayden felt sick to his stomach. Fear began to build up inside of him. For a moment, Jayden didn't know what to do. Why is this guy looking at me? He thought. Swallowing his fear, Jayden stood tall with his sword drawn.

"You are Dion's son, aren't you?" The hooded figure asked.

"Yes, and who might you be?"

"My name is none of your concern, my purpose however is. If you come with us voluntarily, we will let your friends go. If you resist, I will beat you to within an inch of your life; then I will have your friends killed in front of you. Then I will still make you come with us."

"Jayden, don't do it, just get out of here," Sarah yelled. The man holding her punched her in the side. She doubled over in pain.

Suddenly Jayden's fear was replaced with deep seeded anger, "If either of you lay a hand on my friends again, it will be the last thing you will ever do."

"Jayden none of my men will harm your friends again; that time was an accident," he said with a cruel smile. "Look if you go with us, I will make a phone call to my boss, and I will have him release Sarah's parents."

Sarah looked up at him, wincing in pain, "Are they really alive?"

"Oh yes, they are very much alive. In fact, I saw them just a couple weeks ago. We have been keeping them since we destroyed Eiréné."

Jayden looked at Floriana who mouthed he's lying, and he asked "How we do we know her parents are alive and you aren't just telling us a lie?"

"I have no reason to tell you a lie. You will be coming with us either way."

Jayden's mind was going a mile a minute. Since reuniting with Sarah, he had assumed that her parents were dead. Is it possible that they could still be alive? Now that he had an opportunity to help her see her parents again, he didn't know what to do. If I go with them, they will likely kill me to help them in their quest for power. Do I sacrifice my mission for the sake of Sarah's parents? What if he's lying? Jayden wondered. He turned to Sarah hoping for some direction; she stared into his eyes as she shook with emotion, and told him no.

Jayden found his voice and said, "Normally I would go with you, but my dad taught me to never travel with strangers."

The cloaked warrior began to circle Jayden, drawing his black dagger. "That's funny that you should mention your dad to me, because the last time I remember seeing him, I stabbed him in the back with this. You should have seen the shock on his face. The thought of it just makes me smile."

Jayden's eyes flashed red, "big mistake!" he shouted, as balls of fire came falling from the sky.

Chapter 12

The Waters Ran Red with Blood

Jayden's body twitched uncontrollably. His hands and clothes were wet and sticky. As his vision became clearer, he examined his hands and realized that they were covered in blood. He checked himself for injuries and found that he only had one small cut on his bicep. Whose blood is this, he wondered. Immediately, he was struck with worry. Where were his friends?

Standing up, Jayden looked around and found that all of the cloaked warriors were dead. His sword was embedded in the chest, of one unlucky soul. Bullet holes and burn marks covered the rest of his attackers. When he looked down he realized why his clothes felt sticky, they were completely soaked in blood.

He looked around frantically as tried to piece together what must have happened. Then Floriana and his friends emerge from the tree line. None of them appeared to be hurt. That's a good sign, he thought. Tony and Sarah both looked frightened and wouldn't get too close to him. General Floriana's sword was drawn, and she approached him cautiously.

Jayden was confused. "What happened? Why am I covered in blood?"

"Do you not remember?" Tony replied.

"No, all I remember is those jerks showing up. Then, I blacked out and woke up sitting on the grass covered in blood."

"Well, at first, your eyes flashed red, and you summoned fireballs from the sky, which was pretty cool. They hit the guys that were holding us. Then, you moved quicker than I have ever seen you move before. You killed the bald guy, and you shot the rest. You had this crazy look on your face, and we thought you might come after us. So Floriana bonked you on the back of the head, and you took a short nap."

Jayden fell to his knees and stared at the blood on his hands. Did I really just kill someone? The goblins were one thing, but these were people. Even though they did bad things, and one of them helped to kill my father, did he really deserve to die at my hands?

Suddenly, he remembered what Master Thai had told him about revenge. Vengeance was easier to resist at the monastery. But here he had his chance, and he failed. He lost control. He could have hurt his friends, and he wouldn't have known. Jonathan stared at the Daimonia members he killed and asked himself, am I any better than them?

Floriana sat down next to him, "You can't blame yourself for what happened. It will destroy you. It wasn't entirely your fault either. When your eyes flashed red like that, it's what they call "Rage." It makes you stronger and faster but at the sacrifice of self-control. People that can access that type of magic are those who've experienced a lot of pain in their lives. It's happened to many soldiers I've worked with. You can move past this. It's not easy to kill someone, but in this case, you didn't have much choice. You probably ended up saving our lives. Plus, you were able to avenge your father. Isn't that what you've wanted this whole time?"

Her words hit him like a ton of bricks. She was right. He should be filled with joy at this moment. Jayden should be on cloud

9, but instead, all he felt is guilt. Would his dad even be proud of him, for what he's done? Or would his dad be ashamed of him?

Consumed with exhaustion, they gathered in a circle and went to sleep. A few hours later, the sun rose into the sky. Its light illuminated the beautiful forest that surrounded them. Green leaves on the trees swayed in the gentle breeze. Radiant, rainbow-colored sparrows chirped in their nests, while rabbits and squirrels greeted the day with joy.

***

Sarah yawned as she climbed out of the world of dreams. Tony and Floriana were still fast asleep. Maybe she could bug Jayden, she thought. After quickly fixing her hair, she got up. Jayden's bag and sword were lying on the ground where he had been sleeping, but he wasn't there. She glanced around their camp and couldn't see him anywhere.

Considering the events from the previous night, she was feeling really concerned for him. She woke the others, and they began looking for him in the surrounding area and even down the road. He was nowhere to be found. When they came back together, they stared at the large forest that stretched as far as the eye could see. Don't tell me he went in there, they all thought.

"So Tony, did they teach you how to track in the monastery?" Floriana asked.

"Yes, but Jayden is pretty good at making it difficult for you to track him," he replied.

The forest was dark and creepy. Overgrown trees blocked large portions of the trail. Humungous spider webs hung from the branches of the trees. The sound of green forest wolves yapping and howling at each other, echoed throughout the forest.

Tony noticed that the weeds on the trail had been trampled recently. Then he crouched down on the ground and found a shoe print. "Jayden must have stayed on this trail for a while. He wouldn't have left it."

They continued to move deeper into the forest. Then Tony heard a high-pitched scream. Wheeling around, he saw Sarah stomping on the ground like a crazy person.

"What is it?"

She looked up at him flustered and red in the face, "I'm going to kill Jayden for marching off without us. A red-tailed tarantula just landed on me, and I proceeded to stomp him into oblivion."

This made the great General Floriana fall to the ground laughing.

"Ya, ya, laugh it up. Just you wait, one of those giant spiders is going to land on that pretty hair of yours and lay eggs." Sarah said.

Floriana jumped up quickly, "Hey, that's not funny. I hate spiders."

"A General that's afraid of spiders? That's funny! If the Eden army ever went to war against spiders, we would be screwed," Tony said.

"Tony, if I were you, I would sleep with one eye open tonight," she said with a smile.

The trail became wider, and the trees were more spaced far apart from each other. The light was able to pierce through the canopy of the trees. Tony stopped and bent down to examine a set of tracks. He noticed that the set of footprints stopped in the trail and continued into the forest.

They have no idea what lies in those trees, he thought. With his nerves telling him this was a bad idea, he left the trail and the girls followed.

Hiking between the trees was quite tricky. Some of the trees were so close together that they had to squeeze between them to continue. Large tree roots stuck out of the ground. One particular root tripped Floriana, which led to her saying some words that would make a sailor blush.

"Ms. Tonya said the Water Temple would be on the north end of the river. I bet you that is where Jayden is headed," Tony said.

The closer they got to the water, the trees grew even further apart. Tony stopped and pointed, "I think that's him sitting on that rock by the river."

Once they got to the river, they could see that it was Jayden. There was clearly something wrong with him. While he sat by the river, he kept washing and rubbing his arms vigorously with the water over and over again. Floriana gestured for Tony and Sarah to stay back. She walked to him slowly, "Jayden, what are you doing?"

He ignored her and continued to wash. "Jayden," she said a little more firmly, "what are you doing? We've been searching for you. We were all worried."

Finally, he looked up at them. He didn't look too good. His clothes were soaked, and his body was shaking from the icy water. His eyes had rings around them from lack of sleep, and the joy that was normally in his smile was gone and replaced with sadness.

"I wasn't able to sleep the rest of the night." He replied with his teeth chattering. "I couldn't help but think about what happened. So I've been trying to wash off the blood from my hands."

Floriana was genuinely concerned for him. Putting her hand on his shoulder, she replied, "What blood? Your hands look pretty clean to me."

Jayden looked down at his hands and looked back up confused. "You just can't see it. My hands will never be clean again."

Sarah sat down next to him and leaned her head against him. Her presence seemed to calm him. Tony sat down with him on his other side. "Hey man, it's going to be alright. Plus, there might be pretty chicks at the Water Temple."

This made Jayden smile slightly, which got him elbowed by Sarah.

"If you need to, we can sit here for a little bit until you are ready to go," Sarah said.

"No we can't; we should leave," he said, struggling to stand back up.

"Why?"

Lifting his arm, he pointed toward a thick area of trees, "Because we are not alone," he said ominously.

"But Jayden, I don't see anything," she replied.

Tony quickly stood up and drew his broadsword, followed by Floriana. "Hey, Jayden stay by the river. We will handle this."

"Guys! What's going on?" Sarah asked nervously.

SNAP! That sound made Sarah jump to her feet, as she heard large branches break and loud footsteps coming their way. She pulled out one of her pistols and one of her swords. Whatever is coming this direction, is big, really big, she thought.

She looked back, to check on Jayden. He was still just sitting on the ground, completely ignoring the danger that was approaching. I have to protect him, she told herself. He would do the same for me. As their adversaries stepped into the clearing, she instantly became consumed with fear.

Standing in the clearing, were four large Ogres of Eden. They were green, from head to toe and stood over seven feet tall. Their muscles bulged, and their large mouths drooled as they considered their future meal.

The largest ogre stepped forward, "Magic users. My favorite!" he said licking his lips.

"Phillip, I want to eat the little girl with the pistols," said the smallest ogre.

"Wait!" Tony yelled as he pointed at the largest ogre, "Your name is Phillip? Who names an ogre Phillip?"

Phillip's green face turned bright red. Apparently, this was a sensitive subject, "I'll have you know Phillip was my father's name."

"Wow, so you are Phillip the Second? Very original. Now, what are you ogres wanting from us?"

The shortest ogre stepped forward and jumped up and down with excitement, "We are going to eat you all, with potatoes and carrots."

This made Phillip gag, "Eww; I hate vegetables!"

"Remember? Mom said vegetables are good for your cholesterol."

"I don't care about my cholesterol."

"Mr. Phillip," Sarah said, ever so sweetly, while batting her eyes. "I would hate for you to get high blood pressure from eating us. How about I make you a nice salad and some lentil soup?"

For a moment, Phillip seemed to be considering her idea. "What is in this lentil soup?"

"Well, it's awesome like watching a sunset. It's that amazing. If you let me make you some, I might bake you some chocolate chip cookies."

Suddenly his brow furrowed, and he roared, "I hate sunsets!" He yelled, "We will eat you now." He whistled, and five odd looking creatures came out of the woods. Each had the body of a lion and had the head of a King Cobra. They hissed, and venom oozed from their mouths.

"What are those things?" Sarah asked, trying to keep her cool.

"They are called Seraphim," Floriana replied. "Their bites hurt like heck. They can also spit venom, which will burn your skin and give you stomachaches."

Without warning, the seraphim rushed them. Floriana, summoned a block of ice which she slammed into the smallest ogre, sending him to the ground for a nap. Tony summoned a high powerful gust of wind, which knocked two of the Seraphim into the trees. One of the Seraphim rushed Sarah, so she sidestepped it and fired three rounds into it.

Sarah screamed, as burning venom oozed down her neck. She dove out of the way of another Seraphim. The creature changed targets and sped toward Jayden. Sarah yelled for him to run, but he just sat there. When he didn't respond, she aimed her gun and fired, sending the Seraphim to the ground.

Tony ran towards an ogre. The large creature swung its powerful mace at him. Tony ducked and slid under the ogre. Turning around, he slashed the ogre in the back. It roared in pain, as yellow blood poured down it's back. The ogre kicked backward, hitting Tony in the chest, which sent him flying in the air. He landed hard, and his head hit a small rock. Standing back up, his vision was blurry. A Seraphim jumped on top of him and slashed at his chest with its claws. Tony pushed it off, then stabbed it with his sword.

Three more ogres appeared in the clearing, joining the others. Tony ran back to the river, standing next to Floriana, who had apparently turned Phillip, the ogre into half an icicle. She had frozen him from the waist down, which showed that she had quite the sense of humor.

More Seraphim came out of the woods, and Tony said, "I don't think we can fight this many. We may need to jump in the river to escape. There is no way we can outrun them in the forest."

They backed towards the river when a black arrow appeared in the chest of an ogre. Six white arrows rained down from the sky and dispatched the Seraphim. The ogres roared and ran back into the forest. Phillip the Ogre was able to break out of the ice spell, and he yelled back, "That wasn't cool!"

Stepping out from the trees, was a man with a large dark green bow. He had light brown skin and was about 5'7. His hair was black, which matched the arrow, he had notched ready to go. Standing next to him were four elves. They had pale skin and long white bows. On their hips, they had white daggers with light green sheaths. They stood over six feet tall and had light green eyes. Their ears were pointy, and they appeared calm.

Sarah looked at this group of arrow-wielding men and felt uneasy. Tony approached the man with the dark green bow. With a confused look on his face, he said, "dad, is that you?"

Chapter 13

A Warm Welcome

The Water Temple rested at the base of a small mountain, called Zoe. The River of Eden passed through the mountain, and flowed beneath the base of the temple, and cut through the forest. The water was crystal clear and teeming with fish. Swimming in the cool depths of the river next to them, was a blue freshwater crocodile with spikes on its tail. A variety of spiders skated across the waters, while large dragonflies flew just above its surface. Brown-tailed eagles and reptilian birds would occasionally swoop down and pick up fish to bring home to their nests. The River of Eden was quite pleasant and would probably be a perfect place to take a family if it wasn't surrounded by a forest teeming with dangerous animals.

Once the Water Temple became more visible up on the hill, it seemed to brighten Jayden up a little bit. He had pretty much been a ghost of himself, since the other night. However, he did seem to perk up, at the sight of the elves. Tony and Jayden had never seen elves before, and the elves had never met a Jayden before. Jayden couldn't stop staring at their pointed ears.

"Jayden, you're going to make them uncomfortable," Tony whispered.

"Their ears are making me uncomfortable," he said, while cracking a smile.

It was nice to see him smile again. Killing those Daimonia members and going into a rage, really did a number on him. They all wondered if Jayden had completely lost it. During their fight with the ogres, he just sat there in his own world. Will it be just as tough for me, when I have to take someone's life, Tony wondered. Considering how distraught Jayden had been, would it even be worth it?

Jayden and Tony stopped when they reached a set of stairs, which led up to the temple. They were awestruck, at the extravagant beauty of the Water Temple, which loomed overhead. The temple divided into three sections, a ground level, the Central District, and the very top of the building was the sanctuary. The Water Temple was designed like an old pyramid, with a flat roof at the top. The building was painted in a pearl white coat. Blue stripes lined the edges of the steps, which led up to the temple. Three sets of stairs provide access to the three levels of the temple. The entrance to the stairs, which led to the sanctuary, was guarded by two large elves equipped with spears.

Tony breathed in the salty air, which permeated throughout the temple. This smell reminded him of the time his father took him to the beach when he was very young. "Jayden, this is way nicer than the Dragon Temple," Tony said.

"Ya, I wish we would have been brought here as kids. I bet you they've even got a pool." Jayden replied. "Hey Uncle Raiden, what's at the top of the pyramid?"

"That sanctuary is where the Sage of this temple and his top students live. Unless you have received master's level training at a temple, you can't enter it." Raiden replied.

Stepping across the threshold, they entered the lobby which had hallways that went off in every direction. Raiden stopped and turned to address the group, "Tonight they are providing a special dinner, and you all are the guests of honor. These guides will lead you to where you will be staying. Dinner will be in an hour and a half. Don't be late."

Heading to their room, Tony couldn't resist being impressed by the interior of the temple. The painted ceiling had murals with the images of war, angelic beings, and symbols of peace. The residents of the temple were friendly and greeted them with handshakes as they walked by. The Water Temple was a different environment, compared to what they were used to. In the Dragon Temple, the goals were to grow in your abilities and to contemplate the difficult questions about life, through meditation and discipline. The Water Temple sought to embrace those ideas through having a tightly knit community.

The beauty of the building was amazing, but Tony couldn't help but notice that his dad had hardly spoken a word to him. Even after helping to save Tony and his friends, his dad barely acknowledged his existence. In some ways, Tony was annoyed by this, but on the other hand, he really wasn't ready to rebuild a relationship with his father. His dad is the one that left without a word. All he wanted to know was, "Why?"

When they entered their room, Tony and Jayden found themselves both in awe. Their beds floated a couple of inches off the ground. The sound of a babbling brook filled the room, and it smelled like the ocean on an overcast day. On their beds laid a set of aqua green colored elven robes. A necklace rested on each of the robes. They both had a pendant of an eagle attached to them.

"So, are we supposed to wear these?" Tony asked.

"Ya, I think so," Jayden replied. "I don't like them. They look like dresses."

"O, good thing you brought your high heels. These colors will bring out your eyes," Tony added.

"Ha, you're funny said no one ever."

After changing into their robes, they stepped back into the hall. Their guide was patiently waiting for them. He led them to a large dining hall. The dining hall was immaculate. Hanging from the ceiling were large chandeliers. The arches in the doorway glittered with gold. The table was covered in a white cloth, with light blue roses as a centerpiece.

Once they found their seats, they were given plates made of platinum. From one end to the other, the table was littered with foods of all varieties. There was pasta, chicken cooked in every way known to man and elk. Sitting on a long plate, was a roasted pig. They even had large bowls of ice cream, which led to Tony and Jayden giving each other a high five. Floriana and Sarah arrived five minutes later. Their robes were white, and they wore matching high heels. Floriana sat across from Jayden, which bugged Tony a little bit. He was beginning to think she wasn't into him.

"You look beautiful," Jayden said to Floriana, which made her blush a little bit. Sarah rolled her eyes and placed herself next to Tony. Raiden sat at the head of the table, as the rest of the dinner party arrived.

Clinking his glass, Raiden's said, "Welcome all! Today we have some very special guests with us this evening." Raiden gestured for them to stand. "My son and his friends are here to spend a few days with us. I hope you will all give them the same amount of love and respect, which you have shown me all these years. Now, enough with the pleasantries. Dig in."

The food was terrific; everything tasted delicious. After having spent so much time eating lackluster food, this was a nice change of pace. Tony grabbed a slice of pizza, that was as long as his arm, and stuff it in his mouth. If this was how the people at the Water Temple ate all the time, Tony could understand why his dad would want to live here.

Time flew by, as they dined in the Water Temple. The plates of food just kept coming, one after another. After Tony's sixth plate of food, the number of people at the table became less and less. Soon it was just Raiden, a few elves, Tony and his friends.

Throughout the night, as the conversations went on, Tony's dad still acted as if he didn't want to talk to him. He felt invisible to his own father. This intensified the animosity that Tony already felt toward his father. When he couldn't take it any longer, Tony yelled, "How can you go all these years without seeing your own son and act like I'm not here? The least you can do is tell me why you left. Tell me why I had to be raised by my grandparents, only to end up watching them die!"

Raiden turned to Tony, and the stern look he usually carried, was replaced with an expression of deep sorrow. Putting down his glass, he said, "Son, my only regret in this life, is that I chose to leave you. Believe me when I say that it was the hardest thing, I've ever had to do."

Tony was still infuriated. "The HARDEST thing you've ever had to do? I saw the town I grew up in burn to the ground, and my FATHER was nowhere in sight. My DAD wasn't there to protect me. His was," he said pointing at Jayden. "Just tell me why you left?"

"It's a long story, but I'll tell you the truth. Years ago, when you two were still little, we got word that *The Key* had been found during an archeological dig ordered by the Eden Government. Dion and I, along with Sarah's parents, and a few others were given a mission to steal *The Key* away from them. After having done so, we were betrayed by one of our own. The Daimonia had members from our group kidnapped and tortured to find out where we had hidden *The Key*. Once we realized that, we knew that Dion and the rest of us would be in danger. Dion believed, that if some of us moved to Eiréné, we would be safe."

"Who betrayed you?"

"This may be a tougher pill to swallow, but... it was your mother."

For a moment, Tony and the others were speechless. Tony was in complete shock. He was told growing up that his mom had gotten sick, just like Jayden's mother. Tony never knew his mom. He had always imagined her carrying him as a child and them laughing together. He didn't want to believe that she could betray someone, that she could do something so evil.

"How did you know it was her?"

"There was a time when Dion and I, along with your mother, considered switching sides. We were all frustrated because we spent so much time fighting the Daimonia and spending less time on keeping man from destroying itself. The Daimonia have always been good at sticking to their prime directive. During that time, it became apparent that your mother joined them. Her demeanor changed; she seemed so distant then. When we had finished our mission and retrieved *The Key*, she kept asking about where it was, and who had it. That's when we knew she was a double agent. She disappeared after she had members of our team kidnapped and tortured. The reason I left, was because I knew that your mom would come looking for Dion. I thought that if me and him, were far away from you kids, you would be better protected. I couldn't have been more wrong. Dion ended up protecting you more than I did. I wish I would have listened to him. I can understand if you choose not to forgive me. I should have been there with you."

Tony was still angry at his dad. He wanted to hate him, but he couldn't. Not even if he tried. In some ways, he felt sorry for his father. He wanted to protect Tony; he just made the wrong decision. Tony couldn't even imagine, what it must have been like for his dad knowing that his wife was a traitor. Even though Tony never knew her, he felt disappointed and wished he had known her, but on the other hand, he was afraid of her. With tears in his eyes, he got up and hugged his dad.

"I won't ever leave you again," his dad said.

"Promise?"

"I promise!"

***

Midnight fell over the land, and the moon shined brightly in the midst of the darkness. General Floriana, snuck out of her room and moved quieter than an assassin, as she made her way out of the temple. Physically leaving them was easy, but emotionally she was struggling. Her heart was tugging at her; she wanted to stay with them. They needed her help, but she had her duty to fulfill. She was still a soldier, and nothing would change that.

Strolling through the forest at night, was quite surreal. The moonlight pierced through the trees, as she journeyed through. She could hear wolves howling, as she darted through the forest. Owls hooted in the trees, and reptilian birds flapped their wings, as they searched for their prey. The forest was alive and well, and she needed to prepare for anything that might attack her.

After hours of traveling in the twilight, Floriana made it to the edge of the forest. She approached her bike and heard a voice in the darkness say, "Leaving us so soon are we?"

She jumped at the sound and drew her sword. Stepping out from the trees was an archer with a dark green bow.

"Raiden?"

"Did you say goodbye to your friends before leaving?"

She shook her head no.

"Why didn't you say goodbye, and why do you feel the need to leave?"

"I'm a soldier, and I have my duty to my country."

"You didn't really answer my question."

Fighting a back sob, she replied, "I knew that if I tried to say goodbye, I wouldn't be able to leave. I've spent so much time serving this country. Helping people outside of that environment

129

has been nice. I have my duty. I need to speak with the King about the traitors in our midst."

"I can understand that. I do want you to know that you are always welcome to come back." Raiden gave her a small gold colored coin, with the face of an elven warrior on it. "You can use this to communicate with us. Just say the name of the person you want to speak with, flip the coin, and then leave a message. I will give the same coins to the others. Those boys and Sarah will need you again in the future. They need you more than you know. Remember, no matter what happens, seek the good. The path that you are going now will test you and your convictions more than ever before."

"Do you think I am making a mistake by leaving?"

"As you said, you are a soldier, and you have your duty. The mistake would be to stay and not fulfill your obligations."

Hopping on her motorcycle, she sped off into the night. She couldn't help but wonder if she should turn back around. Pulling over to the side of the road, she looked back and knew that she had gone too far to turn back. She wondered what the King would think when he saw her. Would he have her arrested or worse?

Chapter 14
The Darkness Within

That morning they got up and had breakfast. For breakfast, they ate in a small dining room area. Despite the size of the venue, the food was still plentiful. On large ivory plates were pancakes, eggs, sausage, bacon and hash browns. Jayden grabbed a blueberry pancake and some syrup. Sitting at the table with him were Tony, Sarah, and Raiden. Raiden informed them that morning that Floriana had left during the night.

At first, Jayden was angry that she didn't have the common decency to say goodbye. While he chewed on a delicious pancake, he considered how difficult it must have been for her to leave. From the moment they met, in that interrogation room until now, he noticed that she had changed a little bit. She had opened up more and treated them like friends. To the world, she was a General of Eden. For Jayden, she would always be the amazing girl that risked her life to save his.

Jayden swallowed his tenth pancake and felt like he had gained 100 pounds. The two amazing meals he'd had at the Water Temple were the best he's since his mother was alive. He was beginning to feel more like himself. His gloomy attitude had been replaced with the joy he was used to feeling.

A light bulb clicked on in his head, and that's when he remembered why they traveled all this way. He turned to Raiden and said, "Ms. Tonya told us that you might have some information about *The Key*. What do you know?"

Raiden placed his coffee down on the table and said, "In some ways, I know a lot. In other ways, I know too little, but I will tell you what I can. *The Key* is an object that came into existence near the end of the Great War. *The Key* was made to give a person access to weapons and materials that would have ended the war in a very efficient manner. However, the war ended without the help of the items *The Key* would have provided access too. What it opens specifically, we don't know, and The Elders we've asked don't know much about it. What I do know is that it can open up a treasure chest. I believe there is a map in the chest that will tell you where some of the other items are.

"That was kind of confusing," Jayden said. "Where is *The Key*, and why do the Daimonia want it?"

"They aren't the only ones looking for it. I believe King Aelius is after it too. That's why he allowed Eiréné to be destroyed. I don't completely know what the Daimonia are going to use it for, outside of gaining power, but I do think they are planning something big. I don't know exactly where *The Key* is, but I believe that getting in contact with Lady Grace of The Aggeloi would help in finding out where it is." Raiden replied.

"Dad, isn't she dead? How could she help us even if she were alive?" Tony asked.

"That's what the consensus has been, but we had one of ours working the investigation when her convoy was attacked. Her guard and her advisors were all found dead at the scene. The only body that was missing was hers. We believe that the Aggeloi Parliament ordered her to be killed and paid a group of witches to do it. I think they kidnapped her."

"Wait, so you're saying the queen of one of the most powerful countries in the world was kidnapped by a band of nameless women riding on brooms with pointy hats? Why would they simply kidnap her? Why would her own government want her dead?"

"She would be more valuable alive for the witches because her Father was an Elder, and her mother was a brilliant magic user. The Aggeloi Parliament wanted her dead, so they could gain power since she is the last of the royal family. With her dead, the monarchy would have died with her. The witches that we think may have taken her are a part of the Southern Convent, which is run by Lady Clara."

"Where is the Southern Convent? How would we get there?" Jayden asked.

"The Southern Convent is somewhere on the southern continent, Terra. We believe they live in the Chaldean Swamp. Enchantments on the swamp make finding their Convent virtually impossible. You will need to ask for information about the swamp from the villagers that live close to the swamp."

"Are you not coming with us?" Tony asked.

"I can travel with you to Terra, and then I must leave. My current mission isn't to search for *The Key*. I trust you all to find it. My mission is to find out who the current leaders of the Daimonia are and where their home base is." Standing up, he added, "you boys do need to be careful though. Now that you have killed members of the Daimonia, they will come after you. Taking on the witches will be just as difficult. You will need some additional training. Tony, I need you to go out into the hall and speak with an elf named GabriEL. He will teach you some water magic, which you can use to augment your storm magic. Sarah, I need you to head to the Temple library and meet with a lady named Celest. She will teach you some defensive magic. Jayden, I need you to stay here."

Great now I'm in trouble, Jayden thought. After the others left, he said, "Why am I not getting additional training?"

"Because," said a voice behind him, "your hands are covered in blood. You can't continue on your journey until you cleanse your soul." Stepping into the room was a tall elf. He was around seven and a half feet tall. His skin was pale, and his elven robes were a turquoise blue. Resting on his arms was an item that was wrapped in velvet.

Jayden's sense of guilt arose to the surface, and to the point where he couldn't look the elf in the eye. "Who are you? How did you know what I did?"

"My name is MikaEL. I am a Holy Knight and an Apprentice to The Water Sage. You have experienced "The Red Eye." You must climb this mountain to cleanse your soul. There is a darkness in you that is more dangerous than that which is in your adversary." He unwrapped the velvet cloth, which exposed two items, a three-foot long metal chain, and a dagger.

The dagger had an ivory handle that was engraved in gold. The blade was pearl white made of elven steel. The metal chain was a silver color and was slightly heavy. It was held together by links of steel. "You are to climb the mountain that this temple sits on. Near its summit is a cave. Upon entering it, you will know what to do next. The only equipment you can take is this dagger and this steel chain. You may not bring food or water with you either. Anything you need must come from the land."

Jayden looked at him curiously, "Why can't I bring my own equipment or food? I'm already hungry, and we just got done eating." MikaEL bowed and walked out of the room, with Raiden in tow.

Well, that's just great, Jayden thought as he walked out of the temple. Now I have to climb this stupid mountain, and I am currently near the bottom of it. Then I have to find a stupid cave and learn something from it. There are probably bats in the cave, and I hate bats. Jayden wrapped the metal chain around his waist and hung the dagger from it. Well, let's gets over with, so I can get back to eating.

He began his journey by skipping through a meadow filled pink and blue daisies, because no one else was around. The green grass on both sides of the trail was tall enough to reach his knees. Monarch butterflies jumped from flower to flower. This scene reminded him, of the garden at the Dragon Monastery. The sweet smell of the flowers, made him feel at peace.

The further he climbed up the mountain, the older the trees became. Dark green and white vines hung from their thick branches. Large spider webs and moss littered the trunks of the trees. He could sense the energy from the forest, and it was old and powerful. He knew there were dangerous creatures in these woods, and he needed to remain alert.

Jayden stopped to tie his shoe for a moment. That was when he got the feeling he was being watched, which is a terrible feeling to have when you are by yourself. He shook his head and told himself that it was just his imagination.

Moving a little further down the trail, he stopped to get a sense of his bearings. It was very tough to see, even though it was barely midday. There was a bush nearby him that started to shake violently. A large animal came charging out of it. Jayden quickly dove to his left, then rolled over and pushed himself up to get back on his feet. Then he jumped up to grab a tree branch and quickly climbed up it.

Jayden stared down from the tree and his eyes widened as he realized what had chased him. Lurking at the base of the tree, was a male jungle wolf. The animal was three and a half feet tall at the shoulder, and four feet long. The animal's fur was a mossy green shade, and it had yellow eyes, that matched the color of its teeth.

The jungle wolf growled as it paced back and forth. Then it made a low howl. Stepping into view, were two more wolves. One of them had thick black fur and was substantially larger than both of the other wolves combined. The black wolf drooled, as it looked up at Jayden in the tree. As the saliva hit the ground, it burned the grass it landed on. O that's just perfect, Jayden thought, the big wolf can spit out acid.

All three wolves lunged themselves at the tree and began to climb. Jayden's heart began to pound in his chest, as the ravenous wolves pursued him. It was at this moment that, he was beginning to prefer dealing with the ogres.

Jayden quickly realized that the wolves could climb faster than him. He had to be smart about this. He could summon fireball and turn these wolves into hot dogs. However, if he did that, he might end up burning down the forest, he thought. For now, the best option he had, was to get away from them, as quick as possible.

He waited until the black wolf was less than two feet away from him. Then, he broke a thick branch and threw it at the wolf and jumped to the next tree before the wolf could turn him into his next meal.

He climbed as fast as he could. When, he reached the top of the tree with the wolves in pursuit. The light of the sun warmed his face, and he was able to get a better feel for where he was. Most importantly, he could see where the trail exited the forest. He had about 100 or more yards to go.

Ouch! Jayden felt a burning sensation around his ankle. The black wolf had made a clean swipe at his ankle. He winced from the pain. Think Jayden think! You have to put more distance between you and the wolves below you. The wolf went for another swipe. Jayden pulled his leg up just in enough time to avoid it. Then he jumped as far as he could, crashing into a row of trees. He hit branch after branch before catching himself on one. Everything hurt. He had scratches everywhere, and the injury he got from the wolf was bleeding more than he had imagined.

The black wolf barked, and two more green wolves came out of the jungle. He barked again, and one of them jumped into the tree. Well, Jayden thought, at least I know the black wolf is the leader, and apparently a strategist.

The jungle wolf climbed, as the others watched and waited. Jayden slowly unwrapped his metal chain and slid his dagger underneath his belt. He then summoned heat, until the metal chain was bright orange. He swung it at the wolf, sending it to the ground. The animal got up slowly, and there was a burn on its side.

Two more wolves jumped into the tree. Time for me to leave, Jayden thought. He climbed as quickly as he could. Whenever the wolves got too close, he would swing the chain to keep them back. Once he reached the canopy, he jumped to the next set of trees.

This time, he smashed into the top of a tree. His left side burned, as he was impaled by a stick. He pulled it out, just as a wolf came crashing down on top of him. Jayden quickly pushed the animal off, sending it to the forest floor, hitting every branch on the way down. The wolf didn't move after landing, which made Jayden sob a little bit. I hope, I didn't hurt him too badly, he thought.

Now, there were just three wolves left for him to deal with. The animals were following him along the forest floor. He wanted to create a bigger distance, between him and the wolves, by jumping from tree to tree. With every jump he attempted, his body ached even more. His wounds were still bleeding, and he was feeling very dehydrated. He needed to get water and patch up his wounds fast.

Jayden climbed, to the top of the tree that he was in. He needed to get a better perspective on his location. He glanced around and noticed that he only had to go a little bit further, to reach the clearing. Just a few more jumps between the trees and he would be free.

Suddenly, he felt his body being pulled backward. Jayden wheeled around and realized that a wolf was grabbing on to his pant leg. The fabric was tearing. If he didn't do something quick, he was going to be dragged to the ground. With all of his strength, Jayden pushed off from the tree, taking the wolf with him.

Together they crashed into the next tree. Jayden free-fell, smashing through branches on his way down to the ground. He slammed onto forest floor with the force of a rocket. His head was spinning like a Ferris wheel and every inch of his body was screaming with pain.

The wolf was the first to stir, and it slowly approached him. The animal's growl filled Jayden with fear. He was in too much pain to try and get away. He had to think quickly. He glanced around and saw that his metal chain was within an arm's reach. Grabbing it, he slowly wrapped it around his knuckles as the wolf got closer. Once it was within a few feet of him, the wolf leaned its head back and howled. Then, it extended its claws and pounced on Jayden. Just as the wolf landed, Jayden swung and punched the wolf with his metal chain with all the might he had.

Jayden stood up and was relieved to see that the wolf unconscious. Quickly he scanned the area and didn't see any of the other animals. He limped forward as he walked out of the forest, leaving behind a trail of blood.

Stepping back into daylight, the warm sun hit his skin and gave him hope. He walked toward a large green hill. Jayden was only a few feet from the hill when he quickly spun around. Standing at the edge of the forest was a large, black wolf. The creature looked extremely angry. At this point, Jayden was sick and tired of running for his life. It was time that he made his stand. Pulling out his dagger he swung it in an upward motion while yelling, "Fire Wall." A cylindrical column of fire surrounded the wolf. Fright appeared on its face, as it had no way to escape the flames. Jayden's anger burned toward the wolf. He snapped his fingers, and the wall of fire began to close in on the animal. The wolf curled up and began to whimper in despair.

To this day, Jayden has never forgotten that sound. That sound kept him from losing control and almost his humanity. Jayden sheathed his dagger and the fire spell dissipated. The wolf looked up at him and barked, then ran off. Finally some peace, Jayden crumbled to the ground and rested against the hill.

I can't believe, I almost lost control again, he thought. The wolf was just doing what wolves do, but I made it personal. Jayden looked at his hands, and he remembered spending hours cleaning the blood off them. While they looked clean now, they didn't seem that way. His mind trailed off to advice his master gave him. His Master Thai had said, "Learning to use restraint is more powerful than using force. However, the toughest part about restraint isn't knowing when to use it, but to simply use it." MikaEL told me there is darkness inside me. Maybe he was right.

Jayden closed his eyes and didn't wake up again until the sun rose the next day. He woke up to the gentle sound of grass rustling in the wind, and small insects buzzing as they flew from flower to flower. Opening his eyes, he noticed that a family of deer was grazing nearby. The morning seemed so peaceful. Despite the hiccups in his journey, it was all worth it to wake up on a day like this.

He laid there very still until the deer scampered off. His empty stomach growled with the ferocity of a tiger. So he crawled to the nearest bush filled with berries. The berries came in all sorts of colors. Some were red, others were blue, and some were a pearl white. He took a handful and munched on them. They tasted sour, but they provided him with some of the energy he had lost from the previous day. He attempted to stand up, but his balance was still wobbly because his whole body ached all over.

As he struggled his way to reach the top of the hill, he looked up and wanted to cry. The way to the top of the mountain was rocky and steep. In some areas, the walls of rock were completely flat. He also spotted some sections of the mountain, where there were wide crevices that would take a person to God knows where.

Fighting through the pain he felt throughout his body, he climbed for a few hours more. It was very difficult at times. As he climbed, he slipped trying to find his footing climbing on a large rock. Once he gained his footing, he nearly had a heart attack, as a fire scorpion crawled across his hand. Jayden remained still like a statue until the scorpion was completely gone. He vowed to himself that the next time someone asks him to climb a mountain, he was going to choke them.

Jayden pulled himself up, on to a level plain. There was a small grassy hill just a few feet away, with some large boulders resting on it. He limped his way to the hill and sat down on the grass and placed his head on a round rock.

Sitting there by himself, he was beginning to feel fed up with the journey he was on. Tony and Sarah were out there learning magic, and here he was fighting for his life on this God-forsaken mountain. If only his dad could see him, now moping about his problems. He thought again about what MikaEL had said. How could his darkness be greater than his enemies? He didn't destroy Eiréné or kill anyone for that stupid key. How could he be worse than them?

He closed his eyes for just a few minutes when he felt that something was wrong. Jayden discovered what was wrong very quickly. He found himself hanging upside down, which led him to scream like a girl, but in a manly way. Jayden discovered that the rocks he was so generously spending his time with, were in fact not your average stones but were actually the body of a rock troll.

To the untrained eye, they look just like a rock, except it for their red eyes and less than friendly temper. The rock troll roared in Jayden's ear and opened its wide mouth. The monster's teeth were made of sharp rocks and its tongue was as black as night. The monster licked Jayden's face, which felt more uncomfortable than it sounds. Before the troll could turn him into its next meal, Jayden summoned the largest fireball he could, with the amount of energy that he had left, which was almost nothing. He threw the wimpiest looking fireball ever, into the mouth of the rock troll. This seemed only to annoy it, but it annoyed it enough that it threw Jayden up against the rocks on the side of the mountain.

His body hit the rocks so hard that he bounced off them and he spiraled downward until he slammed against a rocky floor.

Jayden looked up see briefly to see how far he had fallen, before blacking out from the pain.

The sound of rushing water woke him up from his pain induced slumber. To his right, he noticed that there was a small creek of streaming water, filled with small, grey fish. Jayden felt dehydrated, so he pulled himself toward the water. With every inch he moved, he screamed with pain. Jayden winced when he touched his left side. A cracked rib maybe? His body hurt like it was going out of style.

Jayden did feel a little grateful, for all the time spent at Dragon Monastery, because it trained his body to endure large amounts of stress without killing him. He grinned, as he could already sense that his auto-healing spell had started to activate. As helpful as the spell was, it wasn't intended to heal people, who have been thrown into crevasses.

Once he reached the water, he took a drink and splashed some of the water on his face. As soon as the water touched his lips, he could feel the pain in his body lessened. It was so effective that he was able to stand up.

He cupped his hands and drank some more water and rubbed it on his wounds. Now instead of feeling sharp, "I feel like I'm going to die pains". He now felt a mildly acceptable amount of pain.

Jayden followed the stream until he reached a dead end. He noticed that the water was coming down from the rocks above. He gazed up at a flat rock wall, and he noticed a darkened area near the top, and he saw what looked like the mouth of a small cave.

The water must be coming from up there. Suddenly, he had a brain blast. This must be the cave he was supposed to find. His heart immediately filled with joy. Then he asked himself, so how am I supposed to get up there? He kicked something on the ground in frustration. "Ouch," he yelled. "What did I just kick?" Glancing down at his feet, he saw an old rusted dagger that was similar to his own. He ran his finger along the blade, and it felt pretty sharp. Then he jabbed it into the rock and it dug into it like butter.

Jayden stepped back and he took a deep breath. This is really going to hurt, he thought. He channeled a speed magic spell, and instantly his body felt more limber. Jayden grinned as he bent his knees and launched himself forward as quickly as he could. Then, he jumped at the wall, planted his foot against it, and used it to spring himself skyward. As his momentum slowed, he jabbed his dagger into the rock, and then he shoved the other one in just above him. Using the two daggers in tandem, he climbed.

The further he climbed, the tougher it became, as the pain in his side came back with a vengeance. Every second filled him with agonizing pain, to the point that his left hand slipped and completely lost its grip.

There he was, just hanging by one hand. "Don't look down! Don't look down," he told himself. So he chose to look up, which was equally depressing. He still had another 15 feet to go. He swung his arm back up. "I can do this." When he finally reached the top, he rolled over on to the ledge and just laid there for what felt like an hour.

The entrance to the cave was barely big enough for a man to crawl into. When he crossed the threshold, he felt a cold breeze that made him shiver. As he crawled further into the cave, his clothes became wet and muddy. The water flowing beneath him felt colder than one of Floriana's spells.

Small, dark, green lizards, skittered along the walls of the cave. Fluorescent webs, made by spiders covered the ceiling of the cave. Jayden cringed as a red-eyed tarantula slowly crawled across his hand. He wanted to scream, but fear silenced him. Once the spider had moved on, he breathed a sigh of relief. That was when it dawned on him, that from the outside, the cave appeared very small, but on the inside, it felt like it was a lot bigger. Maybe, there was some enchantment placed on the cave, that was similar to the one placed on his backpack, which allowed it to expand on the interior.

The tunnel became wider and wider, and he was able to stand and walk. He summoned a fireball so that he could see better. After walking for about an hour, he stepped into an open area. The room he was in, was absolutely amazing. In the center of the room, was a large crystal clear lake, and cascading down from above him, was a waterfall that fed into the lake. The room was bathed in a bright yellow light that made him feel calm and relaxed.

As Jayden approached the waterfall, he noticed a dark figure standing on the other side of the lake. The figure threw a black ball of fire which hit Jayden in the chest, knocking him to the ground. His chest burned, and the back of his head hurt from the fall. He glanced up, just as the dark figure jumped through the waterfall. Jayden rolled just in time to dodge a slash from his attacker's sword. Jayden got up and drew his dagger and his metal chain. His body still ached badly, and his chest was still burning. Even though he could stand, Jayden knew that he was outmatched in this condition. "Who are you?" he asked.

"I am your darkness! I am your hate, and I am here to consume you!" said the dark figure, with a raspy sounding voice.

"What does that even mean?" Jayden asked as he stepped back slowly. "That makes no sense. How can you be my darkness? We just met, and I already don't like you."

"Your heart is filled with anger and hate. Vengeance is all that you seek. I am your anger. I am your hate, and now I will consume you." The shadow replied.

His opponent swung his dark sword, and Jayden tried to avoid it but instead received a gash on his forearm. The next slash came at Jayden's head. He ducked just in enough time; then he did a sweep tripping his opponent. Jayden yelled, "FireWhip!" His metal chain became covered in flames, as he slashed at the dark warrior with it. His enemy howled in pain. Jayden jumped on him, wrapped the chain of fire around his knuckles, and proceeded to punch the dark figure until he became limp.

Jayden pressed the dagger toward its throat, and just as he was about to do the deed, his hand trembled from his anger. Then it clicked, this dark figure is me. Jayden shook his head as he got back to his feet.

"I get it now," he said.

Jayden closed his eyes, as memories from his past played over in his mind. Since I was a kid, I've always wrestled with my anger. I've tried to hide it with humor, but it's always been there. Losing my parents made it even worse. Now that I've killed people with my rage, my anger has come full circle.

In some sense, I didn't think it was there. Maybe all MikaEL wanted me to do, was to simply acknowledge that it was there. Jayden dropped the dagger and the chain, "I may not be perfect, but I refuse to let my darkness consume me. Instead, I will use my darkness for good. I will use my rage and my anger in a constructive way. I will use my imperfections, to make this world better."

Jayden stood up and walked towards the waterfall. Without warning, his body stiffened, and he found it hard to breathe. The salty taste of blood was on his tongue. He looked down and saw that he had been pierced through the chest by the dark sword. His eyes rolled back, and he fell into the lake. The dark warrior stood there laughing as Jayden sank.

Chapter 15

Loyalty and Honor

One of the benefits of being a General in the Army is that you become aware of national secrets. General Floriana was traveling through an ancient tunnel that most people did not know existed. She picked this specific tunnel because of its age. Many of the other escape routes were newer and thus, very well guarded.

This particular tunnel was built so that if the capital of Eden was invaded, the royal family could escape the city from within the palace. The tunnel itself, extended from the Eastern Marine base to the Royal Palace and ended at the Freezing Mountains.

The tunnel was pitch black; the only light she could see was from the glow of her sword. Floriana shivered as she walked through the damp tunnel. Jayden would find this hilarious, she thought. A frost magic user getting cold would have made him roll on the floor laughing.

The smell of mold was thick in the air. Brown colored water dripped from the ceiling and landed in her hair and on her clothes. Gross, she thought. I'm going to have to wash my hair for weeks to get rid of that sewer smell.

She didn't like that the escape tunnel was eerily quiet. Her gentle breathing and the sound of sewer rats scurrying about were the loudest noises she could hear. She tried to walk as quietly as possible, which was quite difficult at times because her footsteps echoing as she walked. Personally, Floriana enjoyed sneaking around. When she was recruited at an early age, she was responsible for recon and clandestine missions.

She still couldn't shake the feeling, that coming here was a mistake. Floriana wondered if she might be walking into a trap.

"Who's there?" Yelled a gruff sounding voice from the other end of the tunnel.

For a second, Floriana thought her mind was playing tricks on her. Then she heard the voice again. Usually, they didn't have any guards patrolling down here. She flicked the light off on her sword and ducked down into a tunnel on her left. She felt around for the wall and rested up against it.

The guard yelled again, "Who's down there? This is a restricted area. If I find you, I will arrest you."

His footsteps echoed, as he passed by her. Without hesitation, Floriana rushed him and put him in a sleeper hold, until he was out cold. She took his uniform and hid her hair under his hat. Floriana took his flashlight and continued on her journey through the tunnel.

General Floriana made a quick right turn down a hall and noticed that the color of the walls began to change from a bright white. I must be getting close, she thought. Using the flashlight, she shined it along the walls. The light landed on a hatch. Hopefully, this is the right one.

With all her might, she tried twisting it open, but it refused to budge. Floriana pulled and pulled, still nothing. She took a closer look at the hatch and noticed that it's base was sealed with cement. She pointed her sword at the hatch and said, "Absolute Zero."

The hatch quickly began to freeze into a block of ice. Floriana almost passed out from the amount of energy it took. Man, that thing was cemented on their tight. Hopefully, it worked, or this is really going to hurt. She crossed her fingers and kicked the hatch as hard as she could, and it shattered into thousands of pieces.

"Now that's more like it," she said feeling pleased with herself.

Floriana crawled onto the other side of the hatch and found a dark, colored ladder. According to her research, this ladder should lead her into the Royal Palace's wine cellar. Floriana grabbed on to one of the rungs and began her climb.

The ascent to the top was physically and mentally draining. It seemed like the ladder went on forever. Her muscles were aching when she finally made it to the top. Floriana opened the latch and found herself climbing out of an old wine barrel. The barrel had a wooden frame, and to the untrained eye, it was just a normal wine barrel. She had to admire the genius of having an escape route that involved climbing into a wine barrel.

She glanced around the room and smiled because there were barrels and bottles of wine in every direction. Maybe if I take one sip, they won't notice. She shook her head, "Come on Floriana, get focused." But it is so tempting, she thought.

General Floriana tried to remember what she read about the wine cellar. There was a rumor she had heard that there was a secret staircase that led directly to the Royal Office. She rummaged around the cellar looking for the staircase, while sampling a glass of white wine.

Floriana stopped when she heard the sound of voices coming from the other side of the room. She placed her glass down and slowly crept closer to the voices. They sounded like King Aelius and Sergeant Jason. Why wasn't Jason at the Army Base, she wondered. Floriana inched as close as she could, but she still couldn't make out what they were saying. How could she get closer without them seeing her?

A light bulb clicked on in her head as a brilliant idea crossed her mind. Grimacing at the thought, she snapped her fingers. Her body started to shift and change. Her muscles and bones contracted. Everything felt like it was being pushed together. She felt her body contracting. As she got smaller, antennae grew out of her head. After a minute of excruciating pain from transforming, she had turned herself into a cockroach. Scurrying across the floor, she hid under a wine barrel that was sitting directly behind King Aelius.

"It has come to my attention that your counterparts have yet to find *The Key*, and they have failed to get the Dion boy to help in the search for it. Is that true?" The King asked.

Jason smiled finding the King's frustration amusing, "It is as you say."

"Wasn't it you that said all those years ago, that the boy would guide us to *The Key*?"

Bowing, Jason replied, "That is correct, my Lord, and I stand by my previous statement. Jayden will find *The Key* with or without our coercion. He's too much like his father, to let a powerful item like that slip into our hands. His desire for vengeance will guide him to it. We must be patient my King."

Pacing back and forth, Aelius grew more agitated, "we don't have all the time in the world Jason. The Aggeloi military is getting stronger by the day. The Elders and their descendants have situated themselves in key positions in both our government and the Aggeloi. Did you know that the Aggeloi are interested in some of our raw materials? Our military is not a big enough deterrent to keep them at bay. We need power and we need it now." Drawing his cutlass, he pointed it at Jason, "Do not think for one second that your life is precious or of any value to me. I can strike you down here and now. Give me a reason not to. I placed my trust in you. Don't tell me that it's become misplaced."

Jason stepped forward until he could feel the tip of the King's blade against his chest. "My Lord, I am but a humble servant in your army. If you wish to strike me down, I will let you, for you are my King. If you choose to let me live and extend your grace upon your servant, I will be forever grateful. I will not rest until *The Key* and the chest it opens, are in your possession."

Taking a moment to think, Aelius replied, "Tell me, where you think *The Key* is now. If your answer is sufficient, I will spare your life for now." He pressed his sword a little harder against Jason's chest.

"My Lord, our investigation has led us to believe that *The Key* has been hidden somewhere on the Southern Continent Terra and is in possession of some associate of "The Witnesses." I have dispatched twenty members of the Daimonia to search for it."

Withdrawing his sword, Aelius seemed to achieve a level of calmness. He grinned mischievously, "so, would you find it prudent for me to have the boys from Eiréné taken out of the equation? Also, may I presume that the Terran government are unaware that *The Key* sits right under their noses?"

"Yes, you are correct in your presumption," Jason replied. "I also agree that the boys may know too much, and that could be a problem. The sooner they are dealt with, the better."

"Lucky for us, I have something planned. The Water Temple that they are staying at will be turned into rubble very soon."

The smile on Jason's face, changed to one of concern, "Wait, why are you going to destroy the temple? That course of action may end up being worse than allowing Eiréné to be destroyed."

"Jason, you are a wise soldier, but your understanding of how to run a country is comical. The elves and humans that live in the temple have been trying to undermine this government for quite some time. Some Elders live among them that have been trying to gather intel on our operations. They want to overthrow the monarchy and Parliament. We can't allow this to happen. Now I must head up to my office to do some paperwork. I need you to inform Commander Drake that he has permission to attack when ready. No survivors this time. Word cannot get out about this!"

Jason watched the King head up the stairs. You old fool, he thought. Do you honestly think your men stand a chance against the Warriors at the Water Temple? While they don't compare to the might of the Daimonia, your men will fail, and I cannot wait for the world to see it.

***

Scurrying to the farthest corner of the room, Floriana transformed back into her normal self. Her heart was beating so hard, it felt like it was going to leap out of her chest. The conversation she just heard, was a lot to process. How could the King do this to his own people? Why did I even bother coming here? I should have known they were this corrupt. Have I been carrying out the orders of a tyrant this whole time? Does that make me even worse than them? What should I do now?

The great General Floriana sat in a corner sulking. He's going to attack the temple. My friends are going to die and here I am hiding in this wine cellar. What kind of General am I?

Her problem wasn't simply with the King, but something much deeper. She was like many gifted youths recruited into Eden's youth program at thirteen. When the opportunity came to serve her country, she leaped at the chance. She became the youngest General in the history of Eden. Sitting there in the wine cellar made her start to regret receiving all of those accolades. Have I fought for nothing? Did the soldiers I've gone into battle with die for no reason? If our leader is corrupt, then what am I? How can he risk the lives of soldiers for a battle that has nothing to do with protecting this country?

She stood up. I can't sit here feeling sorry for myself. I signed up to defend this country, and that's what I'm going to do.

150

Floriana reached into her pocket and pulled out the coin that Raiden gave her. She said Raiden's name, flipped the coin and gave a message informing him about the King's plans, and that she would meet up with them to head to the Southern Continent.

Floriana wanted to get more intel on the King's plan, so she made her way to the Royal Office.

She found the set of stairs which led to the Kings quarters. The old steps creaked as she climbed them. Floriana pushed open a door and stepped into a hall. She was greeted by red carpet made of velvet, along with paintings of the former Monarchs. Floriana continued down the hall until she reached the Royal Office.

Her stomach felt queasy, and her mind was going a mile a minute. The last time she felt this nervous was during her first day of boot camp. What would the King say, when he saw her. Everything in her body told her she shouldn't do what she was planning to do. Her hands trembled as she touched the golden door handle. Taking a deep breath, she entered the room.

The King was dressed in a light green robe. He stood by the window gazing out into the garden. In his hand, he held a clear glass filled with red wine. When he turned back around, he had a surprised look on his face when he saw Florianaa sitting at his desk. ShaKing off his look of shock, he smiled like a politician and said, "my Lady, I wasn't expecting any company. Please forgive me for being less than professional at this hour."

"My Lord, please forgive me for the intrusion. I should have announced myself," she replied.

Swirling his drink, he took a sip and eyed her suspiciously. "Well, what brings you here on this day? I was under the impression that you were as the saying goes, "on the run."

"My King, I am here to seek your forgiveness. I am willing to give up my rank and to start at the bottom again. The only reason I ran off is because I thought that Jason was holding those boys illegally. I feared that we were in the wrong and I did not want the name of this country, and it's military besmirched."

"General Florianaa, I would love to reinstate you. The risk you took to come here is admirable. That tells me that you are dedicated to this country and its welfare. It is that spirit in you, which led me to recommend you to become a General."

She sat up straight, "But will you reinstate me?"

Finishing his drink, he placed it on the desk. "My dear, I will ask the military council to reinstate you under one condition. You tell me everything about the boys you traveled with and what they are trying to do. If your loyalties are with us, that shouldn't be too difficult to do."

She stood up and said, "They are just two simple boys from a small town in the northwest. Both of them are guided by some sense of vengeance. That's pretty much all I know."

"Is that really all you've learned from them? My lady, please forgive my distrust, but I believe you aren't telling me all that you know."

"My Lord, if I knew more, I would surely tell you."

Scratching his chin, he paced back and forth. Stopping by a rack of swords by his desk, he pulled out a cutlass. "General Florianaa, I will be honest. I have been withholding information from you. I allowed Eiréné to be attacked by a group called the Daimonia. They were to retrieve an object from one of the residents. This object would allow me to protect this country from those that want it destroyed. And now, the boys you helped escape are trying to keep me from acquiring it. I want you to travel with them until they find it, and then I want you to kill them."

Slowly, she got out of her chair and placed her hand on her sword. "My Lord, I understand your desire to protect this country. As a General, I am fully aware of the threat other countries pose to our security." Drawing her sword, she looked him dead in the eye.

"But you made a big mistake in allowing Eiréné destroyed. Because of your desire, countless lives have been lost. My uncle died protecting those boys. I don't know what this key that you are wanting is for, or how it can help this country, but its power has already corrupted you. I am a soldier for the people of Eden; I will defend them against all that threaten peace. And you, My Lord, have become that threat!" With lightning quick speed, the King kicked his desk at Florianaa and jumped on top of it, slashing at her.

The King moved faster than she was expecting. His swipes were just as powerful as they were quick. Aelius was able to parry and attack, with minimal effort. Within just a few seconds of combat, Florianaa had already sustained slashes and cuts across several parts of her body. This fight can't keep going like this, she told herself. I have to find his weakness.

Floriana slashed downward with her sword. He blocked it, then spun the blades around until she was disarmed and her sword skidded to the other side of the room. Floriana did a few backflips to put distance between the King and herself. She looked nervously back at the King, and the door, she was wondering when the guards would come rushing in.

Spinning his sword, he said smugly, "I guess the rumors are true, you have started to rely more on your magical abilities instead of your swordsmanship. It's a shame, really. You were trained by some of the best." LooKing at the door, he smiled, "Don't you worry about us being interrupted. This room is soundproof; no one will hear you scream for mercy." He laughed cruelly as he rushed at her and slashed at her neck.

DucKing under his weapon, she stabbed him in the stomach with her knife, then tripped him onto the ground. She threw her knife into his chest, then rolled to grab her sword. Once it was in her hand, she shouted, "Avalanche!" The room instantly became covered in a thick pile of ice and snow. Snapping her fingers, she transformed into a snow fox, and dove into the pile of snow, and ran for the Wine Cellar to escape. Her only thought as she ran was I hope I can make it back to the temple in time.

153

Crawling out of the snow, the King pulled the knife out of his chest. That was fun, he thought. He blew on the snow, and it disappeared. Heading to his desk, he picked up the phone and dialed a number. "Floriana has become a problem. I need you to solve it. When, you ask? Sooner rather than later." Hanging up, he sat back down in his chair and took a sip of his wine. This will make a great story to tell the press tomorrow. A General of the Army betrays her country and tries to assassinate the King.

Chapter 16

Port of Alexandria

Opening his eyes, he saw a bright, blinding light. Am I dead? Man, Sarah is going to be so mad at me if I am.

He blinked his eyes a few times, and his vision became clearer. Jayden looked around and he found himself standing in a lake. The water felt warm as it brushed up against him gently. His body was wet, but his clothes remained dry. Jayden felt stronger and lighter like a weight lifted off of his shoulders.

Jayden glanced around the cave and he wondered where the shadow figure had gone. Was it all in my head? Maybe I am starting to go crazy. Then he touched his chest, and it felt a little tender. His chest was the only slight pain he had. Did confronting my darkness heal me?

Jayden jumped out of the pool, and he noticed that his shoulders were a little broader. His muscles were bigger, and he was a few inches taller. He felt stronger and bolder, like the sins of the past, have been washed by this mystical water.

There was a big smile on his face as he exited the cave. He stared out into the distance, and the memories of his journey up the mountain came back to him. He ascended the mountain filled with fear and anger. Now he was joyful and ready to conquer the world. He grinned and took a few steps back, then he leaped across the chasm, racing down the mountain.

Raiden approached MikaEL, who was standing by the temple steps. Tony and Sarah followed after him. Raiden had received a message from Floriana, which said the Water Temple would soon be attacked by members of the military.

Shaking his hand, Raiden said, "My Brother, our scouts have spotted soldiers in different parts of the forest. They have set up mortars and micro-artillery cannons."

MikaEL paced back and forth, "Are you nervous Raiden?"

Grinning, he replied, "of course not! It was only a matter of time before the army was at our doorstep. I have ordered our scouting team to kidnap an officer once the fighting starts. So we can have evidence to present to the world, that the King of Eden is a power hungry monster."

"Is GabriEL among the scouts"? MikaEL asked.

"Yes, he was of the opinion that he would dispatch more enemies down there than you will from up here with your arrows and magic."

Sarah interrupted them, "Isn't Jayden up in the mountains? What if he runs into the army soldiers?"

MikaEL looked down at her, "Concerned, are we? Have you no confidence in his abilities?"

Sarah gave the tall elf a death stare for his comments. Before she could tell this elf where to shove it, she heard footsteps coming from the stairs below. Walking up to them was Jayden spinning a revolver in his hand and munching on a piece of jerky with the other. She ran and tackled him to the ground, sending him back down the stairs. Laughing, he said, "missed me much?"

Sarah punched him, "I will not admit to such a thing." She looked him over for a second and realized that there was something different about him. "Did you get taller?" she asked.

"Yes, I did."

"How?"

"Heck if I know, I must have found the fountain of youth or something."

MikaEL approached Jayden, grabbed his hands and examined them, "Your hands and your spirit, have been made clean. Jayden, your sin wasn't simply what you did. It's the dark thoughts that you kept inside, which you hid from others and yourself. You have come to peace with the darkness within. But believe me when I say, that you were able to overcome the evil in your heart, but that doesn't mean that it is gone forever. Now, do you still have that dagger I gave you?"

Nodding, Jayden handed it to him. MikaEL touched the tip of the blade, and it began to glow. "The struggles you overcame, have unlocked the magic of this dagger. You may have noticed that you could move quicker than before, but now you will be able to move even swifter. The magic you use to increase your speed and agility will now be even more effective. Jayden, you must be diligent with such power. The previous owner of this dagger was careless. I would urge you to use better judgment. If you decide to give this dagger to someone you care for. You will become even more blessed. Now keep this in mind Jayden. You may have to kill again. Do so only as a last resort. It takes great wisdom to know when that is."

"Hey, Jade where did you get that pistol?" Tony asked.

Spinning it with his finger, Jayden replied, "I almost forgot about it. Well on my way down from the mountain, I ran into some soldiers from the Eden army. They tried to arrest me, emphasis on the word "tried." I ended up getting a new pistol and some jerky out of it. I was planning on giving it to you, the gun, not the jerky".

157

Tony took the gun and mumbled that he would have liked the jerky too.

"So what's going on? Why is the army here?" Jayden asked. Before Raiden could respond, two artillery shells slammed into the temple. Jayden completely lost his balance and fell down the stairs again.

Standing back up, he looked to see where the shells had hit. The damage caused to the temple was minimal, but the idea of shells being fired at them made him feel uneasy.

Raiden spoke, "You three need to get to the basement level of the temple. Sarah, show them how to get to it. The basement will take you to a tunnel that leads underneath the river. It will take you directly to Port Alexandria. Find a boat there and head to the Southern Continent. Sarah, tell Floriana to meet you there. Jayden, don't forget to grab your bag from your room. The road ahead will be dangerous."

Another volley of shells slammed against the temple. The sound was deafening, and the ground beneath their feet shook, from the force of the blast. Tony stood still as Jayden and Sarah started to run to the temple.

"Tony! Go with them!" Raiden yelled.

"No, I'm staying with you."

"Tony, you need to go. They will need you."

"You promised me that you wouldn't leave me; I'm not going to leave you either."

Sarah pulled on his shirt, "Tony, let's go." He pushed her off. "Jayden, make him leave with us."

Jayden approached Tony, "Not a day goes by that I don't regret having to leave my dad. Stay with yours, and we will meet up when we can." Jayden grabbed Sarah by the wrist and ran towards the temple, as bricks fell overhead. "Well son, are you just going to stand there or will you fight? I'd hate to see that all of your training has been wasted." Raiden said while notching two arrows and sending them skyward.

Tony grinned, "I hope you can keep up old man." Spinning his broadsword, he yelled, "Hailstorm!" Dark clouds began to form in the sky, spreading across the forest. Rain and hail the size of baseballs fell from the sky, pelting the advancing soldiers.

***

Climbing down a steel ladder, Jayden and Sarah arrived in the sewers. Rats scurried across their path, and water flowed down the center of the sewer between the two walkways. The smell of the sewer was about as enjoyable as a nosebleed. Together they moved as quickly as they could, to escape the deafening sound of exploding shells.

His brow was drenched with sweat, from hours of running. Feeling exhausted, they took a break and reclined against a cement wall. Jayden noticed that Sarah kept flipping a coin, and whispering into it, over and over again. "Where did you get that coin? Can I flip it next?"

She looked at him with fire in her eyes, "How can you sit there with a smile on your face? While your best friend is out there fighting for his life. Why didn't you make him go with us? What will you do if Tony ends up dying?"

Smiling, Jayden leaned back, "Tony won't die, he and his dad will be able to help fend off the Army. Of that, I am confident."

She punched him in the rib, "How can you be so smug and confident? Don't you see this is exactly what happened to us as kids? The Water Temple will end up just like our homes, forgotten and burned to the ground. Don't you even care? What really happened to you on that mountain? The old you wouldn't have left Tony's side."

Sitting up, Jayden replied, "I left a part of me on that mountain. To some degree, I have come to peace with what happened all those years ago. I understand the darkness within me a little better now. Since I have done that, I now see a greater hope in the world. I do not doubt in my mind that Tony and the Water Temple will survive. It is this hope that will keep me going."

She rested her head, on his shoulder and said, "I'm sorry I yelled at you. I'm just really worried about Tony and the others. I hope they can make it through this. By the way, something just occurred to me. If we find this key, what should we do with it?"

Jayden thought about it for a moment and replied, "I think we need to destroy it. We cannot let the power that can be gained from *The Key* come into the world. Any other option would be catastrophic. On another note, Raiden wanted us to get a hold of Floriana. How are we supposed to do that?"

Flipping her coin, she whispered words into it, and it began to glow. "This coin allows us to keep in contact with people that have a coin like this one. Raiden gave Floriana one before she left, and he gave me this one. She told us about the attack, and we were able to prepare for it."

Jayden squeezed Sarah, and said, "Well, that was so kind of her to do. Maybe her leaving us to see the King, wasn't such a bad idea. Anyway, we gotta keep going. The smell of this sewer is driving me nuts."

They dusted themselves off and continued their trek through the tunnel. The sewers beneath the temple extended a lot further then he was expecting. Jayden looked at his watch and was surprised to see that it had taken them half of the day to reach the end of the tunnel.

Climbing out of the tunnel, they were greeted by the afternoon sun. Jayden could see that the river continued for a few more miles and fed out into the ocean. They found themselves in the middle of an oasis. The beautiful oasis was populated by various palm and fruit trees. A small crystal clear pond was sitting to their right. They took a drink of water and started to collect some of the fruit. Jayden took a bite of a blue apple; it tasted like a combination of a green apple and a blueberry. Next, he discovered the oddest looking oranges in a nearby fruit tree. They were shaped like a starfish and were red on the inside, like a grapefruit. As he put them in his bag, he noticed something odd about an oak tree off in the distance. A person was laying down under it.

Jayden approached the tree cautiously. The individual on the ground looked like he had been roughed up pretty bad. The man's long black hair was a mess. He had a cut on his cheek, and his black robes were torn. Laying by his side, was a halberd with a golden ax head. The pole it was connected to was split down the middle. In his hand, he held a knife that was crusted in blood.

Jayden had a feeling that he had seen this man before. He got closer and spotted a tattoo that was peeking out from a tear in his sleeve. The tattoo looked like a demon called a Succubus, which he had seen in a scary movie. Then he remembered what Ms. Tonya had told him; members of the Daimonia would typically have the tattoo of a demon on their arm.

Sarah sat down next to Jayden and whispered, "he's one of them."

Just as the words left her mouth, the man thrust with his knife. Jayden caught him by the wrist just in time. The man looked wild, as he glanced nervously at the both of them.

Jayden said calmly, "hey, we aren't here to harm you. You can put your knife back down."

Slowly, the man placed his knife back on the ground. He stared at the both of them and smirked. "Who would have guessed that out of all of the people in the world. I would run into you two?" He chuckled to himself.

Jayden and Sarah felt confused, "You know us?"

The man nodded, "Jayden, it's me, Cain."

Jayden took a second glance at the scruff on the man's face and his long black hair. Grinning, he wrapped his arms around Cain's neck in an embrace.

Sarah hesitated, "Why are you here Cain? What happened to you?"

"Well, it's nice to see you too, Sarah. The both of you have grown a lot since I last saw you two. It's nice to see the two of you finally got together."

Jayden fumbled with his hands uncomfortably and avoided eye contact with either of them, while Sarah blushed for a quick second before gaining her composure. "Sorry to disappoint you, Cain, but we are not together. You still failed to answer my question."

Resting against the tree, Cain sighed, "I guess it wouldn't hurt to tell the truth. Over the last couple of years, I have been a gun for hire. Most recently, I started working for a merchant company helping to protect their trucks as they traveled from Port Alexandria to other towns and cities. Earlier today, our convoy of trucks was attacked by a motorcycle group called the Desert Rats."

Jayden and Sarah both glanced at each other and grinned at the name.

"Have you heard of them?" Cain asked.

"Yep, we have run into them a couple of times. They tried to rob us, emphasis on tried." Jayden replied.

"Well, that would explain why they were so aggressive. They started firing at us before we could find out what they wanted. They swarmed us as if their lives depended on it. There were forty of them. I barely made it out. I ran to this oasis to rest and recover."

Sarah sat back stared at Cain. There was still something suspicious about him. She remembered seeing him the day that

Eiréné was destroyed. Looking back on it now, it seemed to be too coincidental that he was there that day. Examining him further, she looked at his tattoo again, and then it all made sense to her. "You are one of them. One of those Daimonia guys. You were there the day Eiréné was destroyed." Pulling out one of her machine pistols, she put it to his head. "Tell me why I shouldn't kill you right now! Our families are gone because of you! How could you betray your own people?"

Jayden looked back and forth at the both of them. He just couldn't believe that the man he looked up to as a big brother could be one of them. Maybe he didn't want to believe it.

"It's not true, is it?" Jayden asked, trying to sound hopeful.

Cain took a deep breath, with the look of an intense sorrow on his face. His eyes watered as he spoke, "when I left home at 13, it was because they recruited me. They gave me money, trained me, and made me feel like I was part of a family. It wasn't easy being an adopted child, but they looked after me. I guess that helped me to justify all the things I did. I liked what I did for the most part until the day I was ordered to go to Eiréné, to talk to Dion about this object called *The Key*. A battalion from the Daimonia, came along with me, to make sure I made it there safely." Tears poured down his cheek as he continued his story, "I had no idea that they were going to destroy the town and kill all those people. I hung back during it because I couldn't stand it. I just waited until it was all over like a coward. After that night, I've never been the same. My work for the group became sloppy, and they put me on probation. I've been a gun for hire ever since." Turning to Jayden, he added, "not a day goes by that I don't regret my part in the whole ordeal. Sarah if you pulled that trigger, you would be giving me what I deserve. Just do it! Pull it now!"

Jayden grabbed Cain by the wrist and lifted him to his feet. "You made a mistake that will probably haunt you for the rest of your life. The best way to make peace with the past is to create a positive change in the present. Join us on our journey to find *The Key* and destroy it."

Feeling completely unsure of himself, Cain responded, "I will go with you if it's okay with her too."

Sarah shrugged, "I don't care either way. We were on our way to Port Alexandria. You can take the lead."

Cain grabbed his knife and led them south toward the Port of Alexandria. Sarah pulled Jayden aside and asked quietly, "How can you trust him?"

"I can't trust him. I'm just trying to give him a second chance," he replied.

The Port of Alexandria was one of the most enchanting places, Jayden had ever seen. Large wooden ships, with white sails, traveled upon the waters, with a spirit of grace. Cruise ships and military vessels sailed back and forth in the harbor. The roads were paved with cream-colored bricks. Horse-drawn carriages and cars drove by as they walked around the city. Many of the houses were designed like haciendas, with beautiful white walls, and red shingle roofs.

The smell of salt from the ocean hung in the air, and a cool breeze greeted them as they entered a cafe. Sarah stood by the bar, and Jayden noticed that she was speaking to a girl with beautiful blonde hair. The girl looked really pretty. He wondered if Sarah would be mad if he hit on her new friend.

Jayden turned to Cain and said, "Do you know who Sarah is talking to?"

"I have no idea," Cain replied, as he and Jayden found a booth to sit in. Jayden ordered a green tea, and Cain asked for a coffee.

Sarah slid into the booth sitting across from them. "Hey, who was that chick you were talking to?" Jayden asked.

Sarah smiled feeling amused at the question, "Why the curiosity?"

"I wasn't curious; I was just wondering who she was."

Raising an eyebrow, she said, "Do you want to talk to her?"

"May I?"

Sarah grinned, "I'm not your mother. Who am I to keep you from speaking to another girl?"

Jayden was up before Sarah had even finished speaking. He walked boldly up to the pretty blonde at the bar. She was wearing a white T-shirt and black jeans. "Excuse me. I saw you talking to my friend over there. I thought I'd come over and introduce myself. My friends call me Jade. I'm a Scorpio, and you look like my next girlfriend. Also, I'm a whizz at cheesy pickup lines."

The beautiful blonde turned in her barstool, "Really? That was your line? Jayden, you had your shot." Patting him on the head, she walked over and sat next to Sarah and sparked up a conversation.

Jayden looked at her bewildered, how did she know my name? And how did that pick-up line not work? I thought it was golden. He sat back down in the booth, looked across the table, and realized that the beautiful blonde looked very familiar.

"You still don't recognize me?" she said, feeling slightly disappointed.

Sarah elbowed her, "told you he wouldn't recognize you with that blonde hair. I believe the bet was that you owed me five gold coins if he didn't recognize you."

Suddenly, Jayden realized who it was. "Floriana? I knew it was you; I was just pretending I didn't."

She looked away from him, "You are shunned for not recognizing me. The only thing I changed was my hair color."

Cain chimed in, "So, Jayden, what was the pickup line you used on her? Rumor has it no woman could resist it, I mean, fall for it."

"I would restate it, but I'd hate for these two lovely ladies to fall for it again." The girls rolled their eyes at his comment. "On another note, why did you dye your hair?" he asked.

"Are you saying it looks bad?" Floriana exclaimed.

"Oh, of course not!"

"So, you know how I went to Central City, to talk to the King right? Well, things got out of control pretty quickly, and we ended up in a fight. So, now I am wanted, for an attempted assassination of the King. That is the reason I decided to dye my hair. By the way, why did you guys decide to go to Terra?"

"We are going there to look for a group of witches known as the Southern Convent in the Chaldean Swamp. Raiden believes that will give us a clue to help us find *The Key*," Sarah replied. Turning to look at Cain, she asked, "You were in the Daimonia; you must have some idea of what *The Key* actually does."

Cain took a sip of his coffee, "I am not too overly thrilled about having to deal with witches, but I can tell you what *The Key* does. It opens up a treasure chest that has a map in it. This map will lead you to an underground cave, where there is a war machine that The Elders left behind after the Great War. The war machine and the other weapons in that cave could change the world overnight. Now, that is what I was told by our commander. Personally, I think that *The Key* opens a lot more than just a simple treasure chest. They are spending too much money just so they can get some war machine. They have plenty of weapons already. I think they are after something bigger than that."

"I can see why the Daimonia and the King, would want an object like that. Likewise, the Eden military already has plenty of warships. If the King is willing to risk his crown over this, *The Key* must give someone access to unimaginable power. Plus, we are at a disadvantage, because we don't know their end game. We need to be watching our backs as we travel. The Daimonia and the King will strike us down if we get in their way. So, sleep with one eye open tonight." Floriana said as she downed the last drops of her coffee.

They left the café, in complete silence. The journey ahead seemed even more dangerous than it already was. Jayden crawled into his bed, and he knew he wouldn't be able to sleep well tonight. Floriana's warning made him paranoid to sleep. He shifted in his bed and tried closing his eyes.

Flashbacks from their travels on the road filled his dreams. Nightmares of his father's death played over again in his mind. The Daimonia frightened him to the core. He knew that he was strong enough to face them now, but they still terrified him. They were a violent, power hungry group, and he didn't know how, or if he could stop them

Sitting up, he glanced over at Cain and was happy to be reunited with him. Part of him, still wondered, if he was making a big mistake, by bringing Cain along. He seemed genuine in his desire to help them, but he had worked for the Daimonia. How much can a guy like that be trusted?

Chapter 17
Sailing the Liberta

The smell of salt water and a cool breeze filled the room. Jayden's bed rocked back and forth gently like he was sleeping on a wave. Sunlight breached through his window, gently coaxing him out of a deep slumber. He opened his eyes and was appalled when he realized that he was now wearing a flowery islander shirt and cargo shorts. On his nightstand, there was even, a pair of red flip flops.

Panic surged throughout his body, and he started looking around. Where am I? More importantly, who got me this ugly T-shirt? Cain stepped into the room, wearing red and white board shorts, a pair of sunglasses, and sandals.

"Morning sweetie," Cain said, in the most demeaning voice possible.

Jayden was instantly annoyed. "It's morning? I usually don't like getting up until noon at the earliest. I do have one awkward question, why am I dressed up as an unattractive tourist? And why is this room rocking back and forth?"

"Oh, we are on a cruise ship called the Liberta, and we are heading to Terra's most northern port."

"Well, that makes sense. I do have one more question. How did I get aboard this cruise ship without knowing it?"

"You sleep like a log. I told the guy at customs you had narcolepsy. For some reason, he believed it."

"Did you buy me this annoying tourist outfit and put it on me in my sleep?"

"Sarah bought it for you. I simply helped to put it on you. She would be upset if you changed out of it."

Jayden felt like a monkey's uncle dressed in his outfit as he left his room. He clutched his pamphlet in his hand and decided to explore the ship. The Liberta was a pristine vessel. According, to the brochure in his hand, the vessel was about 800 feet long from bow to stern. The ship was covered in a pearl white paint, and the wooden deck was dressed in a beautiful cherry oak stain. A six-piece band was playing smooth jazz, on the upper deck. The living quarters were top of the line, and the staff was the most generous people he had ever met.

As he explored the ship, Jayden passed by people from all over the world. He stopped to watch as a drunk elf, and a red pixie argued over a game of poker. He had never seen a pixie before; he thought they only existed in movies. The creature's red hair glistened in the light of the day, and his wings flapped furiously, as he tried to punch the six-foot tall elf in the face. Jayden fell to the floor laughing when the elf kicked the pixie below the belt.

Once the scuffle between the pixie and the elf subsided, he made his way toward the bow of the ship. When he got there, he saw a large telescope, which was connected to the ship's railing. He looked through the lens of the telescope, as he felt the cool spray of the ocean against his skin. Jayden was entranced by the large dolphins leaping out of the water, as a flock of Clouded Sea Dragons, dove into the sea to retrieve their meal.

He took a deep breath of the cool ocean air which made him feel completely at ease. The fears he had deep inside were now as far away from his mind as it could be. Maybe they could stay on this ship, and sail the world forever, he thought.

Suddenly, his vision went black, as hands covered his eyes.

"Guess who?" said a woman with a pretty voice.

"Hmmm, your hands are slightly warm, and your perfume is pleasant and not quite overpowering. You must be either Floriana or that pretty blonde I saw walking by."

Jayden felt a sharp and intense pain in his ribs, as he received a series of punches from the beautiful woman with the dark hair standing behind him. "I knew it was you, Sarah. I was just making a joke."

She laughed with the least amount of enthusiasm possible. "I'm sure you were. What are you doing out here?"

"I'm just enjoying the view. I was planning on climbing on to the railing while swinging my arms out wide and yelling something stupid. But I figured it had been done before."

Nodding in agreement, she asked, "How would you like to go hang out at the pool?"

"I'll think about it. Do you think there will pretty girls and a diving board there?"

She grinned and grabbed him by the hand, "There is only one way to find out. Let's go!"

Jayden was having a blast getting to run with Sarah, from one end of the ship to the other. Sarah was a much faster runner then he had expected; he almost had to use a speed magic spell to keep up with her.

Sarah dodged tourists with ease, as they sprinted through the ship. Jayden was at full gallop when Sarah stopped without warning on the quarterdeck. Unfortunately, Jayden was not prepared for this change in tempo and accidentally ran into the ship's captain.

Jayden picked the man up and said, "So sorry about that." The captain walked away without even saying a word. Jayden tapped Sarah on the shoulder and said, "Hey, crazy lady. Can you turn on your brake lights, the next time you decide to stop randomly?"

"I will ignore that rude comment. I have a question. Did your Masters teach you how to climb at the Dragon Monastery?"

Jayden nodded yes.

"Do you think you could carry me on your back and climb up three levels of this boat to where the pool is?" She asked ever so sweetly.

Jayden looked at her and then upwards and grimaced. "You do know that this ship has an elevator and stairs we could take instead. Right?"

She put a big smile on her face, "Are you saying you couldn't carry me up the side of the ship? I bet you Cain could. Maybe I should ask him instead."

"Well played," Jayden replied. "Sarah, so that you know, I could climb two mountains with you on my back. Now hop on. If you fall off, it's not my fault."

Without hesitation, she jumped on his back, "Well let's go Mr. Strongman. What's taking you so long?"

Bending his knees, he jumped up to the next level. Jayden used the windowsills as footholds to climb up the side of the ship. He was motivated to show Sarah how much stronger he had become. Sarah's peach scented perfume was radiant. He wanted to impress her. Maybe it was stupid of him to try, but Sarah was a once in a lifetime kind of girl.

Once they made it to the pool, Sarah jumped off his back. "You should check out the diving board." She said.

Jayden grinned, as he approached the ladder for the high dive. He cracked his knuckles. I'm going to show these weird tourists how it's done. He grabbed a rung and climbed 45 feet to reach the diving board. Jayden waved to the crowd. Then he took a deep breath and did a triple backflip into the pool, which was followed by a roar of applause from the crowd.

Feeling a little more confident, he decided he was going to try a double front flip. He started to bounce on the diving board to get some air. Then he jumped and completed the two front flips and landed in a belly flop.

He smacked against the water so hard it knocked both the air and pride out of him. How embarrassing, he thought. He tried to hide his face, as people around the pool, pointed and laughed at him.

Trying to divert the unwanted attention from Jayden, Cain climbed up on to the high dive, which seemed to get everyone's attention. He stood on the diving board with his well-defined six-pack, while the rest of his body looked like he started weightlifting when he was a four year old.

Jayden couldn't understand why the girls, and some of the married women, found his friend so interesting. If Cain hadn't already stolen enough attention from Jayden by simply taking his shirt off, he raised the stakes with his breathtaking dive. Jumping off the high dive, Cain did two barrel rolls in the air, then landed on the lower diving board, jumped from it, and did a backflip into the pool. This feat of pure skill was met by a round of applause and a standing ovation by all sitting around the pool.

He got out of the pool and felt like a complete loser, as he watched both of the girls chatting up Cain. Even Sarah, who had previously treated him with indifference, suddenly found him, "Oh so interesting." For a moment, Jayden started walking towards them, then decided he wasn't going to sit with them. He found a green lounge chair, which was all by itself. He plopped down into it and sulked. I thought Sarah wanted to spend some time with me.

How can I compete with Cain? Leaning back, he shut his eyes and fell right to sleep.

***

Cain and the girls finished swimming and made their way to a smoothie station near the stern of the ship. The "Smoothie Hut" was covered by a canopy, and the floor was made of green AstroTurf. For seating, there were couches and lounge chairs.

The smoothies they made were unique because they were poured into a pineapple that had been cut in half and hollowed out. Sarah grabbed a strawberry and banana smoothie and sat down on one of the grey couches. Floriana joined her while Cain was still in line trying to get a drink.

"So, what do you think of him?" Sarah asked.

"In some ways, he seems like an older brother version of Jayden. At the same time, he has this quiet intensity about him. You must have known him from Eiréné. Tell me a little about him." Floriana replied.

"Well, I was pretty young when he was living in Eiréné. He was the big kid that all the boys looked up to."

"That trick he did at the pool was impressive. Almost as impressive as Jayden's belly flop."

Both of them fell into a fit of laughter. "What's so funny?" Cain asked.

"Oh nothing," they said in unison.

He sat in between them, "Did you two see where Jayden went?"

They both shrugged. Sarah grabbed him by the arm, "Hey, so are you as good at dancing as you are flipping off diving boards?"

"Unfortunately, I am. My foster parents made me take dance classes when I was younger. If you tell Jayden that I will push you two overboard." he said, with a tone of voice that sounded like he meant it. "Why did you ask?"

Floriana turned towards him, "Well, while we were in line. We overheard a conversation that there will be a pig roast and candlelight dance tonight around 8. It will be on the promenade deck. We thought it might be fun to go."

"I guess I could go with you two."

Sarah smiled and said, "If you see Jade, tell him to put on a tie. It will look nice with his flowery shirt I got him."

The promenade deck of the Liberta was on the fourth floor of the ship near the stern. The dance floor extended from the ballroom to the promenade deck. Ivory stairs connected the ballroom to the promenade deck. A white canopy covered the promenade deck; yellow and white lights hung from the canopy. Three tables were covered with a silk tablecloth, and on top of each were roasted pigs.

The jazz band was performing in the center of the ballroom, and they changed up their sound to play beautiful classical music. The music reverberated throughout the ballroom and on to the promenade deck. The sweet melodies and harmonies were entrancing.

Cain was waiting for the girls in the ballroom. He was wearing a dark blue suit, with a gold watch. Sarah came down the stairs, wearing a beautiful white dress, with a diamond necklace. Her dark hair was perfectly curled. He bowed respectfully, kissed her hand, and said, "Ciao Bella."

Half blushing, half smiling, she replied, "That was sweet. I have no idea what it means. I thought you were going to meet us on the promenade deck."

"Oh well, I can head up there with you."

As they walked, Sarah asked him, "Have you seen Jade yet?" He shook his head no. Sarah felt a little disappointed and slightly worried. She thought that Jayden would have loved a chance to dance with her. Maybe he was just running late and is still getting ready.

Cain led her out onto the promenade deck. Floriana was decked out in a black dress, with a matching pair of heels. The young General was grinning from ear to ear, as she waltzed with the captain of the ship.

A beautiful crescent moon bathed the cruise ship in a gentle light. Cain took Sarah by the hand and placed his other hand near her waist, and they danced around the deck. Waltzing with Cain made it easy for Sarah to forget her worries. He was a much better dancer, then she had imagined. He was skilled in the waltz and the quickstep. Cain moved across the dance floor effortlessly. Holding him close, she found it hard to believe that he could play any role in the destruction of her hometown. She really wanted to believe that he was still that sweet boy, that looked out for Jayden and her as kids.

A saxophonist stepped forward, as the band played a soft melody. His golden tenor saxophone gleamed as he placed the reed to his lips. He closed his eyes and played a solo as the piano faded into the background. The solo was filled with passion, the kind of passion that comes from pure love.

As he continued his solo, everyone on the dance floor stopped to watch him play.

They were caught up in a melodic trance from the music and were completely unaware of the armed men that were sneaking on to the deck. Two chefs, unbuttoned their uniforms, revealing black T-shirts and automatic rifles. Eight men jumped down from the ballroom roof, crashing through the promenade canopy. The sudden chaos jolted the music listeners out of their trance. Gun shots were fired into the air, and everyone hit the ground.

More armed men, swarmed the deck, bringing with them guests they had corralled from throughout the ship. The ballroom was filled with people. Many of the ship's passengers were confused, didn't what was going on and yelled to be released from their armed captors.

A large boat appeared on the port side of the ship. Armed sailors got off their boat and climbed up to the promenade deck. These men were dressed in blue and white, striped T-shirts, with cheesy white sailor hats. One sailor in particular stood out as he was wearing a purple pinstriped suit with a white fedora. In his left hand, he spun around a modified flintlock pistol. In his right hand, he held a megaphone and on this hip was a cutlass, with a hilt made of white gold.

"I'm guessing he's in charge," Cain whispered.

Floriana looked around, "there are too many of them for us to make a break for it. If we could get to our weapons, we might be able to help." Sitting amongst the other passengers made her feel helpless.

The man in the pinstriped suit, raised the megaphone to his lips, "we apologize for interrupting your dance under the stars. If you can be compliant, we can be out of your hair in a jiffy. Understand, that we are not here to harm you or to sink your ship. We are just here to steal some of your valuables." Lifting his fedora, he smiled his pearly whites. "We are pirates after all."

Cries of defiance rose from the passengers of the Liberta. A man in his forties stood up amongst the passengers and yelled, "they can't take us all!"

Before he could finish yelling, the pinstriped pirate shot the man in his shoulder, sending him to the ground howling in pain. "Understand people, we are the ones in charge. If any of you attempt to get up to resist us again, I will have the pirates on my boat, put enough bullet holes in this ship to sink it." Gesturing to his men he added, "bandage up this man's wound, and get him some painkillers. Please do not try to be a hero. This man and a few others have already had to learn their lesson the hard way. Now just sit here until we are done getting what we want. Just so you aren't bored to tears, I will have the band continue to play. If you have any questions, you can call me Captain Rosso."

***

His pleasant dreams were interrupted by the sound of gunfire. Jayden jumped to his feet and looked around, but he couldn't tell what was happening because it was so dark. Normally, the pool lights would have turned on by now. That can't be good, he thought.

Walking around a pool in the dark was a bad idea, he told himself, right before he tripped over a lounge chair. The chair skidded across the ground, and he cursed under his breath.

"Who's there?" yelled a man that was approaching him with a flashlight in one hand and a submachine gun in the other. "Why aren't you with the others?"

Jayden blinked as he examined the man in front of him. Then he fell to the ground laughing. The man standing over him was dressed up like a pirate. He had a fake parrot on his shoulder and wore an eye patch.

"What is so funny?" he asked, sounding annoyed.

"Have you looked in the mirror? You are a grown man dressed up as a pirate on a cruise liner. How do you not see the humor in that? Did your mother make that outfit for you? Wait, was there a costume party I missed out on?"

The pirate pressed his submachine gun, against Jayden's chest. "There is no costume party, and my mother did make this for me. I am a pirate, and my captain gave me orders to kill any passenger that poses a threat to our mission. Make another joke. I dare you."

"Well in that case," Jayden replied, "Two pirates walked into a bar."

"Shut up!" the pirate yelled as he quickly wheeled around at the sound of footsteps coming from the other side of the pool. He clicked off the safety and raised his firearm. "Freeze!"

On the other side of the pool, a family of four stopped in their tracks as he shined his flashlight in their direction. Their eyes were filled with fright. With the pirate distracted, Jayden seized the opportunity to tackle him to the ground. Then he jumped back up and kicked the pirate in the face, knocking him out.

Jayden signaled for the family to come over. They walked towards him cautiously. The father shook Jayden's hand. "Thank you," he said. His hand was trembling as Jayden held it.

"So what all is going on?" Jayden asked.

"Do you not know what is happening?" the man's wife said frantically. "The ship has been taken over by pirates!"

"I was taking a nap when all this went down. Where is everybody?" Jayden asked.

"They have most of the passengers on the promenade deck and in the ballroom. Their leader is on that deck," her husband said. "We barely got out in time. I'm sure there are other passengers scattered throughout the ship. They have one large boat on the port side of the ship. You know how to fight. You might be able to do something."

Jayden nodded his head, "I can help." Extending his hand, he gave them the submachine gun. "Take this and use it only if you have to. Do you have a place to hide?"

"We were planning to hide in our room," he responded.

"I will travel with you to your room to make sure you get there safely. Then I will take back the ship. Once it is safe, I will throw a gigantic fireball into the sky. Do not leave your rooms until then."

Jayden followed them to their room and then set out to find his friends. He decided to climb down the side of the ship, to get to his room. Unfortunately, he was climbing in complete darkness. While he descended the ship, he almost had a heart attack, when he lost his footing. As he dangled in midair, he felt around for one of the windows. Once he found the window sill, he struggled to lift his feet onto it.

When he regained his balance, he took a deep breath to regain his composure. Jayden looked down and figured that he had another 30 feet to go, which was good news. The bad news was that there were two pirates dressed in black, pacing back and forth on the deck below.

What should I do? He wondered. If he jumped down, they would gun him down. He had to think fast. He waited until both men were standing directly under him talking. "Here goes nothing," he whispered. Then he jumped down and landed on both of them, knocking them out cold.

Jayden pulled them into his room and tied them up. Then, he grabbed his bag from under his bed. Jayden took out his katana, his new magnum pistol, throwing knives, and his rifle. He switched out of his swim clothes and put on one of the pirate's black uniforms.

He checked himself out in the mirror and smiled thinking, I should wear this outfit more often. At that moment, a thought popped into his head. He may have to kill someone tonight. He wasn't sure if he was ready to do that again. Tightening his belt, he took a deep breath and remembered that MikaEL told him that he might have to take a life, and in this situation, there may be no avoiding it. Hope for the best and plan for the worst, he told himself.

Jayden crept out of his room and back on to the deck. He wanted to get to the promenade deck to see what was going, but right now it would be too risky. Glancing over the side of the Liberta, he saw the pirate's ship. The boat was an oversized armored speedboat, with a couple of decks and a large machine gun at each end.

Jayden found a rope that connected from the cruise ship's railing, down to the pirate's boat. This must be how they boarded the ship. Jayden raised his dad's rifle, and he looked through the scope. This scope was rather unique; it was designed to adjust to any light, and it could be switched to a thermal setting.

With the thermal setting turned on, he was able to tell that the majority of the pirates were below deck. "I need to create some chaos on that boat, but how? I know there must be some security force on this cruise ship. They must have been rounded up first, so the pirates could take over the ship. Would they have already killed them? No, probably not. These pirates are after money, not needless bloodshed." Ducking back into his room, he woke up the pirates he knocked out.

Grabbing one of them by the collar, he said, "When you took over the ship, did you take out the security team that is paid to protect this ship?"

The pirate with long blonde hair spit on Jayden's face, "Hey, give me my clothes back! We won't tell you anything unless you give me back my clothes."

Wiping the spit off his face, he smiled a little bit. "You know, that's the first time anyone has ever spat on me before. For that, I've decided to keep these clothes indefinitely. I gave you that nice flowery tourist shirt. Isn't that enough?"

The pirate with spiky red hair spit on Jayden's shirt, "Now it's happened to you twice. Happy birthday, punk! You can keep your stupid shirt and shove it up your..."

Smacking the pirate in the back of the head, Jayden looked at the both of them, "I was hoping you two would make it easier for me. I was hoping I wouldn't have to resort to violence to get information out of you, but I'm on a bit of a time crunch."

"Do your worst! This ugly shirt is torture enough," the other pirate said.

Grinning, Jayden pulled out his magnum pistol. Using heat magic, he made the barrel of the gun exceptionally hot and pressed it against one of the pirates' legs. The man screamed, then Jayden pressed it against the other pirate's temple. He also screamed in pain. Snapping his fingers, he summoned a small fire snake. "If you guys don't tell me where the security team is, I'm going to let this snake crawl all over this room until he burns out. By the time he's done, this room will be burning you to a crisp. You will be dying slowly and painfully, in a closet like a bunch of losers."

The fire snake hissed in their direction, which filled them with fright. The blonde pirate looked away from the snake, "Okay! Okay! I'll tell you where they are. Just get rid of that snake! I'm not scared of being burned to death. I just hate snakes. Right now we have about 30 or 40 guys sitting in the engine room tied up that are a part of the cruise ships security."

"Thank you for that info. Now I have one more thing to ask. How many men are guarding them?"

Taking a moment to think, the red-haired pirate responded, "Last time I checked, there wasn't anyone guarding them. We locked them in the engine room. We do have a couple of guys guarding the door with *The Key*."

Patting them on the head, Jayden thanked them, then knocked them out again. Stepping back out of his room, he knew what he needed to do. First, I need to free the security guards, and then I need to get onto the pirate ship.

Jayden found a set of stairs that led to the engine room. This part of the ship's interior was not as easy to maneuver in. The halls he walked through, were super narrow. Jayden felt like a sardine trapped in a can; only this can was the inside of a ship.

He made a right down a corridor, and then he took a left and found another flight of stairs. When he approached the metal steps, he stopped just in enough time, as two pirates were heading up them. He pressed himself up against a wall and grabbed his rifle. He had just a few moments to decide his next move. Before he had made a decision, they came up the stairs.

Instinctively, Jayden rushed the unsuspecting pirates, hitting them with the butt of his rifle. They crumbled to the ground like a sack of potatoes. Well, that worked better than I thought it would.

He tied them up, hid them down a corridor, and went down the stairs. When he reached the bottom of the steps, he heard a rumbling sound coming from the large ship's engines. The floor vibrated from their immense power, and the air below deck felt really warm.

He found that life in the lower decks was much calmer than in the world above. Jayden really liked that there weren't as many gunmen running around. As he drew closer to the engine room, he spotted two men guarding the door to the engine room. They were trying to light a cigarette but were having no luck.

Jayden approached them saying, "Oi mates, ya need a light?"

They looked at him suspiciously even though he was dressed just like them.

"Why are you talking like that?" said the guard on the right.

"I don't know. I thought it sounded tough," Jayden replied.

"Well, it doesn't. Bring us a light, would ya?"

Jayden approached the two pirates. When he was standing between them, he snapped his finger, and a small flame appeared on his thumb. A look of shock and surprise appeared on their faces. Jayden quickly hit both of them in the throat and conked their heads against the engine room door. Removing their keys, he unlocked the door and entered.

Chapter 18

Save Our Ship

The Liberta's engine room was hot and noisy. He could only imagine what sort of hell it must be to work down here. Even for a fire user, Jayden found the engine room to be hot and musty.

The engine room was filled with wires and large pieces of machinery which were operating completely oblivious to the turmoil going on the rest of the ship. As Jayden moved through the engine room, he started to feel a little claustrophobic. There was hardly enough room to walk. He was beginning to understand how horrible it must be for the security team to be tied up down here.

On his left, he found an area that appeared to be relatively spacious, which in the engine room still wasn't much. As he got closer, he could tell that there were people huddled together. The security team was tied up and blindfolded. Many of their faces, had become red from the heat of the engine room. Jayden felt glad that he was going to be able to help them. They looked miserable.

Jayden knelt down and gently removed the blindfold of a woman. She was in her late twenties or early thirties. Her lip had a small cut, and she had a bruise on her cheek. She looked at Jayden fearfully and tried to pull away from him.

With a calm and soothing voice, Jayden replied, "Don't be afraid, I am not here to hurt you. I'm actually one of the passengers. I am here to help you." Jayden took out his knife, cut her loose and started to untie the rest of them. Once he had finished untying them, a dark-skinned older man, who was maybe in his sixties, approached him and shook his hand.

"My name is Larry," he said. "I am the lead supervisor for security on this boat. Thank you so much for releasing us. It has been quite dreadful being down here. They gathered us up before the ship even set sail and left us down here. We never even had a chance to stop it."

"Well, here is your chance to get back at them. Most of them are on the promenade deck and around the ballroom area. I have knocked out a few of them. I can show you where four of them are. You can take their weapons and uniforms. They have a ship right next to the Liberta, and it has two machine guns on it. I need to take that ship out of the equation before you guys start taking back the ship."

Scratching his scraggly beard, Larry looked Jayden up and down. "You're a brave young man. Your family should be proud, but are you sure you can take over their boat on your own?"

Jayden nodded, "I will be fine. Now, when I throw up a blue fireball, that will be your signal to take over the rest of the ship. Once I've finished my part, I will rejoin you on the promenade deck."

Larry agreed to his plan and gave his crew instructions on how to proceed. Jayden felt uneasy, leaving them on the lower decks. He was concerned for their safety, but he knew he had to carry out his part of the plan, so they could have a chance at taking back the ship.

Jayden reached the railing of the ship, and he began to wonder if he made a mistake by not bringing some of them with him. Could he really take over a pirate ship all on his own? Well, it's too late to turn back now. He took a few steps back from the railing, he ran, and front flipped over the railing and dove into the ocean.

He breached the surface of Southern Ocean with a pencil dive. The cold water chilled him to the bone. The taste of saltwater was on his lips as waves crashed against him. His weapons were pulling him down making it difficult to swim. Jayden swam under water as much as possible as he approached the pirate boat.

When he arrived at the boat, he grabbed onto a ladder that was on the side of it. The metal ladder creaked as he climbed up it. Suddenly, his heart jumped into his throat. Standing above him was a pirate who was gazing down at him. Jayden wasn't expecting to run into one of them so soon.

"Ey, you fall off the ship? We got a rope that's connected to both ships if you need to get back up there." The pirate pulled Jayden onto the boat, and that's when he got a little more suspicious. "Where did you get all those weapons? Let me have that pistol."

Channeling his inner pirate, Jayden said to him, "Naw mate, this one is mine, get your own. There are plenty on the cruise ship." The pirate growled and walked off feeling miffed.

Now that he was on their boat, Jayden felt a little lost. He had this great plan in his head, but he had no idea how he was going to take this boat out of the equation. He knew, because of his dress, that he could blend in with them, but sooner or later they would figure out he wasn't a pirate.

He scanned the deck and counted about six pirates. How many were below deck, he had no idea. If he went below deck, he could maybe find the engine room and get a fire started.

Jayden wandered towards the bow of the ship and examined the machine gun. The machine gun was a military grade weapon. It rotated 360 degrees and loaded with armor-piercing rounds.

A devious smile spread across his face; maybe he could sink their ship with their own gun. At the same time, if he put holes in this boat, he will most likely end up killing, most of the people on this ship. Feeling conflicted by his choices, he turned to glance up at the cruise liner and saw lights flashing on and off. Holy crap, he thought. The security team has already started taking back the ship. He had to make a decision quickly if he was going to help them.

Four pirates came running up from the lower decks, and the ship's pilot started giving him an ugly look. As the group of pirates got closer, one of them raised his pistol at Jayden. Well, I guess I couldn't fake being a pirate forever. Jayden grabbed the machine gun and started firing at the ship's deck. The pirates ran to retreat, and one of them fired off a shot hitting Jayden in his left shoulder.

Jayden dropped to the ground for a moment, as he was enveloped with pain. Putting his hand on the wound, he winced as his shoulder burned with pain. Looking up, he saw that the pirates were starting to advance on his position. What was his next move? Shooting the deck did absolutely nothing. The pirate ship hadn't started sinking at all. He needed a backup plan.

Jayden pulled out his pistol and fired off rounds at the approaching pirates. He managed to drop two of them, and the rest of them hit the deck. Jumping back to his feet, he grabbed the machine gun again and started firing. He must have hit something important because the ship began to leak black oil into the ocean.

Quickly, he let go of the machine gun and ran towards the rope that connected the pirate ship to the cruise liner. Summoning a fireball, he threw it at the oil and jumped onto the rope just as the fire spread and the boat exploded, launching a gigantic fireball into the sky. The pirates on the ship yelled and shrieked as the boat slowly began to sink.

While he climbed, he watched as fire and smoke rose into the night sky. This moment reminded him of the night when his world was turned upside down and burned to the ground. This time he was doing the burning. He didn't know how many pirates were on that ship, but their deaths rested squarely on his shoulders.

Only about twenty more feet to go and he would be back on the cruise ship. One thing was starting to bug him as he got closer to the ship. The sound of gunfire had ceased. That was either a really good sign or a really bad one. He pulled himself over the railing and looked up, just as two pirates were running toward him, with their swords out, hungry for his blood.

Grabbing three knives from his belt, he let them fly striking one in the chest and the other in the neck. Two more sailors came running up from behind him. Before he could react, he heard three gunshots, and the pirates dropped. Turning around, Jayden saw the security lady he had rescued from the engine room.

"Hey, thanks for saving me," Jayden said.

"You're welcome. I'm just returning the favor. By the way, my name is Carol. It looks like you did one heck of a job destroying their ship."

"I did the best I could," Jayden replied. "So where is the rest of the group?"

"Well, some of them are still below deck fighting it out. Chances are they will come out on top. Larry sent a few groups to the upper decks. I'm running around here because I got separated from my group in a firefight."

"It's so quiet right now," he added.

She scrunched her nose, and a worried look appeared on her face, "I'm worried about Larry and his group. I think they've been captured." She noticed that Jayden's shirt was stained with blood. "O my gosh! You got hurt. Let me fix that before we move on."

Scratching his chin to think, Jayden said, "Cheer up! I'm sure they will be fine. Look, what you should do is head below deck and bring that security team to the promenade deck. Get them there as quickly as possible. Make sure you have them take up good firing positions, so we can avoid hitting any of the passengers. I'm going to go there now and cause a distraction until you all get there. Don't worry about me. I will be fine."

She looked concerned for him and wished him luck before she ran towards the stairs to the lower deck. Jayden took a moment to bandage his shoulder. He ripped off a piece of his sleeve and wrapped it around his shoulder. Flexing his arm, he was able to move it somewhat. The pain made his arm motions very stiff.

He looked up the side of the ship and decided that even with a gunshot wound, he would have a better chance of getting to the promenade deck by climbing up the side of the ship, than fighting his way up there. Since his self-healing spell wasn't activating, he was going to have be very careful moving forward.

His shoulder was burning with pain once he reached the pool. The night sky was dark, and it made it difficult to see. The stars were shining about as bright as the depths of the ocean. Not even the moon came out to say hello. To avoid tripping over objects and walking into pirates, he used the night scope so that he could avoid detection. Finding his way to the ballroom was going to be much easier now.

Jayden was surprised by how rarely he saw any pirates on his trip to the stern. Apparently, the security team had managed to put a good-sized dent in the number of pirates on the ship. He had been walking for minutes, and the only pirates he ran into were bodies left on the ground. Normally that would be a good sign, but Jayden knew that the battle wasn't over. Not by a long a shot.

The worst part about navigating through the ship was that it was so quiet. A deafening silence permeated throughout the ship. This sense of loneliness made him feel paranoid and uneasy. Jayden was like a cobra ready to strike at a moment's notice.

When he was close enough to the ballroom, he decided to lie down and scan the area with his scope. His scope revealed to him that the passengers were frightened and forced to sit very close together, while armed pirates walked amongst them. He needed to find their leader and confront him. If he could manage to do that, he would buy Carol and the rest of the security team enough time to get up here. Jayden found a dark corner to the left of the entrance. If he could get to that corner, he could jump up onto the roof of the ballroom. Being on the roof would make it easier for him to spot their leader.

He got low to the ground and moved stealthily toward the dark corner. Instinctively, he ducked behind a metal box as he watched three pirates step out of the ballroom to guard the entrance. One of the pirates was pacing back and forth near the dark corner he needed to get to.

"Crap!" He whispered under his breath. How am I supposed to get to that corner without being seen? He checked his belt. He had just two knives left, not enough to take them all out without creating a sound. He could try to rush them and hope that they are really terrible shots, or he could come up with a distraction so that he could get to the roof of the ballroom.

Using his brain, he decided to distract the pirates with something that entrances guys of any age, fire. He whispered the words, "fire buddy." Within a few seconds, a small humanoid made of fire appeared in the left corner of the ballroom entrance. The "fire buddy" started laughing like a child, as it skipped back and forth. The pirates were intrigued by this latest development and walked over to it cautiously with bewildered looks on their faces.

"What kind magic is this?" one of them said. "Is it a demon?"

"No, you idiot! This is obviously an omen. Didn't you pay any attention in school?" said another.

"Shut up you two!" said the third pirate as he crouched in front of the sprite.

"What are you?" he asked. The "fire buddy" stopped skipping to look at who had interrupted his fun. The sprite smiled as it bowed, then exploded, sending sparks that set one of pirate's clothes on fire. Jayden had to stifle his laughter as the pirates ran away flailing their arms to put the fire out. Now's my chance, he thought, as he snuck to the left corner of the ballroom and jumped onto the roof.

The moment he landed on the roof, he knew he was in trouble. Two pirates were standing on the ballroom roof, carrying high powered rifles with suppressors. As they turned in his direction, he let his two remaining knives fly. Instantly, the pirates crumbled to the ground and began their eternal sleep.

He shook his head. I had no other choice; I had to kill them, Jayden told himself. His hands were shaking, as he walked by their lifeless bodies. He felt nauseated and nearly threw up over the side, as the reality set in. He slapped himself, come on Jayden, you have to push forward. It's too late to change anything now.

While he snuck along the roof, he had this growing fear, that it was slowly becoming easier for him to take a life. He managed to sink a ship full of sailors and kill two pirates without any hesitation. His heart felt heavy, as he began to wonder if it was okay to kill for the sake of others. Was there any other option? Does this make me a killer?

Jayden shrieked for a moment when he realized that he had just stepped onto a glass ceiling. Even though the glass felt sturdy, he didn't want to take the risk of it breaking. He moved to the left, so he wasn't on the glass. Peering down into it, he saw a beautiful chandelier covered in diamonds. The beautiful decorations seemed out of place, in a room filled with the fearful passengers and bloodthirsty pirates. From what he could tell, the number of the pirates had considerably dwindled down. Carol and the others may have a shot at taking back the ship. He knew he was in a time crunch. Jayden had to get to Larry before it was too late.

He didn't see the leader of the pirates in the ballroom. He must be on the promenade deck. Jayden crawled to the edge of the roof and looked over. Sitting in a small semi-circle was Larry and his security team. They were resting on their knees as a man in a pinstriped suit paced back and forth yelling at them.

"My men put you in the engine room before we took this ship over. I told you all that if you cooperated, I would have you released. Now here I am holding up my end of the bargain, and here you are blowing up my pirate ship and trying to take back the Liberta." He spun his flintlock pistol with his index finger, and his pale skinned face turned scarlet red. "Now I have to change up my plans. Since you allowed my boat to be destroyed, I'm going to have to take this one and make the lot of you "walk the plank," as the saying goes."

Larry laughed defiantly, "You are a lunatic if you think that you can make us all walk this mythical plank of yours. There are more of us than there are of you. You only have so many bullets. Plus, once this ship goes missing, the Eden and the Terrain Navies will be looking for you. You lost this battle, long before it even started."

Captain Rosso smacked Larry in the cheek with his flintlock pistol, and a bruise began to form on his face. "Old man, you will be the first to go." He snapped his finger, and a pirate with a patch on his left eye stepped forward.

Captain Rosso gave him his pistol. "Make it bloody," he said, with a sinister grin.

The pirate with the eye patch placed the gun to Larry's head. A shot rang out, and it echoed throughout the promenade. A look of shock appeared on the pirate's face, as he fell to the ground hard. A large pool of blood spread from beneath him. Captain Rosso stepped back and drew his sword, as four pirates came to his side.

Jayden front-flipped down from the roof and landed between Larry and the pirates. Captain Rosso gave Jayden a 'you've got to be kidding me' look. "Who the hell are you?" he asked.

"My name is none of your business, and I'm here to send you and your pirate buddies to Davy Jones' locker. On a side note, what kind of pirate wears a pinstripe suit? Did your mother make you wear it?" Jayden asked.

His comment apparently angered the captain, as he threw a knife at Jayden, hitting him in the same shoulder, which had been shot earlier. Jayden doubled over in pain, as he removed the knife from his shoulder. The pain from his gunshot wound combining with the knife wound, almost made him pass out.

Jayden's head felt woozy from the loss of blood. He knew that he couldn't show any more weakness. He needed to stay alive long enough for the cavalry to arrive. Jayden was going to have to soldier on and put on one hell of a show.

"I apologize for the insult," Jayden said, as he winced. "Considering that you have complete control of this boat. I was wondering if a little one on one fight between us would be out of the question. I mean what harm could it do?"

Captain Rosso grinned, "young man, you have sustained injuries to your shoulder. I would hate to fight you with a handicap."

"Don't you wish to avenge your first mate I just killed? Or how about your ship that I destroyed?"

Captain Rosso's face turned almost the color purple from his anger. "So, you are the one who helped to orchestrate all of this. You will get more than a fight. I will kill you in front of all these people!"

The captain attacked Jayden with slashes from his cutlass, creating a small gash across Jayden's chest. Jayden's upper body was enveloped with pain. He dove to his left and rolled on the deck. He jumped back up and threw his rifle and pistol to the ground. Then pulled out his sword.

The pain in his shoulder was too intense for him to try and use two hands with his sword. Using just one arm placed him at a disadvantage. While his strikes were still quick, he lost a considerable amount of power. He was beginning to think that challenging Captain Rosso to a fight was the stupidest idea he had ever come up with.

He ducked a slash that was aimed at his head. Then he quickly thrust his sword at the captain, impaling him in the rib. He pulled his sword back and jumped out of the way, just as an enrage Captain Rosso, swung his sword at him wildly.

The stinging pain in Jayden's chest and shoulder were taking a toll, as they continued to fight. Jayden's vision was getting blurry, as he struggled to keep up with his lively opponent. His shoulder was feeling stiff, and every swing with his sword took an immense amount of energy. Jayden was starting to think that cavalry wasn't coming. He should have been patient and waited until they were ready. If he continued to fight like this, he would end up having fought for nothing.

While the young Dragon Warrior was lost in thought, Captain Rosso slashed at Jayden. He managed to block the strike, with what little strength he had left. With their blades pressed against each other, the captain gained the upper hand, by pushing Jayden backward and knocking him on to the ground. When Jayden hit the ground, he quickly rolled to his right, avoiding the downward thrust of his opponent's sword.

Jayden stood back up slowly. His equilibrium felt way off. He took a glance at the audience of frightened passengers. Hope was fading from the looks on their faces, and then he noticed his friends sitting amongst the crowds. Sarah appeared distraught, and Floriana looked frustrated as if she wanted to help but couldn't. Cain just looked at Jayden and simply nodded. At that moment, Jayden knew he couldn't give up.

Captain Rosso pulled out another flintlock pistol and fired at Jayden. Big mistake he thought. Jayden's sword glowed as he deflected the bullet, and it ricocheted into the captain's right pectoral. The captain stumbled backward, as Jayden ran at him. He jumped in the air and kicked his opponent in the face, knocking him unconscious.

When Jayden landed, he wobbled back and forth, as the pirates raised their guns to finish him off. He clutched himself, expecting to feel a hail of bullets. He squinted his eyes open when heard the sound of gunfire. Jayden felt confused as the pirates surrounding him fell to the ground, and the rest of them dropped their guns and fled.

His world began moving in slow motion as blood soaked his clothing. He felt weak in the knees and collapsed on to the ground. His vision became blurry, and then it all faded to black.

Chapter 19
Terra

His eyes opened, but his vision was pretty blurry. After blinking a few times to clear his vision, he noticed a beautiful woman was sitting on the chair next to his bed. Jayden sat up and said, "I thought you were Sarah for a minute."

The beautiful woman was reading a women's magazine. Hearing him, she looked up him and replied, "sorry to disappoint you. It's about time you woke up."

"I love you too, Floriana!"

"You better," Floriana replied as she flipped through the pages in her magazine. She appeared to be reading an article on how to turn a bad man into a good one. He glanced around the room, and there were two green reclining chairs with blankets and pillows on them.

"Where am I?"

"You are in the hospital, Jayden."

"I know that, but why? Weren't we on a ship like five minutes ago?"

She got up and sat next to him and patted his head. "Bless your heart, Jayden. We haven't been on that ship for about three and a half weeks now. We made it to Terra and are in the port city Varlden. And you, my good man, are in their general hospital."

Jayden touched his shoulder, and it still felt sore from having a knife thrown at it and being hit by a bullet. "Wait, explain to me why I was out for almost a month. I wasn't hurt that bad. I'm pretty tough, you know!"

"Well, you lost some blood from your injuries. What really did you in was his knife and sword laced with poison from a tree viper. The last time you became poisoned made you more sensitive to the toxins in venom. So, that slowed your wannabe automatic healing spell plus, you were in a mini coma."

"Well, that makes sense. Wait a second. Don't make fun of my healing spell! I'll have you know that it works most of the time. Also, where are the others?" he asked.

"I wouldn't make fun of it if it wasn't so easy to do so. You'd be better off throwing sand on your wounds than using that spell. Sarah left a while ago. I think she will be back pretty soon. I sent her to get us some chocolate candies from the vending machines. Cain is out trying to get information on how to get to the Chaldean Swamp."

Just then, Sarah walked in the room with a bowl full of chocolates of every kind even some with peanut butter. When she noticed that Jayden was awake, she calmly handed Floriana the bowl of candies. Then, she wrapped her arms around Jayden and held him close for a moment. Unfortunately, she was hugging him a little too tight. "If you hug me any tighter, I'll fall back into a coma," he said with a chuckle.

She smiled ever so sweetly back at him before she pulled his pillow out from under him and threw it to the other side of the room. "You should be grateful that I hugged you at all. I even got you chocolate with peanut butter in case you woke up." She sat on the edge of his bed and said, "what did I tell you would happen if you almost died on me again?"

He scratched his head, "I must have forgotten," he said as he reached for a piece of candy.

She smacked his hand and said, "that was for complaining about my hug. When you can get out of bed, you can have a piece."

Jayden looked at both of the girls, and he couldn't help but feel loved and appreciated. Here they were looking after him once again while he was in a hospital. He didn't know what he would do without them. "Hey, I've been meaning to thank you two for keeping an eye out for me. I know this journey hasn't been fun or easy, but I'm glad to have you two by my side."

They both smiled back at him. "You are such a softy," Floriana said. "I guess we kind of like you too. We still like him don't we, Sarah?"

Sarah shrugged, "I'm not sure. I think we usually like him a lot until he opens his mouth and talks."

The girls burst into a fit of laughter, and that's when Cain entered the room. He was wearing a black trench coat with a matching shirt and pants. On his back hung a large claymore and on his belt, he carried his knife.

Cain sat down on the reclining chair and said, "It is nice to see that you are awake. We had a wager going as to when you would wake up. Sarah was the closest."

Immediately, Jayden regretted saying all those nice things about them. "That is a horrible thing to wager on. Sarah, you should be ashamed of yourself!" She pretended to ignore him and took a bite of chocolate.

Grinning, Cain replied, "Jade, I'm mostly kidding. Anyways I have some good news. I have found some guides that will take us to a town called Chaldea. We will be able to find the swamp once we get there. We will meet our tour guides by a set of stables on the southwest side of town. Once Jayden is feeling well enough, head to the stables. I will be waiting for you."

***

Four hours later, Jayden was released from the hospital. He decided to change into his martial arts uniform and wrapped his red sash around his waist. Jayden slung his sword over his back, stashed his .45 in a holster under his shirt and hung his dagger on his right hip. The magic of the dagger made him feel lighter on his feet. The weapon even made the stiffness in his shoulder go away. Grinning, he decided to see how much quicker he could move now.

Taking a deep breath, he sprinted through the City of Varlden. As he picked up speed, his legs became like a blur, and the rest of the world seemed to be moving in slow motion. Pedestrians stared at Jayden in awe as he flew down the streets.

Varlden was a beautiful city located at the base of a valley. This port city wasn't as modern as Alexandria. Many of the residents traveled on bikes and horses. The majority of the roads were made of brick or cobblestone. The builders of the city designed it to embrace the ecosystem it existed in. Colossal tropical trees provided shade and fruit for the residents of Varlden. Beautiful parks with lakes and rivers were spread throughout the city.

This port city was a melting pot of cultures from all over the world. The racially diverse city was filled with elves, humans, and even this odd race of humanoids called Eaglets. Jayden learned that Eaglets were native to the Southern Continent and were one oldest races to live there. The Eaglets were covered from head to toe with feathers and had the beaks of a normal eagle. Jayden was impressed by how willing they were to share their culture with him.

Jayden finished talking with an Eaglet family and continued sprinting through the city until he reached the outskirts of Varlden. He could tell that he was getting close to the stables when the scent of manure hit him. The smell reminded him of the small farms that surrounded Eiréné.

While he jogged down the dirt road, a man was heading in his direction. The gentleman slowed as he approached and that's when things got weird. Jayden noticed that the animals pulling the man in his covered wagon were not your average horses. They were both around nine feet tall. One of the animals had black fur, and the other had red. Their eyes were dark orange. That wasn't even the weird part. A silver horn protruded from their foreheads.

A man in his fifties stepped out of the wagon. He was wearing overalls and a straw hat. After he shook Jayden's hand, he said, "you must be the boy they are waiting on. Your friends are waiting for you by the stables."

The man had a tight Kung Fu grip on his hand. When Jayden was finally able to pull his hand away, he asked, "so what kind of horses are these?"

"Boy, did you bump your head when you were little? Don't you see the horns? These are Aggeloian Unicorns. I had them imported years ago and have been breeding them ever since." Jayden touched the horn of one of the unicorns. The horn felt smooth and warm.

"I always thought unicorns were only in fairy tales."

The old man climbed back on to his wagon and said, "son, they are as real as you and me. Now go catch up with your friends. I need to head into town." Then he cracked his whip, and the unicorns dashed off leaving a trail of dust.

As Jayden approached the stables, he noticed that his friends were standing next to a couple of animals that looked like large red tigers. The large creatures had long whiskers and spiky tails. The tigers were eating grass which he thought was odd.

He also noticed that two small children were having a conversation with his friends. There was a small boy and a girl. They stood just over four feet. The girl had blonde pigtails, and the boy had long brown hair. What he found to be disturbing was that the girl had an ax strapped to her back, two hatchets on her hips and she was holding a small crossbow. The boy was carrying a machete and a bow staff that had an ax head, on each end.

"Floriana, what are those?" Jayden asked.

Pointing at the animals, she responded, "Those are Tigladons. They look a lot like tigers. The differences between them are that their claws are a little bit longer, they run faster, and they are omnivores."

"Why are they here?"

"Bless your heart, Jayden. We will be riding them to the Chaldean Swamp. We will be able to get there a lot faster on them than by walking."

Still confused, Jayden pulled Sarah over and whispered to her, "whose kids are those? Where are their parents?"

Giggling, she replied, "I don't know, Jayden. Why don't you go find out?"

Jayden walked up to the young girl in pigtails. She looked maybe 12 or 14 tops. "Does your mommy normally let you play with axes?"

Jayden knew he made a mistake when the girl's face turned redder than a tomato. She tackled him to the ground and started punching him. While he tried to push her off, he realized a couple of things. This girl was about as strong as he was and his friends were laughing at him.

The boy stood over Jayden as he was being pummeled. Now that he was closer, Jayden could see that he had a mustache and almost a unibrow. "My sister will stop punching you when you apologize for your insult. We aren't children you uncultured swine. We are dwarves."

With his side getting sore from being punched by an angry dwarf, Jayden decided he should apologize. "Ma'am I'm sorry for being insensitive and assuming from your stature that you are a child."

For a moment, she stopped punching him and looked even more flustered with Jayden, "ma'am? How old do you think I am?"

Using his brain for the first time, Jayden chose his answer very carefully. "Well, it's obvious that you are about 18, 21 at the most."

Blushing, she squeezed his neck. "You are so sweet! I'm actually 205 years old, and my brother is 210."

Jayden knew better than to question her anymore about her age, so he decided to change the subject. When he got to his feet, he shook their hands and introduced himself. "Hello, my name is Jayden, and who are you two? You are the first dwarves that I have ever met. I always thought dwarves were in fairytales and books."

"Well, my name is Tammy Reinhart, and this is my brother Romeo. We will be guiding you to the Chaldean Swamp. If we can be done with the introductions, I think we can be on our way."

Jayden approached his Tigladon cautiously, mainly because it had razor sharp teeth and claws. He watched as the others climbed on theirs when Sarah approached him with a big smile on her face.

"We get to share this one." When he looked confused, she added, "aww, don't act too upset about it. You know you will love me riding with you."

Great, Jayden thought, she can already read my mind. I was looking forward to riding this alone. Gingerly, he put his hands on the animal's back and prayed to God it wouldn't turn around and devour him. Pushing himself up onto its back, he grabbed the reigns that were attached to a leather collar on the Tigladon's neck. Sarah jumped on behind him and wrapped her arms around him, which made Jayden smile a little bit.

"Oh, get over yourself," she said. "I'm only doing this so I don't fall off."

Leaning back against her, he replied, "Whatever helps you sleep at night."

Their caravan set off heading south. The dwarves were riding on small ponies while the rest followed them on their Tigladons. Jayden found riding on the furry beast to be quite comfortable. He would be enjoying the ride even more if Sarah would stop trying to tickle him. While they were traveling up a steep hill, she tickled him so hard that he fell off the Tigladon and almost landed on a family of yellow rattlesnakes.

This place was wonderful, Jayden thought. Beautiful palm trees gave them a healthy dose of shade in the humid air of the valley. Nine tailed monkeys swung from vines of the fruit trees. To his left, there was a babbling brook with large frogs jumping from rock to rock snatching insects that flew just a little too close. He even was able to witness the fin of a small freshwater shark darting up and down the creak. This moment, to him, was perfect. It was the first time in a long time that he didn't have to fight or fear for his life. The idea of moving to this part of the world didn't seem so bad.

Leaning back against Sarah, he said, "hey, when this is all over, we should move here."

Resting her head on his shoulder, "I could get used to this," she replied. "If you put two rings on my finger, you got yourself a deal. I will show you the engagement ring I want at the next jewelry shop we see."

That sounds like it might get expensive, he thought. "How about I get you a nice plastic ring for a copper coin?"

Whispering in his ear, she said, "Jade, if you get me one of those rings, I just might have to, I don't know, marry Tony or even Cain instead."

"That last one was a low blow," he replied.

After two hours of hiking, they were able to get out of the valley. On each side of the dirt road, there were tall blades of grass and trees of varying sizes teeming with fruit. Large buffalo snatched leaves from the trees. Small coyotes chased a rabbit across the path in front of them. He stared in awe at a gigantic red nosed giraffe and witnessed light green unicorns racing across the grassland. Jayden was beginning to feel like he was starring in one of those safari movies his dad made him watch growing up. In comparison to the country sides of Eden, Terra's ecosystem was very tropical, and it had a vast Savannah. The biggest difference was the abundant fauna. Many of the wild animals in Eden had been hunted to near extinction. The wild animals in Terra roamed so freely; it was almost poetic.

Jayden felt entirely relaxed as he drank in the beauty of his surroundings. His eyelids were starting to feel heavy, so he gave Sarah the reigns. Leaning back against her, he closed his eyes and fell into a deep sleep.

***

Sarah held him close as she fell in love with the scenery around her. The beauty of this moment was almost impossible to describe. Her view of the sunset was truly breathtaking. This fantastic crescendo to an incredible day gave her a greater sense of hope. The peace and harmony of nature she was getting to experience would be something she would never forget.

The beauty of the Terran countryside contrasted so much with the struggles she had experienced on this journey. Seeing Jayden in the hospital again was just as difficult for her as it was the first time. She really worried about him even though she loved the fact that he was willing to fight until his last breath for the sake of others. He had demonstrated his selflessness, but she also knew recklessness and selflessness had a cost. That cost might be more than her heart could take.

As the sky grew darker, her mind drifted back to that moment when she learned that he was alive. Things between them haven't panned out the way she thought they would. Maybe things like that only fix themselves in the movies. The reality was their relationship had been a little bumpy since that night at the fair. She thought they would have developed a deeper connection by now, but life and circumstance have made that difficult. Riding together on this four-legged beast, she couldn't help but feel that something good was coming their way. If their relationship never flourished, at least they had this moment under the setting sun. She held him close and kissed his cheek right as he began to come out of his sleep.

The moon rose into the sky as a lion with a golden mane jumped on to a nearby rock. Sarah felt entranced as the powerful creature opened its massive jaws and let out a deafening roar. The Terran countryside was truly an enchanted world filled with possibility. This brought her a sense of comfort even though the road ahead was shrouded in darkness and filled with uncertainty.

Jayden touched his face and said, "hey, why is my cheek wet? Did you kiss me while I was asleep? Weirdo!"

She placed her head on his shoulder and whispered, "just go back to sleep. It must have just been a dream."

Chapter 20

An Intertwining Journey

They decided to camp out that night on top of a mesa which overlooked a valley. Cain gathered wood for a fire, and Jayden started it with a flick of his wrist. Sitting around the camp,

Sarah cooked for them some red trout. Jayden was chowing down on a piece of fish when Tammy plopped herself down next to him. Sarah got annoyed watching her try to cozy up with Jayden.

"Jayden, can I ask you a question?" Tammy asked, ever so sweetly.

Scarfing down a bite, he replied, "sure."

Twirling one of her pigtails, she said, "why do you wanna go to the Chaldean Swamp? That place is gross and stinky."

Jayden took a moment to respond; he wanted to choose his words carefully. He wasn't sure how much information he should divulge about their mission to people he had just met. Plus, he was still hiding some info from Cain. Would it really hurt if he told them everything?

Noticing his apprehension, Tammy yelled in a huff, "Fine don't tell me!"

"It's not that I don't want to tell you. I'm trying to think of the best way to say it," he replied. "We are going to the Chaldean Swamp to look for the Southern Convent." Both dwarves gasped. Romeo was now completely engaged in the conversation that Jayden was having with his sister.

"Why would you want to deal with those evil people? Do you know how many dwarves those witches have tortured and turned into their mindless pets?" Romeo asked.

"We believe that we may find a clue there which will help us on our journey."

"What is the goal of your journey?" Tammy asked.

"There is a group called the Daimonia, and we are trying to stop them from finding an ancient artifact which would give them access to powerful weapons." When Jayden mentioned the name Daimonia, Romeo and his sister both looked at each other and nodded. "I take it you two have heard of the Daimonia."

Tammy sniffled as tears began to flow from her eyes. "We don't want to talk about it," Romeo snarled. "See what you did by bringing up such a sore subject. For the remainder of this trip, I don't want to hear you mention that name again."

The tongue-lashing Romeo continued to give Jayden left him feeling like the backside of a donkey. He could tell that Cain was trying to avoid eye contact with them. Jayden could only imagine how uncomfortable he must be feeling.

Tammy reassuringly touched Jayden's hand. Wiping her eyes, she said, "it's okay Jayden. You didn't mean to. It's just that you need to understand that we Dwarves have had a terrible history with the Daimonia. Many Dwarves live in northern Aggeloi up in the mountains, and the Daimonia are responsible for the deaths of many Dwarves. Our older sister Olivia was captured by them a few years ago, and we haven't heard from her since. It hurts just thinking about it."

Putting his arm around her, he replied, "we know how terrible they are. That's why we set out on this mission. The Daimonia destroyed our home and killed people that we cared about. We want to keep them from being able to do that on a massive scale."

Cain pulled back his sleeve revealing the tattoo of a demon. Without skipping a beat, Romeo tackled Cain to the ground and placed his machete to his neck. His face turned a dark purple as he became filled with rage. "How can you say that you are wanting to stop the Daimonia when you are traveling with one?" he snarled.

Jayden got up calmly and walked towards Romeo. "The man that you are laying on top of was with them when they destroyed our town. That day, I lost my father. A part of me died that day, and I will never be the same because of it. I am choosing to give Cain a chance at redemption. If you choose to kill him out of vengeance, the only thing you will end up doing is getting blood on your hands. We are getting close to Chaldea. We can figure out how to get to the swamp from there. If you two want to leave, we will understand. But you need to get off of him in the next five seconds. This is your only warning."

Romeo pushed himself off of Cain, kicked him in the rib, and walked away. Tammy, however, didn't move. She just stared at Cain with a mixture of rage and a silent curiosity. Romeo started to grab his things and placed them back on his donkey. He glanced at his sister and said, "get your things. We are leaving." In defiance, she ignored him. He grabbed her arm and said, "let's go!"

Pulling her arm away from him, she looked at her brother with fire in her eyes. "I am a 205 year old woman. Don't you dare grab me like I'm a child. If you want to leave, then go. I'm going to finish this job we were hired for." Romeo cursed under his breath and climbed on his donkey and sped off into the night.

Touching his tender rib, Cain looked up at the blonde dwarf sitting next to Jayden. For the first time since revealing who he was, he looked her in the eyes and said, "your sister is alive or at least the last time I saw her she was."

Tammy's eyes widened as she struggled to process this new information. Feeling unsure of herself, she said, "you're not lying, are you? How do you know she's alive? How do you know she was my sister?"

"Before I left the Daimonia, I was assigned to our detention area. There was a woman named Olivia who was half dwarf and half human. She's a little taller than you and your brother, but she has the same color eyes that you and your brother have, and she has brown hair like Romeo's. It was heartbreaking working there. Your sister would sit in her cell eating old cornbread and rice. She was one of the kindest people I have ever met, and I knew that I needed to help her escape. Plus, during that time that she was in our custody, I was already contemplating leaving in the Daimonia at the time. So I staged a prison escape in the detention center and made sure that she got away. I gave her my double-barreled pistol and a sword."

Tammy's eyes brimmed with tears as she wrapped her arms around his neck. "Thank you so much for that. I know she must be alive out there somewhere."

Cain was caught off guard by this sudden act of affection, so he awkwardly patted her on the back which Jayden found hilarious.

Clearing his throat loudly to get her attention, Jayden asked, "so Tammy, how is it that your older sister is half human?"

Wiping her tears with her sleeve, she replied, "Um, we have different mothers. Our dad's first wife was a human. My sister got her height from her mother, and her strength from our father." Content with her answer, Jayden volunteered to take the first watch.

***

After hours of sitting at the edge of their camp, Floriana came to take his place. She plopped herself down next to him and rested her head on his shoulder. "If you wanted to be a real gentleman, you could stay up with me until my shift is over."

"Normally, I would love to spend time with you Floriana, but I would really hate for you to miss out on your beauty sleep. And since I am such a gentleman I will stay awake until it's Cain's turn to do watch," he replied.

Floriana sat up and said, "I'm not sure whether I should feel honored or offended. Are you saying I'm not pretty and I need all the help I can get?"

Jayden kissed her forehead. "Of course not," he replied. "Now go back to sleep."

The Eden General stood up and dusted her clothes off. "Thanks for that Jayden. Now I'm going to talk with Sarah about that kiss you just gave me," Floriana said as she walked off. You're the devil, he thought.

The morning came sooner than Jayden was expecting. To help him wake up, Sarah poured water on his face, and Floriana transformed the water into ice. That helped Jayden get out of bed quickly.

This odd caravan of humans and a dwarf had about one hundred more miles to go. Jayden wanted them to pick up the pace, but he also wanted to bug Sarah. So Jayden prompted the Tigladon to pick up speed. Within seconds, the world around them seemed like a blur. Sarah's hair was blowing in the wind as they zipped down the road. A large rock appeared in the middle of the road, and they jumped over it. By they, I mean Jayden and the Tigladon, Sarah didn't quite make it. The animal bucked quicker than she was expecting, and she ended up on the ground.

For a moment, she sat there on the ground with dust on her new jeans. Her hair was a complete mess, and she was giving Jayden the kind of stare that would make any grown man cringe.

She knew that Jayden was trying to mess with her, and she wasn't going to move an inch until he fixed it. Jayden approached her with a massive smile on his face.

"You better wipe that grin off your face," she snapped at him. "Now help me up. I think I broke my tailbone."

To annoy her even more, he smiled even wider and picked her up. While carrying her back to their furry ride which was content to eat grass, Jayden kissed her cheek and said, "Your hair looks so beautiful like that. I'm digging this wild Amazonian look."

"Enjoy that kiss. It will be the last one I will let you give me until you turn forty," she replied.

As Jayden approached his ride, Cain swung around and pulled up next to him. Extending his hand, and said, "Hey Jade, why don't you let her ride with me this time?"

This offer made Sarah perk up a little bit. "Jade, would you be okay with me riding with him?" In his mind, Jayden said no. In fact, his brain was screaming hell no. The last time Sarah spent time with Cain was on the ship, and we all know how that turned out.

Trying to be cool about it, Jayden nodded his head yes and helped her get onto Cain's Tigladon. Jayden jumped back on to his ride and began a slow gallop. He decided to ride in the back of the group to keep an eye on Sarah and Cain. Deep inside he knew that watching them was a little creepy, but he couldn't stand Cain getting to spend time with her.

General Floriana noticed Jayden's distress and decided to ride alongside him. As her beautiful blonde hair blew gently in the wind, she gave Jayden a smile which awakened the butterflies in his stomach.

Catching him staring at her, Floriana said, "Jayden, if I knew I could make your jaw drop just from dyeing my hair, I would have done it years ago."

Embarrassed, he awkwardly turned away from her. "Well, um..." Jayden mumbled as he was at a loss for words.

"It's okay. I will take it as a compliment that I can still get you tongue-tied. So, I noticed you have been very secretive about why we are going to the Chaldean Swamp to find witches."

Jayden nudged his Tigladon closer to Floriana, so he could speak softer. "We are going there because Raiden believes that Lady Grace of the Aggeloi is alive. Her parents worked with my dad to find *The Key*. He believes my dad may have given it to them."

Floriana appeared stunned. "I remember the day when her convoy was attacked, and her body wasn't discovered. The pictures of the crime scene were gruesome; there was blood everywhere. I've met her once, such a sweet girl. If Tony's dad is right, we may finally be a step or two ahead of the enemy. So tell me this, why are you keeping him in the dark?" she said looking at Cain. "Do you not trust him yet?"

For a moment, he sat there in silence. Her question was the same one that he had been wrestling with for quite some time. To be honest, Jayden wanted to trust Cain. When he was growing up in Eiréné, Cain was the cool big brother he never had. For Cain to have been at the center of the worst moment of his life was like watching your biggest hero fall. He wanted to hate him, but his heart wouldn't let him.

He dropped his head and muttered, "I really wish I could. Am I an idiot for bringing him along?"

Floriana took a moment to put her hair up in a ponytail and replied, "Wanting to help a friend doesn't make you an idiot. That makes you a caring person. As a soldier, do I think it was the safest decision? No. Cain is a trained killer and extremely powerful. We both know that to be true. However, he may end up becoming our greatest asset. Only time will tell."

While Jayden thought about what Floriana just said, he became distracted by a high-pitched squeal coming from Tammy.

She started to accelerate on her unbelievably swift donkey up a grass hill. Catching up with her, Jayden was bewildered by her excitement.

Gazing down from the hill, he saw a small town which he assumed was Chaldea. Even from a distance, Chaldea looked relatively unimpressive and slightly depressing. The buildings were off-white, and the shingle roofs looked like they once had been a dark red and were now a soft brown. The surrounding area was even more depressing. The grass plains surrounding Chaldea were a pale green, almost a gray.

Jayden had the impression that at one point this was a thriving savannah, but now the fauna and greenery were quickly fading away. Even the livestock on the nearby ranches looked very questionable at best. The cows were skinny, and many of the chickens were missing feathers. Jayden had a feeling that he would be better off eating dirt than anything in this town.

Tammy led them down the hill, and they entered the small town. Jayden had a bad feeling in the pit of his stomach as they walked by people having an evening stroll. Many of the residents of Chaldea looked like drunk degenerates, and the rest gave them dirty looks. Jayden had the feeling that Chaldea did not get many visitors. He wouldn't have been surprised if Chaldea never had anyone visit before.

General Floriana found them an inn on the north side of town. The inn was called, "A beautiful night's sleep," but judging by the cheap furniture outside the building, Jayden felt that the title might be overselling the experience a tad bit.

"Hey!" Jayden yelled to the others, "I'm going to look around town and see if I can get some information about the Southern Convent." Just as those words escaped from his mouth, he felt a cold chill run down his back, and black crows began to congregate on the roof of the inn. Creepy, Jayden thought. "Anyways," he added, "I might try and find a pub to gather information about it."

Jayden felt relieved as he walked away from the inn. He was tired from riding on an animal for the last few days, and the last thing he wanted to do was spend time in that crummy looking inn.

One thing that Jayden noticed about the residents of Chaldea was that they all seemed to have gloomy looks on their faces. The few children he saw seemed mildly depressed as they played an unenthusiastic game of kickball. Even the sky above seemed to stay perpetually overcast. When the wind blew, it carried with it an ominous chill which caused the hairs on the back of his neck to stick up. Something about this town just wasn't right. Jayden was beginning to think stopping here was a bad idea.

A small building across the street piqued his interest. Based on the individuals he watched stumbling in and out of the building, he guessed that this was a pub. The sign on the building looked as if at one time it used to light up and glitter in the night. The collection of dust and broken lightbulbs appeared to have ended that era of jubilee. The pub was called, "Fire and Ice."

As he approached the door, a small dwarf came barging out of the pub. His face was red with anger and inebriation. He stopped to look at Jayden. He muttered something in Dwarven that Jayden assumed wasn't pleasant. Then he shoved Jayden aside and walked away. Watching that small angry dwarf walk away made him wonder what sort of hell awaited him on the other side of the door. Taking a moment to swallow his fear, he twisted the doorknob and entered.

Chapter 21
The Specter's Curse

The smell of pipe tobacco and cigar smoke was overwhelming. Half finished cigarettes rested on ashtrays strewn across the pub spreading clouds of smoke that filled the room. The floor was sticky from spilled drinks. Peanut shells cracked under his shoes as he explored the pub. The building was so dirty that Jayden was half tempted just to start sweeping the place up.

There were two bars in the old pub, one on the left side of the building and the other on the right. A band of old dwarves sat center stage playing music with the same enthusiasm that one might put into performing a dirge. The bar closest to him was filled with dwarves hiccupping from their alcohol. He smirked when he noticed a particularly bold dwarf peeing in the corner of the room.

The bar on the other side of the room featured a different set of patrons. That side of the room seemed to be serving drinks exclusively to a group of elves. These elves were a lot different than the ones he had met before. These elves were a lot shorter, and many of them were as tall as the dwarves or smaller. Their faces didn't have that ageless look of wisdom that other elves had; their faces were rough, and many had carried battle scars from bar fights in the past. The races were segregated in this bar. Neither one seemed to acknowledge the other.

Jayden located an empty barstool and sat down next to a small, middle-aged dwarf. All of a sudden, Jayden felt the need to duck. He heard a crashing sound behind him as glass shattered against the door sending shards into the air. It was at this point that he realized that he might not be welcome here.

A large dwarf arose from a table on the far side of the room. He stared at Jayden with a level of animosity that caused his heart rate to increase. This dwarf stood at just under five feet tall. He was a little overweight and stumbled slightly as he walked toward Jayden. In his hand was a pitcher of beer which he lifted towards his lips and drained of its contents. Then he threw the pitcher at Jayden's forehead. Ducking just in time, Jayden placed his hand on his dagger and kept glancing around to see if any of the others in the bar were going to jump in. It appeared as if all the dwarves and elves in the bar were taking a break from drinking to watch this strange human who had just interrupted happy hour.

"What are you doing here?" the dwarf snarled. "Humans are not welcome here unless they are accompanied by a dwarf or one of those snooty elves." His snide comment caused a small elf from the other side of the room to throw a glass bottle at the dwarf. The bottle missed him by a mile. The dwarf shot a look at the elf momentarily, then returned his focus to the human standing near the doorway. Sniffing in the air, he looked at Jayden and snarled, "Not only are you a disgusting human, but I can also smell the blood of The Elders running through your veins." Spitting on the floor, he looked back up at Jayden, "clean that up you maggot."

"That boy is here with me," said a voice in the background. The angry dwarf fumed as he looked around to see who would utter such a thing. Appearing by Jayden's side was Romeo with a sawed off shotgun in his hand. "You said if he were accompanied by a dwarf he would be welcome here. Well, I'm a dwarf, so unless you want a problem with me, then I'd suggest you go and find your seat."

"How can you hang out with such filth? His kind are nothing but traitors and cowards."

Jayden watched the angry dwarf stomp off in a huff. That's when he realized that his hands were trembling. The level of restraint he had been using was way more than he knew he possessed. Turning to Romeo, he said, "thank you for doing that. What are you doing here? I figured that you would have made it back home by now."

"It was nothing. I despise seeing the prejudice that some of my own kind still hold." Guiding Jayden to his table, Romeo plopped down into his seat and took a huge bite of a fried turkey leg.

"So, why are all the people in this bar looking at me funny? Do I have a big pimple on my face? On a more serious note, how was that guy able to tell that I have the blood of The Elders in me? Do I smell that bad? I didn't know I was related to them."

Romeo took another bite of his turkey leg, and replied, "Elder blood gives off a distinct scent. To those that can sense it, it smells like cinnamon. It's not surprising that you wouldn't know that you had some ancestors that were Elders. Many humans and elves descend from them. You are special because your blood isn't as deluded as most people. I think some of your relatives must have been half or full-blooded Elders. Now, the reason that some dwarves, and those Pigmy Elves, hate humans so much, stems back to events during the "Great War." There is a legend that close to the end of the war, the younger race of humans was approached by the "The Elders." During their meeting, they convinced the humans to back out of the war in exchange for technology and leniency. The humans agreed to the deal and during one of the final battles, the humans withdrew allowing many dwarves and others to be slaughtered. To be honest, I am not sure if that story is true. It is one that has been passed down through the ages. However, I can tell you this. Since the Great War, the younger race of man has oppressed dwarves and the other races. At one point in time, Dwarves lived all over the world. Now, the only territories that they control are in pockets of Aggeloi, the Northern Continent, and parts of Terra. Since you descend from both the Elder race and the younger race of humans, you will find that some Dwarves and other races might distrust you."

Jayden found it hard to believe that flowing in his veins was the blood of tyrants and traitors. He couldn't blame the dwarves for hating him. The fact that Romeo and Tammy had been so accepting of him said a lot about the quality of their character. For Romeo to even sit with me with my heritage is quite humbling, he thought.

Jayden turned his head and spotted an elf sitting in a corner who proceeded to give him the finger. Luckily, the elf was too drunk to flash him the right finger which made him chuckle. Suddenly, Jayden had a thought. "Hey Romeo, I thought all elves were members of "The Elder Race." Why would they fight against their own kind?"

Lighting up a cigar, the dwarf took a drag and blew a ring of smoke. "Boy, didn't you pay any attention in school? Most humans don't care about anyone outside of their race. They barely care about their own race unless money is involved. The truth is that many elves are a part of The Elder race, and many others descend from them. However, that is not true for all elves. The Pygmy Elves, for example, are a race that are just as old as The Elders. Elven Elders and the Pigmy Elves share a common ancestor from a precursor race that they call Elfion. The Elven Elders thought they were superior because they were able to use powerful magic. So they felt like they could enslave all the other elves. So, when the "Great War" started, all the other elves decided to rise and fight against "The Elders." See, if you had paid more attention in school, I wouldn't have had to give you a history lesson. Now, tell me why you came to this bar. A boy like you ain't the drinking type."

"When they threw that first bottle at me, I was wondering the same thing. The reason I came in here was because I wanted to get some information about the Southern Convent." As those words left his mouth, he felt the hairs on the back of his neck stand up and felt a cold chill pass through his body. Even though he said those words quietly, an older dwarf on the other side of the room was staring right at him. He waved for Jayden to come over to speak with him. Jayden was a little unnerved by that. How could he hear me from the other side of the room?

He got up and placed himself on a barstool to the left of the dwarf, and Romeo sat on one to the right. The dwarf they were sitting with had a long graying beard. His eyebrows were practically white, and the few hairs he had left on his head were dyed black. In the dwarf's left hand, he held a goblet filled with mead, and on the bar, he spun an old revolver. His hands were arthritic, and the bags under his eyes were evidence of a great many sorrows he had experienced. He tried placing his drink down and spilled some of it on the bar as his hand twitched. The dwarf's expression turned cold, and he said, "what you seek you might find. What it may end up costing you, are you willing to pay?"

Cryptic much, Jayden thought. He watched as the dwarf went back to drinking as if Jayden wasn't there. Well, that's rude. Who asks someone an awkward question and then quickly ignores them before a response? Jayden was beginning to think Dwarves were naturally rude; then he remembered his dad telling him not to make stereotypes. So maybe eighty percent of the Dwarves out there were rude, with Tammy being the only the exception. Turning to the dwarf again, Jayden asked, "What makes you think I am seeking something? And were you able to hear me from the other side of the room?"

The dwarf placed his drink down and replied, "We dwarves have ears that hear just as well as elves. I know what you seek because I know who you are."

Perplexed, he asked, "Well who am I Mr. Dwarf?"

The dwarf continued to sip his drink absentmindedly, "You are Jayden LoneOak."

Jayden felt like he had just been hit in the stomach. Here he was in the most depressing town in the world, and this dwarf who was older than dirt knew him and his last name. "How did you know that? How did you know my last name?"

Turning to Jayden, the dwarf fought back a sob and said, "I knew your father and mother. I was there at the hospital in Mirage the day you were born. I still remember the look of joy on your parents face when they first held you in their arms. I wish life would have treated you better. Alas, I am to blame for your sorrow."

Jayden felt a tug in his heart. He had not thought about his mother in years. He tried to cling to good memories he had of her, but he was so young when she passed. The memories that have stuck with him the most were having to watch his mother slowly waste away. Tears brimmed in his eyes, as he remembered holding her hand, until the very moment she passed away. He missed his mother dearly and wished he could see her one more time.

Patting Jayden's shoulder, the dwarf said, "you have lost a lot already. Can you handle losing more than what you already have?"

The truth was, he couldn't. If he lost Sarah or any of the others, he knew he might break. Since his trial up in the cave, Jayden was able to keep a more positive outlook, but being in this town was eroding at his joy. All the pain he had pushed away was starting to resurface.

"Why do you blame yourself for my sorrow?" He asked.

"Young man, my name is Silvanus. I am six hundred years old, and I was a recruiter for The Witnesses. I recruited Dion when he was 13 and your mother Maria when she was 15. If I had not recruited them and pushed your father into doing that mission,0 they might both still be here."

Feeling confused, Jayden thought back to when his dad would talk about how he met his mother. His father had told him that they met in school, and he courted her. Was all that a lie? He couldn't imagine his mother fighting off The Daimonia with a sword. When she was alive, she had a gentle spirit. His mother wouldn't even let Jayden kill the bugs in the house. He would have to catch them, and then release them outside. He had another question that was getting to him, "So, Mr. Silvanus, how could my mother being part of The Witnesses have contributed to her death? My dad told me when she got sick that she had a type of cancer."

With a big gulp, Silvanus drained his glass of mead and avoided making eye contact with Jayden and replied, "My boy, you aren't ready to hear that truth."

Slamming his fist on the bar, Jayden felt his rage building up inside of him, "I want to know the truth about my mother. If it wasn't cancer, then what was it? I can handle more than you think." Lifting his fist up from the bar, he realized that he had made a small dent in it. His anger had almost consumed him again.

"Young man," he yelled, "that rage within you is proof that you aren't quite ready. I can tell that you have already tapped into the power of "The Red Eye." Do you have a death wish? Is that why you are looking for the Southern Convent?" The temperature of the room immediately dropped twenty degrees at the sound of those words.

"Raiden believes that Lady Grace of the Aggeloi may still be alive. He thinks that my father may have passed *The Key* on to her parents before he died." Jayden replied.

"Heh, that Raiden is quite the gambler," the dwarf muttered.

"What do you mean?" Jayden asked.

Silvanus ordered another glass of mead and said, "Raiden is taking a big risk by sending you all here. Finding the Southern Convent is difficult enough. You also take the risk of revealing the connection between Lady Grace and *The Key* to the witches there. I will help you to find it, but you need to remember that those witches cannot be trusted."

"I will keep that in mind. Now how do I find those witches?"

"Boy, you are brash. You think you can simply just walk around their swamp like you own the place? My boy, the only way to find the Southern Convent is if you are invited. The enchantments they have on that place make it impossible to find. You would lose your mind long before you found it."

"How do I get an invitation?"

Silvanus took a swig of his drink. "Well, that answer requires me to tell you a story. Many moons ago, a young man began to court a beautiful woman. They both lived here in Chaldea back when it was a small beautiful Kingdom. They both knew each other since birth. Sounds like a match made in heaven, right?"

"Right," Jayden replied feeling confused as to why he had to listen to this sappy story.

Silvanus smacked Jayden in the back of the head before he continued his story. "Well, you'd be wrong my boy. No relationship worth having falls in your lap. You see, this woman wanted a long-lasting relationship, and so did he, but he soon forgot that. After a few years of marriage, he wanted a son. They had two kids, both of them were girls. He grew frustrated with his wife. Instead of focusing on helping his growing family, he became infatuated with a young woman from across the street. One day, this man took this young lass out for a picnic by the Crystal Pond in the Chaldean Swamp. In a fit of lust, he tried to take advantage of her. Luckily for her, his wife had followed them to the pond. His wife stepped out from behind a tree with a wand made of oak and pointed it at her husband. He stopped trying to harm the younger woman to turn and laugh at his wife who was approaching him with a stick. What her husband didn't know was that his wife was descended from a witch from the Northern Convent and was trained in magic. With a flick of her wrist, she summoned a spell known as "The Specter's Curse." This spell killed her husband and cursed his soul to live forever in the Chaldean Swamp. His wife was a forgiving woman and allowed the young woman to live. Together, along with her daughters, they created the Southern Convent. Until those witches release the man's soul, his ghost is bound to the swamp, and he must obey the wishes and desires of the witches."

Jayden still felt confused, "I'm still not sure how that helps me."

Silvanus smacked him in the back of the head. "Boy, are you thick in the head? Were you paying attention at all during my story? You need to draw the ghost out, so he can take you to the Southern Convent. If you can get his attention you might have a shot, but, you will have to appear as unthreatening as possible. Do you have any pretty ladies traveling with you?"

"What kind of question is that?" Jayden replied.

The old dwarf smacked him in the back of the head. "My boy, it's always important to have a pretty lady by your side. If you can find any pretty ladies to take with you to the swamp, have them put on a white dress."

"Why?" Jayden asked.

"Because while that ghost must do the bidding of the witches, he is still a snake of a man, and the presence of a pretty woman might encourage him to show up. And you," he said, turning to Romeo, "you cannot enter the forest with him. Those witches are known to experiment and torture male dwarves. Jayden, I wish you luck. If you find *The Key*, you know where to find me."

Chapter 22
The Path of Least Resistance

Stepping out on to the dusty road, Jayden stared down at the old revolver in his hand. Silvanus had given him his old pistol name FireBrand. The gun looked impressive, but he couldn't quite figure out how it worked. The weapon was built on a revolver frame, but he couldn't see how you could load the weapon. The cylinder for the pistol was sealed so that you couldn't load any bullets in it. Since you can't put any bullets in it, maybe Silvanus used it as a club, he thought. So Jayden grabbed the handle and swung it around like a sword at Romeo. Romeo was not amused at this sudden change of events and decided to cock his shotgun.

Jayden rotated the weapon in his hand and tried to remember what Silvanus said about FireBrand. He was told that this gun possessed magical properties and in the hands of the right person, they would be able to access such power. Unfortunately, Jayden wasn't the right person; he was told to give this to someone he cared about and wanted to keep safe. Why couldn't he have the gun though? With a name called FireBrand, Jayden assumed it used elemental fire magic, and that happens to be his forte.

Spinning it around on his finger, he wondered how many battles this gun had seen, and how many more could it handle. The gun had been made for Silvanus by an Elder blacksmith who lived in the Freezing Mountains of Eden. The quality of the firearm exceeded any of the guns Jayden owned. He could feel the ancient power emanating from the weapon in his hand; he was beginning to understand why the Daimonia would seek such power.

Romeo and Jayden made their way down the street, toward the inn to catch up with the others. They heard a loud yell that made them jump, as they looked to see where it came from, they were both tackled to the ground by a short blonde dwarf.

"Jayden, we looked all over the place for you. We couldn't find where you had gone," Tammy yelled in his ear. Turning to her brother, she said, "you stubborn ass don't you ever walk away from me like that I again." Giving Romeo a big squeeze, her eyes widened with excitement, "Hey brother, did Jayden tell you our sister is alive. Cain helped her to escape."

Fighting to show any emotion, Romeo replied, "And you believed him? How do you know he didn't say that to get you to trust him."

Tammy huffed, "Can you stop being stubborn for once in your life, and be happy that our sister is still alive and has been set free?"

Jayden had to listen to the dwarves argue back and forth as they walked to the inn. Cain was sitting outside on the deck, sharpening his new sword with the sun setting in the background; the image seemed ominous. Jayden couldn't shake the feeling that Cain was still hiding something from him, but it was too late to change anything. It was his idea to bring Cain along this journey. Jayden knew that if they manage to find *The Key* or the treasure box it opens, he had to keep them as far away from Cain as possible.

He pushed open the door to the inn and was immediately impressed by it. At his feet was a small burgundy colored welcome mat and he was greeted by a beautiful elf with curly brown hair that stood behind the counter. She had a toothy smile, and her aura was pleasant. "My name is Colinda, and you must be Jayden. The rest of your friends are sitting in the living room by the fireplace."

The Dragon Warrior smiled and gave her a nod before heading into the next room. He was greeted by the sound of wood crackling and the smell of smoke coming from the fireplace. Cain followed after him and sat next to Sarah on the couch. Even though they had just entered the room, Cain seemed to be sneaking flirtatious glances at Sarah who didn't seem to mind the attention. General Floriana was relaxing in a recliner which rested in full view of the fireplace. Romeo and his sister chose to sit on the smaller couch, and Jayden was forced to take a seat on the rug.

Floriana cleared her throat and asked, "so Jayden what's our next move?"

"The plan is to go into the Chaldean Swamp and find a ghost who will guide us to the Southern Convent," he replied.

"A ghost? Jayden you can't be serious" Sarah said. Even Tammy looked bewildered by Jayden's statement. Cain seemed to be a little intrigued by what he said and stealthily placed his other arm around Sarah.

Before Jayden could let his jealousy consume him, Romeo stood up and said, "Jayden is right about what we need to do." He explained to all of them about their encounter with Silvanus.

Cain's interest quickly turned into skepticism, "Jade, you can't tell me that you believed the words of some random dwarf you met at a bar. I was hoping your information came from a more credible source. How could you trust someone so easily? How do you know he wasn't part of The Daimonia or the Eden government or even drunk."?

For a second Jayden began to doubt himself. Maybe Cain was right; maybe I was too quick to trust Silvanus. It is possible that the dwarf was sent there by someone and was provided with enough information about Jayden to get by. Using a dwarf to get Jayden to find *The Key* is just the type of thing they would do. Did I put my faith and trust in a drunk dwarf? Then he remembered the tears Silvanus fought back when talking about Jayden's mother and father. Those emotions were too real to be fake.

Jayden found his courage and said, "I chose to trust him for the same reason I've chosen to trust you."

"And what reason is that?" Cain asked with a hint of sarcasm.

"Faith" Jayden replied, "I have faith, and I have to be able to trust people to make it through this. That is why I trusted Silvanus, and that is why we will try his plan. Plus, I thought you said that The Daimonia hated dwarves?"

"I never said that," Cain replied. "The Daimonia have recruited many dwarves into their service over the years. It is true that The Daimonia have oppressed a few dwarves over the years, but they haven't oppressed all of them. Anyway, that's not what this is about. My issue Jayden is that you are trusting someone that you just met. Are you willing to risk the lives of the people you care about over what one person said?"

Cain's words hit Jayden like a ton of bricks. Since he left the Dragon Temple, he had been willing to risk his own life for the cause. Not once did he give much thought to the sacrifices that the others were making. He turned toward Floriana and realized that she has not only has risked her life for his, but she was willing to sacrifice her career for him.

Then he realized that he had taken Romeo and Tammy for granted too. Romeo stood up for him when he had every reason not to. Lastly, he looked at Sarah, even though she sat there leaning against Cain, he couldn't help but feel grateful that she decided to come on this journey at all. Even if she never fell for him, he was at least happy that she was around, and he couldn't ask her to give up more than she already had.

As took everything in, he found his voice again. "Honestly, I can't ask any of you to give up more than you already have for me.

The danger in simply traversing the swamp, coupled with trying to infiltrate the Southern Convent is too much of an undertaking for me to ask of you which is why I have decided to go to the swamp by myself."

Floriana rose from the recliner to go and stand over by Jayden. The stern look on her face reminded Jayden of the first time he met this female General from Eden. She pulled out her sword and placed it to Jayden's neck, and Floriana said, "don't you ever tell me what I can and cannot do with my life. I have given up my livelihood for you, so don't tell me that I can't join you on this potentially suicidal mission. There will be a cold day in hell before I let you go into that swamp alone. You understand?"

Jayden took a moment to appreciate the strong and beautiful woman, whose sword was touching his neck. He looked into Floriana's pretty brown eyes with her newly blonde hair tied into a braid and resting on her right shoulder. He now knew why she was so adamant about him not going on his own; she cared for him on a deeper level then he thought. It had taken him all this time to figure out that truth. He knew that trying to talk her out of going wouldn't work and talking Sarah out of going would have been equally difficult. So he decided to take the higher road and sneak out after they had gone to bed.

Putting on a fake smile, he said. "Fine. You win. You can go. I won't try and stop you."

"Ahem," Sarah said while giving him the death stare.

"You too" he muttered.

"Well, what about us Jayden? Can we still go"? Tammy asked in the sweetest tone of voice.

"Tammy, you should know that I wouldn't mind having you along. However, your brother knows why it might not be wise to bring you two along." Tammy pouted at this and ran over to her brother to find out why. Turning to Cain, Jayden said, "I also think it would be better for you to stay here."

Cain jumped to his feet, his eyes bulged with anger, "Why Jayden? Why can't I go with you? Have I not earned back your trust? Don't you remember that I was there for you when your mother died? I was your friend before you even met Sarah. If you think you can't trust me, you should ask yourself, how can you trust anyone else here?" Cain stomped out of the room and slammed the screen door heading out into the night.

"Way to go Jayden," Sarah said as she ran after Cain.

The others began to leave, as Jayden sat staring into the fireplace. He couldn't blame them for being mad at him. He didn't want them to give up more than they already had. Jayden wanted them to know that he cared for them, and in the end, he belittled them. Maybe they will be too mad even to want to help him.

***

The hours rolled by as he sat in that living room. He didn't even stop to check on Cain when he and Sarah came back. Somehow, he knew Cain might still be angry with him. He heard the sound of footsteps on the wooden floor. Waltzing into the room was Floriana in a T-shirt and gray sweats. She parked herself right next to him and rested her head on his shoulder.

"Hmm for a second, I was beginning to think the only outfits you had were either armor or camo. You don't look too bad, dressed like a normal person," he said.

She responded to his statement with an elbow to his rib, "admit it, I look good in sweats." Jayden's wide smile told her all she needed to know, "Now why all of a sudden are you concerned for our welfare? We have been traveling together for a while now and you never once asked us to absolve ourselves."

Before he could reply, she got up and moved to the couch. Jayden joined her and said, "Cain made a great point. I haven't thought much about the risk I was asking you all to take. The whole reason I started this journey was to find out who killed my father and I was going to make them pay. Things are different now; I'm not just after vengeance. I'm out to save the world. And you guys have come along for the ride. I never once considered the price that ride might cost."

"Well, that's sweet of you Jayden. You need not worry. We all picked up our swords knowing what it might cost in the end. I picked up my sword long ago. I have seen some terrible things as a soldier. I am fighting alongside you for the same reason I chose to serve, to make this world a better place," she replied

While trying to chew on the things she just said, he reached into his pocket and pulled out the pistol that Silvanus had given him. He spun it on his finger and said, "Silvanus gave me this pistol, it's called FireBrand. He told me to give this to someone that I care for and want to keep safe. So I have decided to give it to you."

Floriana was caught off guard by the gift that he was presenting her. As she held it in her hand, she was able to sense that this was no ordinary firearm. This sentiment caused her to place her arms around him and gave him a big kiss on the cheek.

Floriana felt confused, "but why would you give this to me? Why wouldn't you give this to Sarah?"

"Well mainly, because I don't know how to use it. Plus, she already has two guns, and you weren't able to bring any with you. Honestly, I'm giving this to you because I care for you and Sarah. The road ahead is uncertain, and I'm not sure how it will end for any of us. If something happens to me, I want you to use that gun to protect yourself and Sarah. I don't care if I lose my life. What I couldn't handle is either of you two getting hurt. And that is why I decided to give this to you." He watched as Floriana processed what he had just said. For a moment he could have sworn that she was fighting back the tears.

Then Sarah came rushing out of the hallway with tears in her eyes and she jumped on to the couch and wrapped her arms around him and Floriana. The couch teetered backward, and they all fell on to the floor laughing.

"What was all that about weirdo? You probably just broke the couch." Jayden laughed.

"Are you calling me fat?" Sarah replied as she crossed her arms.

Jayden shook his head, "No, no, no that's not what I meant," he said frantically.

"So you are saying that I'm the fat one and I broke the couch," Floriana said as she scooted to sit next to Sarah.

"You two are the worst, and no you aren't fat," he replied. "Sarah why did you come running in here like a crazy person."

She wrapped her arms around him again, "I heard what you said. That's the sweetest thing I've ever heard you say."

Jayden cocked his head to the side, "wait, so you tackled a couch because I gave her a gun? When did my life become a romantic comedy?"

"Since you got two hot babes like us hanging around you, am I right sista," Sarah said while fist bumping the blonde lady sitting next to her.

"You two are so weird. Anyways, I'm going to head to bed, big day tomorrow."

***

The time was about four in the morning when he decided to get up. He grabbed a pair of jeans and put on a black shirt. Grabbing his dagger, he placed it on his left hip and his dad's .45 on to his right hip. Then he picked up his magnum pistol, he slid it into the holster he had tucked under his shirt. After slinging his sword onto his back, he picked up his rifle from the bed then stared at his reflection in the mirror. With a grin on his face, he whispered, "I look like a badass."

Quietly he unlocked the window to his room and closed it behind himself. Pulling himself onto the roof, he walked to the other side of the building, where the chimney was. Slowly he climbed down the backside of the chimney until his feet touched the ground. He felt a gentle nudge against his hand, which gave him such a fright that he almost jumped out of his shoes. looking to his right, he noticed that it was one of the Tigladons. He petted the animal affectionately, and the large jungle cat licked his face. Such sweet animals he thought. When this is all over, I'm going to get me one.

The early morning was dark and cold. He was greeted by a light drizzle and a gentle breeze that was cold as ice. As he walked, cold moisture dripped down his face and he was beginning to regret not bringing a jacket. Large cicadas and crickets chirped and welcomed him on his morning stroll to the swamp. Red-eared coyotes howled as they chased down their prey in the darkness. Jayden found it strange that there could be such harmony of nature in a world filled with such disharmony. Maybe people could take a lesson from experiencing the peacefulness of nature. Would that make the world a better place, he wondered?

Jayden knew that he was starting to get closer to the swamp because the air around him was beginning to feel a little humid. Beads of sweat began to congregate on his forehead. The closer he got to the swamp, the more depressing the landscape became. Soon the broad fields of grass turned to patches of weeds. The bright greenery slowly changed into light browns and grays. Part of him wanted to turn back; he felt an increasing sense of dread as he reached the outskirts the swamp. Dark energy filled the air; he knew he had to cautious. The magic in this swamp was ancient and powerful.

Jayden realized that he had officially arrived at the swamp, not simply because of the awful smell, but because there was a sign that said, "Welcome to The Chaldean Swamp, the largest swamp in all of Terra." A couple centuries ago, this swamp was probably quite the tourist attraction. The sign looked as if at one point in time it used to be dark green. The green was now a faded gray, and the steel was bent and rusted.

The worst part wasn't the fading paint or the bullet holes it had in it, but the two skeletons hanging from it. Being the wise person Jayden was, he approached the skeletons to see if they were real. Breathing a deep sigh of relief, he realized that they were fake probably purchased from a party store or something. He was happy that at least someone in Chaldea had a sense of humor, albeit a twisted one at that.

Above him, the skies were gray and overcast. He turned to back examine the road he came in on. Then it became clear to him, that the overcast sky was only hanging above the swamp. The rest of the plains were bright and sunny. The power of the dark magic in the swamp able to the climate.

The temperature outside of the swamp averaged around seventy-five degrees. In the swamp, the temperature seemed to fluctuate between extreme heat and uncomfortably cold.

The swamp itself was about as pleasing to the eye as watching paint dry. The grass and weeds looked like they had died centuries ago and the trees were a chalky white. Scurrying across the path were white and gray bunnies with red eyes. His heart almost jumped into his throat when he tripped and landed right next to a three-foot long black rat. Luckily, it was as afraid of him as he was of it.

Jayden decided it would be best to walk around the outer rim of the swamp to get a sense of his barring. As he walked around the swamp, he tripped over a root for the sixth time and landed in a white thorn bush. His body burned as he picked the needles out of his body. The needles felt like a burning match on his fingertips.

Once he dusted himself off, he was approached by a small, thinning hyena. The animal's dark gray fur and brown spots were slowly fading from a lack of nutrition. The hyena opened its mouth to growl at him, and Jayden smiled and whispered a healing spell which caused the hyena to glow. Then he threw one of the sandwiches to the animal. That should help, he thought. The poor animals that live in the swamp deserve better.

Jayden made his way over a small hill and gazed down at a small pool of water. Initially, he wanted a sip until he got closer to it. He noticed that the water was black and thick like oil. The water bubbled and steamed, and a small green octopus emerged from the water to look at Jayden before quickly submerging again. How the animal wasn't boiled alive is beyond me, Jayden thought. He glanced up and spotted rivers of this hot boiling liquid which flowed towards the center of the swamp.

Jayden began moving toward the interior of the swamp, and he was starting to get the feeling that he was being watched. Pushing through some white thorn bushes, he entered a clearing. He knew something was watching him, but he couldn't tell what or who it might be.

Being alone in this swamp did not feel good. Maybe he should have stayed with the others because once they wake up, they will come searching for him anyway. That's when he realized that by sneaking out, he was encouraging them, even more, to come to the swamp. The truth was that he needed them more then they needed him. Silvanus told him to bring a pretty lady to get the ghost to reveal it's presence, yet here he was in the swamp without a pretty lady. Jayden was hoping the ghost might show up anyway, because, let's be honest, how often do pretty ladies wear white dresses and walk around creepy looking swamps?

Branches from the trees behind began snapping as something was stomping through the small forest. The ground beneath him shook, and birds frantically flew into the air to escape from the approaching terror. Jayden's heart was racing as he tried to imagine what could be coming his way. He wanted to look back, but he was frozen with fear. Even with all of his magical abilities and the weapons he had, he knew that he wasn't invisible. Escape was not going to be an option, he was going to have to stand his ground and hope for the best.

Two trees came crashing down as a large animal that looked a lot like a rhino entered the clearing. The creature's skin was the color of moss covered in brown spots. On top of the animal's head were three sharp horns and its mouth was filled with razor-sharp teeth. The animal had a round body and stood at just over six feet at the shoulder; hot steam oozed from its nostrils.

The creature's hooves pawed at the ground, and its large red eyes were fixed on Jayden. Slowly, he chambered a round into his rifle, placing his thumb on the safety. Generally, at this range, he would switch to one of his pistols, but he wasn't sure that the bullets would pierce its hide.

Once he flicked off the safety, the animal darted after him. The creature moved with such incredible speed that Jayden had to dive to his left at the last minute. As he rolled to his side, he landed on a sharp rock. He watched as the rhino spun back around and headed right toward him. The animal was so quick that he had to fire a shot without using the scope. When he got back on his feet, the rhino rushed him again and managed to butt him with one of his horns, launching Jayden into the air. He crashed on to the ground so hard the wind was knocked out him. His rifle was knocked out of his hands, and his torso had a small gash from the rhino's horn. He watched in horror as the animal licked its lips and drooled as it circled it's wounded prey.

Chapter 23
Taranis and the Lost Boy

Her chest was burning as they ran down the dirt road. When she woke up that morning, she was planning on having a pleasant breakfast. Instead, she had to run ten miles. Why you may ask? That morning Sarah had discovered that Jayden had ditched them before they had woken up. Now she was on the verge of having an asthma attack hoping that they will find him alive and once they did, she was going to strangle him for leaving.

Cain was running alongside her and seemed to be more focused on what was down the road, then anything surrounding them. His face looked tense, and she was wondering what must be going through his mind. When Jayden allowed Cain to join them, she was apprehensive about it at first. It wasn't until their trip on the Liberta that she felt able to trust him again. In all reality, it was nice to have a childhood friend traveling with them. Sarah lost a lot the day Eiréné was destroyed. Cain's presence made her feel safe.

"Are you worried about him?" She asked.

"Huh?" Cain said, with a confused look on his face.

"Didn't you hear me? I said, are you worried him?" She replied.

"Worried about who?" He asked. Sarah shook her head in frustration, "Jayden? Who did you think I was talking about? Is your head in the clouds?"

Cain shrugged, "I'm sorry, my mind was on something else, and no I am not too worried about that."

What else could he be thinking about? During the previous night, she spent some time alone with him chatting and learned how the destruction of Eiréné almost destroyed him. How he felt like he owes Jayden, and her, his life for the small part he played in its destruction. She also was able to gather that he didn't enjoy being part of The Daimonia as much as he let on, but they treated him like family. His only regret was not appreciating the parents that adopted him as much as he should have. Since their talk, Sarah was able to see why Jayden would want to give him a second chance.

"It must be difficult for you to be carrying so much guilt," she said.

He replied, "It sure makes it difficult for me to look in the mirror and not hate myself for what I have done." As Cain finished his statement, he sped up to run alongside General Floriana. That girl has some power over the boys. They always seem to gravitate towards her eventually, Sarah thought. First Tony, then Jayden, and now Cain, I don't know how she does it. If Romeo's not careful, he could be next. She chuckled at the thought of that dwarf trying to keep up with Floriana who seemed to enjoy running.

Once the swamp was visible on the horizon, Sarah had a feeling that she was going to hate it. She had never really been the biggest fan of camping and being a part of a search and rescue party in a swamp seemed like it would be even worse.

The skies above were blanketed with gray clouds that were slowly getting darker. Thunder rumbled amongst the clouds while lighting filled the sky with a brilliant light. The rain started to come down as a light drizzle, and the wind began to pick up as it rustled against the trees.

Despite the rain, General Floriana and the others continued to examine the ground intently which to Sarah found to be quite amusing to watch. She knew that they were trying to track Jayden, but she had no idea how to track or even what to look for.

The rain began coming down in sheets. They continued to search for hours on end and found nothing. Sarah was starting to understand why the Southern Convent would use this swamp to set up shop; it was the most depressing place on earth. The few animals she saw were wary and seemed to keep their distance which was good because she didn't like the idea of having to fight in the rain.

Thirty minutes later the rain started to let up, and the clouds began to clear. Unfortunately, that's when an icy gust of wind started to blow. The cold chill from the wind sliced through their wet clothes like a knife. Despite the cold, General Floriana continued to look frantically at the ground for even the smallest clue of Jayden's whereabouts. Sarah was utterly impressed by the sheer determination of this blonde haired General from Eden.

Whatever was driving Floriana to look for Jayden with such conviction was difficult for Sarah to understand. Floriana was searching for someone that she barely knew as if her life depended on it. What kind of friend am I? Here I am worried about being cold while she is risking getting sick to find Jayden. If something terrible happened to Jayden, Sarah knew it would destroy her.

Cain, being the magical genius he was, started a fire to warm everyone up. Which for most people would be very difficult to do, seeing as all the branches were soaked from the rain. Cain created a fire using powerful magic, but not just any magic, he summoned a black fire.

As the black flames danced across the logs and broken branches, Sarah noticed that the dwarves refused to get close to the dark flames. Tammy had an anxious look on her face as she stared

J. Edwards

at Cain and then back at the fire. Romeo seemed to tense up, and his face turned scarlet red with anger, "How dare you summon that sorcery in our presence and in this cursed swamp no less. Why don't you grab a megaphone and announce our presence?"

Cain was focusing on the fire and keeping it lit; he acted as if Romeo had not said a word.

Romeo's lightly tanned skin turned bright as he became inpatient. "Hey, you with the long black hair! I'm talking to you. How can you sit there and casually summon the black fire as if it's nothing? How twisted is your soul?"

Cain looked up at him with no expression on his face, "it's more twisted then you will ever know. Plus, I had to do something. We can't be walking around here with our clothes soaked. If any of you got sick, it would be all over but the crying. The nearest hospital is in Chaldea and it looks like you would die of an infection just coming in the door."

"Hey, guys calm down. I don't get what the big deal is. Jayden can summon fire too. Are you going to get mad at him also?" Sarah interjected.

"The difference is that he summoned the dark flame. That's a type of Chaos magic." Tammy said nervously.

"I still don't get the difference," Sarah said feeling utterly confused.

Poking a stick into the fire, Cain turned to her and said, "Chaos magic is a type of magic that is only used to cause harm. The fire spells that Jayden summons are designed to hurt and injure a person, so they won't try to continue fighting. They hurt enough to get the point across. The black flames are intended to hurt and kill someone. In fact, this spell is one of a few fire spells, that can actually hurt a fire user. This is probably one of the few occasions that the black flames have been used to help save lives and not take them. But thank you, Romeo, for pointing out my folly. Next time it rains, we can walk around in wet clothing and see who get pneumonia first."

"Why you mouthy son of a... "Romeo shouted before his sister put her hand over his mouth.

"Brother calm down, it's obvious that Cain is just looking out for us. Thank you for that Cain, I think this is a very nice fire" Tammy said as she scooted to sit next to Sarah.

She was right Sarah thought. The fire was pretty nice; it was most definitely a different breed of magic than what Jayden used. Just sitting near the black flames for a few minutes her clothes dried rapidly. In some sense, the flames were too hot. The intense heat made her wonder how often Cain would have used this spell. What frightened her the most about it was that this spell could be used against Jayden. She shook her head; there is no way that Cain would use this on him.

From off in the distance, they heard someone yell. Sarah quickly wheeled around to see where the noise had come from. She waited until she heard it again, glancing at a grove of trees she saw Floriana come running. The General from Eden waved at them to follow her. Sarah suddenly felt a burst of excitement and jumped up to run after her.

While Sarah ran after the Eden General, she began to wonder if Floriana had found Jayden. If she had, why wasn't he with her? Could he be injured? Or is he just hiding and planning to scare them? Or could it be something even worse?

With her head filling up with doubts, Sarah sped up and pushed through a grove of trees. She immediately noticed that something was odd about this grove of vegetation. This small forested area looked as if something big had smashed through there recently. Splintered and crushed branches littered the ground in front of her, and small trees were bent over as if something big and powerful had pushed through them. If something this large could cause this much destruction, Sarah didn't want to imagine what it could do to Jayden.

General Floriana was standing off in a clearing. She waved at Sarah to catch up. She was staring at the ground for some reason, "Do you see it? Tell me that you see it?" Floriana asked, with a tone in her voice that made her sound a little crazy.

Sarah examined the ground, and all she could see were weeds and rocks. She shook her head and replied, "no, I don't see anything."

"Look closer, tell me you see it." Floriana gestured toward a patch of crabgrass, with a crazed look on her face.

Sarah was beginning to think that Floriana was having an episode, so she decided to play it off cool and shrugged her shoulders and said, "ahh yes I do see it. It looks awesome; I can't believe it was right here all along" that may have sounded a little more sarcastic then she intended it to be.

Shaking her head, Floriana said, "you're impossible." She bent over and picked up something from the ground and shoved it in Sarah's face, and then it clicked. In Floriana's hand was rifle shell that had specks of blood on it. Her eyes widened as she was processing this new information, she stared down at the weeds where Floriana was pointing.

The blades of grass that brushed up against her skin had a scarlet red tint to them which meant only one thing, Jayden was hurt. Suddenly, she was running around the clearing searching for more evidence of the battle with the hopes that they would lead to Jayden.

Lying on the ground beneath a patch of crabgrass, was an empty magazine for a pistol with some shells lying next to it. Whatever chaos took place here must have been intense for Jayden to have to use his rifle and one of his pistols. She discovered another clip ten yards away only this one had been crushed by something large and heavy. On what remained of the clip there were small traces of blood on it, the blood was still wet, which meant he had here recently.

Her frustration was getting the best of her. She couldn't believe that he could be so selfish and arrogant to think he could handle this swamp by himself. I mean, how many times have I visited him in the hospital over the last couple months?

"Ouch!" Sarah yelled as she hit the ground hard. Sarah was so busy being frustrated, that she wasn't paying attention and tripped over a large object. Sarah winced as streams of blood began dripping from her knee. She glanced down to see what she had tripped on, and she couldn't believe her eyes. Sarah was speechless, as she stared at a creature that filled her with pure terror. She felt numb, she couldn't move, and it was hard to breathe. Sarah felt glued to the spot where she stood, this monster was something straight out of a horror film.

It took a gentle nudge from Floriana for Sarah to find her voice again, "do you see what I'm seeing?" Sarah asked.

General Floriana nodded, "I have never seen something like this before. It looks like a rhino, but I've never seen one with teeth like that. This thing is huge."

Laying down amongst the weeds and grass was a large animal that looked a lot like a rhino. The creature's body was covered in scars from bullet holes to cuts from a sword or a dagger, and there were some burns on its hide. Most of the injuries looked superficial, however, some of them were deep enough to be fatal. On the animal's largest horn, they noticed some blood stains that were not from the creature itself. This was a gruesome scene to behold, but as they stood over the dead animal, they were slowly beginning to piece together what may have happened to Jayden.

"They call it a Tryno," Romeo said as he tried to squeeze between Sarah and Floriana to look at the creature. "It looks like Jayden gave this Tryno one hell of a fight. Bringing one of these down by yourself is very hazardous to your health. These animals are omnivores like the Tigladons only they are a lot more aggressive. Their tough hides are almost impossible to pierce. If Jayden walked away from this fight he did so limping, let's hope there weren't any more of them nearby."

Both girls knew he was right which made it a tougher pill to swallow. At any moment they were expecting Jayden to pop up from amongst the trees or jump out of one of the small ponds, but instead of being embraced by his warm spirit they were greeted by the uncomfortable silence of the Chaldean swamp.

Tammy discovered something that was only a couple of yards away from the Tryno. She picked up the item from the ground and let out a sob. She whimpered, "come and take a look at this."

In her hand was a black T-Shirt that was covered in mud and dirt. There were two holes in the shirt, one was near the collar, and the other was in the center of the shirt. The fabric was stained with blood. Sarah grabbed the shirt, and the smell of Jayden's cheap cologne still radiated from the T-Shirt.

This was the undeniable truth that Jayden had been here and fought this Tryno. If the animal made the holes in this shirt, then there was no way he walked away, and that fact hit her like a ton of bricks. She fell to her knees and began to weep into the shirt. Floriana plopped down right beside her and placed her arm around Sarah. Even for the great General Floriana, it was difficult to stop the tears from flowing.

Feeling overcome with emotion, Sarah got up and walked away from the group. She didn't care where she went; she just wanted to be away from here. Images of Jayden collapsing in this swamp from his wounds played over and over in her mind. If she could see his smile and hold him one more time that would be enough. The thought of him dying all alone on this cursed plot of land was too much for her to bare.

As Sarah walked, she passed by a river with water as black as oil. Intense heat radiated from the stream, hot steam and bubbles breached the surface. She followed the river, and it led her into an area of thick vegetation. Large vines and moss hung from the trees, and white rose bushes with six inch long thorns covered the path. One of the thorns managed to scrape her as she brushed up against it and even though her arm bled. She didn't care and just kept on going.

The deeper she went into the swamp, the more the scenery changed. The trees seemed to become larger and greener. The air in the swamp started to feel cooler and less humid. A light fog was beginning to build as she moved toward the center of the swamp. Before too long, the fog was as thick as a blanket and Sarah could not even see her hand in front of her. She tried to turn back around, but her body just wouldn't listen. Her lack of control made her feel very afraid. Whatever magic was controlling her was strong and malevolent.

Her hair blew into her face as she picked up speed from being pulled by an invisible force. She passed by tree after tree in a matter of seconds. The path in front of her looked like a blur. She felt like she was sitting in the front seat of a rollercoaster. Before she could pass out from moving so fast, she came to a sudden stop. Her stop came so abruptly that her equilibrium was thrown entirely off course. Sarah's world was spinning around so much that she leaned over and lost her lunch.

When some color had returned to her face, and her world stopped spinning like a Ferris wheel, she looked around to see where she was. Sarah found herself alone in a clearing. It was dark, and the only light she could see came from a nearby pond.

A bright light from beneath the water's surface bathed its banks with a luminescent glow. Swimming in the crystal clear waters were fish of every size and color. Red alligators rested under lily pads, and they weren't as big as the ones she had seen on television; they were about the size of a sheepdog. The vast array of fauna in the pool of water wasn't even the best part of it. Resting along the bottom of the pond were rows of precious jewels. There were emeralds and sapphires, platinum and gold. The jewels rested on a bed of rocks that were made of pure crystal. Sarah was beginning to wish she had brought along her scuba gear; diving into this pond would make her a rich lady.

A light bulb clicked on in her head, and she realized where she was. Sarah was standing next to the Crystal Pond. This was the place that Silvanus had talked about in his story, which meant it must be mostly true, minus the ghost part. Since they've been in the swamp all day, she had yet to see anything close to a ghost, a zombie, or anything of that nature.

Sarah felt parched and wanted to wash her face, so she got down on her knees and scooped up some cold water. When the cool liquid hit her lips, her thirst was quenched instantly. The water from this pond was the best she had ever tasted. Sarah splashed it against her face, and she immediately felt less woozy and more energized. She took another scoop, and as she did so, the light underneath the pond flickered and became dim. Her heart began to beat faster as she took a nervous gulp of the water.

She sipped another handful of water, and then she heard the sound of weeds being trampled by foot behind her. Sarah shook her head; it's nothing she told herself. I'm alone in this clearing. There is nothing to worry about. Then she heard a tree branch snap and almost jumped out of her shoes. She wheeled around and saw nothing in the clearing, and the footsteps stopped. Breathing a sigh of relief, she returned to try and take another drink of water, and that's when she felt a cold hand touch her shoulder, and then a quiet voice whispered in her ear, "Sarah."

Sarah was so frightened that she jumped out her shoes and landed in the pond. Now that her clothes were all wet, she looked up at the banks of the pond, and there was no one there. Chills crawled down her spine as she recalled the cold hand touching her shoulder. Sarah wanted to run and scream for help, but she had no idea where she was and let's face it, screaming probably wouldn't help either.

Sarah climbed out of the pond, sat down on a rock, and began putting her shoes on. Out of the corner of her eye, she saw something moving on the other side of the pond. There was a dark shadowy figure playing among the reeds. What scared her the most, was the fact that the shadow wasn't making a sound. She watched as the shadow jumped into the water and the figure made ripples as it broke the surface. The absence of splashing sound made her heart beat like a drum in her chest. At this point, she knew that either she was going deaf or she must be going crazy. How can something jump into the water without creating a sound?

For a moment Sarah thought she could hear the sound of someone breathing right behind her. She looked around, and there was no one there. Goosebumps began to form on her arms, as the air around her became colder than the inside of a freezer. She was hoping she was having a mental break and everything she was experiencing was all in her head.

Sarah shook her head; please tell me this isn't happening. Tell me this a very elaborate nightmare. She covered her eyes out of fear, and then she heard a blood-curdling scream. Within half a second, she jumped to her feet and quickly pulled out one of her machine pistols. Her hands shook violently as she scanned the dark waters of the Crystal Pond. Her jaw dropped when she saw the shadowy figure approaching her from the other side of the pond. Her heart was pounding in her chest, and her mind was yelling at her body to run. While she watched the shadow gliding across the large pond, she became exceedingly alarmed as the water beneath it grew darker and started to boil.

The shadow stopped at the edge of the pond and gazed upon her. Light from the moon pierced through the clouds above revealing the ghostly figure floating above the pond. His body was a pale grey as it shimmered in the light. The specter's eyes were a pale blue, and his hair was short and combed to the side. He was dressed in a nice overcoat that he must have worn the day he died. The ghost had broad shoulders and large, powerful hands. His height was difficult to judge as he was missing the rest of his body from the knee down but, judging by his build, she gathered that in life he was probably just under five feet. Analyzing the ghost a little more, she noticed he had a similar facial structure to Romeo and Tammy he must have been a type of dwarf when he was alive.

At that moment, she understood why the Southern Convent might not be the biggest fans of male dwarves. The creepy smile he had on his face, and all of the theatrics he put on made it clear to her that his ghost was a jackass.

The closer he got, the more she wanted to run and hide. She wasn't quite sure what a ghost could do to her, but she had seen enough scary movies to know that ghosts can be mean. And considering the story she heard about this specter, she knew he was not the kind of person to let your guard down around.

Sarah gulped down her fear and raised her machine pistol at him. "Don't you come any closer!" she yelled with all the courage that she could muster which wasn't much. His creepy smile turned into a maniacal laugh. Well, I guess that means he's daring me to shoot him, she thought. She flicked her machine pistol to fire in bursts, squeezed the trigger and let off three rounds.

Just as the bullets past through the ghost, it disappeared, and all she could hear was a gentle splash as the rounds hit the water. Great, she thought. I scared away the ghost. Whose help I do actually need

As quickly as the ghost disappeared, he reappeared right in front of her. His sudden appearance made her scream. "You aren't the sharpest tool in the shed, are you? I'm a ghost woman; did you really think bullets would hurt me?" He asked in a snarky tone.

Sarah felt accosted at the insult, "excuse me? How dare you talk to me that way!"

"How dare you enter my swamp without permission? I am Taranis the Cursed One, the swallower of souls, and you look like my next victim. I'm hoping your soul is better than your taste in clothing. I remember when ladies used to come into my swamp in white, flowy dresses. Those women I would let live for a short time, but you I will consume."

Again, Sarah felt wholly insulted by this stupid dwarf, shaped ghost. She had just about enough of his nonsense. Taranis opened his gaping mouth to consume her soul, and Sarah smiled as she looked him dead in the eye and yelled, "Repel!"

A ball of blue light slammed into the ghost knocking him back towards the pond. Then she flicked her hand like she was holding a whip and yelled, "Ensnare!" Suddenly blue chords of energy wrapped around the ghost and started to squeeze him, which caused him to howl in pain.

"You are going to apologize to me for that comment!" Sarah yelled as she snapped her fingers, which caused the chords to wrap around the ghost even tighter, "You will take my friends and me to the Southern Convent. You will not give us an ounce of trouble or else I will make this Ensnare permanent, do we understand each other?"

"Yes, ma'am," Taranis replied with a struggle.

"And?" She said with a hand on her hip.

The ghost bowed his head, "I'm sorry for making fun of your outfit."

Sarah gave him a brilliant smile, "now that's more like it. See, if you were that nice in the first place and not trying to turn my day into a living nightmare you wouldn't be in this predicament."

Chapter 24
The Wicked Witches of the South

In the blink of an eye, they were consumed by a brilliant light. The light that surrounded them was warm and comforting as a blanket. General Floriana woke up and found herself staring up at a beautiful night sky. Bright lights streaked across the sky as they bore witness to a lovely meteor shower. The stars glittered in the night changing colors as the seconds went by, from neon green to yellows and reds. Watching the stars change color made her wonder if she was in some dream. Sitting up, she looked around and saw that the others were laying down nearby. Getting to her feet, she wiped off the dust that was on her clothes that she had picked up from the cobblestone street they were sitting on. She quickly roused the other, and they all had a bewildered look on their faces.

"Where are we?" Tammy cried

"Does anyone remember how we got here?" Cain asked.

They glanced at each other, and they all shook their heads no. Great, Floriana thought, one minute we were following this dwarf spirit and the next they are waking up on some random road.

The General wanted to get her bearings. She looked to the east of their location there were acres of blue grass spread across a series of rolling hills. A hundred yards behind them was a large vineyard filled with green and white grapes. About a half a mile north, the cobblestone road led them to a small village. In the center of the village was a large castle which was surrounded by a moat. The Eden General was beginning to think they had entered into a fairytale as they decided to walk towards the castle.

Floriana led them to the village. She was impressed by the unique culture of this magical town. The small town was relatively modern in some ways, and in other ways, it was relatively old-fashioned. Many of the residents they passed traveled around on horse-drawn carriages, while others rode bikes and Segways.

What really blew her mind was the population of this village. There were so many people living in this small town that it was as if all the former residents of Chaldea decided to pack their bags and move into the Southern Convent. She was expecting to see women walking around wearing pointy hats and riding on broomsticks. It was quite the contrary; she witnessed people wearing the same types of clothes that she had in her closet

The people in town were quite pleasant, with many of them waving as they passed by. A flirtatious young man ran up to give the girls flowers, and a nice young lady even slipped Cain her phone number. The reception they received from the residents was unbelievable; they seemed to be just as accepting as the elves were at the Water Temple.

The young General was feeling a little confused by the harmony and sweet nature of this community. When she was training for the military, they warned her to be very cautious around witches, especially those of the Southern Convent. She was amazed by the witches and wizards that were using their magic for entertaining their kids, instead of using it for murder and mayhem. Everything she was told about this community was the opposite of what she was seeing.

Snap out of it, she told herself. This place cannot be as good as it seems, or could it be? In a way, the level of community they were experiencing, would make anyone want to live here. There has to be something more to this place; there is no way it could be this perfect.

They approached the moat, and Tammy rushed towards the water's edge. Her face was beaming as a pair of yellow dolphins breached the surface. The animals nuzzled her, and she petted them gently. She giggled as more dolphins came to greet her. Romeo made it to the edge of the water and accidentally pushed his sister into the water. She smiled as the dolphins came up to examine this blonde headed dwarf.

Floriana crouched down as she petted one. This was the closest she had ever been to a dolphin. These are some pleasant and amazing creatures, she thought. Cain sat down next to her and appeared to be as interested in them.

"You've been a little standoffish lately. What's the deal?" She asked.

"I don't quite know." Cain murmured, "part of it is that I'm concerned for Jayden's safety; the other part I don't quite have figured out. This place is amazing though. It makes you want to question all the things you've been told about the Southern Convent, doesn't it?"

Floriana didn't quite know how to answer that. She had read the reports about violent acts of aggression caused by alleged members of this Convent. Spending the last couple of minutes in their heartland was making those facts harder and harder to believe.

The sound of metal creaking brought them back into focus. A drawbridge descended and a small procession of witches, wizards and knights came out to greet them. A man in a navy blue three-piece suit stepped out from amongst the medieval looking crowd. He appeared to be a man in his fifties, his brown hair was slicked back, and they could smell his cinnamon scented cologne from the other side of the drawbridge. He bowed before them and said, "Welcome, welcome my name is Peter, and you all are our honored guests. We have been looking forward to your arrival. Would you honor us by having a meal and meeting with Lady Clara and the High Council?"

"How did you know that we were going to be here?" Cain asked sternly.

Peter smiled back at him, "Well Taranis told us he brought you here and your friend informed us that you might be arriving here shortly."

"Jayden's here? He's alive? Where is he? How did he get here?" Sarah asked earnestly.

Peter yawned, "calm down, calm down. He is here and alive."

"Where is he? We would like to see him," Floriana interjected.

"Well, come have dinner, and we will discuss your friend." Without waiting for them to respond, Peter and the rest of the precession walked back towards the castle.

With a hint of caution, they followed after them. The draw bridged creaked as they walked across it. The guard towers surrounding the castle were protected by soldiers carrying assault rifles and crossbows with explosive tipped arrows. This military presence made Floriana feel quite uneasy.

An iron gate slowly lifted as they entered the castle, sharpened spikes protruding from its base. Those spikes locked into the ground when the gate was shut, however they did serve as a warning for all who might enter the castle.

When they entered the front courtyard, there was a path that split in three directions. Patches of grass and rose bushes separated the paths and filled the courtyard with a sweet aroma. A young woman with platinum colored hair approached them from the central path. She was wearing a violet colored robe which glittered as she walked. She signaled for them to follow her.

Along the path, there was a fountain that depicted images of witches standing triumphantly on top of a globe. A little full of themselves, Floriana thought, but I guess if you were able to hide a place as brilliant as this with just a few enchantments, maybe you have right to think a little more highly of yourself.

The one thing she found most interesting about the statues they walked past was that some of the statues depicted males with magical abilities in a positive light. Based on the story that Silvanus had told Jayden she assumed the witches here were all dwarf hating feminists.

The young woman led them to a set of large black doors that opened on their own and granted them entrance to the Great Hall. Chefs dressed in white uniforms greeted them with silver plates containing hors d'oeuvres from all of over the world. Each bite of the small appetizers filled her body with a sense of warmth and joy. A waiter wearing a white button-up shirt with black pants handed her a glass of sparkling wine. She took a few sips from her glass, and it magically refilled itself. Immediately a big smile pursed her lips; this is the best glass ever she thought. I wonder if they wouldn't mind me keeping it.

When Floriana drained her glass for the second time, they stepped into a dining hall that was literally a life changing experience. From the moment she entered the room, the smell of her most favorite foods filled her nostrils. Pleasant memories of meals past filled her mind.

The marble table at which they were to sit was shaped like a T. Sitting at the cross-section of the table were the 13 members of the High Council, six of them, men, the rest, women. The woman sitting at the center of the council, Floriana assumed, must be Lady Clara. If Lady Clara had been standing she would have been about six foot, her long, dark, red hair was tied up into a ponytail that hung over her shoulder. She had on a gold necklace with the symbol of a black tiger hanging from it and resting on her table within an arm's reach was her wand. The wand was painted silver and hanging on her belt was a dagger. Her facial expression appeared calm, but

Floriana got the feeling that Lady Clara could go from calm to violent in a matter of seconds.

Lady Clara did not wait for them to get settled into their seats and jumped straight into business. She tapped her wand against her champagne glass to get everyone's attention, "ahem" she said as she cleared her throat, "to our honored guests, on behalf of the Members of the Southern Convent and all of the residents living here in Paradiso, we welcome you." Raising her glass, she took a sip of her champagne, and took a quick glance at Cain and smiled. She snapped her fingers and instantly everyone's most favorite foods appeared on their plates. "Soups on," she said with a sly grin. "While you all eat, let us have a small chat and tackle the issues at hand. My initial question to you is why did you come to my swamp?"

"We came here looking for my friend, I mean, our friend Jayden. He snuck out of the inn we were staying at last night, and we came here looking for him." Sarah answered, "Is he really here? Is he okay?"

"That is quite unfortunate. You all must be great friends to be willing to risk your lives for him. He is safe by the way, for now." She replied.

"What do you mean for now? You aren't planning on harming him are you?" Cain interjected.

Lady Clara took another sip of her sparkling wine and put on a cruel smile, "Of course we aren't planning on harming him. Although, we would be well within our right to do so. Your friend was caught hunting and poaching one of the Trynos living in our swamp. Hunting animals in our swamp without a permit is illegal. A price must be made for this infraction."

Cain laughed sarcastically, "so what? You want money?" Reaching into his pocket, he threw platinum and gold coins onto the table. "There take it and release our friend."

J. Edwards

Lady Clara's pale skin turned almost violet as her extreme anger became apparent, "don't you ever insult us with your petty cash. The taking of a life is a price that no amount of money can repay. What I want is the truth, and so far I haven't received it. You cannot tell me that you came here armed to the teeth, just to simply admire our swamp. Provide me with an appropriate answer, and your friend just might get released."

Just as she finished her statement, Jayden entered the room in shackles. He had a bruise under his eye and a cut lip. Under the orange jumpsuit, he was wearing, some bandages wrapped around his torso. He looked gaunt as if had gone weeks without food.

"What did you do to him?" Floriana, yelled as she got to her feet.

With a flick of her wand, Lady Clara forced Floriana back into her seat. "My lady, don't you make another outburst like that again. Please be civil. We have done nothing to your friend. He wanted us to make him look roughed up when you got here. He said it would give him street cred."

Sarah rolled her eyes at him and said, "You're an idiot."

Lady Clara flicked her wand again which made Jayden's body morph back to normal, and his prison garb became a white T-shirt and a pair of blue jeans. "Now tell me why you all came here. I will not ask again," she demanded.

Sarah responded by sharing the story of the adventure with all who were present. She shared the heartbreaking story of how Eiréné was destroyed, and how they all ended up on this journey to find *The Key*. Many of the members sitting on the council nodded, while others wiped tears from their eyes. Lady Clara sat their stone-faced. When Sarah mentioned that they were searching for Lady Grace of the Aggeloi, Lady Clara became increasingly interested in her story.

A wizard in green robes whispered in Lady Clara's ear, and she shot him a quick look that said I've got this handled. "Your story is very intriguing. If it is true, we might be able to help you. However, I am a little curious as to why you would travel with a member of the Daimonia when they are the sole reason for the destruction of your hometown, and the loss of your families." The whole group became silent after her statement. Tension filled the air as the others didn't quite know how to answer the question.

The awkward silence was getting on Romeo's nerves. Finding his voice, he turned towards the council and said, "To be honest Lady Clara, I'm not quite sure. But Jayden believes in giving people second chances, and I trust his judgment. Therefore we are giving Cain a chance to redeem himself. Plus, if Cain breaks that trust, I get to break his neck."

"A chance at redemption and breaking someone's neck, you all are quite an unusual bunch. Thank you for your input, Master Dwarf," she replied.

Lady Clara snapped her fingers and Jayden's shackles disappeared, and she instructed him to have a seat at the table. Before she had even finished her instructions, Jayden rushed to the table and began to scarf down fries and chicken nuggets.

"Jayden you don't have to eat so fast," Sarah said.

"Thanks, mom, I will keep that in mind for next time," he replied sarcastically which caused her to kick him under the table.

"Ms. Clara, why were you so nice to my brother? I thought you all didn't like dwarves?" Tammy asked ever so sweetly

With a toothy grin, the red-haired witch replied, "My dear, you can't believe everything you've been told about us. Contrary to popular belief we aren't bigots or male hating feminists. Some of the earliest members of the Southern Convent were dwarves and male wizards. The story about Taranis took place long after the Southern Convent was established. He just happened to have made the mistake of trying to harm a lady in our swamp."

As Floriana struggled to finish eating the biggest sundae she had ever seen, three prison guards entered the room escorting a young woman who was wearing a black jumpsuit similar to the one Jayden had been wearing. The young lady's hair was black with red tips, the same shade of red that Lady Clara had. Her eyes were a royal blue and on her left forearm was a tattoo of an angel with a broken wing. Her expression was intense, and her fists were clenched.

"For those of you who may not know, this is Lady Grace of the Aggeloi. Please forgive her attire as she's had a rough time the last couple of weeks. She will help guide you all to where you need to go." As she was talking, the guards released Lady Grace who walked over and sat in the chair next to Jayden. Jayden nudged her flirtatiously, which led to her punching him in the side. "As you can see Jayden and Grace have already become acquainted with one another. You do need to be careful while you are traveling with her. She can get a little rambunctious at times. You will be traveling by StarDoor to your next location. You are to find *The Key* and bring it to me is that understood?"

Sheepishly, Tammy replied, "But why, Ms. Clara?"

The witch smiled warmly back at Tammy and replied, "Because I let your friend live, *The Key* is the price for his life and your freedom. If any of you have a problem with that, I will have young Jayden killed right here in your presence." At this statement, they all stood up, except for Grace and Jayden who were both happily chowing down on some spaghetti and meatballs.

Breaking the awkward silence, Jayden said, "It's okay you can have *The Key*." Everyone turned to him with varying expressions of anger and frustration on their faces. Glancing at all of them he shrugged and said, "It's not worth losing my life over. I'm grateful to be out of those chains, and I will be grateful to be rid of that stupid Key. She can have it."

"Well I know it's late, but it's time for you all to start on your journey again. One final thing before you go." She pointed her index right at Cain, "You may not under any circumstances join them. You are to remain here until they return."

Floriana wasn't surprised Lady Clara didn't want Cain to join them. Like most people, she didn't trust him. It must be utterly humiliating for him to be treated like that. She really wanted to stand up and defend him, but it would have been of no use. The most challenging part of Cain's road to redemption hasn't come from seeking forgiveness, but in rebuilding trust and creating a new identity. General Floriana knew a little something about creating a new identity. Her hair was now blonde and in a ponytail. She was even beginning to wear her armored uniform less often in favor of more traditional clothes. The soldier she had been was slowly adapting to her new mission. She was beginning to wonder if she would ever be able to go back to wearing the fatigues and leading soldiers on the battlefield as she once had.

When Floriana took her last bite of her sundae, Lady Grace stood up and beckoned them to follow her to the castle's basement. Typically, she would have resisted following anyone into a basement. In fact, she was surprised how willingly their band of miscreants was to walk down into the dark depths of the castle.

They were forced to climb down ten flights of stairs to get to the basement because the elevator was out of order. The steps creaked and moaned as they walked. It was as if the stairs themselves were advising them to take the risk of riding the broken elevator.

Before they were even halfway to the bottom, Floriana was starting to contemplate just falling down the rest of the stairs. The Eden General had never been a fan of stairs. During her boot camp training, they would make her run up and down stadium stairs all day. Ever since those days, she made a personal vow to use an elevator whenever possible. She was flabbergasted that in this castle full of wizards and witches, they couldn't find one spell to fix the elevator.

General Floriana breathed a sigh of relief when they reached the final set of steps. Her clothes were drenched in sweat, and she decided that she would never climb a set of stairs again up or down. Her body was burning up from going down ten flights of stairs, so she whispered a cold weather spell to let her body relax.

The basement was dimly lit, and the few lightbulbs that were working flickered sporadically. Floriana was following behind Lady Grace, who was guiding them down a hall. On each side of the hall, there were hundreds of doors which led to God knows where. The guards opened a door on their right that had a sign above it that said, "Do Not Enter." Behind the door was another set of stairs, these set of steps were made of bronze.

Once they reached the bottom, they entered a large open room, and it was at that moment the guards left them. Grace led them into the room, and the others followed her cautiously. Something about this room didn't sit well with Floriana. She wasn't very comfortable with following a girl that had been introduced to them wearing iron shackles. Lady Grace was a troublemaker, that much to was clear.

Looming above them was a twelve-foot round door. It was covered in dark blue paint, and bright stars were spread across the door. The door looked entrancing like the evening sky. Floriana touched the door. It felt ice cold which was weird because the room felt really warm.

Jayden turned to Grace and said, "so what are we supposed to do here? And where does this door go?"

"We go through the door so that it will take us somewhere else. That's how doors work, Jayden," she replied in a snarky tone.

Grace reached for the door and touched a large star in the center of the door. The star began to glow a bright red, and she whispered into it and said, "Terracina." As the words left her mouth, the sound of a great wind filled the room. Floriana felt her body being pulled towards the door. She tried digging her heels into the ground to fight it, but it was impossible. She sped toward the door and put her arms up to cover her face, and then it all went black.

Chapter 25
Troll and Trouble

His body felt warm and relaxed. The type of relaxation that comes from laying in your own bed curled up with a freshly dried blanket. He felt like he was caught up in an amazing dream, and he half expected to hear an alarm go off or his dad banging on his door to wake him up. Instead, he was greeted by the beautiful morning light. Normally he would greet the morning sun with scorn and a few choice words. This time around, he embraced the morning with a smile and a renewed sense of hope. Jayden was rested and restored; he felt so good that he decided that he was going to give all the girls and Romeo a big hug.

He glanced around and noticed that they were all lying on the floor of a beautiful hacienda. Everyone was still sleeping, except for Floriana who was now sitting up. He ran up to her and attempted to give her a big hug and a kiss on the cheek. His plan backfired when she pushed him away the moment tried to wrap his arms around her.

"Not right now, Jayden. I haven't even had coffee yet. Go and hug Sarah. I'm sure she will love it."

Ignoring her comments, he squeezed her anyway. Once everyone was up and on their feet, they asked Lady Grace where they were and how they had gotten there. "We are in the seaside village known as Terracina. We got here by going through the StarDoor. Was nobody paying attention when we walked through that big door with the stars on it?" She replied.

"Thank you for the sarcasm Gracey," Jayden said patting her on the back.

She shot him a death stare, "I told you before not to call me that! Can't you come up with a nickname that's at least somewhat original?" Before Jayden could respond to her, she marched out of the hacienda and on to a sandy beach.

The sound of the ocean roared in their ears like a lion. The cool mist from the waves splashed against their faces. Without a moment's hesitation, Jayden and Tammy began to take off their shoes to go for a swim.

"What the heck are you guys doing?" Grace yelled. "We are here to get *The Key*. Jayden! Are you even listening to me?"

They ignored her cries for them to stop and ran into the warm tropical waters.

"Please forgive them. Jayden has selective hearing, and Tammy is a very excitable person. So, what makes you think *The Key* is here?" Sarah asked.

Grace ignored her question for a moment and found a nice beach chair. When she sat down, she stared off into the distance and replied, "to be honest, I'm not 100% sure, but I can tell you what I do know. I was told that when the witches took me in, there was a key on the necklace that I was wearing at the time. My parents must have given it to me before they died. When they brought me to Paradiso, a witch named Lady Coral stole *The Key* from me while I was sleeping. Members of the Southern Convent believed that *The Key* I had was the real deal. So they tracked her down to Mount Vulcan," she said while pointing east toward a mountain that wasn't quite too far away.

"Wait, so you don't remember your life from before?" Sarah asked

"I can remember what my parents look like and that's about it. Lady Clara told me that when they saved me, I must have bumped my head really hard," she replied.

Sarah and Floriana glanced at each other trying to weigh what they should ask next. Before Sarah could press the issue, Floriana posed a question. "Grace, can you tell me how the StarDoor works? I'm just a little curious. It was at night when we left the Southern Convent and its daytime now. And I know that the Chaldean Swamp is pretty far away from Terracina."

"Well Floriana, it works like most doors do. You walk in them, and they take you somewhere else. From what I know, if you enter the StarDoor at night, you will arrive at your destination in the daytime, and if you enter it during the daytime, you will arrive at night. It's not the most efficient method of travel, but it can sometimes get you to a destination quicker than you could travel by airship or glider. The StarDoors can only transport you to another StarDoor, or to a location that is owned by the Southern Convent. Since Terracina is owned by the Southern Convent, we were able to travel here with ease," she replied

"Isn't Terracina owned by the Terran Central Government?" Floriana asked.

"Nope, the land here has been owned by the Southern Convent for centuries. The Terran government leased the land from us and then sold the lease to the Eden Government. The Eden government uses this land for tourism and meetings with government officials." She replied.

This made Floriana feel a little uneasy. She was still on the wanted list for an attempted assassination on King Aelius, and the Eden government was still after *The Key*. She knew that they needed to get moving to avoid any suspicion. So, she whistled for Jayden and Tammy to come back in.

Jayden dried their clothes with a heat spell, and they began travelling along the Terracina Beach. It became apparent to him that they stood out like a sore thumb. Even though they were dressed differently, the residents of this beach community were nothing but kind to them. Surfers that walked by gave them high fives, and one of them even got Tammy to stand on their surfboard. The friendliness of this town made Jayden consider living here when their journey was over.

He looked around the city and was impressed by the beautiful architecture. Each building was covered with tropical colored paint. Many of the skyscrapers were designed to look like bananas and pineapples. The houses in Terracina were built in the hacienda style with balconies that gave a perfect view of the ocean. There were also small shacks that were scattered throughout the beach. These shacks were made out of steel or palm trees, and they could be rented for 100 gold coins a night. At those prices, Jayden would be homeless within a week.

Only a handful of the roads in Terracina were paved. The vast majority of the streets were made of soft white sand. The residents and tourists that filled the city streets seemed to prefer traveling on beach cruisers and dune buggies instead of cars. Jayden figured that the city planners wanted their residents to feel like they were never too far from the beach.

Lady Grace waved at him to catch up. She led them up a hill on the outskirts of town. When they arrived at the top of the hill, Jayden stopped to look back. From where they stood, they had a panoramic view of the beautiful city. Jayden wanted everyone to experience this moment of peace for he knew in his heart that the rest of their journey was going to be far from peaceful.

While they paused to enjoy their tropical view, the wind began to pick up. The trees nearby started swinging back and forth as if they were experiencing a powerful storm. The wind howled as the branches of the trees crashed against each other and shattered. Then a cold breeze blew across the trees to their right and covered them beneath a pile of snow.

Jayden heard a loud roar which sent chills up his spine. He wanted to turn around to see what was coming, but his body wouldn't move. His fear intensified as they became enveloped in a dark shadow. Jayden looked up and saw the white underbelly of a dragon.

The dragon's body was covered in blue and white scales. He watched in fear and awe as it flew towards the water. The large animal shrieked as it dove into the Western Ocean. After a few seconds, the animal resurfaced with a large shark squirming in the dragon's claws. With one flap of its wings, the dragon launched itself into the sky and flew right over them. Jayden was crossing his fingers and praying to God that the dragon lived far, far away. Life can be so cruel sometimes he thought as the dragon flew directly towards Mount Vulcan.

"What the hell was that?" Romeo exclaimed.

"That would be a fully grown female Ivory Wyvern," Jayden replied with his face beaming from his moment of brilliance. Everyone in the group turned to him with shocked looks on their faces. "Why are you all surprised that I knew that? In case you all forgot or didn't know, I was trained at the Dragon Temple. Besides learning how to fight there, I also learned a lot about dragons. Of course, that was the largest and scariest dragon I've ever seen."

"Jayden, should we be worried about the Wyvern since it went in the same direction we are going?" Sarah asked.

Jayden pulled his rifle out of his bag, "well, that shark she took should be able to keep her fed for a little while. Wyverns don't typically eat people, but they can be fearlessly territorial if you get near their nests. So when we get to the mountain, we need to be very cautious."

Grace smirked and didn't even wait for Jayden to finish talking and decided to keep walking toward the mountain. Floriana ran to catch up with her to ask a question, "you seem to be pretty comfortable traveling toward the home of a Wyvern. Have you done this before? And please explain to me why are those witches sending you to find *The Key*? Why don't they get off their lazy asses and get it themselves?"

"Not much gets past you, does it? From what I was told the members of the Southern Convent couldn't go anywhere near Lady Coral's palace. She set up some enchantments and barriers that make it impossible for Southern Convent witches and wizards to reach her. This is the third time I have been forced to take people to Mount Vulcan. The first time was six months after I was brought to the Southern Convent. The sad part is that those damn witches will kidnap people who visit the Chaldean Swamp and use them to try and bring back *The Key*. They try to act like they are good people, but I can see right through their BS." Grace replied.

"Wow, that's crazy. Why do you even bother helping them?" Jayden chimed in.

"They send me because one of the few things I can remember from my past is what *The Key* my dad gave me looks like and because they know I won't try and run away." She replied, "You probably think that I'm stupid for always coming back. Every time that I have had to come out here I have ended up going back to Paradiso all alone. All of the people I have traveled with to that stupid mountain were either killed or abandoned me while trying to find that stupid key. But what else am I supposed to do? Lady Clara and the others have taken care of me since I was a kid. It's a sad truth, but they are the only family I've ever known. Even when I've tried to run away, I always end up coming back. Doesn't that sound pretty pathetic?"

Jayden didn't know what else to say to her. He wanted to tell her that they were using her to get what they want, but he had a feeling that she already knew that. In some twisted way, she found comfort in it. He was beginning to wonder if he should tell her that Lady Clara had her entourage killed and kidnapped her for the sole purpose of finding *The Key*. He couldn't imagine how lonely she must feel. Just like her, he missed his parents significantly, but he found solace in the fact that he at least had memories of them.

Grace, on the other hand, had her memories stolen. He wanted to make Lady Clara pay for messing with Grace's memories. All she wanted was to be with people that cared for her, and they denied her that common decency. At that moment, he vowed to help her as much as he could.

Grace led them to a road that sliced right through a forest and ended at the base of Mount Vulcan. Further down the trail, there was a family of black panthers moving across the dirt path. The panthers took a moment to stop and look at Jayden. Then one of the animals lifted its head and sniffed the air. The mighty creature raised its head and let out a deafening roar, and then the panthers ran back into the forest as if they were startled by something.

A low rumbling sound echoed throughout the tropical forest. The mechanical noise was getting closer, and it appeared to be coming from the hill behind them. The group ducked into the dense foliage to see what was interrupting their pleasant stroll.

A giant dust cloud was kicked up by four off road vehicles and a large SUV covered in military camo. The occupants of the vehicles were dressed in army garb and were carrying assault rifles. Standing up in the lead vehicle was a man who was barking out orders at the driver and on his Walkie-talkie. Their C.O. was equipped with an assault rifle, a short sword, and hanging on his back was a navy-blue longbow with a matching quiver. As the lead vehicle passed by them, the commanding officer glanced their direction.

Floriana sat there in shock and was afraid to move. She couldn't believe what she had just seen.

"We might be in trouble. I think those were soldiers from Eden," she said in a hushed tone.

"How do you know?" Jayden asked, "Why would they be heading to Mount Vulcan. Were they following us?"

"Maybe someone from the military noticed us while we were in Terracina and made a phone call. I can confirm that those were Eden soldiers because their C.O. is a man named Jason. He has been working with King Aelius to find *The Key*."

Jayden was beginning to get nervous; his hands started shaking uncontrollably. "Is that the same guy who interrogated Tony and me?" Floriana nodded her head yes. Great, Jayden thought, that Jason guy is nothing but bad news.

Tammy blushed, "I thought he looked a little cute."

"I was just thinking the same thing, Tammy." Sarah giggled, as she looked right at Jayden and smiled.

"Sometimes Sarah, I think you say things just to hurt me," Jayden interjected.

"A few years ago I thought the same thing as you two," Floriana said in a louder voice then she intended. Her face turned bright red as those words left her lips.

"Make that four of us Floriana," Grace added.

Jayden felt annoyed by this impromptu slumber party talk and shouted, "what is wrong with you women? Jason is a total jerk and a bad dude".

"Jayden," Grace said, "it's not you, it's me. I just prefer a man in uniform, plus if he's a bad boy that's even better."

Feeling unloved, Jayden turned to the only other male in the group, "I'm guessing you think Jason's cute also."

"Naw, he's not my type. I'm not really into blondes," Romeo replied. At his response, they all fell down and laughed. Once they had composed themselves, they decided to travel through the dense foliage just in case more soldiers came running down the dirt road.

Hiking through a tropical forest is an experience that every person should do just once, Jayden thought as he admired its immense beauty. The humidity, however, was something he could do without. His clothes were drenched in sweat, and he was having to swat at the mosquitos and large flies that were trying to eat him.

If that wasn't annoying enough, Jayden decided to trip over a vine accidentally and landed on a large fourteen-foot python. While the snake was wrapping itself around him, his friends continued to laugh at him in his predicament. Before the large snake could choke the life out of him, he summoned a small fireball and threw it into the snakes gaping mouth. Within half a second, he was released from the snake who was now scurrying off wishing that he had never met Jayden LoneOak.

Jayden was leading the group when he stopped in his tracks. His ears perked up when he thought he heard the sound of firecrackers being set off in the forest. That seems a little unsafe, he thought. Isn't it a fire hazard to set off firecrackers in a forest?

Then he glanced up and noticed a pillar of smoke rising into the sky. Suddenly, he realized that the popping sound he was hearing, might not be coming from fireworks. Jayden wanted to use caution as they proceeded, but Floriana had different plans. The General from Eden pushed passed him and started sprinting towards the column of fire. The others followed after her leaving him the dust. He shook his head thinking this isn't going to end well.

He stared down range toward a clearing which was near the base of the mountain. Jayden was shocked to see four armored vehicles that were entirely engulfed in flames. Their SUV was covered in scratches, and its windows were broken. Sergeant Jason was standing on the SUV, firing arrows at a horde of green and frost goblins. Four soldiers stood alongside Jason, and they were shooting their rifles at a group of Brown Mountain trolls, which were throwing large rocks at them. Resting next to the burning vehicles, were soldiers that were killed in combat. This was the most hopeless situation that Jayden had seen in quite some time.

General Floriana was not deterred by the violence; she continued to dash toward the fallen soldiers. Jayden quickly grabbed her and pulled her to the ground. "Jayden! What the hell are you doing? You need to let me go. They need help." She pushed him off, but he grabbed her again and pulled her to the ground.

"Floriana, get a hold of yourself. I know you want to help them, but you have to be smart about it. We have to have a plan of action." Jayden yelled.

"Just let me go! We don't have time to wait," she shouted.

Her eyes widened as two army soldiers were snatched off the SUV by the trolls and dragged off into the forest. Then a large Frost Goblin summoned an icicle into its hand and threw it at Jason. Luckily, he was able to catch it in his hand at the last second. Once Jason had thrown the icicle back a green goblin jumped onto the SUV. The monster slashed across his chest. As he fell backward, he notched an arrow and dispatched the creature. When he hit the ground, he quickly got back onto his feet and fired five arrows at the goblins rushing down the mountain.

A massive troll started pushing the SUV to flip it over. Jason pulled a black arrow from his quiver, firing it at the troll as the vehicle rocked back and forth. When the arrow struck the monster, a small bolt of lightning came down from the sky electrocuting the troll.

"Did you see that lightning arrow? That was totally badass!" Jayden exclaimed. He loosened his grip on the General and said in a soft tone, "Floriana, if you really want to save Jason, then you will need to calm yourself and think. We can't just rush out there and get killed. We need to have a plan."

Floriana took a deep breath and regained her composure. Time to think like a General. She stood up as Jayden released his grasp. She snapped her fingers, and her clothes changed into her armor. "Okay, here is what we need to do. Jayden you stay here and try to take them down with your rifle. Sarah, I want you to use your explosive magic on the group of goblins to make them disperse. Tammy and Romeo, we are just going to rush them and hope for the best. If we can take the trolls out of the fight, we have a chance."

"I think you forgot about someone. What about me? Can I help?" Grace said.

"Well, can you fight?" Jayden asked

"Of course I can you dummy. I did live in the Southern Convent remember. I'm trained in summoning magic and I am handy with a sword." She replied.

"Grace, I want you to stay here and watch Jayden's back. He will be vulnerable shooting here amongst the trees. If you can cast any spells from here that will be perfect," Floriana said.

Jayden reached for his belt and removed his elven dagger and handed it to Grace, "take this just in case any goblins get too close to us." Then he turned towards Sarah and said, "please be careful out there."

"Aww, that concern is cute Jayden. But just so you know, I'm going to take more of them down than you." Sarah replied with a little sass.

"We will see about that," Jayden added, " If you don't mind Ms. Floriana, I think I'm going to get this party started."

Jayden laid down in a prone position and placed his rifle on a log for stability. Taking a deep breath, he zoomed his scope in on a goblin that had just jumped on to the SUV and was about to make Jason its next meal. Taking another deep breath, he squeezed the trigger and goblin dropped. A few moments later, he heard Sarah yell, "Grenade" and a yellow explosion sent the goblins surrounding the SUV back peddling.

Jayden switched targets and was now aiming at a large brown troll that was advancing towards him and Grace. A second troll with two golden hoop earrings joined the advancing troll. The monsters swung their large clubs wildly against the trees as they advanced, and sent splinters flying into the air. Jayden knew that he had to make the next few shots count. He loaded a round, and he aimed the troll with the shiny earrings. Just as he was about to squeeze the trigger, Grace jumped right in front of him.

Startled, he yelled, "what the hell are you doing Gracey? Are you crazy? I was just about to pull the trigger!"

"Shut up!" She snapped. Grace put on her bravest face and turned toward roaring trolls who were now less than twenty yards away. She cleared her throat nervously, and yelled, "Bees and Locust!"

A dark cloud of insects appeared in front of Grace. There were bees with gigantic stingers and locusts as big as your hand buzzing around them. She snapped her fingers, and this swarm of insects zoomed towards the trolls. Both of the beasts roared and howled in pain as the bees and locusts swarmed upon them. Lumps from the bee sting spread across their body, and small bite marks from the locusts covered their faces and hands. The trolls swung their arms wildly as they tried to get away from the endless swarms of insects.

Jayden patted Grace on the back, "That was brilliant. I didn't know you could do that." Grace's face beamed with pride. While giving her a high five, the cloud of bees and locusts stopped pursing the trolls.

The sound of insects buzzing filled the forest as the bugs turned back toward Jayden and Grace. Feeling alarmed, Grace took a step back and said, "Um, Jayden, I forgot to tell you something. You know how I have been trained in summoning magic? Well, I sort of lied. I was never actually taught how to use summoning magic. It's a magical ability I was born with. Today was the first time I've ever made a summon attack a target. I really don't know how to control them or make them go away. We might have to start running soon."

Grinning from ear to ear, Jayden replied, "so you are admitting that you had no idea what you were doing, and you jumped in front of my rifle like a crazy person to try something you had completely no control over."

Grace appeared nervous as she backed up, "yes Jayden! I admit it! Now can we please start running? Those bugs are getting closer, and I HATE bugs."

Grace turned to run, but Jayden stood his ground as the cloud of bugs drew closer. He pointed his index finger like a gun at the cloud of bugs and yelled, "Bang!" Instantly, the insects were engulfed in a large ball of fire.

Grace stopped running and placed her hands on her hips and said, "I'm not impressed."

With a toothy smile, he replied, "Don't lie, you know you loved it. By the way weirdo if you're afraid of bugs why did you summon them in the first place?"

She shrugged her shoulders and said, "I don't know. I figured since I don't like bugs that the trolls wouldn't like them either." Jayden laughed and grabbed her wrist, and they ran to catch up with the others.

The remaining goblins began retreating into the mountain while the trolls retired into the forest. Sarah rushed into Jayden's arms with Tammy running behind her. As Jayden enjoyed the oddest three-person group hug he ever had, he checked to see if they were hurt. Besides some minor scratches and a small cut on Sarah's cheek, both of them seemed to be okay. looking around, he noticed that Jason was sitting down and resting up against the SUV. Floriana was crouched next to him and was trying to dab at the wounds on his chest. Jason had deep gashes spread across his chest, a bruise on his shoulder and a cut on his leg. Compared to the rest of his men, he was in the best shape. Lying next to Jason, was a soldier named Carl. He had suffered a broken leg because one of the goblins had attacked him with a club. Carl had a gash on his forehead that Romeo was dressing. Jason and Carl were the only Eden warriors that had survived the battle. It was a terrible sight to see.

Jason opened his eyes to look at Jayden with a halfhearted grin he said, "of all the people in the world who would come and save me from an ambush, you had to be one of them. I bet you are happy to see me like this."

"I'm not going to lie; I like this new look of yours. Although I'd prefer to be the one to have given it to you," Jayden replied. Floriana shot him a look that said she would cut him. The jab Sarah gave him in the side echoed Floriana's sentiment.

Jason blinked for a moment as he examined Jayden, "so what do you plan to do with me?"

Scratching his chin, Jayden replied, "what would you do if you were in my shoes?"

"I know what you're thinking. You think I would simply kill you if the roles were reversed?" Jason asked. "Well, you couldn't be further from the truth. Regardless of my allegiances, I am not a monster. I wouldn't kill a man injured by some blood thirsty trolls. I would bring you back into town and let you heal up. Only when your strength had returned would I seize your life."

Jayden placed his hand on his heart, "that was such a sweet thing of you to say, Jason. I have decided that I will let you and Carl live. I will have Floriana, Romeo, and Tammy cart you to the hospital at Terracina. They will wait there in town until we get back. If you or any of your buddies try to harm them, I will come after you with no hesitation. Does that sound okay to you?"

Jason bowed respectfully and shook Jayden's hand. Floriana and Tammy hugged him before leaving. Jayden waved goodbye as Romeo lifted Jason on his shoulders. Romeo didn't seem too pleased to be leaving, but he still managed to mouth the words "Good Luck."

Chapter 26

The Bitter Climb

They began their climb up the base of the mountain. Dirt filled their shoes and thorns scratched against their ankles. This incline was relatively gentle, but the scenery was about as attractive as a black eye in a school photo.

Jayden was more concerned about what lay ahead of them. From what he could tell the higher elevations were separated into two sections. The middle section of the mountain was entirely covered in snow and ice. The summit was blanketed by dark thunderstorms. It seemed odd to him that the thunderclouds would be up that high. He had a feeling that magic must be involved with that anomaly. He could already sense magical energy in the air, and it only seemed to get stronger with every step.

Sweat glistened across his forehead as they continued to climb. His muscled burned as the hours dragged on. He couldn't tell if he was feeling out of shape or if the magical powers in the mountain were draining his energy.

The climb was feeling more difficult as the incline became steeper. Jayden was hoping they could find a nice, gentle trail that led them further up the mountain. He was starting to wonder how

Jason was planning on driving up this mountain without a trail. Maybe he had known something that Jayden didn't.

Jayden glanced back to see how the girls were doing. Sarah's face was bright red, and she was huffing and puffing from exhaustion. Grace had a big smile on her face and seemed to be enjoying their hike up Mount Vulcan. Since she had spent most of her life in the Southern Convent, this hiking trip must be a pleasant change of pace for her. Jayden wanted to stop and take a break, but he wouldn't suggest stopping unless the girls wanted to.

He looked back again and chuckled as Lady Grace tripped over a root and face planted into a shrub. Fighting the temptation to laugh, he helped her to get back on to her feet. Other than a bruised pride she seemed to be alright. He took a moment to look down the mountain to see how far they've traveled. As he stared down the mountain, he realized that they weren't that far from where they had started and that he missed the companions they left behind. A feeling of dread was creeping into his mind. He had a feeling that leaving them to look after Jason was a bad idea but what other choice did he have?

They looked up and cheered when they saw a line of trees just a few yards above them. Travelling with the sun beating down on them like a drum, was getting old and they could use the shade. With what energy they had they raced up the mountain to be the first one to sit and relax. Sarah pushed passed Jayden and reached the first set of trees and collapsed on to the ground. Instinctively, Jayden grabbed her and rested her against a tree. He gave her a bottle of water and watched her take a few sips.

"Sorry about that. I must have gotten a little dehydrated. I'm feeling a little better now though," Sarah said as she gulped down the rest of the bottle.

"Oh good, I was worried I might have to finish this trip with just Gracey," Jayden replied.

"Please, Jayden you'd love that too much. I, however, would want to kill myself before we made it halfway to the top," Grace chimed in.

"That was too mean. Just for that, you don't get a chocolate bar," Jayden replied as he handed Sarah a chocolate bar with peanut butter. Reaching into his bag, he grabbed another chocolate bar which Grace quickly snatched out of his hand and took a huge bite and handed back to him.

"Jayden how much further do you think we should go before calling it a night?" Sarah asked

"Hmm...I'm not quite sure. Hey, Princess Gracey how much further do you think we need to go?" Jayden asked.

"Don't call me that! Honestly, I've never made it this far up the mountain. Which is kind of depressing when you think about it. Personally, I think that Lady Coral lives near the top of the mountain. Where, exactly, I have no clue." Grace replied.

"Well, in that case, I think we need to travel a little bit further before stopping for the night. We don't want to be trying to find a place to sleep in the dark," Jayden said

They gathered their things and resumed their climb. He knew that if they were to make any progress, they needed to find a more efficient way to hike up this mountain. Jayden decided to use a spell called Dragon Sight. This spell would allow him to see the aesthetics of the mountain in greater detail which would make it easier to spot trails and gentle gradients for them to hike.

The sky above them began to change from a light blue into colors of red and purple as the hours drew on. With the sun setting in the west Jayden decided that they needed to find shelter for the night. He was hoping to find a cave that they could spend the night in. Pushing through a set of trees, they came upon a pile of large gray rocks stacked up against a small hill and at the top of the rocky hill was an entrance to a cave.

Climbing up to the cave was a lot tougher then he had imagined it would be. The rocks were jagged, and when Jayden slipped on one it made a long scratch across his leg that left droplets of blood on the rock. He didn't feel too bad about struggling; the girls were having just as rough of a time. When he had made it halfway up the rocky hill, he heard a high-pitched scream. Quickly he turned around to see what had happened. Grace's face was redder than a tomato, and her body was trembling.

Fearing the worst, he yelled down to her, "what happened? Are you alright?"

Feeling flustered, Grace replied, "Does it look like I'm alright? A green snake just tried to crawl down my shirt. I feel so violated!"

Jayden laughed, and replied, "Did the snake at least ask you for your name or give you flowers?"

"Jayden! Can you be serious for once? Grace could have been bitten while you are up there laughing. Now come down here and help her climb up the rest of this hill." Sarah demanded.

"When did you become my mother?" Jayden replied

"Excuse me?" Sarah said.

"I'm kidding Sarah. I love you, "Jayden replied.

"You better," she said.

After being berated by both girls, Jayden felt like the backside of a donkey. He decided to be nice and carry Grace up the hill on his back. The moment Grace climbed on to his back he began to regret this act of kindness. Not because she was too heavy but because she thought it was hilarious to kick his side like he was a horse. On top of that, Sarah was slightly annoyed with him. The worst part was that he was going to have to spend a night with them in the cave and he had a feeling they would make him do most of the night watch.

They reached the entrance to the cave, and it was a lot larger then he had imagined. Green moss and thick vines covered the entrance. A foul odor filled their nostrils as they crossed the threshold. Jayden had a feeling that something had died in their recently which was going to make sleeping in the cave less enjoyable.

The deeper they went into the cave, the stronger the smell became, the more uneasy Jayden felt. His ears perked up when he heard the sound of something grunting in the dark. Reaching into his bag, he pulled out a flashlight and gave it to Grace. She flicked the switch and directed the light towards the back of the cave.

At first, they could only see green moss on the cave walls and spiders crawling along the ceiling. They stopped when they heard the sound of crunching and a low growl. Grace lowered the light beam until it landed on something that was moving in the darkness. Sitting on the cave floor was a rare, Red Mountain Troll munching on a green deer. As the light shined on troll's yellow eyes with the deer's blood running down its mouth, it let out a deafening roar that made Jayden and the girls jump back. At that sign of weakness, the troll stood up and scratched at the ground with its sharp claws like a bull.

Before the monster could attack them, Jayden stuck out his right hand with the palm facing outward, and he yelled, "Meteor!" A giant red ball of fire with an iron core appeared in Jayden's hand. The troll rushed at them, and Jayden threw the ball of fire and metal at the troll striking it in the chest and sending it stumbling backward. Then he pulled out his pistol and fired five rounds at the creature while Sarah emptied half a magazine into it from one of her machine pistols. The large monster crumbled to the floor landing on the deer he had just been eating.

Grace pointed the flashlight at Jayden and seemed to have been shaken up by what just happened. "Does it ever bug you to take a life? Even if it's the life of a monster?"

Jayden looked down at the troll and choked back a small tear, "it will always bug me to take a life whether it's an animal, a human, or even a monster. I know you are still getting used to stuff like this, and I know you have had some experiences with violence in the past. This situation is similar and yet different then what we faced down the mountain. This was about life and death; it feels different than when you are simply trying to save the day. In a battle like this there is no hero; just the ones who walk away and those that fall to the sword. Taking a life should never be easy or something you grow too accustomed to. But as we continue on this journey, you will have to wrestle with that. When we run into Lady Coral, you may have to choose to take her life or lose your own. And believe me when I say that ending the life of another person isn't an easy thing to do."

Jayden bent over and began the tall task of dragging the carcasses out of the cave. While Jayden was doing some of the heavy lifting, the girls cleaned up the blood and cleared away some of the brush and rocks, so they would be able to sleep. Sarah reached into her bag and pulled out a small bottle of perfume and sprayed it around their sleeping area.

"That oughta do it," she said, "now it smells a little more heavenly and less like death."

Grace grabbed Sarah's perfume, "that smells pretty nice. What's this perfume called?"

Sarah replied, "it's called, a Sunny Dream."

"You should get your money back because the cave smells like a slumber party and a nightmare," Jayden said as he rejoined the girls.

"I put it on every day, and I haven't heard any complaints from you....or Cain," she replied with a devilish grin.

"Well, that's because Cain can't smell, and I respect you too much to comment," Jayden said with a chuckle.

"O hush he can too, and for just being difficult, you won't get to have marshmallows for s'mores. They will just be for Grace and me." Sarah said as she reached into her bag and pulled out graham crackers, chocolate bars, and marshmallows.

"I've never had s'mores before," Grace said.

"Oh, you poor thing," Jayden said while patting her on the head.

Together they munched on s'mores and beef jerky. When the girls began to nod off and go to sleep, Jayden was tempted to draw on their faces. He decided against it, mainly because he didn't want them to kill him in his sleep. He dusted himself off and moved to the entrance of the cave.

Staring out into the darkness, he watched as a shooting star raced across the sky. He knew he should make a wish, but what should he wish for? Deep down he knew that his wish was for everything to go back to the way it was. He watched another shooting star, and he wished for the destruction of Eiréné to have just been a dream and that he was only asleep in his old bed. The sad truth was that he knew his wish wouldn't come true. He just really wanted to see his dad again even if it was just for a moment.

Tears brimmed in his eyes and his heart ached as he thought about his dad. If he wouldn't have asked his dad to save Miss Mara would he still be alive? No matter how much time has passed since that day, he still felt guilty for father's death. If only he could have been a little stronger, a little braver, then maybe those that died protecting him would still be alive.

Jayden clenched his fist as he became more frustrated. Truth be told there was probably nothing he could have done about it. The odds were too stacked against them that day. Sulking about it won't change anything. So he decided to close his eyes and meditate.

As he closed his eyes, he took a deep breath. When he exhaled, he began to feel a sense of calm, and he was able to be entranced by the beautiful sound of nature. He could hear the gentle wind brushing against the trees which helped him to feel more at peace with his past. Off in the distance, he heard wolves howling into the night. Mountain cats and trolls roared in the darkness, and their voices echoed in his ears. This mountain was mighty, and it deserved his respect.

Jayden found this sudden abundance of nature sounds to be quite peculiar. While they were traveling up the mountain, they had seen very few animals. He was beginning to think this mountain was critter free. It became clear to him that at night Mount Vulcan came alive.

The hours passed by as he meditated in silence until he heard someone yell, "Boo!" right in his ear. Startled, he jumped to his feet. He was looked around frantically until he felt a tug on his shirt. Then he glanced down and saw Sarah who was grinning from ear to ear, until she burst out laughing.

"You know, Sarah, sometimes I want to replace you with another woman," he said to her before sitting back down and resting his back against the cave wall.

With tears in her eyes from laughing, Sarah replied, "you couldn't replace me even if you tried. Plus, as of right now your options are Grace or Floriana, and they both would have done the same thing."

"Why aren't you asleep?" He asked sounding slightly annoyed.

Grabbing his arm, she placed it around her shoulder and her head on his chest, "I couldn't sleep. I'm worried about the others."

"Me too. Part of me wonders if I made a mistake by letting them take Jason back. Maybe I should have just killed him," Jayden replied with a clenched fist.

"Jade, I have known you for years. You wouldn't be able to live with yourself if you killed a man who couldn't defend themselves. I couldn't handle seeing you lose yourself again." She said, "after you killed those men from the Daimonia, I thought I would lose you forever."

"I thought I'd lose myself forever. But I don't think that will ever happen again. And I hope I never do that Red Eye thing again. So, what do you want to do when this is all over? "He asked.

Sitting back up Sarah replied, "I don't know. Maybe we could go back to Eiréné and rebuild it?"

Jayden eyed her suspiciously. "Is that your passive aggressive way of saying you want to keep me around for a while?"

She stared back into his eyes with a cheeky grin and replied, "maybe."

"But I thought you liked Cain" he said.

Sarah raised an eyebrow, "what makes you think that? Have you been getting jealous? To answer your question, I do like him a little bit. But you see, Cain is so guarded and complicated. I don't think he will ever drop the walls he has up and you aren't as complicated."

The last few words Sarah said stung like an angry wasp. He wasn't quite sure that being as complicated as Cain was a good thing. In fact, Jayden thought he was plenty complicated. Both his parents were dead. He had killed people through an uncontrollable rage, and he had no home to go to. Wasn't that complicated enough?

Sarah's words made him feel second rate like he was a fallback plan. He didn't want to be the guy she turned to if all her other plans fell through. In all reality he felt like he had slowly been growing closer to Floriana and Grace and that he was moving further and further away from Sarah. He loved her, but he wasn't sure how much she loved him. As the thoughts in his head grew heavy, so did his eyelids. Eventually, he stopped fighting his body and drifted off into a heavy sleep.

***

The morning sun climbed into the sky, and the cave was bathed in extravagant colors. The walls of the cave shimmered like they were painted in gold. He tried to sit up straight and realized Sarah was resting her head on his left leg. Fearing he might wake her and experience her morning wrath, he slowly adjusted himself, so he could sit up against the wall. He had a slight kink his neck from sleeping on a rock, but other than that he had a restful night.

Then he heard the sound of feet dragging against the ground from the other side of the cave. Apparently, Lady Grace was now awake. She wiped the sleepiness from her eyes, and said, "so, this is where you two went off to. Did I miss anything?"

"Oh Gracey, I hope you don't feel too left out. I plan on snuggling with you tonight," Jayden replied.

"No, you aren't," Sarah said sounding a little groggy from sleep.

Snapping her fingers, Grace said, "You heard the lady, Jayden. No snuggling for you."

"I have a habit of doing the opposite of what Sarah tells me to do," Jayden said defiantly.

"Oh, well, in that case, you won't get to have any of the bacon I brought," Sarah said as she walked toward the back of the cave.

"Wait, you have bacon? Won't it get spoiled in your bag?" Jayden asked.

"Didn't Tony tell you? The enchantments on our bags can allow you to store food in them for six months before they spoil. I've had this bacon in my bag since we left the Water Temple."

Jayden jumped up and made a fire near the back of the cave and Sarah set up her iron skillet for cooking. From her bag, she pulled out bacon, eggs, sausage, and bread. The moment the food hit the skillet, Jayden's stomach growled like a lion. This meal was going to be amazing, he thought.

Once the food had been prepared, Sarah pulled out some paper plates from her bag and a bottle of red sauce. Jayden's eyes widened "Is that the hot sauce that your parents used to make?"

"Yes, it is. Before Eiréné was destroyed, my parents taught me how to make it. I keep a bottle on me for good luck," she replied.

"Can I try it?" Grace asked ever so sweetly. Sarah handed her the bottle, and Grace poured a few drops of it on a piece of sausage and took a bite. "It tastes pretty good," she said. After a few more bites, Grace's face turned bright red, and she stopped chewing.

"O my God!" She yelled, "it's so hot! My tongue is on fire! Jayden give me your water."

Before he could respond, she reached into his bag and grabbed his water and began to chug it as if her life depended on it. Jayden and Sarah fell back laughing their heads off at the spectacle.

Jayden grabbed a piece of bread and presented it to her. "You know, when your mouth is on fire, drinking water makes it worse. You should drink milk or eat this nice piece of bread I got you." Grace snatched the bread out of his hand and whispered something under her breath that would make a sailor blush.

When Grace had regained her composure, and they gathered their things, they continued their trek up the mountain. As they climbed, Jayden was beginning to gain a greater appreciation for the size of the mountain. The easiest trail he could find wrapped around the mountain which made climbing easier, but it meant their progress was slow. He knew sooner or later they would need to attack the mountain more directly. Jayden felt uneasy about pushing the girls too hard, not because they were out of shape. He was concerned about the dangers that may be lying in wait for them. The night before helped him realize that there were very dominant creatures on this mountain. Since they didn't know the terrain or even where their destination was, they couldn't afford to fight in the dark or fall into an ambush.

Jayden felt a cold breeze as they passed through a grove of evergreen trees. The hairs on the back of his neck began to stand up on their own and goosebumps formed on his arm. The tree branches around them started swinging violently as the wind picked up. The bitter cold sliced through his clothes like a knife. This sudden change in the weather seemed unnatural, he thought. They still had another thousand feet to climb to reach the snowy section of the mountain. There was no reason for it to be this cold.

He sensed powerful magical energy in the air. The mountains aura felt cruel and malevolent. This reminded him of how he felt when they arrived in Chaldea. Something about this place was off. He was beginning to understand why all of Grace's trips to the mountain failed. Everything about this place seemed off.

His ears perked up at the sound of wings flapping in the sky above. Jayden glanced up just as blackbirds began to congregate in the branches overhead. The birds opened their beaks and let out a haunting scream. As the blood-curdling sound filled his eardrums, hundreds of birds began appearing in the sky and joined this choir from hell. Every shriek echoed across the mountain like the haunting cries of the damned. Jayden quickly covered his ears, and he wanted to get as far away from their obnoxious sound as possible. If this was just a dream, it was the creepiest one ever.

The canopy above was now as black as night from the thousands of birds that filled the trees. The branches above them snapped as the wind began to rage. They wanted to run and hide, but they had nowhere else to go but up. The crows continued their song of terror while the ravens swooped down and pecked at Jayden and his crew. They sprinted up the mountain covered in scratches from their avian attackers. They hoped and prayed that it would stop.

Just as quickly as the terror began, it stopped without warning. The mountain became as quiet as the grave. While Jayden appreciated the renewed silence, he was still absolutely terrified by the sea of blackbirds that filled the trees. Their beady, yellow eyes filled with malice stared down at him. Jayden had never been more afraid of birds until today. These creatures filled him with primal fear. So much so that he wanted to walk down the mountain and never return.

They were all thoroughly exhausted from trying to get away from those blackbirds. He wasn't sure if they might attack again, so they decided to take a break. Jayden grabbed the trunk of a nearby tree and pulled himself forward. When he took another step, he stopped instinctively as a large branch snapped and landed right in front him. The impact of the branch made a dull sound, and the ground beneath him reverberated.

Just as he flicked off the safety on his pistol, a dark shadow came down from the tree above crushing the branch beneath it. Standing two feet in front of him was a dark green imp with black eyes, razor sharp teeth, and six-inch claws on each hand. The creature's breath smelled worse than rotten eggs. The imp licked its lips with its forked tongue, and that's when Jayden realized that he was on the menu. He wanted to yell for the girls to run, but he was frozen with fear. Jayden wanted to raise his gun, but the imp might strike him down before he got the shot off. Even if he could fire off a round, he would only be able to manage one shot before the imp would overtake him. He was screwed no matter what he chose to do.

The green monster drooled as it sensed fear in its prey. Jayden saw a blur as the imp swiped at his throat. Instinctively, he stepped back and narrowly avoided the creature's razor-sharp claw. While stepping backward, his foot landed on loose dirt, and he stumbled. The imp charged him knocking him down the mountain. He screamed as the monster sank its teeth into his left shoulder.

The pain was excruciating as they tumbled down the mountain, locked in an epic struggle. The monster's teeth sunk deeper into his shoulder, making the pain almost unbearable. He needed to do something quickly before the imp or tumbling down the mountain killed him. With great difficulty, Jayden managed to lift his pistol just enough to squeeze off three rounds into the imp's chest. The monster's toothy grip lessened slightly, but it's lockjaw held on to his shoulder tight and wouldn't let go.

They continued to roll down the mountain and Jayden saw that they were heading right towards a tree. With all the strength he could muster, Jayden rolled quickly, so the back of the imp slammed right into the tree. The impact knocked the wind out of him.

For a moment he laid there struggling to breathe. His world was spinning, and his vision was blurry. Jayden was struggling to maintain consciousness when he heard the girls scream. He shook his head and with his knife, he pried open the mouth of the dead imp. Slowly Jayden rose to his feet, and his world was still spinning a hundred miles an hour. His shoulder was bleeding and hurting so much that he almost passed out from the pain. He put pressure on the wound and looked up the mountainside. When he realized how far he had tumbled, he was filled with despair. Three imps were bearing down the mountain to attack the girls, and there was no way that he could get to them in time.

Jayden knew that he still had to try and do something. He picked up his pistol from the ground and tried to aim it at the monsters. Jayden felt even more discouraged because at this range he was going to be lucky if his bullet hit a tree, let alone an imp. If that wasn't bad enough, the bag with his rifle was snagged on a root higher up the mountain.

Jayden felt entirely out of options, so he desperately tried to run to help the girls as the bloodthirsty imps drew closer to them. His head was spinning like a gyroscope as he tried to do the most straightforward task of making his legs move forward. Blood was trickling down his forehead, and the immense pain in his arm was zapping his energy. Jayden slipped on loose dirt, crashing to the ground. With his arm stretched out he tried to yell, but his words got stuck in his throat. Then everything went black.

Chapter 27
Cold Fury

He awoke to a roaring pain in his shoulder. His head was throbbing; his body felt like he was hit by a bus and then hit by another bus. Jayden tried lifting his left arm, and his nerves signaled to his brain that he was a moron for trying to move. When he attempted to sit up and open his eyes, he became nauseated and was forced to lay back down feeling utterly defeated.

He heard the sound of footsteps approaching him, and he forced his eyes to open. Sarah was sitting on her knees next to him, her hands glowing. As her hands shined a radiant yellow light upon him, his body became warm and relaxed. The pain he felt all over his body lessened, and he was able to move his left shoulder without experiencing the kind of pain that makes a grown man want to run to their mother.

"It's about time you woke up. You had me worried for a little bit," Sarah said.

"I'm sorry," Jayden croaked. "How long was I out for?"

"About a day and a half," she replied.

"A day and a what?" Jayden yelled.

Jayden forced himself to sit up, and his eyes met hers. He kissed her cheek, and for a moment they sat in complete silence. As her beautiful brown eyes gazed into his, Jayden became wholly mesmerized by his childhood friend. She was the smartest and bravest girl he had ever met, and he began to realize how lucky he was to have her on this journey with him.

"You know you're very pretty right?" He said feeling a little star struck.

She blushed and pushed him back down gently, "that better not just be the pain talking. You are lucky that you have such a hard head. You took quite a tumble. I need you to do this still," Sarah said. She began chanting, and her hands started glowing again.

"Are you speaking elvish?" Jayden asked, "When did you learn to do that?"

"While you were out hiking when we went to the Water Temple. They taught me a few healing spells. When you fell down the mountain, you bruised a few of your ribs, and there is some damage to your shoulder from the bite. This spell will help to boost your auto healing spell and lessen the pain and fight infection. Healing magic can't bring you back from the dead. You need to be more careful. How many more times do I have to tell you to do that? Now sit still."

Sarah continued to chant for the next fifteen minutes. Slowly the glow in her hands decreased, and Jayden found a renewed strength in his body. The pain in his shoulder and his head were now just a distant memory.

Finally, he had the strength to sit up without getting dizzy. Jayden leaned back against a wall and closed his eyes to rest. The wall felt cold against his skin like he was leaning against an ice slab. As he surveyed the world around him, he not that they were in a cave filled with crystals that were covered in ice. The room was bathed in gentle blue lights from the crystals. As he became more conscious, he started to realize how cold it was. Sarah must have read his mind because she placed his black jacket on him.

"Hey, isn't it the guy's job to give the girl a jacket and not the other way around?" He asked.

"If you wouldn't have gotten knocked out, you could have had the chance to put a jacket on Grace's shoulder," Sarah said with a devilish grin.

"That was cold. Speaking of cold, where the heck are we and why is it freezing in here?" He asked.

She grabbed his hand and led him to the entrance of the cave. He looked down the mountain and saw snow. Then he looked up and saw more snow. Feeling a little confused, he turned to Sarah and shouted, "how the heck did we get way up here?"

"Lower your voice you don't want to cause an avalanche. While you were taking a nap and those imps were attacking us, Grace summoned three large monkeys. Once we had finished off the imps, two of the monkeys ran away, and the third stayed behind and helped us carry you up the mountain. So in between stops to heal you, we were able to make it up here."

"Gracey was able to control one of her summonses? That's pretty cool," he said with a smile.

Avoiding his gaze Sarah shrugged and replied, "control might be a little bit of an overstatement. When the monkey brought you to the cave, he kind of just dropped you on the ground. Then it tried to braid your short hair and when that didn't work. The monkey tried to take a bite out of you. Luckily, it dissolved before it could bite your other shoulder."

"The monkey tried to what? Where is Grace? I'm a shove some snow in her face for that. The woman isn't allowed to summon anything anymore," he yelled.

"I'm down here you moron. Next time, I'm just going to leave you at the bottom of the mountain," Grace said while building a snowman. "Now come help me finish this snowman."

While Jayden assembled the head for the snowman, the temperature dropped dramatically. Cold wind sliced through his body like a knife. Quickly, he and Grace ran back into the cave. The wind roared as the snow blasted the mountain. Sarah started a fire with some difficulty in the damp cave, but the cold, treacherous wind was weakening the flame.

"Jayden!" She yelled, "I know you're not feeling the best but, I need you to use your magic to get this fire going again."

While Jayden concentrated his energy to summon a blaze, Sarah pulled out quilts from her bag. Jayden snapped his finger, and a small spark appeared on his thumb. He extended his arm to place the spark of magical flame on the wood. Then a gust of cold wind blew through the cave and extinguished his flame.

Shaking his head in frustration, he snapped his fingers again. The sound of the snap bounced off the walls of the cave, but no fire appeared. Attempt after attempt, Jayden failed to summon any source of heat. Instead of snapping his fingers, he opened his palm and whispered the word "Fireball," nothing happened. Not even a small spark. In fact, the temperature in the cave dropped as if the weather outside was mocking him for his failure. Sarah patted him reassuringly on the back and with a book of matches she helped Jayden to get the fire started again. Together they helped to fan the flame to keep it going.

As the fire blazed brightly in the cave, they huddled together. Even with the bright yellow and orange flames dancing on the wood, the cave still felt like the inside of a freezer. Sarah and Grace rested their heads on Jayden's shoulders. Normally this level of attention would have made his day, but all he could feel was a sense of failure. Since waking up in this cave, his magical energy had been wavering, and he assumed that was due to him almost dying again. But it was also possible that the cold weather was draining him of his magical abilities. Either way, he felt thoroughly defeated.

He examined his hands and began to wonder if he would be able to protect the girls. Would he be able to survive the rest of the climb without his magic? Jayden was so frustrated that he seethed with anger. He had never felt so useless or embarrassed in his life. Well, not since the day that Eiréné was destroyed. Back then, he couldn't fight. All he was able to do was watch people die in his place. He made a vow never to be that weak again, but now he was sitting in this cave with his teeth chattering because he couldn't summon a simple fire.

Sensing his frustration, Sarah kissed his cheek which managed to make him feel warmer than that quilt did. "Don't beat yourself up about it. Pushing you to do that on the same day you woke up from your mini coma was too much to ask of you. I'm sorry," she said.

"I'm sorry I let you two down. I feel like I might fail you two again," he said glumly.

"What makes you say that?" Grace asked as she sat up to look at him.

"Well, when I was trained to fight at the Dragon Temple, and it became obvious that I would be a fire user because I'm hot stuff." He said which made Sarah laugh and Grace roll her eyes. "Ever since that day, I have become a lot more sensitive to cold weather. The more cold and wet moisture in the air, the more difficult it becomes for me to use my magic. Even though fire magic works well against ice, it takes a lot more of my energy to use my abilities when it's cold. Even the magic that makes me physically stronger and agiler becomes tougher to do when it's cold. The worst part is that the magic that helps me to recover quickly isn't going to work as well in this weather. So we need to be careful the rest of the way."

"Jayden, we are a team. This whole mission is not dependent on you alone. Mine and Grace's magic isn't affected by the weather. Now with that being said, I agree that we do need to be more careful. We will have to start rationing our food more. Losing two days of travel was not the best thing for us. Plus, I have about half a magazine in each of my machine pistols. How many bullets do you have left?" She asked.

Pulling out his dad's gun and his Chrome pistol out of his backpack, he emptied the magazines. "I have about five left in my dad's gun, nine bullets in this one, and three rifle rounds."

"Well, that sounds encouraging. We are lucky that taking down Lady Coral will be as easy as walking in the park." Grace said without any attempt at hiding her pessimism.

Normally Jayden would have commented back, but he knew that she wasn't that far off base. They didn't have much ammo left and what good will it do for them while trudging through the snow. Even if he was able to recover enough energy to use his magic it still might not be enough. He punched the ground in frustration. The girls were strong. He couldn't deny that fact, but the challenges ahead will put them in greater danger. He couldn't handle losing either one of them.

Sarah nudged him flirtatiously, "hey, cheer up. I told you that it is going to be okay. By the way, I have some good news for you. I got in touch with Floriana and the others."

Jayden perked up with a grin on his face, "did you really? How? Are they doing okay?"

"How come you never perk up like that when you see us?" Grace asked.

"Hmm, that's a good question," Jayden answered.

Sarah raised her eyebrow with an expression that said his response was going to get him smacked. After smacking him, she said, "They are doing fine. I used the communication coins to talk to her. She told me that they are staying at a hotel near the outskirts of Terracina."

Feeling a little better after hearing some good news, Jayden reached into his bag and rummaged around for something. A shocked look appeared on Grace's face as Jayden handed her his Chrome 44 magnum pistol. At first, she refused it, but Jayden pressed her into taking it. "This gun has a wicked kick, but it will drop anything that might get too close. When you pull that trigger make sure you have your big girl pants on."

Grace laughed, "okay last time I checked, Sarah and I saved your butt the other day. Maybe you need to put your big boy pants on. Do you want your fancy dagger back?"

"That was a low blow, Gracey. Maybe I should have let those bees you summoned sting you. I want you to keep the dagger. It was given to me, and now I want you to have it. The magic in that dagger will let you use some Speed magic. You'll be able to move almost as quick as me," he replied.

"If only your moves worked," Grace chuckled. With his pride feeling slightly wounded, he laid down next to the fire and closed his eyes.

***

Sunlight pierced through the cave like a knife through butter. The bright morning sun signaled the end of the blizzard. Still feeling half asleep, he shuffled his way to the entrance of the cave. A hundred yards down the mountain, he watched a white momma bear play with her two cubs. Brown and white squirrels climbed up a nearby tree. A beautiful golden hawk with outstretched wings soared in the skies above them. A smile grew on his face as he watched the mountain come alive again.

The best part of this beautiful morning wasn't even the breathtaking view all around them. Jayden could feel his strength returning, and during the night, he also managed to raise the temperature of the cave with a simple heating spell. After two days stuck in the cave during the blizzard, he felt ready to take on the world.

He turned around and helped the girls pack up camp, and to get started back on the winding trail that led up the snowy slopes. The snow crunched beneath their feet as they walked leaving a trail of footprints behind them. While they climbed up to a higher elevation, the trees became scarcer, and because of the snow, many of the thorny bushes were hard to see. Grace learned that firsthand when she tripped over a prickly bush that was covered in snow. Jayden could have stopped her fall, but instead, he chose to laugh loud enough to cause an avalanche.

After Grace got back to her feet and threatened to strangle Jayden for not catching her, she led them along a ridge that wrapped around the side of the mountain. The further they traveled, the narrower their path became. The danger of climbing this mountain was growing. There was a chasm on their right side that was so deep that if Jayden sneezed and fell into it, the chasm would take him straight to the gates of Hades.

As their path continued to shrink in width, they were soon forced to walk in a single file line. Jayden pressed his back up against the rocky mountain, to shimmy himself down the path.

The three travelers shimmied like a group of weirdos until they reached a break in the path. About two feet to his left, there was a small ravine. The distance across the gap was almost five feet. Normally that wouldn't be a problem except for the fact they didn't have any room to get a running start. Jayden was going to have to jump and rotate his body in the air and hopefully grab the ledge.

When Sarah and Grace caught up with him they saw the gap, their eyes opening wide. Grace slipped out a word that would have gotten her detention in school. Jayden stood near the ledge and thought about the jump they needed to make. If he jumped and missed, he would die a quick and efficient death. If he didn't jump, he might still die on this cold mountain. Taking a deep breath and closing his eyes, he said a quick prayer. Turning to Sarah, he gave her a quick kiss on the lips which made his heart pound in his chest. Her lips tasted just like fresh cinnamon. Once he pulled away, her face turned a bright red and then he jumped the gap.

Jayden reached the ledge and slipped on the wet snow. Before he could plunge to his death, he grabbed on to the ledge and pulled himself back up. With his heart still pounding like a steel drum, he gestured for Sarah to jump and grab on to his hand.

She was still dazed and red faced from his kiss and him almost falling off the ledge. Sarah nodded her head and jumped. Jayden grabbed her while she was in the air and sat her next to him. The wind picked up again as he stretched out his hand for Grace to grab. She looked nervous and shook her head no. Jayden stretched out his hand and yelled for her to jump.

"I can't do it Jayden," she said with a sob. "I'm afraid of falling."

"Don't you mean heights?" Jayden asked.

"Don't correct me! I'm afraid of heights, falling, and snakes. I'm not going to jump. You guys go on ahead. I will wait here," she said crossing her arms.

The cold wind blew her hair into her face and for a second, she felt unbalanced and almost leaned too far forward. Tears rolled down her cheeks as she looked back and forth at the ledge and the cliff below.

Jayden yelled, "just jump already before the wind gets too bad. You can do this!"

"No, I cant!" she yelled, "I'm too afraid."

"It's okay to be afraid." He replied in a soothing tone, "you can do this Gracey. I promise to catch you. I won't ever let you fall."

Choking back another sob, she took a deep breath. "If you even think about trying to kiss me, I will plummet to my death". She took a step back, then bent her knees and lunged herself across the gap. Instinctively, Jayden stretched both his arms out to catch her. She grabbed on to him for dear life as she hung over the ravine. Sarah grabbed Jayden by the ankles and pulled him as he held on to Grace's wrists. Once they had all made it on to their small narrow walkway, they took a breather.

Luckily, the wind had died down, and the snow was now just mere flakes falling from the sky. Jayden hung his legs over the side and sat in awe as he stared down at the mountain below them. The sheer power of nature and the respect the mountain demanded was something Jayden was beginning to appreciate

Grace was still pretty shaken from the jump. Her breathing was heavy, and her heart rate was still up. Jayden put an arm around her and kissed her cheek, "it's going to be okay," he said.

"I thought I warned you about kissing me. Now I want to jump off of this thing!" She replied.

"Please," he scoffed, "that kiss was the highlight of your week. You're probably going to write about it in your pink diary before you go to sleep tonight."

Glancing to his left, Jayden noticed that Sarah had not said a word since the jump. He had a feeling her abrupt silence had nothing to do with their recent near-death experience. Her mind was thinking about something else. Maybe kissing her before he jumped was a mistake, he wondered.

After swallowing a few sips of water, they continued their trek along the narrow pathway. The sun above them had begun to set. With the day coming to a close, Jayden was starting to get nervous. He was worried about finding a place for them to spend the night.

Grace discovered a large cavern that pierced into the mountain. She called for Jayden to take a look at it. The mouth of the cavern was about fifteen feet wide, and the ceiling was easily over twenty feet high. An eerie light pulsated from deep within the cavern. Jayden thought that this would be a great spot to spend the night. Truthfully, he found the cavern to be just a little too creepy. Together, they decided to continue down the trail to see if there was a better place for them to set up camp.

Their path led them straight to a dead end. A wall made of rock and ice impeded them from going any further. The flat rock's face was over 100 feet high, and without any other options to choose from, they decided to set up camp at the dead end.

Sarah pulled out a blue tent from her bag that was surprisingly roomy. Jayden placed the stakes firmly into the ground just in case the wind picked up. When the tent was fully assembled, Sarah handed out blankets for everyone to use. Before the sun had completed setting, the girls went to sleep.

Jayden decided to sit at the entrance of the tent. He unzipped the tent to look out into the darkness. The clouds above were now just a distant memory. In their place was a beautiful crescent moon and stars that sparkled in the night sky. This night reminded him of his first winter at the Dragon Temple. Jayden couldn't believe, how cold it was back then. He enjoyed getting into snowball fights with Tony and watching the neon glow of the Northern Lights. At this moment, the mountain seemed just as peaceful as it did at the Dragon Temple. It was hard to believe, that they had fought through a blizzard, and took a leap of faith to get to where they were now.

Jayden took a deep breath and began to meditate. As his body became calm and relaxed, he could feel the magical energy building up in his body. Heat began to radiate from within and the snow beneath his feet started to melt.

He examined his hands and decided that he would try it again. While he meditated with his eyes closed, he snapped his fingers. No spark appeared, but he could feel the heat coming off of his fingertips. With his confidence rising, he opened up his right palm. Then he whispered the words, "Flame Ward."

Jayden felt a boost of energy from within his body and a tingling sensation on his fingertips. Suddenly, a purple flame appeared in his hand. He smiled as power surged through him again. He thrust his arm out of the tent and snapped his fingers with his other hand. The purple flame began to float on its own outside the tent filling the air with a gentle warmth.

"What is that?" said a sweet voice from behind him.

Jayden jumped in his seat and turned around to see that Sarah had come to sit next to him. Clutching his heart, he said, "woman, you need to stop sneaking up on me when I'm doing guard duty. You're going to give me high blood pressure."

She smirked, "you still didn't tell me what that was? I'm guessing this means you are back to normal?"

"This is called a Flame Ward. It's a protective spell. If a monster or anything comes too close, that little sprite will smash into them. It is a pretty effective deterrent. I do feel like I am getting some of my magic back, but the weather here is still going make it difficult to use" he replied as he watched the sprite dance back and forth.

"Well, can I ask you something else?" She said softly. Jayden nodded his head yes.

"Well, I've been thinking about what happened back there. And I just want to know why did you kiss me?"

"Honestly, I thought I was probably going to die. It seemed like the good idea at the time," he said with a gentle smile.

Sounding annoyed she replied, "so the only reason you kissed me is that you thought you were going to die and I just happened to be there as a convenience?"

"Again, I honestly, thought I was going to die. I would have kissed Gracey if she had been the one standing next to me," he said.

"You're such an ass!" She yelled as she stormed off to the back of the tent.

Not again he told himself. This trip up the mountain was already unbearable, and now he has pissed off the girl he cared for the most. Why do I always put myself in this position? Why couldn't I have just been honest with her? Maybe I should have told her how I really felt.

Jayden shook his head and continued to sulk until he heard footsteps coming from behind him, and lucky for him, Grace plopped down right next to him.

"Hey loser, why the long face? Did you repeat something stupid? Don't tell me you would have actually tried to kiss me?" She asked.

"Oh, you heard that?" he replied. Grace nodded yes. "Then I probably would have. You are kinda cute; it might not be such a bad idea."

Grace rolled her eyes and said, "wait so now I'm just a probably and kinda cute? Jayden, I enjoy your company, but I'd hate for my first kiss to happen just because you thought you were going to die," she replied.

"So, I will take that as you wouldn't have refused it. Score one for this guy," he said pointing his thumbs at himself.

She nudged him, "you are so weird, I hope you know. In all seriousness, I, um, wanted to thank you for everything back there. Honestly, if it weren't for you, I wouldn't have even tried that jump. I was so scared on that ledge. Traveling with you is helping me to discover a lot more things about myself. Even though, I still don't remember much about my past. The one thing I do remember is that I hate heights."

"And snakes," he said. "Don't worry about it. I was glad to help out Gracey. I meant what I said. I will always be there to catch you."

"What did I tell you about that nickname? Do you really mean that? I mean after you guys bring back *The Key* to Lady Clara.

You are just going to leave me. You don't have to pretend to be my friend".

He scratched his chin, then took her by the hand and walked her just outside the tent. Jayden laid down on the snow and she laid down next to him and stared at the stars.

"The truth is Gracey. I really don't know what's going to happen. Honestly, if we find *The Key* and are somehow able to take it from Lady Coral and make it back down this mountain alive, that will be a miracle. Even then, I have no intention of giving Lady Clara *The Key*, not in a million years would I do that. Originally, I set out on this journey to seek vengeance on the people who killed my father. I'm starting to realize, that there are more important things in this world than my desire for retribution. I want you to get to see that too. I want you to get to explore this big world as I have gotten to, and hopefully, you will do it with better motives. Once we get *The Key*, you are welcome to stick around and help us to destroy it. You can travel with me as long as you want. You could even travel back and live with the Aggeloi; it's up to you. But I will give my life if I have to so you can have your freedom. Believe me, when I say this, I'm not pretending to be your friend. I do care about you."

She sniffled and wiped a tear from her eye as she sat up and kissed him on the forehead, "That was nice of you to say. I don't know what I will decide to do, but I'd hate to have my freedom at the expense of your life."

Jayden sat back up and stared into her eyes, "you are just the sweetest. I think you are starting to get a little soft on me, Gracey". Those words he would soon regret as she punched him in the chest and it hurt quite a bit.

Chapter 28

Illumination

Jayden awoke to the sound of gunfire. His heart jumped into his throat as he grabbed his equipment and stumbled out of the tent. He drew his sword and glanced up only to see Sarah standing next to Grace.

"That is two gold coins for me, "Sarah said. Grace handed her the coins and turned toward Jayden.

"You just made me lose money! "She yelled.

"What the heck are you two doing? I thought we were trying to conserve bullets!" He shouted.

"We were trying to wake you up, and you wouldn't get up. You were screaming in your sleep; it was scary. So Sarah bet me that it would take two gunshots to wake you up, and I told her it would only take one. You let me down, Jayden," Grace replied.

Jayden raised his eyebrow and gave Sarah a look of disappointment. She just smiled at him as she walked passed him.

While Jayden was removing the tent stakes the air around became colder. The gentle breeze that had been blowing had stopped entirely. The mountain was now eerily quiet. This sudden change made Jayden feel a little uneasy about continuing further.

Grace wanted them to proceed through the cavern instead of climbing up the vertical wall. His gut feeling told him that it would be safer to fight gravity. Then to explore the dark, and possibly haunted, cavern. Jayden didn't even try to argue with her because he figured that Grace was through with anything which had to do with heights.

They stood outside the entrance to the cavern, and there was a bright yellow light emanating from deep within it. Stepping across the threshold into the cavern gave him chills. Jayden told the girls to be careful and to watch out for the black ice that was on the ground. Even with the yellow light bouncing off the rocky walls, it was still quite difficult to see. Sarah pulled out a small lantern and twisted a knob on it. The lantern's white light shined just bright enough for them to see a couple of feet in front of them. The way she swung the lantern back and forth reminded him of the scary movies he and Tony used to watch together. Jayden was half expecting to hear creepy music playing in the background and a man with a chainsaw running after them.

He had no idea where they were going or even why he even agreed to enter the cavern in the first place. Everything about this place was just wrong. The cavern seemed to grow wider the further they went into it, and the ceiling above them was getting higher and higher. The floor was made of smooth stone, and in some sections, it was covered in black ice. He couldn't believe how smooth the flooring was. How many mountains out there, could boast about having a stone floor like this, none he told himself. This cavern must have been manmade.

Sarah stopped in her tracks and shined the lantern toward the ceiling. From what Jayden could tell, the cavern's ceiling was filled with stalagmites covered in ice and green crystals. Small red-tailed bats, hung upside down from the ceiling, lunging at small insects as they flew by. Jayden wasn't the biggest fan of bats, but he didn't mind their presence because he could see them. It was the monsters in the darkness that he couldn't see that worried him.

Out of the corner of his eyes, he swore he could see shadows moving in the darkness. When he would look away for a moment and look back, they were gone. He was tempted to use a spell that would help him see in the dark, but he really didn't want to find out what was following them.

Truthfully, it was his fear that made him a liability on this journey. The others would never say it. He hated that he has been caught off guard so many times and ill-prepared for this journey. His training was partially to blame. The Dragon Temple can turn any person into a weapon, but they are also taught to hold back and to demonstrate self-control. It still wasn't a good enough excuse; his mistakes have put the girls' lives in danger, and he needed to step up. His power scared him, but no longer would he be unprepared. Whatever was lurking in the darkness waiting to pounce on them was going to be in for a rude awakening. Jayden LoneOak was equipped for war and ready to give them hell.

While he was lost in thought, he bumped into Grace who had stopped in her track. She started gagging and was holding her stomach like she was going to lose her lunch. Jayden found this to be quite disturbing and not very ladylike. He gently patted her back.

"Are you feeling alright?" He asked.

"No!" She yelled, "can't you sense that awful smell? It's making me sick."

Jayden sniffed the air, and now he wanted to hurl. A strong, musky odor was filling the cavern; it smelled like dirt mixed with the scent of rotting flesh which is bad enough to make any strong stomached person want to lose it. It was so bad that he was doubling over and feeling light-headed. Sarah, being the genius woman that she was, pulled out one her perfumes and started spraying it in a circle. Her perfume helped to relieve some of the stench, but now it smelled like someone had died on a beautiful bouquet of flowers.

Jayden reached out his hand to stop Sarah from spraying. He put a finger to his lips signaling the girls to be quiet and whispered for them to listen. He closed his eyes and concentrated on listening to the sounds of the cavern. It took him a few moments, and then he found it; the sound of shallow breathing and of claws scratching against a rock. His body tensed, and Sarah screamed. As Jayden looked up at her, he watched as yellow goo came down from the ceiling and landed on her shoulder. The liquid looked like the grossest drool he had ever seen.

Sarah gulped down a heavy dose of fear and raised her lantern skyward. Staring down at them from the ceiling was a light blue frost goblin who was licking its lips. Running back and forth beside it on the ceiling was another odd creature. It had the face and tail of a lion with the body of a medium-sized dog, sharp crooked teeth, and yellow eyes.

A LawDog is what they were called. Jayden remembered hearing about them in one of his science classes. He remembered learning that they traveled in packs and would eat anything that ran into their path, the fact that it and the frost goblin were working together was a bad sign.

The large animal opened its mouth and let out a roar that was so loud, it shook the stalagmites and made some of them fall and smash on to the stone floor. Before the creature could finish its act of intimidation, Jayden threw an explosive tipped knife into the monsters gaping mouth and fired two bullets into the frost goblin. The explosion from the blade lit up the cavern, and that's when everything went wrong.

Jayden wheeled around saw that a large group of goblins and LawDogs had been stalking them. He raised his gun to fire and then he remembered that he only had three bullets left. Quickly, he holstered his pistol and yelled at the girls, "Run!".

He drew his sword, let loose his last two throwing knives, turned on his heels and ran as they exploded. Jayden was trying to fight a grin as he felt like an action hero from a movie; the main difference was that he actually was in danger. Still, he felt like a boss.

While he sprinted through the cavern, he stopped when he realized that the monsters were catching up. He spun around, and he swiped his sword in a line and yelled, "Wall of Fire." A yellow wall of hot flames appeared in front of him. The line of fire was about 49 feet long and ten feet tall. Unfortunately, a few unlucky frost goblins did not stop in time, and were melted as they ran into the wall of flames.

Jayden was impressed with himself that he was able to cast the spell. The sad truth was that he knew it wouldn't last much longer. The amount of energy it took to conjure that much magic was too much. He stood and watched in despair as the flames began to fade, and the monsters rushed after them.

He ducked as a group of frost goblins threw snowballs that were as hard as rocks. Jayden tried to avoid a few more before he caught a snowball in the shoulder. He groaned as the pain in his shoulder felt like getting slapped by an ice pack on a fresh sports injury. He had to rotate his shoulder as he ran to keep it from going numb.

His heart was racing as they continued to run. He was so anxious that he was constantly looking back to see how close the monsters were getting. While he was distracted, Sarah accidentally dropped her light, and it's bulb shattered on the rocky floor. Darkness fell over them, and Jayden slipped on the lantern as it rolled his way. He fell hard to the ground and yelled at the girls to keep running.

With his head throbbing, he tried to reach for his sword which was now lying on the ground just a few feet away. He stopped reaching for it when he heard a low growl coming from right behind him. The hair on the back of his neck stood straight up, and he had goosebumps on his arms.

Slowly he moved his head and found himself face to face with a fully grown LawDog. Out of the corner of his eye, he noticed a few Frost Goblins were approaching him from his right. Jayden closed his eyes, expecting to be monster lunch. Instead of the sensation of sharp teeth on his neck, the animals began circling him, snapping at him and blocking any chance for him to escape.

He tried to reach for his gun, and a small goblin slashed at him with its claws. Jayden quickly ducked to avoid it and received only a tiny scratch on his cheek. More and more monsters began to swarm around the young Dragon Warrior from Eiréné.

Jayden hoped that the girls were quite far away because he had feeling things were going to get ugly soon. He was grateful he was still breathing, but he knew something was up. The monsters should have attacked by now; it seemed like they were up to something. He also found it odd, that they were focused on him and had forgotten about chasing the girls which was good for Grace and Sarah, but not so good for Jayden.

He wanted to defend himself, but all the options he had would get him eaten. Jayden was beginning to think there was no way out of this. He was starting to accept that this was the end. Was he to die cowering in the face of the certain death? Did he spend all that time training at the Dragon Temple, only to die quietly?

Maybe I should unleash my real power, he wondered. He shook his head no. What if I go overboard and the girls get hurt in the process. There has to be another way out of this.

While he was lost in his thoughts, the monsters began to close in on him. Quickly, Jayden lunged for his hunting knife just as a LawDog was about to pounce on him. Once the animal became airborne, it stopped midjump and crumbled to the ground. That's when he heard the gunfire, and the monsters began falling back, as the bullets made contact with their targets.

Suddenly, Jayden was really grateful that Sarah had decided to join them on this journey. He kept his head low as bullets filled the air and then he heard a voice in the distance yell, "Salamanders of the Flame," which was the oddest thing Jayden had ever heard.

A bright red light flashed, and the monsters went into a full retreat, as twenty red salamanders with wings made of fire advanced on them. One salamander landed on a Frost Goblin and burst into flames, sending the goblin into the air screeching in pain. Two more salamanders landed on a LawDog and were biting and scratching at the large beast just as a ball of yellow energy landed at the animal's feet and exploded.

Jayden opened his eyes after the large explosion and noticed that the circle of monsters that had been surrounding him was now nonexistent. The creatures appeared to have crept back into the darkness. Jayden wiped the sweat from his brow. Whew, that was close, he thought.

He looked for the girls and twenty yards away from him was Sarah holding a smoking gun and a ball of explosive energy in her hand, and Grace pointing her dagger that was glowing red as it sent forth salamanders. At that moment, Jayden decided he was going to start being nicer to the girls and probably buy them a nice dinner. Then he remembered the lack of control Grace had over her summons, and he decided he better get up quickly before the flaming salamanders turned on him. He grabbed his sword, sheathed it and ran to give the girls a big hug.

While embracing them, a loud roar ripped through the room, shattering stalagmites and sending them to ground. Jayden threw a light green fireball to see where the noise had come from. His fireball bounced off the chest of a LawDog that stood eight feet tall and standing next to it were two six-foot Frost Goblins. Without saying a word, Jayden and the girls started running again as if their lives depended on it.

Jayden had a feeling that they couldn't outrun the monsters, but he also knew they couldn't fight them head on. That was weird, he thought. Those monsters should have caught up to them by now.

Their loud footsteps and constant roaring made them sound like they were right behind them.

Jayden was too afraid to look back, so he closed his eyes and tried to imagine how close the monsters were. When that didn't work, he looked over his shoulder. The giant Law Dog and his pals appeared to be content on just hanging back. Jayden wasn't sure what to make of it. Were they leading them into an ambush? Were these animals teasing them or were they waiting for Jayden and the girls to get tired of running.

He was beginning to wonder if the monsters were just out of breath and out of shape. Somehow, he knew that might not be the case. He perked up when a dim yellow light shined off and on in the distance. The light was quite odd because it seemed to be emanating from the ground. With the increased visibility, Jayden spotted a staircase that led skyward. Jayden shook his head in disbelief. How could there be a staircase inside of a mountain? He crossed his fingers and was hoping that the girls would just run past the staircase.

He whimpered as his hopes evaporated in front of him. When Sarah proceeded to dash up the staircase, followed by Grace who was huffing and puffing from exhaustion. If the monsters didn't kill her, running up the stairs would, Jayden thought.

Jayden slowed down before catching up with the others; he watched as the monsters stopped at the base of the staircase. He had a feeling they could jump up to where he was with no problem. Something about them ending their pursuit did not sit well with him. He wondered if the whole reason the monsters had attacked them was to get the girls running up this staircase.

He looked up and saw that the stone steps went on for what seemed like an eternity. Jayden was dreading the climb; he almost wished the LawDogs and the goblins had eaten him. This much exercise was bringing back memories of training at the Dragon Temple. He remembered the cold nights of running up and down that mountain. Those were fond memories he wanted to keep in the past, but here he was climbing up some random staircase that led to God knows where.

After a mixture of jogging, walking and crawling up the staircase, they finally decided to take a break. Sarah had found a flat slab of stone that served as a break between the sets of stairs; it was long enough for them to collapse on it without the risk of falling over the side.

Grace fell to the ground from exhaustion. Her breathing was heavy, and she was holding her stomach; she must have gotten a cramp from all of the running. Jayden rested against the wall that served as a barrier for the spiraling staircase. Unfortunately, this barrier was only on one side of the set of stairs, so the risk of falling to their death was still a possibility. He sipped on some water and took a bite of a peanut butter and chocolate bar. The smell of the chocolate was all the inspiration Grace needed to sit up and take a bite of his chocolate bar.

"You think you're cute doing that don't you? If you weren't pretty I'd push you off the stairs for that," Jayden said.

Stretching her arms, she rested her head in his lap and replied, "Jayden if you were a little more of a gentleman, you would have offered it to me."

"Ya, like that will ever happen," Sarah said while sitting at the edge of the stone slab with her legs dangling over the side.

"Ouch." Grace grimaced, "bet you felt that one, Jayden."

She was right, that line from Sarah did sting a little. Not because it wasn't true, but because it meant Sarah was still mad at him. The woman confused him. One moment she is saving his life and the next she goes back to being mad at him.

The girls decided to lay down and go to sleep. Jayden couldn't tell if it were night or day; back in the cavern, it felt like it was perpetual night. He couldn't blame them for being so tired, running for their lives and climbing a staircase would be exhausting for anybody. Jayden summoned two Flame Wards and placed one on each side of the stone slab they were on. He summoned them not because he felt any imminent danger, but it just seemed like a good idea considering the bad luck they have.

His eyes became heavy, exhaustion consuming him, and he went to sleep. Jayden only intended to sleep for a short time, but he ended up closing his eyes for hours. He awoke to the sound of crunching and laughter. He sat up and saw Sarah and Grace munching on crackers with ham and cheese. Normally that would be a great snack, but Jayden knew that was a sign that they were running low on food. Jayden rummaged through his bag and found three strips of beef jerky. He removed one piece from his bag, he broke it into three pieces and handed two of them to the girls. His tummy growled as they ate their pitiful lunch.

"So where do you think this staircase will lead us?" Grace asked.

"To heaven, if we're lucky," Jayden muttered as he munched down on a cracker.

"And, if we are not so lucky?" Sarah asked. "Grace, do you think we should see where this staircase goes or should we turn back?"

Grace scratched her chin and replied, "I think this is where we need to go. I just have this feeling that this staircase will lead us to *The Key*."

They rested for a few moments before gathering their things and leaving their comfy stone slab to climb the next set of stairs. It didn't take long for Jayden's legs to ache with every step they took. The last time he felt this out of shape was his first day of training at the Dragon Temple. The girls seemed to struggle just as much as he did. When they had first started climbing up the stairs, it didn't seem so bad. Now that they weren't running on adrenaline, this climb felt like a chore from hell.

Grace decided to take the lead. As she climbed the steps, she started wheezing and coughing. Sarah handed her some water which helped to relax Grace. Jayden felt sorry for her since she had to spend most of her life in the Southern Convent. It wasn't fair that she didn't have many opportunities to prepare her for this. The advantage Sarah had was that she had trained with Ms. Tonya and she had already done a fair amount of traveling with Jayden up to this point. He couldn't blame Grace for being tired, he, too, was feeling exhausted and didn't seem like they had climbed that much. They had to keep moving regardless; it was only going to get more difficult from there. Suddenly, a scary thought popped into his head. If this staircase takes them to Lady Coral, they might not have enough energy to fight her if things got out of hand.

Jayden smiled and picked up Grace. He was quite strong, but he wasn't Goliath, and he was a little clumsy. He realized that he was a lot clumsier than he had thought as he had to juggle carrying Grace and climbing up steps. Grace would yell rude comments in his ear if started teetering too far to his right. With the wall on their left, Jayden could understand her desire to react, but her yelling was killing his eardrums. Being the genius that he is decided to get as close to the edge as possible just to mess with her. Doing that was a bad idea because she kicked him in the side. Now he knew what it was like to be a horse.

It took them hours to make any headway up the stairs. They would have to take breaks from climbing every twenty or so minutes. At this point, Jayden's body felt so worn out; he could no longer carry Grace on his shoulders. His legs and his calf muscles were screaming at him with pain. This climb had become a battle of wills; his body wanted him to stop climbing, but his mind knew that if they continued to stop they would never make it to wherever this staircase led.

Once it had become nearly impossible for his legs to keep moving, he used his arms and the wall on his left to propel himself forward. He tried to lift his right leg on to the next step, but his body revolted, his leg spasming. He crumbled to the ground. His heart was pounding in his chest, and it felt like his lungs were about to explode as he struggled to catch his breath. Every inch of his body ached. He leaned back against the wall behind him. He moved his neck ever so gently to look below him. He saw that Sarah and Grace had already stopped on the flight of stairs below him. His mind was so obsessed with the climb up the stairs that he hadn't even noticed.

They seemed to be doing alright and weren't yelling at him, so he decided not to worry too much. Rummaging through his bag, he found that he had only half a bottle of water left. He wanted to drink it all in one gulp, but he knew he needed to save some of it. He begrudgingly took two small swigs and put the rest in his bag. As the cold water descended throughout his body, the small amount of liquid seemed to strengthen him a little bit. He checked on the girls one more time as his eyes became too heavy, and they slowly closed. His only thought at that time was that he hoped that he up would wake up back in Eiréné surrounded by his family and friends.

He awoke with a jump. Why you might ask because Grace poured ice cold water down his back. Before he could strangle her, he had to struggle to get his eyes open. His difficulty wasn't due to anything being wrong with his eyes, but from a bright light that was shining down on his face. Once his eyes adjusted, he felt the need to strangle Grace yet again, because she was now shaking him to get him to move.

"What is your problem?" Jayden grumbled.

"Jayden, get up you have to see this! At least keep your eyes open for a little bit," she said sounding quite chipper which was quite odd for her.

How could someone be so happy when it's bright and cold? Cold, he thought, why did it feel colder all of a sudden? Finally, Jayden decided, it was worthwhile to keep his eyes open. Grace was pointing up, and Jayden leaned back to see what she was trying to get him to look at. The white light shining from above them was blinding. Staring down from the midst of the bright light was Sarah and floating down through this hole in the ceiling were tiny snowflakes. Then it hit him; something was wrong about this. Something terribly wrong was happening. The light above them was about three flights up. Before Jayden went to sleep, he swore that there were more stairs above them.

Sounding startled he said to Grace, "Where did that hole in the ceiling come from? How did Sarah get up there? Was that there before I went to sleep?"

Grace glanced up at where Sarah was and then looked back at Jayden and frowned, "I'm not quite sure where it came from. I remember seeing the staircase going on forever. When I woke up, Sarah was gone. So I climbed up the steps past you, went up a little further and there she was standing under a door hatch she had found. Together we pushed it open and voila! We were back outside. And then I ran down here to wake you up."

"Why didn't she come down to wake me up?" He asked.

"Well because she chickened out on pouring ice water down your back and because of other reasons I'm guessing," she replied.

"What other reasons would she have?" He asked. Grace smiled and started to head back up the stairs. Jayden wondered if Grace knew the answer to that question or if she was messing with him, but then again, he wondered if he wanted that answer.

Trying to adjust to the bright sunlight was difficult but standing up was even more of a pain. Not only were his legs sore and stiff, but he had this awful kink in his neck from sleeping. Gritting his teeth through the pain, he trudged up the steps. As he got closer to hatch, he could see the ceiling above them. The ceiling was flat, slightly rocky, and quite similar to the floor below them. The placement of the ceiling and hatch were just low enough for a person to climb up through the hole, once the hatch was opened.

He climbed through the hatch and found himself standing in a few inches of snow. Jayden could see the summit from where he stood. Powerful thunderclouds blanketed the mountain's peak. Bright lights flashed from within the clouds, and he could hear the thunderclap so loud that it shook him to the bone. This powerful storm that was forming just a couple hundred feet above them filled him with absolute fear.

Chapter 29

The Key

His hand slipped on a rock as they climbed toward the summit. He cursed to himself as he struggled to regain his grip. The rain made it almost impossible to climb. Visibility and traction were almost nonexistent. Normally, he wouldn't climb a mountain under such conditions, but they had a mission to complete. He knew they must be close; the magical energy in the air was so strong there was no doubt they were getting close to the finish line.

Beads of sweat appeared on his brow. The rainwater was cold to the touch, but the air around them felt tropical and humid. In other words, it was a little unusual. Just a couple hundred feet below them there was still snow on the ground, but now they were caught in a tropical thunderstorm. Even the rocks that they were climbing on looked odd. Most of the stones were triangular and diamond in shapes. The rocks felt smooth like they were made of metal. These metallic stones were stacked on top of each other like the steps of a pyramid that was leading them to the top of the mountain. The rocks themselves were so cold it was like clutching ice. The corners of the rocks were so jagged they scraped Jayden's hands as he tried to pull himself up.

Lightning pealed across the sky, and the thunder boomed so powerfully, he could feel it reverberate in the rocks. He thought it was terrifying to be climbing a mountain in the middle of a thunderstorm. He wished they could turn back, but that was out of the question at this point.

As the lightning flashed, Jayden swore he could see something a couple of yards above them. From what he could tell, there was a flat area about hundred or so feet above them. When the lightning flashed again, he thought he caught a glimpse of a roof.

The closer they got to the building, the more Jayden wanted to turn back. He knew the building they were heading to wasn't some five-star hotel or a beautiful beach house. They were headed to the home of a witch who was willing to betray her own people.

Even though his body had reached some level of exhaustion, he could feel his magical energy returning. He knew that he would need every ounce of it. If Lady Coral was half as strong as he thought, he might have to tap into his real power. He didn't want to, but if she tried to hurt the girls. Jayden would burn this whole mountain if he had to.

Jayden pulled himself up on to a landing. Standing just a few yards in front of him was their destination. The outside of the building matched the color of the metallic rocks they had just climbed. It was both gray and depressing. The windows on the building were tinted black with a pale white door. The structure in front of them looked just like an old chapel. Black crows congregated on the statue of a gargoyle, which rested on top of the building. The blackbirds stared at them coldly daring them to enter the building.

Grace decided to plop down in front of the entrance. Sarah joined her and pulled out ham and crackers from her bag. She distributed the small meal to everyone. Jayden reached into his bag and handed out the rest of the jerky. He figured there was no point in saving it.

"This is probably the most depressing place to have a picnic," he muttered as he chomped down on the ham and cracker sandwich he made.

"I think you are right," Sarah replied. A look of shock appeared on Jayden's face. Did Sarah just acknowledge my existence? He wondered if that meant he was out of the doghouse now.

Grace glanced around them nervously, "Jayden, I don't like this place. Do we really have to go inside?"

Jayden wanted to tell her that it was going to be okay. He wished that he could say that inside this building they were going to find cookies and candy. The reality was he had no idea what they were going to face. The fear in Grace's eyes was unsettling. She knew something that he didn't. Grace had met Lady Coral, and the fear on her face said everything he needed to know. He felt bad for her because she had never made it this far before. She probably never expected to retrieve *The Key*. Now she was going to have to be in the presence of that evil witch. Jayden wished he could give her another option.

Jayden placed his hand on Grace's shoulder and said, "I know that you don't want to go in there, but we have to check it out. When we go in there, you can stand behind me. Everything will be okay I promise."

That was a flat-out lie, and he knew it. His words seemed to reassure Grace a little bit or at least she was pretending they did.

"By the way, I think we should leave our bags out here. If things go south we need to be ready to defend ourselves," he said.

Jayden dusted himself and got back to his feet. He approached the pale white door with caution. What waited for them behind it, he had no clue. Jayden grabbed the door handle and made a gentle twist. The doorknob snapped off and clanged as it hit the ground. The door creaked as it opened on its own. Normally when something like that happens, one should run and hide, Jayden.

He stepped into the room, and the wooden floor creaked beneath them. The room was pretty dark, so Jayden snapped his fingers, and a small flame appeared just above his thumb.

Large picture frames hung from the walls with nothing in them. Further into the room he noticed a small round table. Resting on it was a vase made of crystal. Inside of it was a single long stemmed black rose. The flower was cold to the touch, and its thorns were razor sharp.

A musty smell filled the room. This smell reminded him of rotting flesh which he considered to be a bad sign. The room temperature dropped by twenty degrees, and a cold breeze swept through the building. The flame flickering above his finger went out.

He snapped his fingers, but nothing happened. He tried again to no avail. Sarah flicked on her small flashlight, and as the light came on, she let out a scream. Grace followed suit as the look of fright appeared on their faces. Jayden tried to see what they were gazing at and instantly concluded that the girls were well within their right to scream. In fact, if the girls weren't right next to him, he would have screamed too.

Sitting on throne twenty feet in front of them was a rotting corpse. The corpse was leaning to the side against one of the armrests as if the person had died right there in the chair. The body was a moldy gray and covered in white linen. Long strands of thin white hair covered its head. The cheeks were sunken in, and the eye sockets were empty. Wrapped around the neck was a gold necklace that had faded over time. Hanging from the necklace was a bleached white key made of ivory.

"That's it!" Grace yelped, "that's *The Key* my Father gave me."

"Wait, that's it? That's *The Key* we have been looking for this whole time?" Jayden asked as his heart began to fill with emotions of hate, anger, sadness, and relief.

"Ya, I think so. That key is one of the few things about my dad that I can remember," she replied as tears brimmed in her eyes.

Sarah put her arm around Grace. "Hey, if that's *The Key*, then the person sitting in the chair must be..."

"Lady Coral," they all said in unison. Once those words escaped their lips, the ground beneath them shook. Purple flames sprang to life dancing on the tips of the lanterns and torches that hung on the walls. Then a bright white light flashed, and then they heard something pop like a firecracker. A thick cloud of smoke appeared and enveloped the throne.

A strong wind charged into the room and blew away the smoke. The corpse on the throne disappeared and sitting in its place was a beautiful woman. She looked like as if she was in her mid-thirties. Her hair was black with blonde highlights, extending down to her ankles. She was wearing a beautiful black dress, with earrings made of platinum. In her right hand was a black wand with a small green snake wrapped around it. She had beautiful brown eyes and cruel smile that made him want to run. The witch cracked her neck and gazed into their eyes as if she could see into their very soul.

"Lady Coral? Is that you?" Grace asked nervously. Her lips trembled as she addressed the witch who was slowly approaching them.

A malevolent grin appeared on Lady Coral's face. As she approached them the air in the room felt colder. Dark magical energy radiated off of her body; it was frightening to gaze upon her. He knew that if he showed any sign of weakness that Lady Coral would pounce without any hesitation.

"You are quite perceptive Grace. My hair was a lot shorter the last time you saw me. I am honored to have the future Queen of the Aggeloi on my mountain." Lady Coral said as she bowed before Grace. "I must commend you two ladies for rising above the challenges you faced to get here. It is evident that the blood of The Elders flows within your veins. However, it is quite unfortunate for you, that your companion is both the son of Dion LoneOak and a Dragon Warrior. Now can you tell me, what brings you here to my neck of the woods?"

Grace glanced around nervously, "Well, we came to here um...we wanted to ask you about something," she mumbled as she trembled with fear.

Finding his courage, Jayden stepped forward and rested his hand on Grace's shoulder, "look here lady. What's with all of the cheesy horror flick theatrics, and why do you have a problem with me? Better yet, how do you even know who I am. Have we met before?"

Lady Coral switched her focus from Grace to him. She stared at him like he was a nuisance that needed to be snuffed out. She smirked and then she raised her wand, and a bright light flashed off the tip.

Jayden felt the sudden sensation of cold steel against his skin, as a large serrated knife appeared out of nowhere. The blade pressed lightly against his neck. He could feel a small cut begin to form. A light stream of blood began to trickle down his neck staining his shirt. Normally, he would have been freaking out at this point, but he knew that he had to stay calm.

He stared into Lady Coral's eyes, and there was something very familiar about her. Jayden had a feeling that this was not her first encounter with him. Regardless of how she knew who he was, he had to maintain eye contact. He had to be brave.

Lady Coral raised her wand and spoke, "the Dragon Warrior will speak to be me with the honor and respect that I deserve. I know your father taught you better than that. If there is one more disrespectful outburst from you, I will cut your throat open without hesitation. Is that understood?"

"Yes," he said begrudgingly.

"I said, do you understand," she replied.

Dropping his head, he replied, "yes ma'am."

She smiled back at him ever so sweetly and lowered her wand. Once her arm was back by her side, the knife disappeared within a cloud of smoke. She cleared her throat and said, "I know you must be wondering as to why I made your trip up this mountain quite difficult. The main reason is that I like to have a little fun, and sometimes I get a little bored. This sorry excuse of a Dragon Warrior was not meant to survive. He's a lot tougher than I had imagined. Anyway, I hope you all had as much fun traveling here, as I did watching you struggle."

"It has been nothing but fun," Jayden muttered to himself.

"Lady Coral, how do you know Jayden? Why do you want to hurt him?" Grace asked cautiously.

Lady Coral smirked and let out a cruel laugh, "his dad and I don't see eye to eye. You see many years ago when *The Key* was rediscovered, Jayden's father and his band of do-gooders stole it from King Aelius. I saw this as a golden opportunity for the Daimonia. So I tried to convince Jayden's father to put the power of *The Key* to good use and to switch sides. He shot me down, so I convinced Raiden's wife, Moriah, to steal *The Key* and to join the Daimonia."

"Wait a second; you knew Tony's mom too? I thought you were part of the Southern Convent?" Sarah asked, feeling really confused.

"Yes my dear, she is my cousin. Once she joined the Daimonia, I had her try to get *The Key* by any means necessary. I have been a member of the Daimonia for quite some time. Through an exploration of some their literature, I realized that I appreciated some of their ideals. Unfortunately for you Jayden, your father couldn't see that the Daimonia had the world's best interests at heart. Instead of being part of the solution, he went into hiding like a coward."

Her insults made Jayden's blood boil as the witch continued her speech. If the opportunity presented itself, he vowed to kill her.

Lady Coral chuckled as she watched Jayden become increasingly frustrated. She twirled her bangs and said, "As the years went by we had no idea where your father had hidden *The Key* or where he was. I was the one who discovered that he was living in Eiréné and I passed that information on to the Daimonia," Lady Coral said.

Clenching her fist, Sarah said, "So you are the reason our village was destroyed, and our friends and families were killed?"

Grinning, she replied, "I don't think I implied that at all. Now that I have shared some of my skeletons, it's time for the princess to share hers." Her face turned a shade of red as she became filled with anger. "Now tell me! Where is the real Key?" She yelled as she ripped off her necklace and threw it at Grace.

The Key made a loud clanging sound as it struck the ground. The three of them looked at *The Key* on the ground and felt instantly confused. Isn't this *The Key* we've been looking for, Jayden thought. She must be trying to mess with us or forgot to take her crazy pills he decided. There is no way they could have gone through all that they had on this journey to end up chasing the wrong key.

"Lady Coral are you saying that's the wrong key? "Grace asked. "I'm pretty sure that's the same key my dad gave me when I was little. In fact, that's the only major thing I can remember from my past."

The witch replied "Yes Grace, I am sure that's the wrong key. I know this because I found the treasure chest that *The Key* is meant to open."

Lady Coral swiped her wand, and a light clicked on near the back of the building. The shallow lighting illuminated the room just enough to reveal a large cabinet made of iron. Resting in the center of the cabinet was a small treasure box. There was an image on the top of the box of a Pegasus inlaid with white gold. This was an old symbol of The Elders.

She pointed at the treasure chest and said, "*The Key* I took from you does not open that box. Now search your memories and tell me where the real key is, or you will face a punishment until I get what I want."

Grace shook her head as she struggled to recall anything. "I'm sorry I can't remember anything else. The only memory I have about a key was when my Dad gave me that one and he said that it would protect me and keep me safe. Why can't I remember anything else?"

"Well, that answer is simple. When The Southern Convent, was hired by the Aggeloi government to kill you and your entourage. I told them not too because you would be an asset to us and your connection to *The Key* was invaluable. Lady Clara had the brilliant idea of using memory modification magic on you. She wanted to make all of your memories fuzzy except the strongest memories you had for a key. The downside of memory modification magic is that you risk losing vital information. She did that to control you and to keep information about *The Key* all to her bitchy self. When I realized that you had hidden *The Key* that your father gave you, I took it from you to protect you. She was going to kill you once she got all the information she needed. In a way, you owe me your life. If you can search your memories for *The Key*, I can help you recover all of your memories. Help me so I can help you."

Grace tried to concentrate but the harder she tried the dizzier she became. She teared up in frustration, "I'm sorry! I just can't do it!"

Lady Coral grinned, "Don't you worry my dear, I will give you a little incentive" she raised her wand and pointed it at Jayden. She smiled at him sweetly, "Dragon Warrior, I am assuming that you are quite resistant to traditional fire magic? In fact, I'm guessing that sometimes when you are hit by normal fire magic, it helps you to regenerate some of your energy. Would that be a correct assumption?"

Jayden nodded yes, feeling quite unnerved by her question and the wand that she was pointing at him. With a devilish grin, she flicked her wrist and said, "Freeze Flame."

Instantly, Jayden was engulfed in a sea of light blue flames. He dropped to his knees as his body was overwhelmed by a burning cold sensation. His nerves were screaming with pain as it felt like a thousand needles were jabbing every inch of his body. He tried to yell as the pain became too much but the cold flames snuffed away his voice.

The girls all stared at him in horror. Sarah rushed to his side, and she reached out to grab him. Once her hands had touched the blue flames, she yelped and pulled her hand back.

"Make it stop! You are going to kill him!" Sarah yelled.

Lady Coral chuckled and flicked her wand and the fire consuming Jayden disappeared. "Now Grace did that jog your memory? Do you remember anything more about *The Key*?"

Grace shook her head in frustration. She wanted to lie and say yes, but she knew that would have been a bad idea. She was terrified of the potential repercussions of her honesty.

Lady Coral's hair became staticky and dark energy filled the room as her anger grew. "Tsk, tsk, this is not what I wanted to hear. You see I am trying to be the good guy here. I really don't want to kill your friend to fix your memory. So, I will give you one more chance. I need you to think really, really hard or else I will bleed him dry. I will give you five minutes to search your mind. In the meantime, let's see how strong this Dragon Warrior really is." With a flick of her wand, she lifted Jayden into the air. Coral summoned a staff made of oak and slammed it into the ground and chanted, "Souls of the Dead come forth and fight for me! Rise with the sword, rise with the shield. The depths of Hades bring forth the Nekron!"

The ground beneath them shook, and a wave of energy shot out across the floor and then vanished. She flicked her wand again and sent Jayden flying out the door.

His back smashed against the door, as he crashed through it. He hit the ground and rolled over in pain. His body was still reeling from the fire spell Coral had cast, and now his back was aching from being thrown into a door. What the hell is that lady's problem, he thought?

He grew nervous as the ground beneath him rumbled, and the gravel beneath him shifted violently. Just as quickly as it started, the mini earthquake stopped. Then he heard a low growl that sent chills up his spine. He wanted to keep his eyes closed, but his fear forced them open.

Coming up from beneath the earth were old bones and sharpened swords. The bones began connecting to each other slowly locking into place with their necessary counterparts. Soon whole skeletons were surrounding the building picking up their swords as they took form. Jayden looked up and standing above him, was a large skeleton with a black crown on its head. The large skeleton was grasping on to a double-bladed katana painted in gold and dripping with blood. The monster looked down upon him and let out a deafening roar.

Chapter 30

A Lapse in Judgement

Sarah couldn't stop her body from trembling. She was frozen with fear and shock. Her eyes couldn't look away from the door, Jayden had been thrown into. She had no idea how much pain he must be in. The sound of monsters growling and shrieking just outside of the building made her stomach churn. A feeling of dread was starting to consume her; she had a feeling that this time they might not survive. Sure, they have had plenty of close calls thus far, and have been able to rise above the previous challenges. However, standing in the presence of Lady Coral on top of a mountain seemed rather hopeless.

Then she heard it. The sound of metal clanging against metal. The walls of the building muffled the sound somewhat, but she swore she heard it. There it was, the glimmer of hope she was needing. Jayden must be alive, and he's got enough strength to fight whatever monsters Lady Coral had conjured up. A gentle nudge from Grace brought her out of her momentary stupor.

Lady Coral cocked her head to the side and had an evil smile on her face. "Your friend, the Dragon Warrior, is a lot tougher then he looks. You know, if he weren't Dion's son, he would make a great addition to my collection."

"What do you mean by that?" Sarah asked, as she seethed with anger.

"Oh, never mind darling. He won't be your problem for much longer. Now, Grace, I do apologize for having to push you so hard to get your memories back. It might take a little longer for you to remember everything. So I have decided to keep you here for a while."

She slammed her staff into the ground and wall of green flames spread around the four corners of the building. The fire created a perimeter making it impossible for them to escape without getting burned.

"You may have noticed that those flames don't give off much heat. This spell is called Bio-Flame. If you touch it, you will feel a slight burning sensation and of course get dreadfully sick. Forgive my absentmindedness; I forgot to tell you, Sarah. I will need to keep you here also."

Sarah's eyes flashed with anger. She drew her two short swords and lunged herself at the evil witch. Grace quickly grabbed her by the wrist and pulled her back. She whispered in Sarah's ears to remain calm. The idea of being calm was the furthest thing from Sarah's mind. She wanted to make Coral pay for all of the lives she's devastated. Sarah would rather die than become another pawn in Coral's game.

As Sarah struggled to remain calm, Grace gently let go of her. Grace then took a step forward which seemed to catch Lady Coral off guard. Feeling a little confident, she took another step forward and put her prettiest smile on and said, "Ms. Coral, why would an all-powerful witch like yourself even need the Daimonia?"

Lady Coral opened her mouth to respond but hesitated for a second. She scratched her chin as she contemplated, how to correctly answer this question. She cocked her head to the side and smiled.

"You really are your father's daughter. That flattery you most definitely picked up from him. Truthfully, I don't need the Daimonia. They would still be chasing their tails if it weren't for me. You see young lady it is I who is using them. I feed them just enough information so that they can do the leg work. You see that box back there with the map in it; the Daimonia have no idea that I possess it. While I have had them looking for *The Key*, I was searching for the chest that it opened. Once *The Key* is found, I will become the sole possessor of the..." The witch stopped mid-sentence to quietly observe that Grace and Sarah were slowly moving closer to her.

"Of the what?" Sarah asked, "You didn't finish your statement. Also, why do you need me? What is so important about me? I understand you needing Grace, but what's so special about me?"

"Like Grace, you are quite special Sarah. You will learn how special you are before too long. For now, you are simply leverage. Now to answer your other question, when I can open that chest, the map in it will lead me to..." Lady Coral stopped mid-sentence again to cover her nose, "ACHOO!" She sneezed, "Sorry about that, as I was saying. I will become the sole possessor of the... Achoooo!!!"

Lady Coral's eyes started to tear up, and her cheeks became puffy. She continued to sneeze so hard it felt like it shook the building. She looked around frantically as she continued to sneeze. She wheeled around to look back at her mantle. She screamed as she spotted four black cats resting on it.

Her face turned bright red, and she turned back towards Grace and said, "How dare you summon cats in my presence! ACHOO! You know I have an allergy!"

Grace responded by bursting out in laughter, "You have got to see the humor in this, with you being a witch and having a cat allergy." She snapped her fingers and summoned more cats into the room. Soon Lady Coral was sneezing uncontrollably at that moment Sarah lunged at the witch.

329

A yellow ball of energy appeared in Sarah's hand, and she yelled, "FlashBang." The ball of energy slammed into Lady Coral's chest and exploded filling the room with a blinding light and smoke. The which stumbled backward, dropping her staff and wand.

Sarah summoned two balls of orange energy and yelled, "Thermal Grenade!" She tossed the orange balls of energy at the staff and wand upon contact they exploded. The force of the explosion sent each girl flying in a different direction. Lady Coral slammed hard against the mantle while Grace and Sarah were pushed up against the green wall of fire.

The moment Sarah felt the heat on the back of her neck, she tried to redirect her momentum away from it. She knew immediately that she had just brushed up against the BioFlame.

Besides the slight burning sensation, she didn't feel too bad. Maybe Lady Coral was lying about the adverse effects of the green fire. She glanced to the left side of the room and watched as Grace pulled her arm out of the BioFlame. Then she watched Lady Coral get up from the other side the room. As the witch drew closer to them, Sarah's vision started to blur. She struggled to keep her head steady because the world around her was spinning. Her stomach was beginning to churn while Coral let out a cackle. Her laugh sounded cruel; it rang in her ears like the piercing sound of a morning alarm.

Sarah's head was throbbing, and for a moment she thought she heard Grace dry heave. Her stomach continued to churn and burn with pain. Soon she started coughing up a lung as Lady Coral moved to the center of the room.

Lady Coral giggled, as she witnessed the girls misery, "I see you two have been bitten by a little dose of karma. You pretended to be nice to get me to drop my guard and then you thought by summoning cats that I would be easily defeated. You believed that by destroying my staff and wand that you would somehow cripple me? The thought of that is laughable. I see the BioFlame is working it's little magic." She laughed to herself, "normally, when someone trifles with me. I kill them slowly and painfully. Unfortunately, your lives are a little too important for me to take at this time. However, I can make you wish you were dead. The both of you have experienced plenty of terrible things in your lives. How about you relive those traumas?" She grinned as she snapped her fingers. Her wand reformed and appeared in her hand, "magic of this caliber cannot be destroyed so easily. This next spell I'm going to use is a personal favorite. I hope you can appreciate it as much as I do. Flashback!"

Green light filled the room, and as it faded away, Sarah became increasingly dizzy. Her stomach churned, and the ground beneath her started to shift. She blinked for a moment, and when she opened her eyes, she found herself back in Eiréné.

Sarah was sitting on her bed with homework in her lap and headphones in her ears. She glanced around her room and admired the posters of her favorite bands that covered her ceiling. Even her yellow bookcase was filled to the brim with novels and magazines. Resting on her nightstand was a journal her grandfather had given her before he died, and a glass of chocolate milk her mom had made her. She took a sip of her drink while she stared out her window. It was starting to get pretty dark. looking down at the paper in her lap, she realized it wasn't homework she was staring at. It was a letter that her ex-boyfriend Bryce had passed to her in class. He wanted to get back together with her. She shook her head and tried to remember what she saw in him in the first place. Truth be told, she wished Jayden had asked her out, but he never even tried. No matter how many hints she dropped, that boy must be thickheaded.

Something about this moment in time seemed just a little too familiar. Maybe it's just a minor case of déjà vu, she thought. She picked up a school book when her mother ran into the room just as she heard the sound of firecrackers going off just outside her window. Her mom's dark hair looked wild, and her face looked frightened, and in her right hand, she held a machine pistol and on her back was a short sword.

"Get up!" She yelled.

Sarah replied, "mom, calm down. Why are you barging into my room with a gun? Where did you get that?"

"Sarah Lynn! I said get up! We have to go now. Leave your stuff and let's go."

As she spoke, Sarah heard more fireworks going off, and it sounded like they were getting closer. She got up and ran to her mother's side. Her mother grabbed her wrist and as they ran toward the kitchen. The kitchen window shattered, and she heard the sound of metal clinking against the tile floor. Her mother grabbed her and pulled her to ground before they reached the kitchen. Within seconds, the kitchen exploded launching shrapnel into the walls.

Sarah blacked out when her head hit the ground and was awoken by a splitting headache, her ears ringing, and her mother shaking her to get her conscience again. Sarah winced as a bruise began to form on her left cheek from a piece of the ceiling tile that had fallen on her during the explosion. Smoked filled the house, and the fire alarm began to blare.

"Mom," she coughed, "What just happened?"

"I think that might have been a grenade." Her mom replied nonchalantly. She rose to her feet and extended her hand, "if you can stand, we need to get out of here now. We will find your father and go from there okay." She grabbed her mom's hand and stood up.

Then she heard people trying to bust down their front door. Her mom led her back into her bedroom. Bullets crashed through her bedroom window, sending fragments of glass into the air making six holes in the wall. Her mom drew her gun and slowly approached the window; she had Sarah wait in the hall. The sound of gunfire outside of the window was intense. It lasted for about five minutes and then there was complete silence.

"Hey Donna, it's me. It's safe for you to climb out of the window," said a familiar voice.

"Dave? David is that you out there?" She asked.

Jumping through the window was a man who stood about 5'10. His gray hair was slicked back, and there was a tattoo of a blue dragon on his forearm. In his right hand was a machine pistol and, on his back, rested a short sword that was now stained with blood.

"Dad!" Sarah yelled as she ran to embrace him.

"Dave! What's going on out there? It sounds like a war zone. Those bastards blew up my kitchen!" Donna said as her rage grew.

"We can't discuss it now, but we need to get Sarah as far from Eiréné as possible, "David replied.

They climbed out of the window just in the nick of time as a small rocket blasted the front of the house. They ran east to get out of town.

The sky above them was filled with smoke and painted with an orange hue from the fires. Screams and gunshots filled the peaceful streets of Eiréné. While they ran, Ms. Tonya joined them in their escape. Her lip was bleeding, and her hair was matted but other than that she looked fine.

White lights flashed behind them. Sarah looked back and saw men in black coats chasing them and firing bullets in their direction. She couldn't process what was going on. Sarah pinched herself hoping this was all a dream and that soon she would wake from this nightmare. Her parents stopped as the men in black cloaks were gaining on them. They handed Ms. Tonya the guns and the swords.

"Tonya, take her. We will catch up with you" Dave replied.

"But Dave." Tonya pleaded.

"Go now! While there is still time," Dave demanded.

"Daddy, no!!" Sarah yelled.

J. Edwards

Donna and Dave embraced their daughter, "look, baby, we will be right behind you. We are just going to slow them down. I promise you; we will catch up with you, and I'll make your favorite breakfast in the morning." She kissed her daughter, "now go!"

A wall of sand and dirt sprung up from the ground separating Sarah from her parents. Just as she tried to reach for her parents, the image became distorted and twisted.

The distortion made her head spin more than it already was which contributed to her losing some of her lunch. She closed her eyes as the spinning in her head became unbearable just when she thought she might throw up again, the spinning slowed.

Nervously, she opened her eyes and found herself standing in a hospital. Her vision was still blurry; she realized that she had been crying for quite some time. Her nose was runny, and she could feel a mild pain from someone squeezing her right hand nervously. On her right side stood Tony whose eyes were puffy from tears and whose determined facial expression was struggling to hold back a wealth of worry. Sarah noticed that there was a hand, gently patting her back to try and comfort her. Standing next to her was General Floriana, her stoic poise seemed forced. What were they comforting her for?

They were standing in a blue room with a large window about two feet in front of her. She stepped forward to see what was on the other side. Once she had pressed her face up against the cold glass, she noticed that there were a few surgeons and nurses frantically working on a patient.

She could see a heart monitor, and the digital image on the screen did not bode well for the patient. Sarah watched as the heart rate of the patient skyrocketed and then quickly plummeted. The heart monitor was beeping out of control; the patient had begun coding. So the medical staff brought out the defibrillator and pulled out the paddles.

One of the doctors yelled, "Clear!" He tried again. "Clear!" The line on the heart monitor went flat, and the doctor tried one more time. Nothing happened. The doctor yelled furiously, "Call it!"

The doctors and nurses began to disperse, and Sarah pressed her face closer to the glass to see who the patient was. A nurse dressed in blue moved to the left and Sarah could finally see who was lying on the operating table.

His brown eyes stared right back at her like he was gazing into her soul. They were expressionless, and his smile which would normally light up a room was now vacant. The patient laying on the operating table was Jayden.

The nurse came back into view and pulled a sheet to cover the body something in Sarah snapped, and she banged on the glass. Sarah yelled, "Jayden, get up! Please get up! That's not how this is supposed to end! You are supposed to make it through this!" She banged on the glass again and again. "Come on, get up! Please don't leave me like this," she whimpered.

The tears flowed from her eyes, and while she was reliving this twisted and painful memory, one clear and coherent thought came into her mind. What she was seeing wasn't real. Then she remembered Lady Coral had cast a spell on her and Grace. How could this all be fake, she wondered. These emotions, this scene, they felt so real. She glanced at the lifeless body on the operating table one more time, and she remembered that the real Jayden was in danger. As long as she was reliving this nightmare, she wouldn't be able to help him.

Think, she told herself, how do I get out of this nightmare? Sarah began sifting through the various spells her parents and Ms. Tonya had taught her, and the magic she learned at the Water Temple. She could not think of one single spell that could help her escape a twisted world filled with horrible memories.

J. Edwards

Between the sensation of Tony's hand trembling as it held hers and Floriana patting her back gently, a lightbulb turned on in her head. She had an idea that could work, but then again it could totally backfire. It didn't matter if it worked or failed, she wanted to wake up from this hellish dream.

She closed her eyes and tried to concentrate. Sarah had to envision herself back in Lady Coral's creepy house. She had to imagine herself lying down on the floor with that witch standing in the center of the room. Sarah could almost see it in her mind. She took a deep breath, summoned all the energy she could muster, then she yelled, "Rebound!"

A bright blue light flashed, and in an instant, she was back in the real world. Sarah was still dizzy from the BioFlame. She watched as Lady Coral recoiled and took a few steps backward. The spell she had cast on the girls had been rebounded back to her. Lady Coral screamed and covered her face as she relived the most traumatizing moments in her life. Sarah tried to get up, but her legs felt like jelly. She needed to attack the witch while the opportunity was there.

Lady Coral continued to reel backward as she was caught up in her memories. Her face was filled with shock and tears filled her eyes.

"How dare you use my own spell against me! I will kill you all!" She wiped her eyes, and just as she raised her wand, a red spot appeared on the right side of her chest. A gunshot rang out, and a second red spot appeared on her left shoulder. She smiled ever so sweetly, "you three are full of surprises. My young Dragon Warrior, one day you may even surpass your father." As her words exited her lips, her body became translucent, and she slowly faded away.

As the witch's body slowly disintegrated, Jayden appeared a couple of feet behind her. His shirt was torn, and there were cuts on his arms and across his chest. He lowered his gun and glanced at the girls who were laying down on the ground shaking.

"What happened to you two? I was out there fighting off skeletons, and here you are napping." With tears in her eyes and her head still spinning, Sarah got up and ran into his arms. "Ouch!" he said," I was just kidding about that. I'm sorry I made you worry".

She continued to sob into his chest. He turned his head to take a look at Grace, who was now sitting up with her head between her legs. Her tear drops stained the floor in front of her. Jayden walked over to her, while still holding Sarah in his arm. He bent down and took her hand, "Hey," he said softly, "it's okay now. You're safe."

Grace looked up at him nervously, "is she really gone?"

With a cheeky grin, he replied, "I hope so because I have like one bullet left."

A brief smile creased her lips. More tears started to brim, and she flung her arms around his neck.

"She was so awful." Grace said with tears streaming, "All of them were awful to me. Whatever you do, don't take me back there. I can't stand being around those awful people ever again."

"Gracey, I was never planning on bringing you back there. Plus, you are a part of the group now. You are one of us," he said.

She crossed her arms, "I told you not to call me that, but thank you for looking out for me. So where do I go from here? What do I do now?"

"That's a million-dollar question Gracey," Jayden stood up and scratched his chin, "Well, let's start off with something simple. Why don't you pick up the necklace your father gave you. I will get that treasure chest, and when we get back to civilization, I will get you an ice cream."

"Well, what about me?" Sarah chimed in, "do I get ice cream?"

J. Edwards

"On second thought, you two can share the ice cream. That hug you gave hurt a little bit when you squeezed me," he replied

"This punch I'm going give you will be a lot worse," Sarah said with a grin.

Chapter 31
The Elder's Daughter

He kicked open the door, and his foot landed on solid ground. The sun shined upon him, and his body felt safe and warm. A gentle breeze blew through his short curly hair. He took a deep breath, and he could almost taste the peppermint wafting through his nose. If he could describe this moment in a word, it would be peace.

Jayden looked down and resting in his arms was an old chest. This was peculiar, he thought, I wonder where this came from. He looked around and found himself standing on a grassy hill, near the base of a mountain. Feeling panic-stricken, he let go of the chest to slap his face to see if he was dreaming. The heavy box landed gracefully on his big toe, and he was instantly filled with pain.

"Shit!" He yelled as he started hopping on one leg to make the pain stop.

"What is your freaking problem?" Grace asked, as she watched a moron hopping on one leg.

"I'm not going to use my healing spell if you are going to be so clumsy," Sarah laughed.

Jayden cried out, "Shut up that's not funny it hurts. How did we get here? And why am I carrying this stupid chest?"

"Umm..." Sarah said as she gave him a blank stare. "I can't remember a thing. I don't know how we got here. What about you Grace?"

Grace grinned as she tried to think, "Well I know enough not to drop a chest on my foot. But other than that, my mind feels blank. I feel like I woke up from a bad dream. There was this witch from the Southern Convent, and her name was..."

"Lady Coral?" Jayden and Sarah said in unison.

"Yea, how did you know? I thought it was just a horrible nightmare. Then how did we get here? What happened to our wounds?" Grace asked frantically as images from their last battle came flooding into her mind.

"It's going to be okay," Sarah said trying to reassure herself and Grace. "Lady Coral must have used an enchantment similar to what the Southern Convent uses to keep their town hidden. That's why they could never find her; you could only reach her if she let you. Which means Jayden has the treasure chest that *The Key* was made to open."

Jayden picked up the chest and held it in his hands. The container was obviously an antique, the images on its face were slightly faded due to the passage of time. There didn't seem to be anything extraordinary about it that would make people fight for its contents. They didn't even have the right key to open it, so it was essentially useless junk. He would be saving the world a lot of heartache if he just really destroyed it with a fire spell.

He sat down and tried prying it open with his Kung-Fu grip. Nothing happened. So he tried to pry it open with his knife. Still, nothing happened except for the girls looking at him like he was dropped on his head a few times.

"Hey Gracey, could you hand me your key?" Jayden asked. "I want to try something. Sometimes with keys, you just gotta jiggle them around to get them to work. Grace rolled her eyes, and with a sarcastic tone, she said, "I don't even care, just take it. I mean, what are the odds that Lady Coral wouldn't know how to use a key."

Grace removed *The Key* from the necklace her father gave her. Then she stretched out her hand to give *The Key* to Sarah. When Sarah's fingers touched *The Key*, the object began to glow a light green color. Grace pulled her hand back out of fright, but Sarah held on to *The Key* and her eyes became fixated on the object. Her sun-kissed skin became a pale white. Static electricity filled the air around her. Sarah's dark locks were turned blood red and her hair became staticky as magical energy filled the air. The whites of her eyes became black as night, and her irises became emerald green.

Her smile was absent and her expression was empty. Magical energy radiated from her, the power was so great that Jayden became unnerved. The power he could sense from her transformation rivaled his ultimate abilities. If she lost control or turned on them now, he might not be able to stop her. Ignoring his gut, he decided to hand her the treasure chest gently.

Sarah placed the old treasure chest in her lap. Then she put *The Key* inside of the lock and turned *The Key*. The lock clicked, and the chest opened on its own. Sitting on black felt was an old piece of parchment that was wrapped in twine. She reached into the chest and grabbed the parchment.

Once she removed the map, the material became engulfed in a pure white flame. Within seconds the map was destroyed, but Sarah's hands were perfectly fine. Then pictographs and calligraphy began appearing on her arms. The glyphs shimmered and rotated on her skin. The glyphs he was seeing looked familiar. He recognized them from one of Master Thai's books. The pictographs were words from an ancient Elder dialect. He had no idea what they meant, but it must have to do with the map.

Sarah turned toward Jayden and gave him a gentle grin. Then the glyphs on her body disappeared in an instant. Her eyes rolled back into her head, and she collapsed on to the ground. The treasure chest sitting in her lap became encased in the Holy Fire. White flames covered the old relic, and Jayden became quickly alarmed. He instinctively grabbed the chest, stood up and absorbed the fire into his body.

Instantly he felt more powerful. His biceps and shoulder muscles bulged as the holy flame filled his body. Jayden's magical energy felt like it had doubled from absorbing such power. He felt renewed and restored; then he looked down at Sarah's collapsed body.

Jayden turned to Grace and said, "do you think we should leave her here?"

Grace shrugged, "probably, she looks possessed."

"You are so mean," he replied. "If she wakes up still possessed, I'll let her eat you."

Chapter 32
I See Fire

His forearms were getting tired from fanning his childhood friend. He felt like a royal servant fanning his queen. Instead of working in a fancy palace, he was sitting by a river with flies buzzing in his face, and mosquitos trying to drain him of his blood. Sarah stirred as he smacked another mosquito that tried to bite him. Her eyes blinked, and her pale skin began to return to its perfect golden tan.

She sat up and looked into his eyes and said, "Normally, it would be me taking care of you. This is a nice change, Jayden. What happened to me? And why are you fanning me like I'm a deity?"

Before Jayden could respond, Grace blurted out, "you went crazy and looked like you were possessed! Your hair turned red, and your eyes changed color too!"

"My hair did what?" Sarah shouted as she ran to the banks of the river. "What the hell happened to my highlights? Why are my highlights red now? Jayden did you do something to my hair?"

"Highlights? That's what freaked you out your highlights?" Jayden said sounding flabbergasted. "So you aren't worried about your eyes changing color or the fact that you were able to turn Grace's key into *The Key*? Now the treasure chest is gone, and the map is destroyed. But no, let's worry about your hair. By the way, your hair went back to being black right after you collapsed. The only thing different is that your highlights are red now instead of yellow."

Sarah cocked her head to the side and said, "You are telling me that this whole time, you thought my highlights were yellow? You are hopeless. So how did the treasure chest get destroyed?"

Grace dusted herself off and began to retell the story of Sarah and her possession. She seemed to be taking in the information in stride. Jayden was impressed by her strength and composure. Any other person would find this truth hard to believe or would be petrified with fear. He still couldn't shake how much power she was able to produce. He began to wonder if that amount of magical energy had been in her this whole time.

"Since the map and the treasure chest are gone. Does that mean we win?" She asked.

"Wouldn't that be a little anticlimactic?" Grace added.

"I don't think it's over with. I think you absorbed the magic from the map. The calligraphy that appeared on your skin was an old Elder dialect. The directions to wherever the map leads could have been in them. Do you have any idea where the map leads?" Jayden asked.

"Nope, not in the slightest. I do feel a little different, but that might be the highlights," she replied.

"Plus," Jayden said in a hushed tone, "*The Key* didn't burn up like the other objects which tells me it must be used for something else. Your magical power skyrocketed when you activated *The Key*. Whatever else that thing can open must be extremely dangerous. We need to keep you and *The Key* safe.

"That explains why I feel a little different. Why do you think I was able to use *The Key*? Lady Coral wanted to keep me for something; maybe this was the reason why. Am I really that special?" Sarah asked.

"Of course you are special. You are one in a million." Jayden replied." I don't know why you were able to activate it. I was just as shocked as you."

Sarah blushed, "Thanks for that. Since we don't know where to go and I don't know how to access that magic. What should we do for now?" Sarah asked.

Jayden grinned, "Hey Sarah is that cockroach on your shoulder?"

"Did you say a cockroach?" She exclaimed, "Get it off! Get it off!"

With a cheeky grin, he replied, "well if you insist." He placed his hand on her shoulder and then pushed her into the river. Before Grace could react, Jayden got up and grabbed her before she could run away. He carried her to the water's edge and dropped her into the river.

Once Grace came up for her air, she said with her arms crossed, "Hey Sarah should we bury him alive?"

Sarah replied, "That doesn't sound like such a bad idea. Maybe we could pass out flyers for the people in town to watch."

"I love you two," Jayden said, before blowing them a kiss and doing a cannonball into the river.

As soon as he touched the water, he began swimming up and down that river. For Jayden, this break in their crazy lives felt like a moment lost in time. If he could, he would swim and live along this river forever. They had gone through so much on this journey, and now they had some decisions to make. They technically found *The Key* but had no idea what else it can open or how to destroy it. They also technically found the map but all that information is locked in Sarah's brain. Maybe they could go back home, he thought.

While he was lost in thought, Jayden felt something squeezing his big toe. He ducked his head underwater and saw that a Green Crab was clinging on to his big toe. He whispered a heat spell to make it release his toe which was now the color of purple.

He kicked his legs and dove deeper into the river to snatch up a few more crabs and some Leopard Eels. Jayden dove one more time and found a purple fish with tentacles on its body. He grabbed the creature to see if he could convince the girls to eat it. Once he got out of the water, Sarah brought out her frying pans and began cooking. Within about thirty minutes they were dining on some fresh seafood.

When Sarah jabbed her fork into a tentacle, she posed a question, "How are we going to dry our clothes? I don't feel like changing into another outfit in this forest. That's just weird and creepy."

"I agree," Grace said.

"Lucky for you ladies, us fire users are trained in basic heat magic," Jayden said.

He closed his eyes and concentrated. Then he extended his right fist and said, "QuickDry." Immediately, Jayden's wet and soggy clothes became dry and warm. It felt like he just put on a fresh pair of pants that had just come out of the dryer. The warm clothing and the wind's gentle breeze made him feel pleasantly relaxed. He leaned back against a tree and closed his eyes for a brief moment and fell fast asleep.

It was close to midnight when he was dragged out of his sleep. The heavy scent of smoke filled the air. Gray ash and dust fell from the sky like snowflakes, covering his shirt in debris.

Jayden stood up fully alert. He looked around but couldn't sense anyone else besides them in the forest. The sky was dark, and it was difficult to see anything, but there was no doubt in his mind that something was on fire. He found a nearby tree, that was pretty tall. Bending his knees, he jumped up and grabbed the first branch and began to climb. He had to find out where all this smoke and ash was coming from. His biggest fear was that the witches from the Southern Convent were waiting for them. The idea of having to fight more than one witch at a time did not sound like a task he wanted to volunteer for.

When he reached the highest branch, he scanned the forest in every direction. He spotted a pillar of smoke rising into the sky. The gray smoke was tinted with an orange glow, from the scorching flames. The haunting memories of Eiréné's destruction came flooding back to him with a vengeance.

Before his eyes could brim with tears, he quickly climbed down the tree. Once he hit the ground, he grabbed his bag and pulled out his rifle, and switched the night vision on. Jayden roused the girls who were startled by him standing over them with a rifle in his hand. They tried to speak but he put his index finger to his lips and mouthed the word "danger."

The smell of smoke grew stronger with every step they took. His black shirt was now a dusty gray from the falling ash. The temperature in the forest seemed to be rising from the raging fire. They were still miles from the source, but he could already tell that the fire was out of control.

Together, they reached a hill that overlooked Terracina. This whole time, he had been wondering why Floriana had not tried contacting them with her FlipCoin. Standing on that hill, it became clear to him that she was trouble.

Bright orange flames shot into the sky and smoke billowed from the roofs of the city. Even at a distance, he could hear the loud sound of guns peppering the buildings of Terracina. Grace tapped his shoulders and signaled for him to look into the sky. To his horror, he watched as witches flying on brooms fired spells at the soldiers on the ground.

He raised his rifle to get a better view of the chaos. Through his night scope, he spotted a warrior dressed in a black coat, striking down an advancing Eden soldier. Two more men in black robes corralled around him, and they gave a respectful bow in his presence. The man lifted his sword as he gave his men orders and they rushed back into the fray. Jayden zoomed in on their leader. His sword looked very familiar, the platinum hilt on that weapon was unmistakable. He knew exactly who the man in the dark cloak was. That sword belonged to the leader of the Daimonia, the murderer of his father, calling himself the Dark Prince.

Jayden dropped his rifle, and intense heat began radiating from within his body. Sarah grabbed his wrist with a look of concern on her face. He yanked his arm away.

"Don't touch me. The Daimonia, Eden Army, and the Southern Convent are down there. Floriana and the others are in danger. You two are to stay here until I bring them out safely. Is that understood!" He demanded.

"Jayden no! You can't go down there by yourself? Why do you always have to put yourself in these situations!" Sarah shouted.

"Down there is the man who killed my father. I will strike down anyone that comes in between me and that goal. Tonight, I will save our friends, and I will have my vengeance!

His pupils became blood red as columns of orange and white flames began to swirl around him. The dragon tattoo on his forearm and his jade necklace began glowing. The trees surrounding him quickly turned into ash and cinders. Jayden drew his sword, and with unbelievable speed, he launched himself toward the burning city.

Chapter 33
My Rival

The demon tattooed on his forearm, began to glow as his adversary approached. His blonde, spikey hair blew gently in the wind and a grin creased his lips. He gripped his platinum hilt and unsheathed his sword, as the moment he had been waiting for would soon be upon him.

The Dark Prince, began to channel his magical energy as his enemy drew closer. Normally, he wouldn't have called upon such power, but the battle he was about to be involved in was not going to be your average skirmish. This fight would be the beginning and the ending of a powerful crescendo, the very peak of a mountain. As powerful as he was, he couldn't take any chances, as the warrior who was challenging him was the son of Dion LoneOak.

His grin grew wider, as he watched the young Dragon Warrior descend from the mountain like a God of War, thirsty for vengeance. White holy flames of righteousness and red fires of rage, swirled around Jayden like a tornado. The heat being expelled by his magic, was even greater than the fires consuming the city just few yards away. His magical energy at this moment, was beyond what most could conjure in a lifetime. For the Dark Prince, this would be the first worthwhile fight he's been in, since he destroyed

Eiréné all those years ago. He signaled for three of his guards to attack their advancing quarry. The moment Jayden's foot touched the ground, he summoned a large white serpent that was covered in Holy Fire. The creature slammed into two of the Daimonia warriors that were approaching him, vaporizing them instantly. He raised his sword and it began to glow bright red, as his next opponent threw explosive daggers at him. With ease, he deflected the projectiles and as they exploded, he absorbed the heat from the daggers. Then he struck down his opponent, before he could even reach for another weapon.

The boy was stronger than he had originally thought, one more test would show if Jayden LoneOak would truly be a worthy challenge. He summoned for one his captains to come to his side and he instructed him to strike down the son of Dion. His captain drew this twin short swords, and he advanced on his target.

Jayden slowed his approach, as the cloaked warrior launched himself in the air. He spun in a circle as he hung in the air, building up intense speed. A bright light flashed as he continued spinning, and then he dove with blinding speed towards Jayden. The Dragon Warrior jumped back, as the Daimonia Captain slammed into the ground. He raised his sword to deflect a series of slashes from the twin blades. With each deflection his opponent moved faster and faster.

He ducked as the twin blades converged together to slice his neck. Then he sent blast of fire into the stomach of the Daimonia Captain. His enemy staggered backwards, as he was reeling from the fire spell. Jayden drew his knife with his left hand, and he whispered a spell to increase his speed.

The cloaked warrior regained his composure and continued slashing at his enemy. Jayden used both of his blades to deflect and counter, as the barrage of attacks grew more intense. He abided his time, until an opening became present. The Captain's swords began to glow bright, as he made a double vertical strike down on Jayden. Using the Jade Blade, he blocked the strike just long enough to rotate and move his body around. The Daimonia warrior continued to fall forward, as Jayden managed to spin around him. As his blades slammed into the ground missing his target, Jayden's Katana pierced through his back. He crumpled to the ground and began his eternal sleep.

The Dark Prince smiled cruelly, as he watched his captain's defeat. Finally, he could have the battle he had been craving for. With his Tainted Alona Blade, he could bring an end to the line of LoneOak and retrieve *The Key.*

The white and orange flames spiraling around Jayden, intensified. Anger churned inside of him, with the ferocity of a volcano. His sword was stained with blood and his hands shook as his desire for vengeance grew. Magical energy filled the fields, as he stared down his rival.

The Dark Prince smirked, as he pointed his sword toward Jayden. He summoned a blast of wind, that knocked Jayden off his feet and slammed him onto the ground. Then he channeled electrical energy into his sword and sent streaks of lightning toward Jayden as he was trying to get back to his feet. The bolts of lightning slammed into the chest of the Dragon Warrior, sending him skyward and then crashing him onto the ground.

The column of fire that was surrounding Jayden, dissipated as he laid on the ground. His chest felt like it had been hit by cannonball. His magical energy was dropping, and blood began to soak his shirt. He reached for his weapon and pulled back his hand quickly as the Dark Prince stepped on his blade.

His enemy knelt down and said, "I always wondered, if your Father was holding back during our last and only encounter. That thought has plagued me for years, and I was hoping that defeating you would bring me true satisfaction. But you…you disappoint me. After all of these years of training and anticipation that you have had. Is this all the strength you can muster? Your Father was a warrior and you disgrace his name with this lousy attempt at revenge."

The Dark Prince's smile vanished, as he glanced behind himself with just enough time, to watch a small fireball with an iron core speeding toward him. The meteor exploded against his back, sending him to the ground, covering his cloak in ash and flame. Jayden grabbed his sword and jumped back to his feet. He summoned four fireballs into his left hand and threw them at his rival.

The Dark Prince rolled out of the way, of the onslaught of fire attacks. Once he regained his balance, he used a gust of wind to launch himself towards Jayden. Their blades clashed with tremendous speed and power. With each slash, sparks of metal and electrical energy filled the air.

Many of his warriors, began to fill the field to watch their bout. He had to finish this fight soon, as he could sense that *The Key* was nearby. The Dark Prince deflected two strikes from Jayden and thrust his sword towards his opponent forcing him to step back.

Jayden made a sideswipe at the Dark Prince. His enemy ducked beneath his blade and then did a front sweep which knocked Jayden on to the ground. As the Dragon Warrior fell, he raised his sword to deliver the final blow.

Chapter 34
A Solemn Reunion

All his eyes could see was complete and utter darkness. He struggled to take a deep breath as there was something heavy resting on his chest and pressing against his forehead. Jayden tried to push it off, but his energy was zapped. He tried to push harder to no avail. Then he heard a loud voice yell, "we've got one over here. Don't move we are coming to get you!"

"We are here to help!" a man yelled. "Remain calm. Half of a building fell on top of you, just give us a few minutes to get you out." The men and women above him rummaged through the cement and tiles that were crushing Jayden. He saw a speck of light piercing through the pile of debris. As his eyes adjusted to the shining light, he was able to catch a glimpse of a group of firemen and a nurse removing shingles from on top of him. He raised his hand up, and one of the firemen grabbed it and pulled him out of the pile.

The nurse handed him a bottle of water and placed a blanket on his shoulders. They guided him toward a nearby bench and sat him down. Jayden sipped on the water, and a fireman crouched down in front of him.

"Hello, my name is Ryan. I am a volunteer firefighter. Do you know your name?" The firefighter asked firmly.

"What did you say!" Jayden's voice cracked. His throat felt dry and scratchy from the ash, and his ears were ringing.

"I said, do you remember your name?" Ryan asked again.

This time around, Jayden scratched his ears and pulled out a clump of black ash. "My name is Jayden. I can hear you a little better now. What happened?" He asked.

"Well I'm sure your memory is a little foggy, but last night all hell broke loose. There was like a three-way battle going on down here, and we got caught in the middle of it. Apparently, you ran into this building to get shelter from the bullets flying, but they decided to fire a shell that went right through the roof. Boy, you are lucky to be alive. Now are you a resident of Terracina or were you here vacationing with family?" Ryan asked.

"I was here on vacation with friends," Jayden replied. A very screwed up vacation he thought. Could I look around for them? We got separated during the night."

"Normally young man, I would make you wait here until we can get you all checked out. Unfortunately, our equipment is all over the place. Now I am going to need you to do me a favor, don't go too far and come find me later." He patted Jayden on the back and went out to look for more survivors.

Jayden struggled to get to feet because his right ankle felt stiff and was throbbing with pain. The extreme pain from each step helped to bring his mind back into focus. He had to find his friends. Hopefully, they were all okay.

As he walked along the edge of town, he watched as gray smoke exited through the roofs of nearby homes. The outskirts of Terracina looked like a complete war zone. Buildings in every direction were covered in bullet holes and burn marks from magic. Citizens and tourists covered in bandages, and some lying under white sheets were a common sight as he walked through the streets of Terracina. How many people had to die because of this stupid key? How many lives were permanently scarred by this destruction? The citizens of Terracina and Jayden LoneOak now had one thing in common; the impact of greed and violence has drastically changed their lives.

Despite the depressing look of the city, Jayden was able to find one ray of hope. The vast number of volunteers running around town looking for survivors and bringing them water gave him a sense of peace that this city might heal. A tear brimmed in his eye as memories of Eiréné came flooding back. Unlike here in Terracina, his hometown wasn't blessed with volunteers running to save the day. Instead, it was left to die alone with no one rushing to answer the cry for help.

He proceeded to wipe the tears from his eyes away as he trudged along the outskirts of town searching high and low for his friends. He needed to know that they were safe. Off in the distance, he saw a young man roughly his age running straight toward him. Jayden was naturally apprehensive as the man sprinting his way had a shotgun slung over his shoulder and a broadsword swinging in its sheath as he ran. Something about this boy seemed familiar, a face he had not seen in quite some time. Before Jayden could stop the young man, he was tackled to the ground.

"Hey loser, how have you been?" The fully-grown man shouted.

Jayden coughed as he tried to breathe, "hey, Tony get off! Firemen just saved me, don't make their work end in vain because you are crushing me."

"Ha alright." Tony stood up and extended his hand to pulled Jayden to his feet.

Jayden was still in shock at seeing his old friend. He swung his arms around him. "Man, it's been so long. I honestly thought I'd never see you again. So much has happened since we left you.

Better yet, how did you get here? When did you get here?" He asked full of enthusiasm.

Tony laughed, "Jade, what's with the 21 questions? Can't a guy randomly show up in war-torn city?"

"I haven't been called that in quite some time. You still aren't off the hook yet. You have to answer at least one of those questions!" Jayden said sounding feeling a little annoyed

"I'll give you short version for now. I'm here because Floriana sent me a message a couple of days ago that you all might need help down here. Then she sent me another message once the bullets started flying," he replied.

"Wait, wait, you heard from her? Why didn't she try and contact us?" Jayden asked.

"She told me that she didn't contact you because you were busy with some super cool mission. Plus, she figured that if you found out she was in danger, you would come running down the mountain to save her, which is kind of funny because that's what you tried to do anyway. But hey we can talk about this later, let's go catch up with your friends," he replied.

Jayden appeared confused, "My friends?"

Tony led Jayden through a small hay field that had been mostly burned to the ground. His friend guided him toward a small barn in the middle of the property. The steel barn was blackened from the fire, and it had a few very noticeable bullet holes. Jayden wasn't sure if he was stepping into a barn or a crime scene.

His childhood friend walked up to a small wooden door and knocked four times. A latch clicked, and he entered the building. The barn smelled like thick smoke, and he found it tough to breathe. Jayden coughed while he followed Tony and his footsteps echoed as they walked down a dark and narrow hall. Tony stopped to lift a latch and pushed open an old, wooden door.

Jayden entered after his friend and found himself standing in a large room where some of the hay and tools were stored. On his left side hanging from hooks was an old wooden spade, a sickle, and a large rake. His ears perked up when he heard familiar voices coming from the back corner of the barn.

Sarah jumped up from sitting on a pile of hay and wrapped her arms around him. Tears streamed from her face as she held him close. Minutes passed by as she held him in complete silence. He didn't mind the silence. The truth was, he learned more from her tears then words could ever say. Whatever horrors she witnessed from the night before was only an encore of the death and destruction that seems to follow the lost children from Eiréné. Sarah could hold him forever, and he wouldn't mind.

She loosened her embrace and whispered in his ear, "I thought I was never going to see you."

He released her from his arms and walked towards Grace, Romeo, and Tammy. Tammy's youthful and fun-loving face was now a mixture of cuts, small bruises, and pure sadness. Her right hand was bandaged, and there were beads of dried blood across her knuckles. Romeo, on the other hand, looked even grimmer than he usually did. He had a gash on his left cheek, his left arm was in a sling, and there was bandage wrapped around his right leg. Grace was in a little better shape than the dwarves. She had a few scrapes on her elbows and a small bruise on her right cheek, but other than that she was her usual self.

Grace looked up at him and then looked away. Romeo raised an eyebrow, "Look what the cat dragged in. You missed it; we were just taking bets on whether you would walk in here or if Tony would be carrying you."

"Well, I am thankful for your vote of confidence. What happened to you guys? I don't remember anything that happened the other night," Jayden replied.

Romeo scratched his chin "That is somewhat of a long story. So, when we left you guys to bring Jason back to Terracina, we stayed at an inn for a while. Not too long after we got settled back here, The Daimonia were sneaking into town and hanging around at night. Obviously, they came here to try and trap you guys and steal whatever you found. The witches from the Southern Convent thought the same thing and did not like them being here. So that led to a few small skirmishes breaking out. Then when some of the Eden soldiers tried to take Floriana into custody, Jason stepped in to defend her. When his men wouldn't stand down, the Daimonia attacked the Eden soldiers, and we were caught in the middle of it. We were pretty grateful when Tony and members of the Water Temple came to the rescue. They helped to save us and anyone who was caught in the crossfire."

Tammy sulked, "we are lucky to be alive."

"You left me!" Grace shouted as she stared Jayden dead in the eye.

"I did what?" He said feeling perplexed.

"You said you would be there for me, but you just left us on that hill. Your eyes went red, and then you just ran off, " she replied with her arms crossed.

"His eyes did what?" Tony asked raising an eyebrow.

"They flashed red, and then he ran off like a crazy person," she said sounding more frustrated.

Jayden crumbled to his knees. For a moment he sat in silence and shook his head. Not again, he told himself. Not again. I thought I was past this. How could this happen again? Did I hurt anyone? How many lives did I take? I thought I was stronger than this.

Tony pat his shoulders, "it's okay man."

"Don't be too hard on yourself," Romeo said, "it might surprise you, but I, too, have experienced the red eye. I know the damage it can cause, and I know what part of the heart it comes from. The truth is this, you running down that hill like a fireball out of hell, was probably the best thing for us. While you were causing all of that ruckus, it drew a lot of the chaos from inside the city to the outskirts. Your anger saved lives, so don't beat yourself up over it. Pick up your chin and stiffen up boy!"

Jayden sat back up straight and looked at their concerned faces. Even Grace was less frustrated with him, and her face showed that she did care for him. There was something they weren't telling him.

"Where is Floriana?" He asked. "Is she okay?"

Grace shrugged, "We have no idea. I lost track of her during the chaos."

"Well... I've wanted to tell you all something. It hurts for me to even think about." Tammy said as tears streamed down her face. "I saw Floriana during the battle. She saved me from three Daimonia soldiers that were trying to kill me. She pushed me out of the way and took them on without a second thought. I watched her as she fought, and I thought....everything was going to be okay. But then, there was a huge explosion. I was knocked to the ground, and when I got up, Floriana was gone. I ran over to where she was, and the only thing I found was blood...and this."

Her hands shook nervously when she reached into her bag. Tears flowed down her cheeks as she pulled out a rapier and handed it to Jayden. The room became instantly silent, as Jayden cradled the cold steel in his hands. The handle and the blade were stained with blood. As he clutched the weapon, he didn't know what or even how to feel. He had only known Floriana for such a brief time in his life, but the moments he spent with her made him feel like he's known her his whole life. She saved his life and put her career on the line for him and Tony. The Great General Floriana gave her life for them, and this reality was too much for him to handle.

The weight of the moment sat heavy on his shoulders. Teardrops began to appear on the blade, and his knees felt weak. He wanted to crawl into a hole and never come out. Sadness and guilt filled his heart. If only he would have stayed at the Dragon Temple, she would still be alive. Her life for his, it just didn't seem fair. Master Thai was right, the road of vengeance is a lonely one.

"Have I failed?" He asked. "It seems like wherever I go, chaos follows me. If I would never have left the Dragon Temple, none of this would have happened. Floriana....would still be alive, doing what she loves."

Grace got up and sat next to him, "do you know how you ended up with a roof falling on top of your head?" Jayden shook his head no.

"Well, you went into that building to draw gunfire away from a family that was trying to escape the city. In your rage, you risked your life to save people you didn't know. You almost died in the process. You started this journey searching for vengeance and to obtain answers about your father. Has it been perfect? No, but how many journeys are? Take a moment to think about all the people you have helped along the way. Check the bigger picture; you wanted to keep *The Key* out of the hands of people who would use it for evil. You even gave Cain a second chance at redemption. And the greatest thing that you did is you befriended a troubled girl that you didn't even know. You gave her a nickname and helped to give her freedom. Jayden, I wouldn't trade my freedom for anything in the world." She smiled and kissed his cheek.

Her words made him feel a little better, but he still felt the pang of guilt. He didn't know how to process everything, and honestly, he didn't want to. Part of him wanted to believe that she was still out there in her suit of armor taking on the evils of the world. But the truth was that she was gone, and now all he had was memories.

Jayden got up and found a corner to be in by himself. He plopped down on a pile of hay and sat down in complete silence.

Tony followed after joined his childhood friend. Together they wept just as they did so many years before. Tony wiped his eyes, "do you remember when you won that giant teddy bear for her?"

Jayden laughed, "Ya and Sarah was super pissed because she only got a slinky."

Tony leaned back and said, "I'm going to miss her. I wish we could have gotten here sooner."

"Me too," Jayden replied, "It's not fair!"

"What isn't fair? She was a soldier Jayden. She knew what she was getting into and what it might cost. The least we can do is honor that sacrifice." Tony said, without meeting his friend's gaze.

"Is it really just that simple?" Jayden asked.

Tony sniffled as he fought back a tear, "I really wish it was."

For a moment they sat in silence, as they worked through their thoughts. Jayden felt emotionally and physically exhausted, so he laid down on a pile of hay and tried to sleep. As he rested, his mind was gifted with nightmares that melded the destruction of Eiréné with the battle of Terracina. Once he was finally able to fall into a deep sleep, he was awoken by Tony summoning a small rain cloud and using it to drench him in ice cold water.

After cursing his friend out and throwing fireballs at him, they gathered their belongings and headed to the docks. Tony rented a boat for them to travel on the open seas. Where they were going, Jayden didn't quite know.

As they had pushed off from the docks, he felt a tinge of sadness to see Tammy waving at them as they moved out to sea. Jayden was going to miss those two dwarves a lot, well, he was going to miss Tammy just little more. He understood why they didn't want to join them; they wanted to find their long-lost sister. If the roles were reversed, he knew he would probably do the same thing.

While the ocean waves rocked back and forth, Jayden stood up in the boat and waved back one more time. Since his friend was distracted, Tony accidentally pushed Jayden overboard.

"What the hell was that for?" Jayden yelled as he struggled to catch up to the boat.

"Sorry about that it was an accident and you were blocking my view of the ocean." Tony replied

"You jerk! Slow the boat down; I can't swim that fast." Jayden yelled.

Sarah pulled him back into the boat, and he used his magic to dry his clothes. He reached into his bag to try and find a pair of sunglasses. Then he noticed something was missing. "Do any of you know what happened to my sword?"

Grace nodded and handed Jayden a metal case. He opened it, and for a moment he couldn't believe his eyes. His heart pounded in his chest like a hammer, and his breathing became heavy. Resting on the red velvet, was his sword. It had been shattered into four pieces.

"How did this happen?" He shouted.

Grace replied, "It shattered when you were fighting that Dark Prince guy. You guys were fighting so intensely, that it shattered when the blades connected. It was scary to watch."

"Hey, buddy don't worry about it. My Dad told me of this super cool Blacksmith that could fix any blade and make it better. In the meantime, you should use this." Tony reached into Jayden's bag and pulled out a black scimitar and handed it to him.

Dark magic radiated from his Father's sword. As he rotated the sword in his hand, he felt the temptation to seek his revenge on the Daimonia. His desire was for them to feel his wrath, he wanted them to know his pain. He didn't want to see Floriana's name to become forgotten and lost in the pages of history. The truth was that she wouldn't want him to seek vengeance; she would want him to find peace again.

Jayden grinned from ear to ear, as he clutched his Dad's old sword in hand, "well Tony, I think it's time that we head home."

Chapter 35
Those Who Lived

His hammer made a thud as it slammed into a nail. Only one more board to go, and Grace's new home would be done. She was willing to move into one of the older houses, but Jayden thought she deserved a place of her own. Together he and Tony built her a beige two bedroom house with an outdoor pool because she's a princess. The house itself wasn't anything fancy and compared to the beauty of the Southern Convent this house was downright ugly. But for Grace, it was chance at a new beginning.

Storm clouds began to form in the skies above Eiréné. Droplets of rain fell gently against his skin; the coolness of the weather was greatly appreciated after day's work. The change in precipitation also meant that it was time for the celebration. He wasn't looking forward to it, but he couldn't hold it off much longer.

He jumped down from the ladder and ran to his house. He opened the red door and entered the home that he grew up in. With Tony's help, he was able to restore what was destroyed all those years ago. It still felt weird to walk into his room and not hear the sound of his father yelling at him to do something. Jayden knew he might not ever get used to silence in this house, but he was happy to have a place to call home.

Jayden stretched out his arm and reached into his old closet. The closet was filled with clothes that were twice the size of the ones he wore in grade school. He grabbed a blue collared shirt and black pants. Once he was dressed, he tried to comb his short, curly hair. As he admired himself in the mirror, he was impressed by how much he had grown from the last time he looked at it.

Tony was waiting for him outside. Together they walked toward a field on the outside of town, close to the Dragon Mountains. Grace, Sarah, and Ms. Tonya were sitting in a row of chairs as he approached the newly made cemetery. This new gravesite was made to honor all those who lost their lives when Eiréné was destroyed.

The powdered white gravestones were beautiful and stretched as far as the eyes could see. In the center of the cemetery was a small cross that was made for his father, a rifle, and a rapier. Jayden wanted Floriana to be buried alongside her uncle, Robert.

As he stared down at these memorials, sadness began to rise to the surface. He wished he could see their faces just one more time. The rows of gravestones would forever be a reminder of the consequences of greed and power. He vowed to make the world a better a place.

Jayden turned around to face his friends who were patiently waiting for him to speak. He cleared his throat and fought back the next wave of tears. He looked into each of their eyes and said, "today we take the time to remember, not that we would ever forget, but we remember because everyone whose names are on these stones, their memories should never fade from this earth. Snuffed out too quickly by the hands of those that harbor evil and hatred in their hearts. Their violence will not determine our future; we will use it as a tool to seek peace and reach out a helping hand to those we meet as we travel through life. I am grateful and blessed to have you all in my life. Let us look upon this cemetery, not as a place for the dead, but as a home for those who will live on in eternity. Our hearts ache in this life for them, but we will see them again in the next. But until that time, let us live on!"

J. Edwards

His friends stood up slowly, and with tears in their eyes, they gave him a standing ovation. They hugged each other and talked before they all gradually dispersed. Jayden decided to hang back; he had one last goodbye to make. He walked toward the makeshift cross, where his father was buried. He knelt down and touched the wooden fixture, and he began to wonder if his father was proud of him. Jayden missed him so much, but he just wanted to know if his father was glad of the man he became.

A gentle breeze picked up, and white feather from an eagle landed gently into his hand. He held the feather close as he looked up into the darkened sky and gave a prayer of thanks. For he knew his father was at peace and that his future was bright.

He stood up as it began to rain and went to catch up with the others. As the young Dragon Warrior walked away, Floriana's rapier began to sway gently in the wind. A bolt of lightning struck the ground near the sword, and as the thunder roared in the sky, the blade shattered into a thousand pieces that will be blown away by the wind.

First Draft Previews

Edited by Meagan Lasitter

Baptized by Magic

"The Witches Pendant"

Chapter 1
A Beautiful Ceremony

Droplets of water were falling from the sky, with no sign of stopping. The wind was blowing gently against his coat, insuring that he would never forget how cold that morning was. Clouds, as dark as night, were spreading across the city of Eureka. Thunder cracked and lightning raced across the sky, to provide a comforting sense of danger and urgency.

A puddle of ice-cold water was beginning to develop beneath his feet. His new, suede shoes were completely soaked, and his dress socks were starting to resemble a wet sponge. If that wasn't terrible enough, their commencement speaker was only a quarter of the way through his awful speech. Considering how large of a budget the federal government had, you would figure they could afford someone with a little more charisma.

All of this ceremony and fluff was complete nonsense, he thought. Why do they need to spend two hours talking, when they could just hand him his diploma, and call it good. Sure, he was little bitter, but he had good reason to be. He scored higher than anyone in his class on their written exam, and he even won a game of BINGO the night before. Yet, he was still placed at the end of line, all because he was terrible at magic.

Why would he even bother joining the Federal Crimes and Supernatural Investigation Agency, anyway? Before his parents died, they wanted him to be a lawyer or join the family business. He hated baking, and he thought that most lawyers were full of themselves. No, he joined because he wanted to make a difference in the world. What a bunch of hog wash! How could he make a difference if he can't even get his magic to work half the time?

"Jonathan Silver!" yelled a voice from the podium.

Johnny was still daydreaming when he heard his name called. It took him a moment to realize that he was actually going to graduate from this program. His heart should be bouncing with joy as he approached the stage. All of his accomplishments led up to this moment, and all of his failures.

Commander Johnson, shook his hand and said, "You will do great out there son. Make the agency proud."

Johnny took his diploma and stepped down from the stage. He found his spot on the grassy field and joined his classmates. He looked out at the audience that was cheering them on. In this crowd of over a hundred, there wasn't one person that was cheering for him. The only friend he had in the world was his buddy, Todd, who joined the Agency with him. He wanted to shake hands with his friend and have a few drinks. But instead, they had to stand in this formation until the Commander saluted them to be released.

A large silver dragon flew gracefully above them as the Commander saluted them. Maybe this was a sign that things would turn around for him. Maybe he could really be the agent he desired to be. If the Commander could believe in him, maybe he should too.

The new agents saluted their Commander, as the trumpets blared the national anthem. Today, Jonathan Silver became a Federal Agent. He was going to prove to those who doubted him wrong. He was going to uncover the secrets of his parents death's, and save the world

Chapter 2

My First Assignment

His hands shook uncontrollably as he clutched the envelope that would determine his future for the next two years. Johnny knew that he would eventually have to leave the FCIS University and begin his new life as an agent. He didn't expect to receive that information the day after his graduation.

Johnny stared intently at the manila colored enveloped. The thickness of the paper was to the point that he couldn't tell what exactly was inside of it. The young lad who gave him the envelope, said that there was an encryption spell placed upon it. In order to open it, he had to figure out the riddle. The riddle was, he had to say something about himself that no one else knew.

He could say a million different things that most people didn't know about him, like he wasn't the most popular person in the program. That Jonathan Silver had both book smarts and street smarts. He was decent at breakdancing, and could cook a mean steak. But apparently, the establishment knew all of that. It didn't help that he sucked at magic. There's about a million different spells that might be able open this letter.

Johnny closed his eyes. He tried channelling whatever ounce of luck he had and said, "I am a Scorpio." Nothing happened. Okay, that was probably a dumb choice since the FCSI already knows his birthday.

Then he shouted over 30 different things he thought no one knew. Still, nothing. He was feeling frustrated and wanted to give up. When he considered all of the obstacles he's had to face to become an agent, the one that has stumped him the most, was this stupid envelope. Maybe he could open it with a knife.

He pulled out his custom-made pocketknife. Johnny unfolded the knife, and its silver blade glistened under the light of his room. Gently, he pressed the blade under the lip of the envelope. Taking a deep breath, he slid the blade across the top.

"What the hell!" He yelled, "Is this envelope made of steel? My knife should be able to cut through this like it's butter. I flipping hate magic."

"Did you learn nothing at the academy?" Said a voice that made Johnny jump and drop his knife on the ground.

"Todd! Can't you see that I am doing something important right now?" Johnny shouted.

"Correction, that is Special Agent Todd Washington to you." Todd said with a grin.

"Oh wow, a little full of yourself now aren't you? Don't think that I forgot the night when you were crying in your bed because you missed your Mommy." Johnny replied.

Todd's fair skin turned bright red. "Hey! You promised to never mention that again. Plus, at least I can open a Damn envelope."

Johnny slicked back his curly dark hair in frustration. "Tell me how you opened it! You know I suck at this magic stuff."

Todd slapped his friend in the back of the head. "Moron, I don't know."

"What do you mean you don't know?"

"No you idiot, that's the answer. I don't know. The riddle is, to say something about yourself that no one else knows. Well, you can't ever truly know what people do or don't know about you. Just say I don't know!"

Feeling absolutely confused, Johnny swallowed his pride and said, "I don't know."

Suddenly, a gentle breeze blew through his room, and the flaps of the envelope unlatched themselves. As the flaps began to unfurl themselves, a small sheet of paper slowly floated out of the envelope. From the looks of it, there didn't seem to be anything special on this sheet of paper. There was no discernible writing or codes on it, and not even a scribble on either side of the pearl white sheet of paper. Johnny tried to shift the position of the note, to see if the words would appear in a different light. Still, nothing appeared on the sheet paper.

Johnny Silver shook his head in disbelief. "Are they really just trying to humiliate me? Is this some kind of end of the semester prank? Yea sure, let's prank the one guy who sucks at using magic. I hate this place sometimes."

"Look, as much as everyone would love to prank you on the last day, this time, no one is trying to mess with you." Todd said. "All you have to do is tap your index finger in the middle of the page, and the magic will do the rest."

"Oh." Johnny replied, as his light caramel colored skin started to turn burgundy from embarrassment.

He raised his right index finger and pressed it against the center of the page. A yellow light appeared in the center, and rings of bright energy began to fan out toward the corners of the page like ripples in a pond. The parchment in his hand started to feel warm, as a loud screechy voice pierced through the paper.

The obnoxiously high voice said, "Congratulations Johnny Silver on becoming a Federal Agent. You were one of our most talented academic students, and I hope you are prepared for the road ahead. We believe in rewarding excellence and have decided to assign you to the beautiful city of Eutopia. For your first assignment, you will serve in advisory role and assist the local police department. If you have any questions, you can contact your supervisor in nearby Teleia, his name is James Walker. He is a well-trained Special Agent and he will be a great asset for you. We wish you the best of luck, and make sure that you represent the agency with pride and professionalism, wherever you go."

A big smile appeared across Johnny's face. Joy and excitement was building within him, like a powder keg ready to explode. Finally, he felt as if he was receiving the respect he deserved, and was ready to prove all of the doubters wrong. He was going to be a great Federal Agent, maybe even one of the best.

"Are you done gloating already?" His friend asked. "Have you even been to Eutopia?"

"Huh? What do you mean? Of course I've heard of Eutopia. It's supposed to be a nice place right?" Johnny replied.

"Yeah, if farmland and cobblestone roads are your thing. It's a little dinky town, they probably haven't had a decent crime in a century." Todd said.

"Are you serious? Why would they send me to such a small place? I mean the note clearly said a beautiful city, why would they lie?" Johnny asked, as his joy was slowly beginning to evaporate.

"Look man, I don't know. Usually they send new recruits on easy assignments to get their feet wet. Instead of getting upset and feeling like this system is trying to screw you over, why don't you see this as an opportunity to show the agency just how talented you are? And just because it's a small town, doesn't mean you won't run into your fair share of problems. Have fun, soak up the experience, and if you're lucky, you'll meet a nice country girl and live happily ever after."

Johnny smirked, but there was no joy in his grin. His friend was probably right. He should look at this as an opportunity to learn and grow from. All he saw in front of him was just another slap to the face. Yes, he did well academically and was an amazing talent on the rifle range, but those skills didn't matter to the establishment. To them, he was nothing more than another recruit that they hoped would just fail and quit. Johnny Silver was no punk, he was not going to be bullied or forced in to quitting. He decided in that moment to go Eutopia. Even if he hated every second of it, he was going to prove to him that he was something special, and that he could make a difference in any place that they send him to.

Those who Lived by the Sword

Book Two:
The Seeds of our Destruction

Chapter 1
Home Sweet Home

The winds howled like a banshee in the night. He clutched on to his coat as his body shivered uncontrollably. The cool breeze sliced through his three layers of clothing with ease. His socks were soaked, and his gloves were being just as effective as using a squirt gun to fight a forest fire. He was beginning to think that if the hypothermia didn't kill him, frostbite or gangrene would.

Wisps of snow blew through his hood, but he could hardly notice. His face was so numb from the cold, that he could get punched in the nose and not feel a thing. With each step Cain took, he was beginning to feel a growing sense of regret. He pulled out an old wand from his bag and a large Firestone. The items he held didn't seem that special. The wand was made centuries ago from an old redwood and was completely covered in cobwebs. The only thing remarkable about the wand was the head of this magical item. It was shaped like a diamond and there were three ruby power stones embedded in it. There was no magical energy emanating from the stones, and they were pretty much useless. The large Firestone in his right hand was equally unimpressive. There was no magic left in the stone. Normally, the rock would be a bright orange or red color and feel warm to the touch. Instead of being nice and vibrant, the stone was cold and blackened from repeated use.

Despite the complete uselessness of the magical items in hand, that he had to risk his own life to steal, he knew that the Daimonia had bigger and better plans for these items. The Orias sect of the Daimonia was notorious for finding new, creative ways to cause pain and destruction. To a degree, Cain was able to understand why their sect was the most violent and aggressive of the Daimonia factions. The Orias branch were considered to be "the bastards of the party," the black sheep of the demonic family. Their sect wasn't one of the original 12 Daimonia organizations, and they were begrudgingly included as the 13th member. The Orias group was the most underfunded Daimonia group, which was why he was trudging up this God forsaken mountain. Unlike the other Daimonia groups that had beautiful tropical island bases, and offices in top-of-the-line skyscrapers, his sect had to set up shop in northernmost mountain range in Aggeloi, called the Devil's Corridor. The mountain range was given that title because it was home to the second largest mountain in the world, and the range was virtually unlivable.

The Daimonia chose the most desolate mound of dirt of them all, called Mount Dirge. The mountain was filled with rocks, caves, and insects. There was practically no vegetation, saved for a few thorn bushes that just loved to entangle travelers. No animals lived on this mountain; even the birds and dragons avoided Mount Dirge like it was the plague. On top of that, if you didn't know which cave to enter, you could be eaten by one of the giant earthworms that made the interior of the Mountain Range their home.

He hated this place and if he could turn back time, he would have never left Eiréné. Nothing good has come from his time in the Daimonia. Yeah, he got to see the world and he discovered that he had one fully related brother and two half-brothers. The Dark Prince, Drake, and Jason, were the best brothers a boy could have, if that boy wanted to become a murdering psychopath. But what was he to do? The only other home he had was burned to the ground.

Plus, Jayden and Sarah didn't need a guy like him around, not with his past.

A blast of wind knocked him backwards as he struggled up the left side of the mountain. As Cain slid down the mountain, he reached for a protruding branch to stop his descent toward a cliff. The moment his hand gripped onto the branch, he felt a sharp, burning sensation. Red droplets of blood stained the snowy ground. He took a moment to examine the bush that saved his life and realized that he gripped on to the thorns of a Poison Berry Bush. That's just great, he thought. Not only is my hand bleeding, but now I'm going to have a serious migraine from the poison.

Cain regained his composure and got back to his feet. Then he heard a voice shouting down from the mountain. "You alright down there? You look a little lost. I can get a bandage for you."

The young man from Eiréné looked up and saw a warrior dressed in a dark cloak. Cain could see blonde hair protruding from beneath the hood. He had a large bow slung across his back, with a quiver full of arrows of different shapes and colors. Hanging on the left-hand side of his hip, was a long sword.

Cain grinned, "Well if it isn't my half-brother Jason. Back from the war already."

Jason smiled, "My first name is 'Sergeant,' and don't you forget it."

"That's hilarious, it's kind of hard to be a Sergeant without a real army. Did you even leave the Army a two weeks notice? Or was helping to destroy a city a clear enough message for them?" Cain replied.

"Despite my pretense for joining the army, I am proud of the work I did and was honored to serve. But this cause is bigger than any one army." Jason continued, "Now let's get you inside. Just a forewarning, the heater has been malfunctioning." Jason said, as he led his brother back up the mountain.

They travelled along a bend on the western side of the mountain. The ground beneath their feet became slicker; the closer they got to the cave. The mouth of the cave was a dark blue color from the ice, and the magic crystals that filled the cave. Sharpened icicles hung from the ceiling, giving the visual impression that they were walking into the jaws of an Ice Dragon. Cain held on to his coat even tighter as he felt the temperature drop below zero. The negative energy exiting from the cave was overwhelming. It was too late to back out now, he made his decision. Plus, Cain could sense that the Fallen Wizard was here, and there was no way that he would let him go.

His ears perked up to the sound of old sandals shuffling along the icy floor. A shadowy figure was approaching him slowly from deep within the cave. An old, wooden cane gently tapped the ground as their greeter drew closer. He was wearing a mossy green cloak that had become faded over the years. His cheeks were sunken in, and his orange colored eyes were now as pale as a ghost.

The wizard struggled with every step, wheezing as he breathed. His arm and leg muscles were about as thin as a piece of paper. To most people, he would have appeared about as threatening as butterfly. There was a level determination about him that made the wizard so imposing. The old man had survived for thousands of years in this broken state, with a combination of wit and exceptional magic power.

"Young man," the Fallen Wizard said in a hushed tone. "Were you able to acquire the items I asked for?"

Cain bowed before his master and removed the items from beneath his cloak. "I retrieved them successfully, but I don't think these items are going to do any good."

The wizard reached out for the Firestone and examined its smooth surface. For a second, his pale eyes widened and began to regain their normal orange color. What value the Fallen Wizard saw in that magic rock, Cain could not imagine. The old man didn't even bother looking at the old wand. Cain was beginning think that this was just a set up to get him back.

His master stared at him, as if he could peer directly into Cain's mind. With a toothy grin, the Fallen Wizard said, "Things are not always what they may seem, my young warrior. The magic in objects like this never truly goes away. In truth, these items will be just as important to us as The Key. Now, I want you to come with me down to the dungeon. There is someone I want you to meet."

Magic Spell List

Absolute Zero- Anti-Object spell is not one to be used on living beings. This ice magic spell is the ultimate version of Flash Freeze. Absolute Zero will turn any object into pure, and destructible objects. Requires Master Level Training.

Absorb- Is a technique typically used by elemental magic users. This ability allows the caster to absorb the energy of an attack spell. The energy absorbed can sometimes heal injuries and restore, or even increase magical power temporarily. Caution should be given when trying to absorb more powerful spells, as the energy increase can damage the human body.

Auto-Heal (Fast Acting)- A simple healing spell that only activates upon mild to severe bodily injury. The healing magic in this technique is intended to keep the user alive. It cannot fully heal broken bones nor can it seal up open wounds. Once this spell activates, the user should seek medical attention.

Avalanche- A magical spell that causes an intense blast of snow. If the user is trained well enough, they can also summon blocks of ice along with the snow.

BioFlame- Green flames, are a rarity amongst fire users. This spell uses a green fire that is intended to immobilize an opponent by making them extremely sick. BioFlame is intended to be a non-lethal spell and is a Master Level technique.

Control- A Telekinetic spell which allows the user to control bodily movements of another human being, creature, or object. This is a very difficult technique, as it requires a wellspring of magical power, and an adept opponent that can resist this spell. Control, is a Master Level Magic spell.

Cyclone Blade- This sword magic spell causes a user to spin either in the air or on the ground, while swinging a weapon. Cyclone blade can create speeds of up to 65 mph. This is a very risky technique, as it requires the ability to adjust at high speeds.

Dark Flame- A Master Level technique. This spell conjures a dark fireball or wave of fire. Dark Flame is a lethal spell that can be used efficiently against fire users and can be moderately effective on water magic casters.

Deflection- A technique made to deflect and rebound projectiles. Originally was intended to combat arrow and high-speed magic attacks. Deflection is a spell that can be combined with Enhanced Reaction to deflect bullets. Requires a mild amount of magic to use.

Dimension (Enchantment)- Powerful magic that was created by The Elders. Magic of this type is designed to protect locations or property, by creating a dimension for them to be stored. Magic of this type requires physical objects to serve as a boundary for the item or location.

Dragon Sight- A technique invented by the Dragon Monastery. This is a difficult skill because it enhances the user's ability to see and survey the details of the land around them. This increase in sight ability can cause strain on the eyes and shouldn't be used for an extended period of time.

Eagle Eye- This spell is similar to Dragon Sight, but its intent is to be used for an extended period of time. Eagle Eye is a technique used with Arrow and a Firearm magic. This allows the caster to see long distances, without straining the eyes. Caution should be used when using this type of magic, as there is a delay in adjusting back to normal vision.

Elemental Arrow- A magical technique used by bowmen, or wizards. If using a bow, the user must have an arrow that is designed for the magical element the individual intends to use. A wizard can summon and use this technique without a bow by summoning the arrow, using magical energy. Caution should be used with this technique, as the greater distance between caster and their opponent will lessen the potency of the spell.

Enhanced Jump- This is a spell that gives the caster increased jumping ability, and also allows them to land safely when jumping from a great height. The greater power the magic user has, the higher the jumping ability they will have.

Enhanced Movement- Similar to Enhanced Jump, Speed Magic users created this spell. Enhanced Movement, if channeled properly, can allow the user to dodge arrows and bullets. There is no guarantee that you will dodge them, it simply gives the user the ability to do so. Users are even able to move so quickly, that it appears as if they have gone invisible and teleported to another location. That technique is sometimes called Invisibility Speed.

Enhanced Reaction- A technique that comes out of Speed Magic. This spell was originally intended to be used with Enhanced Movement. With this spell, the user is able to react to rapidly moving targets and stimuli. When coupled with deflect, a talented caster gains the ability to deflect some bullets. Caution should be taken, as this spell drains a lot of magic, and causes incredible strain on the human body.

Ensnare- A blue energy blast, that can be used effectively to trap and ensnare living creatures, and the undead. Once the energy blast has wrapped around the target, the user can make the energy beams constrict and choke the target.

Esplosione- The most basic explosive spell. Creates a yellow ball of energy, and it explodes on contact. Esplosione can be charged to create a ball of energy as large, or as small as the caster requires. This spell is not intended to be lethal and is better used for crowd control.

Expanding Object (Enchantment)- An enchantment that allows an object, such as a bag, to expand. The volume of the expansion will be determined by the power of the enchantment itself, and the material of the item being expanded.

Fire Armor- A master level spell that surrounds the caster in fire. The powerful magic causes the fire to spiral around the user, creating a barrier of protection. Fire armor toughens the user's skin, amplifies their speed, and intensifies any fire magic spell they posses. The downsides of this spell is that it requires a massive amount of magical energy, and the user can typically only maintain it for a short period of time.

Fireball (Basic)- One of the earliest combat spells a fire user will learn. A ball of fire is created in the hand of the user and it can thrown to cause modest amount of damage. This is a non-lethal spell, and should be used as a deterrent.

Fireball (Advanced)- This is an intermediate spell that requires more concentration than a normal fireball. The Advanced Fireball allows the user to create multiple projectiles of varying sizes. The temperature and the color of the fireballs can be adjusted based on the user's needs. If the temperatures and size of the fireballs are significant enough, they can be made to be lethal. Fireball (Advanced) only permits use by Dragon Warriors, who are prepping to complete their trials.

Fire Buddy- Is a small Sprite that is created, using a minimal amount of magical energy. For a young Dragon Warrior that chooses the path of fire, this is the first fire spell that they will learn. The Sprite can be conjured to reflect any personality or color desired by the caster. If threatened, or commanded by the fire user, the Sprite will explode causing burns on the aggressor.

Fire Snake- Similar to Fire Buddy, the Fire Snake is conjured by the young Dragon Warrior. Fire Snake is usually the second or third fire spell that a Dragon Warrior in training is taught. In order for the caster to learn Fireball, they must master this spell. Fire Snake is considered a summoning spell, so the user must concentrate on creating its likeness and functionality. The creature can be used to create irritation on an opponent's skin, by having it crawl along an attacker. The snake can also explode, which can cause first degree burns in extreme cases.

FireWhip- The caster summons a fire spell that attaches itself to an object. The object develops the qualities of a whip and gives the user great mobility in a combat scenario.

Fire Wall or Wall of Fire- A powerful spell that requires intense concentration to be used successfully. The fire user channels their energy and is able to create a protective and destructive barrier. The shape and size of the barrier are at the user's discretion.

Flame Ward- A small purple or red sprite is conjured by the spell caster. The sprite is designed to protect the user when they are in vulnerable state, I.e. sleeping, injured. If someone breaches the established territory of the flame ward, the Sprite will slam and explode against the invader. Advanced versions of this spell, allow multiple sprites to be created. Master level versions of this allow the Sprite to reform after explosion, and to continue to attack the transgressors.

Flashback- A spell that comes out of the school of Psychological Magic. This spell activates the parts of the brain that are associated with long-term and short-term memory. The spell caster can then choose to amplify the emotions attached to those memories and twist the way the events in that memory take place. The receiver of this spell can re-experience the images of the memory in real time. Caution should be taken when using this spell, as it can cause permanent brain damage and can cause suicidality.

FlashBang- A bright white or yellow light is created by magic user. The ball of energy can explode on contact or can have a delayed detonation. If done correctly, FlashBang will cause temporary blindness and deafness on the intended target. If it is not done correctly the spell can rebound and affect the caster.

Flash Freeze- Is an anti-object spell. Flash Freeze creates a temporary area of ice that can last from 5-10 minutes. This spell requires a moderate level of magic to cast and should be used sparingly.

Freeze Flame- This is a hybrid spell that was originally created by a wizard from the Southern Convent. Freeze Flame combines the traits of fire and ice magic. A blue or white flame is created, and the opponent will feel a burning sensation similar to what one would experience from jumping into a frozen lake. Freeze Flame is a very powerful spell and is capable of killing a fire or heat magic user.

Grenade- A spell that comes from the school of Explosive Magic. The spell caster summons a ball of yellow energy, and the object explodes on contact. Depending on the skill of the magic user, the explosions can be delayed or amplified. This spell can be used in a lethal and non-lethal capacity.

Hail Storm- A deadly storm that is typically conjured by the use of a staff or other magical weapons. Hailstorm is an immensely powerful spell that creates intense gusts of wind, dark clouds, sheets of rain, and hail that can get as large as a soccer ball. This spell, like most storm magic, is difficult to control and can last longer than the magic user intends. Dragon Warriors that are taught this spell are forbidden to use it within cities or large communities.

Holy Flame Armor- White flames form around the caster when this spell is channeled. This magic increases the user's resistance to piercing weapons, holy magic, and minor fire spells. Holy Flame Armor, like all armor spells taught at the Dragon Monastery, will increase the user's speed, agility, and reaction time. This spell will automatically switch the user's normal fire magic spells, into holy magic spells. With this change in spell properties, this armor makes it an effective tool against the undead and dark magic users. Holy Flame Armor is resistant against dark and death magic to a point. If too much negative energy is absorbed by the armor, then the armor will likely dissipate; or it will change to what is called, Tainted Flame Armor.

Holy Fire- A type of fire magic spell that uses holy and positive magical properties. Holy Fire is effective against dark magic users and the undead. This type of spell can also be mildly effective against water magic spell.

Holy/Fire Armor Hybrid- A highly volatile master level spell. This armor spell combines the properties of fire, and holy armor spells. This hybrid technique can double and even triple the user's movement speed. In addition to that, the user's magical spells have an increased potency. A benefit of this armor for fire users, is that they hide moderately increased resistance to water and intense ice magic spells. However, caution should be used when attempting this spell, as it drains the individual's magic quickly, and it has the possibility of burning up and killing the spell caster.

Holy Seraph- A hybrid spell that combines fire and holy magic. This master level spell creates a large powerful snake, covered in white holy flames. The snake smashes into a target, and if the target isn't powerful enough, they will be vaporized.

Lightning Blast- This is a spell that is popular amongst lightning and storm magic users. In its most basic forms, the caster summons a series of lightning bolts at a target. For storm magic users, this spell by itself is weaker as their lightning attacks are stronger, when caused by an actual storm. Lightning magic users have greater versatility with this spell. They are able to modify range of the lightning at will and can summon multiple bolts.

Icicle- A lethal shard of ice between 3-10 feet is summoned by a magic user. The edges of the icicles are sharp enough to cut through metal. More devious and advanced ice magic users can even cause the icicles to splinter and spread shards within the flesh of their intended victim.

Instant Duststorm- With a flick of the wrist, the magic user conjures a Dust storm. Unlike most storm spells, this one does not have a delay in summoning. Due to the quick nature of this spell, the caster needs to have complete awareness of their target and have the required magical energy to summon it.

Inner Turmoil- A spell that comes from the field Psychological magic. This spell was invented near the end of the Great War by The Elders. Inner Turmoil allows the caster to aggravate an individual's insecurities and even twist their morals. This spell, if used as intended, can functionally be used to control a person's actions and even their mind. Inner Turmoil is a rarely used spell because it requires a wealth of magic and concentration. The caster is at risk splitting their own mind, while trying to control their target. Inner Turmoil is a banned spell throughout the world, even amongst the Witch Covenants; it's considered a spell of pure evil.

Melodic- A beautiful sound enters the intended target's ear, and in that moment, they feel a complete sense of calm. More advanced versions can create delusions and deep sleep. Melodic is a spell that can be created by an individual's vocal chords, or through an instrument. This spell was originally developed to address high anxiety and individuals who have night terrors.

Metallo Thermotata- A simple heat magic spell that is able to warm up metallic objects. Metallo Thermotata is a spell capable of melting metal, if the user is able to channel enough magic power.

Meteor (Basic)- A spell that was created by the first Dragon Sage. Only the best trained and self-controlled Dragon Warriors are taught this spell. Meteor is a spell that is conjured by thought or by vocalization. A medium to large sized fireball is created in the hand of the spell caster. An iron core is created in the center of fireball, and then it is launched towards an adversary. This spell can only be used as a last resort and is one of the few lethal fire spells taught to Dragon Warriors.

Meteor (Advanced)- This is one the most powerful fire spells taught to Dragon Masters. When the magic user summons this spell, a large fireball is created with a core made of iron. In its advance forms, the user can control the meteors with their mind and can even conjure them at a distance. A true master of this technique can summon multiple meteors at a time. Caution should be used when attempting this spell, as it can drain a lot of magical energy.

Monsoon- Storm magic spell that creates a powerful monsoon. This is like most weather control spells, in that it requires conditions in the area of effect to be favorable for this type of storm. If conditions are in the area that the spell is conjured, magical energy can be drawn from a person's life force.

Nekron- A powerful spell that brings the dead to life. Typically, the conjurer will summon skeletal warriors from the ground around them. More advanced versions of this spell can even allow flesh to form on the skeletal bodies. The use of a staff or a wand can amplify the power of this spell. A caster using this type of magic should be cautious, as the Nekron are vulnerable to fire and holy magic.

Quick Change- Is a transformation spell that allows the caster to change their outer garments in the blink of an eye. In order for this spell to work, the caster must be able to imagine whatever garments they intend to wear.

QuickDry- A Heat Magic spell that can be used to dry skin and a variety of other materials. Caution should be used when attempting this spell, as it can cause skin burns and combustion if used on clothing.

QuickFreeze- Is anti-human/anti-monster ice spell. The target becomes encased in ice and becomes immobilized. QuickFreeze is a non-lethal ice spell, and its effects are temporary. This spell is not effective against most fire or heat magic users and can sometimes be effective against water magic conjurers.

Rage (Uncontrolled)- This spell is almost as old as magic itself. When Rage is activated, the user's eyes turn bright red. Usually, the rage is activated by intense pain or anger. The caster's magical and physical abilities are doubled, or even quadrupled in this form. Due to amount of energy expelled when the spell is activated, the rage cannot last more than ten or thirty minutes. Caution should be used when activating this spell, as the magic caster loses all sense of control; and when the spell is over, the user is extremely vulnerable. Intense depression, anxiety, and psychosis can occur after the spell is casted.

Rage (Semi-Controlled)- Ancient magic that was created during the Great War, also known as the Red Eye. In this iteration, the user has semi control of their rage. The individual's base magic and physical abilities can become doubled or tripled. With the added control, the user is able to take fuller advantage of the power increase. Caution should be used when attempting this spell, as it takes years to be honed. In addition to that, since it is semi-controlled, the rage does not last as long and it's very easy for the user to lose control of their rage.

Rebound- This is a defensive magic skill, that is capable of bouncing any spell back against an enemy. Rebound is an advanced magic spell and requires an extreme amount concentration to work. The user must be able understand how an oncoming spell is intended to work. With that understanding in mind, the caster can then say, "rebound," and the spell will strike back at the enemy. Depending on the power of the caster, Rebound is also able to amplify the magic in the spell. Caution should be used when trying this spell, as there is a 50% chance of failure.

Repel- A blue ball of energy is expelled from the energy. Repel has the ability to affect both living creatures and non-living beings. This is a type of defensive magic and requires minimal amount of energy. Caution should be used when activating this spell against powerful magic users, because it can be deflected and cancelled out.

SandWall- A powerful earth magic spell. The user conjures a wall of earth that becomes impenetrable. Sandwall requires objects to create the wall. If the dirt or sand products are buried beneath concrete, the magic user must be strong enough to some the dirt to the surface.

soZo- One of the most powerful healing spells taught by individuals of elven descent. This magical ability requires the user to chant an elven parable. The spell is powerful enough to stop internal bleeding, heal some bone fractures, and moderate organ damage. Due to the amount of energy required, a healer best conducts this spell.

Split Arrow- An ability that is traditionally used by qualified bowmen and magic users, who summon elemental arrows. When an arrow is fired or summoned by the user, when the projectile is launched, it gains the ability to split into multiple objects. An adept user has the ability to adjust the size of the projectiles when they are split. Master level bowmen and wizards can even combine this spell with elemental magic and amplify the arrows accuracy.

Summoning Spells- Magical technique that allows the caster to conjure monsters or objects to do their bidding. Intense concentration is required to summon creatures, and to control them. Most summons will last only a few minutes. A rare skill within summoning magic, is the ability to summon familiars. A familiar is a specific summoned creature or item that can be conjured up repeatedly. For example, a creature that is a familiar, will remember its summoner.

Thermal Grenade- A orange and yellow ball of energy is formed by the user. This is one of the most powerful grenade spells. Thermal Grenade combines the energy of a normal explosive spell, with the heat and burning damage of fire magic. Caution should be used when attempting this spell, the fire energy in this spell is lethal and destructive.

Teleport (Enchantment)- Similar to its spell form, teleportation via enchantment requires extreme concentration by the caster initiating. An enchantment that uses teleportation magic, can only transport the individual to a corresponding location. Depending on the enchantment placed on the object, it is possible for an individual to recover from injuries while teleporting.

Teleport (Spell)- In spell form, teleportation is very difficult to use. Teleport is a technique that requires extreme concentration. The caster must have an exact picture of the location they are going to in their mind, in order for the spell to work. Teleportation is only instant if the traveler is going fifty miles. Any distances that exceed fifty miles, may take an hour or a day for arrival. Teleportation is technique that is usually taught to masters and dark magic users.

Transformation- A rare skill for any magic user to have. This type of magic is usually passed down hereditarily, but how aspects of it can be taught. Transformation in its base form can allow a person to transform a limb, or an item into whatever the caster desires. The more drastic the change, the more magic is required. Transformation in its more advanced forms allows the user to transform their whole body, and even their clothing. Caution should be used when attempting any transformation magic. If the user is off by a fraction they can experience severe physical injury, and even a permanent transformation.

Wind Gust- A basic storm spell that conjures a gust of wind. Formally trained storm magic users and mature practitioners can acquire this spell. An adept spell caster can use this spell and intensify the speed and power of the wind. More advanced users are able to use the wind gust to launch themselves forward, and even glide in the air. Some have reported that master level users have been able to use this spell to fly for short periods of time.

Made in the USA
Middletown, DE
28 August 2021